MRS. LINCOLN'S DRESSMAKER

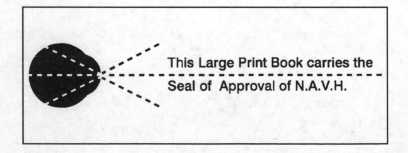

This Large Print Book carries the
Seal of Approval of N.A.V.H.

MRS. LINCOLN'S DRESSMAKER

JENNIFER CHIAVERINI

THORNDIKE PRESS
A part of Gale, Cengage Learning

Detroit • New York • San Francisco • New Haven, Conn • Waterville, Maine • London

GALE
CENGAGE Learning·

LIBRARY OF CONGRESS CATALOGING-IN-PUBLICATION DATA

Chiaverini, Jennifer.
  Mrs. Lincoln's dressmaker / by Jennifer Chiaverini.
    pages ; cm. — (Thorndike Press large print basic)
    ISBN-13: 978-1-4104-5542-0 (hardcover)
    ISBN-10: 1-4104-5542-4 (hardcover)
    1. Keckley, Elizabeth, ca. 1818-1907—Fiction. 2. Lincoln, Mary Todd, 1818-1882—Fiction. 3. Women dressmakers—Fiction. 4. Female friendship—Fiction. 5. First ladies—Fiction. 6. Large type books. I. Title.
PS3553.H473M77 2013b
813'.54—dc23   2012045003

Published in 2013 by arrangement with Dutton, a member of Penguin Group (USA) Inc.

Printed in the United States of America
1 2 3 4 5 6 7 17 16 15 14 13

To Marty, Nicholas, and Michael,
with love and thanks

CHAPTER ONE

November 1860–January 1861

On Election Day, Elizabeth Keckley hurried home from a mid-afternoon dress fitting to the redbrick boardinghouse on Twelfth Street where she rented two small rooms in the back. Although she never failed to carry her license attesting to her status as a freedwoman whenever she ventured out, on that day of the presidential election of 1860 she was eager to be safely indoors well before curfew. The city hummed with breathless excitement even though the white citizens of Washington City, District of Columbia, were not enfranchised to vote. In this, the capital's colored residents, both slave and free, were their equals, although Elizabeth prudently refrained from remarking upon this similarity to the wives of the city's social and political elite for whom she sewed the beautiful gowns they wore to balls and levees and receptions. Her patrons were

7

united in their suspicion of and disdain for the Republican candidate, a lawyer from Illinois they disparaged as an unpolished rube from the West and a radical abolitionist. They disagreed, however, on which of his three rivals ought to succeed President Buchanan, who, if ineffectual, had at least done their home states and the South's "peculiar institution" no enduring harm.

If a spontaneous parade sprang up and turned into a riot, as happened far too often those days, Elizabeth wanted to be well away from the furor. Already the streets were filling with men hurrying from tavern to hotel for news of the election, gathering on corners with like-minded fellows and glaring across the way at their rivals, crowding anxiously around the doors of the telegraph office on Fourteenth Street although the returns wouldn't be in for hours yet. Many folks had obviously been enjoying the free whiskey dispensed by the various political clubs that dotted the blocks near the White House, and from time to time their bursts of raucous laughter drowned out even the unceasing clip-clop of horses' hooves and the more distant whistles of passing trains. As she made her way home, Elizabeth tightened her grip on her sewing basket and kept her bearing serene and composed, flinching only once, when a young man wearing a campaign button boasting a tintype of Mr. Breckinridge jostled her in his haste to reach the bulletin board outside the National Hotel.

She breathed a sigh of relief when she reached her own quiet neighborhood, a haven in what had been an unfamiliar city only months before. She had come to Washington City that spring after a few failed weeks in Baltimore, where her struggle to find work convinced her to seek her fortune elsewhere. Not long before that, she had lived in St. Louis, where, after years of toiling and saving, she had purchased her freedom and her son's. Now George was a student at Wilberforce University in Ohio, and she was a successful mantua maker, a businesswoman with an admirable reputation, independent and free. She could more easily bear the miles separating her from her only child knowing that he was acquiring the education she herself had always longed for and had been denied, and that no man could claim him as property ever again.

Virginia Lewis, her landlady and dear friend, must have seen her approach through the front window, for she met her at the door. "What's the news?" she asked, breathless, studying her expression as if to read the answer there. "I know how your ladies talk. If anyone knows what's happening, they would."

"I'm afraid they don't know any more than we do." Elizabeth set down her sewing basket and unwrapped herself from her shawl. "Nothing's changed from what we heard this morning. Mr. Lincoln's favored to win, but we won't know for a fact until they count the ballots."

"I suppose your ladies wouldn't care much for a President Lincoln."

"Not one bit. Most of their husbands like Mr. Breckinridge, and so they do likewise. A few of them like Mr. Bell too." Elizabeth lowered her voice conspiratorially. "As for Mr. Lincoln, they fear he wants to free all the slaves."

They shared a laugh. "Well, then, God bless him," declared Virginia. "If that's true, I pray he wins."

Elizabeth nodded, but private doubts troubled her. No matter what the Southern partisans inhabiting the city said about Abraham Lincoln, as far as she knew, he had never promised to end slavery, only to keep it from spreading. But even if he had placed his hand on a Bible and declared himself a staunch abolitionist, her few months in Washington had taught her that candidates often made promises that they found impossible to keep after taking office. Whatever Mr. Lincoln's intentions, and whether they boded ill or good for Elizabeth and the Lewises and other colored folk, when Mr. Lincoln's people swept into the city to take over, most of Mr. Buchanan's would be swept out, among them the husbands of several of her best patrons. She could only hope that enough of them would remain behind to keep her business thriving.

It was perhaps too much to hope that the new First Lady would have a taste for finery, and that Elizabeth might somehow attract her notice.

It was well after midnight when she was startled awake by the sounds of shouting on the streets outside, of jubilant songs and speeches, and soon thereafter, of the firing of pistols and shattering of windows. She sat up in bed and strained her ears in the darkness, sifting sense from the jumble of noise and fury until she understood that the votes had been counted, the result announced.

Abraham Lincoln would become the sixteenth president of the United States.

■ ■ ■ ■

When Elizabeth had first arrived in Washington, she had no money, no friends, no place to call home, but she had soon found work as an assistant seamstress for two and a half dollars a day and took a room in a boardinghouse. Before long she decided to strike out on her own, and she had a sign and business cards made. She advertised herself as a skilled mantua maker, capable of sewing the complicated, snug-fitting bodice of the style that well-dressed ladies most desired. Slowly but surely, she acquired a few patrons, who recommended her to their friends and acquaintances. One generous lady, a friend of the mayor, persuaded him to waive the fee for the license that, like all free Negro females over the age of fourteen, Elizabeth was required to obtain within thirty days of her arrival if she wished to remain in the city. And she had already decided that she did wish to stay, even though the daily sight of slaves in chains being led through the muddy streets from shipyard to auction house and the restrictions upon freedmen like the license and curfews sometimes made her feel as if she were not truly free.

In October, a few weeks before the election that threw Washington City into uproar, Elizabeth sewed a gown for the wife of the cavalry officer Colonel Robert E. Lee. "Spare no expense," the colonel had urged Elizabeth as he entrusted her with a hundred dollars to purchase lace and buttons and ribbons for his wife's attire. Elizabeth gladly did as he bade her, and when Mrs. Lee wore the gown to a private dinner party at the White House in honor of the Prince of Wales, the other ladies in attendance were so impressed by the gown's beauty and elegance and excellent fit that they sought out Elizabeth's services. Her reputation grew as one delighted patron after another recommended her to their friends, and soon she had almost more work than she could handle.

Not long after the election, one of Elizabeth's patrons recommended her to a neighbor, Varina Davis, the wife of Senator Jefferson Davis of Mississippi. Informed that the Davises were late risers, Elizabeth offered to come to their I Street residence in the afternoons rather than first thing in the morning. That way she would have steady work sewing for the senator's family in the afternoons, and her mornings would be free to devote to other patrons. Mrs. Da-

13

vis agreed to the arrangement, and so the autumn days passed pleasantly and productively, despite the growing tension in the city that the election seemed to have augmented rather than diffused. The Davis residence was a hub of Southern activity, with politicians and statesmen from the South racing in at all hours and disappearing into Senator Davis's study for clandestine meetings in hushed voices that occasionally broke out into angry shouts. Mrs. Davis's mouth would tighten a trifle at each outburst, but usually she would barely glance at the door and carry on as if nothing had happened. If she were in a particularly cheerful mood, she might make a small joke about men and their tempers, but Elizabeth suspected that she was as concerned as they were about the widening divide between North and South, if not quite so loud about it.

Elizabeth liked the Davises. The senator struck her as a considerate, dignified gentleman, and Mrs. Davis — dark-haired, with large dark eyes and a complexion less fair than was fashionable — was well educated and witty, and she seemed to have friends in every corner, Republicans and Democrats alike. Mrs. Davis looked to be in her early thirties, perhaps a decade younger than

Elizabeth, perhaps a little less. She loved to read and to quote poetry, and whenever Elizabeth called, she usually found her in the midst of writing a letter, reading a book, or enjoying a visit from a friend.

One gray December afternoon, Elizabeth arrived at the Davis residence just in time to see one of Mrs. Davis's friends, the pretty and vivacious Mrs. Samuel Phillips Lee, leaving in a huff. "She doesn't look well pleased," Elizabeth murmured to Jim, the colored doorman, a slave who had come north from Mississippi with the Davises. "I'm almost afraid to come inside and find out why. Did she and Mrs. Davis argue?"

Jim nodded. "Not long, and not too loud, but enough. I heard Mrs. Davis say she's not gonna associate with Republicans anymore."

"Why, that's just silly." Elizabeth shifted her satchel to her other hand and gestured to Mrs. Davis's departing guest, who was picking her way carefully down the street. The winter chill had frozen the mud into hard, deep ruts, which made walking treacherous. It was difficult to say which was worse, the thick, sodden mud that soiled skirts and stole shoes from one's feet or the frozen variety that tripped one up and turned one's ankles. "Mrs. Davis has lots of

Republican friends."

"Not many of them show up around here anymore." Jim glanced over his shoulder and leaned toward her confidentially. "Guess how many angry Democrats can squeeze inside Mr. Davis's study."

"Ten?" Elizabeth replied, curious. "A dozen?"

"Twice that, I saw it for myself. They came in yesterday at dusk, senators and secretaries and the like, one by one, all quiet, and they stayed till near three o'clock this morning, talking secession."

Elizabeth's heart thumped. The first time she had heard the word secession, she had been obliged to ask her landlord Walker Lewis what it meant, and the sound of it still had the power to unnerve her. "Talking war too?"

"Talk of one usually leads to talk of the other, don't it?"

Elizabeth nodded. It did, and ever more so. "Maybe it won't come to that. Maybe it's all just a lot of political bluster." She knew that Senator Davis was working day and night to come up with a compromise to keep the slave states in the Union. She wanted to believe that something might yet come of his efforts, but the two sides' differences were so sharp and strongly felt that

16

an agreement seemed impossible.

"Maybe so," Jim said as he showed her in, but she knew he was merely being polite. Perhaps he wanted war, if the war would bring him his freedom. She could not fault him for that.

She found Mrs. Davis in the parlor, a book on her lap, her gaze faraway. "Good morning, ma'am," she greeted her. "I've finished basting the lining for the day dress if you'd care to try it on."

Mrs. Davis looked up with a start. "Certainly, Elizabeth." She rose and beckoned Elizabeth to follow her upstairs to her boudoir.

The senator's wife said little as Elizabeth helped her into the muslin bodice and skirt. Elizabeth firmly believed that investing the time and effort into the cut and fit of the lining was the secret to a well-fashioned dress, and she could only shake her head at seamstresses who hastened through that most essential part of the process. First Elizabeth would make a pattern for the lining by pinning inexpensive muslin or paper upon her patron's figure. Next, she would remove the pieces and baste them together. Her patron would try on this rough garment, which Elizabeth would fit and adjust and offer to her patron to try on again, over and over, for more fittings and adjustments until Elizabeth was satisfied. Only then would she risk putting shears to the more expensive satins and silks and moirés that would comprise the outer garment. After that, the carefully constructed pattern was the only model Elizabeth needed to sew the gown, a step she would complete in the privacy of her own rooms. The process was laborious and time-consuming, but Elizabeth insisted that it was the only way to ensure a perfect fit. She wondered what her patrons would think if she told them she had learned the technique of cutting on the figure by sewing clothing for her fellow slaves back in Virginia — not for the sake of fashion, of course, but so as not to waste any of the rough osnaburg cloth the mistress provided.

As Elizabeth took in the vertical pleats in the back of the bodice and pinned them carefully, Mrs. Davis sighed and said, "I wonder . . . I wonder if I should have chosen a fabric more suitable for a Southern summer."

"The sateen complements your complexion, and it won't be too warm except on the very hottest days." Studying the bodice, Elizabeth plucked two more pins from her pincushion and slipped them in place. "Why should you wonder? Are you going home to Mississippi for the summer?"

"Home, indeed." Mrs. Davis laughed shortly. "Mississippi is the state of my birth, but Washington is the home of my heart. I should hate to leave it, even if the place is overrun by Republicans."

"I should hate to see you go." Elizabeth thought of Mrs. Samuel Phillips Lee, her pretty features drawn with irritation as she stormed away from the Davis residence. "As I'm sure your friends would too."

"I doubt my dearest friends will linger. Some of them have already declared themselves eager to depart for friendlier states. None of us has much choice in the matter." Sighing, Mrs. Davis obligingly allowed Elizabeth to move her arms apart so she could better fit the sleeves. "It's our duty as wives to accompany our husbands. If they say we stay in the Union, and thus in Washington City, then we stay. If not —" Mrs. Davis forgot herself and waved a hand in helpless dismissal, tugging the muslin sleeve from Elizabeth's grasp. "Well, we go where they go, willingly or not."

"If you must go, and it seems to me there's still a good chance you won't," said Elizabeth, "you'll be the best-dressed woman in Mississippi — if you hold still

19

and let me finish."

In spite of herself, Mrs. Davis laughed. She patted Elizabeth's hand where it rested on her waist, but after that, she stood perfectly motionless as Elizabeth bade her until the task was done.

As December passed, the subject of war came up often in the Davis household — between the senator and his wife, Mrs. Davis and her friends, the senator and his numerous visitors. The senator worked increasingly long and erratic hours, and when Mrs. Davis wasn't tending to her young children, she distracted herself with writing letters, reading books, and entertaining friends she probably thought she must soon part with and might never see again. A deep, hushed anxiety permeated the city, the sense that time was running out, and Elizabeth felt it most intensely within the Davis household.

As the holidays approached, Mrs. Davis kept Elizabeth busy sewing everyday clothes for her and the children, and one special garment for her husband — a fine silk dressing gown meant for his Christmas present. As Mrs. Davis wanted it to be a surprise, she asked Elizabeth to keep it out of sight whenever the senator was home. Once, Mrs.

Davis dashed into the sitting room, where Elizabeth was busy sewing, and flung a quilt over her — the pieces of silk, her sewing basket, and Elizabeth herself from shoulders to shoe tops — only moments before Mr. Davis walked in, home earlier than expected from the Capitol. There was no time to adjust the quilt so that the draping was less ridiculous, so Elizabeth merely sat and nodded a greeting while Mrs. Davis whirled about to kiss her husband. The senator accepted the welcome with distracted affection, but then he looked past his wife to peer curiously at Elizabeth. "Are you cold, Lizzie?"

"Not anymore, Mr. Davis," she replied. Mrs. Davis flashed her a quick, secret smile and led her husband from the room, asking about his day. Muffling laughter, Elizabeth threw off the quilt, folded up the silk, and hid the pieces in her sewing basket before the senator returned.

It was a rare lighthearted moment in a season of increasing worry and dread. A few days before Christmas, all of Washington was shaken by the news from the South — South Carolina had voted to secede from the Union. Within the Davis household, the debates Elizabeth overheard immediately shifted from whether it was legal and right

21

to dissolve the Union to which states would follow South Carolina and how soon. As the calls for secession increased, Mrs. Davis's ambivalence persisted. One day, she would champion the cause of states' rights and praise the slave system, while on the next, she would confide to a friend that she could not bear the thought of leaving Washington City, where she had resided so long and forged such enduring ties. "I would rather remain in Washington and be kicked about than go south and be Mrs. President," she said. And when her friend exclaimed in surprise, Mrs. Davis assured her that it was the true sentiment of her heart.

That more Southern states would follow South Carolina out of the Union seemed all but certain. In all the disquiet, Elizabeth had found very little time to work on Mr. Davis's dressing gown. After weeks of swift, clandestine, off-and-on sewing, on Christmas Eve, the dressing gown remained unfinished.

Although Mrs. Davis did not rebuke her, Elizabeth knew she was anxious to have the dressing gown completed, lovingly wrapped and ready to give to her husband Christmas morning. "I'll stay and finish it, if you like," Elizabeth offered as the afternoon waned, though she was already weary after a long day of sewing, her fingers tired, her head and back aching.

Mrs. Davis gladly, gratefully accepted, so Elizabeth kept on, sewing with neat, quick, flawless stitches in the sitting room by gaslight while her patron decorated a Christmas tree in the parlor for the children. Her thoughts wandered to her son, who would be spending the holidays with a school friend in Cleveland. It would be their first Christmas apart. Elizabeth had sent George a gift — candies, a book, and two fine shirts — but she had not heard from him. Watching Mrs. Davis bustle about preparing for her family's celebration made her miss George more acutely than ever. When she was still a young woman, her beauty and natural grace had drawn the attention of a powerful white man, Alexander Kirkland, who could not be fought off and would not be denied. Her master had done nothing to protect her, and so George had come to be — the child she had not wanted but had come to love with all her heart.

The closing of a door elsewhere in the house snatched her from her reverie, and when her gaze fell upon the clock on a nearby table, she saw that it was a quarter to midnight, well past the ten o'clock curfew for colored people. She could not walk home now, even if she dared brave the streets at so late an hour, what with crime on the upswing even in fine white neighborhoods like the Davises' and respectable middle-class colored neighborhoods like her own. She decided that when she finished the dressing gown, she would present it to Mrs. Davis and request a bed for the night in the attic with the servants. With any luck she could snatch a few hours' sleep and be well rested enough to enjoy the Christmas service at Union Bethel Church in the morning. Virginia and Walker Lewis had kindly invited her to join them and their young daughters for a Christmas feast later that day, and Elizabeth had gratefully accepted. She was accustomed to a good deal of time alone — after more than thirty-seven years as a slave denied all privacy, a bit of solitude still felt luxurious — but on the day of the Lord's birth, she wanted to celebrate in the company of friends.

She was adjusting the tie cords when she heard Senator Davis in the hallway between the sitting room and the parlor. "How festive you've made everything, my dear," she heard him praise his wife, though his voice was devoid of merriment. "The children's eyes will light up with joy when they behold that tree." He leaned against the doorway, and suddenly he glanced over his shoulder into the sitting room. "That you, Lizzie?" he exclaimed, turning her way. "Why are you here so late? Still at work? I hope Mrs. Davis isn't too exacting."

"No, sir," she answered, startled by his gray and careworn look. Elizabeth knew he was ten years older than herself and that he often suffered from poor health, but clearly the events of the past few weeks had aged him drastically. Taken aback, she had missed her brief opportunity to hide the dressing gown. She had no choice but to explain herself, although she tried to conceal as much of the surprise as possible, without lying outright. "Mrs. Davis was very anxious to have this gown finished tonight," she told him carefully, glancing toward the parlor to be sure Mrs. Davis would not overhear, "and so I volunteered to remain and complete it."

"Well, well, the case must be urgent." The senator crossed the room and took the hem of his Christmas surprise in his hand. "What is the color of this silk? This gaslight is too deceptive to my aging eyes."

"It's a drab changeable silk, sir." She almost added that it was a rich, handsome color and would suit him well, but she decided to let him discover that for himself when he opened his gift the next morning and could admire it in daylight.

He nodded, smiled curiously, let go of the hem, and left the room without another word. Elizabeth knew then that he had easily guessed that the dressing gown was his wife's Christmas gift to him, and he did not want her to know that the surprise had been spoiled. She found herself touched by his thoughtfulness. She would never concur with his views on slavery and secession, but she couldn't help admiring him for the small kindness he showed his wife.

She finished the dressing gown just as the clock struck midnight. Her thoughts drifted unexpectedly to her own husband, how he had deceived and disappointed her, until she had been obliged to tell him that they must live forever apart. James Keckley, who had pretended to be a freedman among other things when she agreed to marry him, was likely still a runaway slave hiding out in St. Louis if his drinking had not killed him yet.

Carefully she folded the dressing gown and pushed thoughts of her estranged husband aside. It was Christmas, and she would not wish anyone ill on that sacred day, especially not the man she had once loved.

Just before midnight on December 31, the bells at Trinity Church at Third and C streets rang out "Hail, Columbia" and "Yankee Doodle" to welcome the New Year, but any lingering chance for reconciliation between North and South had been left behind in the old. New Year's Day was usually a festive, merry holiday in the city, or so its longtime residents told Elizabeth, but on the first day of 1861, no crowds celebrated in the inns and taverns, and few neighbors ventured out to pay calls. Those who did bore anxious and troubled expressions, as if urgent business rather than a wish to spread New Year's greetings had compelled them from the comfort of their homes on that bright, frigid morning. A neighbor, a former slave employed as a butler at the White House, later told the Lewises that only a small fraction of the usual number of guests had attended the traditional New Year's Day reception. The guests were as courteous to one another as gentility required, but some boldly wore Union or secession cockades in their hats so that no one would mistake their loyalties. Not even President Buchanan was immune from barbs and bitter words as he shook hands in the receiving line, but as the host as well as the leader of the land, if only for a few more weeks, he bore it with diplomacy and tact.

On January 9, Mississippi voted to secede, and Jefferson Davis told his wife that he was resolved to follow his beloved state out of the Union. Within days, the senator fell ill and took to his bed, which was where the unceasing stream of friends and politicians and statesmen conferred with him. Elizabeth did not doubt that the strain upon him as the leader of the Democrats' Southern faction contributed in no small part to his poor health. Mrs. Davis nursed him tenderly, and when Elizabeth remarked upon her sure hand in the sickroom, Mrs. Davis replied matter-of-factly, "I've had a great deal of practice."

One evening, as Elizabeth was dressing Mrs. Davis for one of the few social gatherings the couple attended that bleak winter, Mrs. Davis suddenly said, "Elizabeth, you are so very handy that I should like to take you with me."

Something in her voice told Elizabeth that this was no idle compliment. "When do you go South, Mrs. Davis?" she asked.

"Oh, I cannot tell just now, but it will be soon. You know there is going to be war, Elizabeth?"

She had long suspected, but Mrs. Davis spoke as if she had certain knowledge of it — which, as Senator Davis's wife, she very well could have. "War? You cannot mean it."

"I tell you, yes. The Southern people will not submit to the humiliating demands of the abolition party. They will fight first."

Elizabeth fought to keep her voice even as she fastened the last of Mrs. Davis's buttons. "And who do you think will win?"

"The South, of course," replied Mrs. Davis. "The South is impulsive, and the Southern soldiers will fight to conquer. The North will yield when it sees the South is in earnest, rather than engage in a long and bloody war."

Impulsive and earnest, perhaps, but Elizabeth didn't think that was enough to win a war. She also thought, although she would not be impudent enough to say so aloud, that Mrs. Davis underestimated the determination of Northerners. Those of Elizabeth's acquaintance did not seem particularly yielding, or any more afraid of a fight than Southern folks. "Mrs. Davis," she said instead, in her most reasonable tone, "are you certain that there will be war?"

"I know it." Suddenly she turned in her chair and clasped Elizabeth's hand. "You had better go South with me. I will take good care of you."

Elizabeth was so startled that without thinking she snatched her hand away.

Mrs. Davis seemed not to notice her rudeness. "When the war breaks out, the colored people will suffer in the North. The Northern people will look upon them as the cause of the war, and I fear, in their exasperation, will be inclined to treat you harshly."

Reluctantly, Elizabeth acknowledged the truth of her patron's words with a nod. Secession would cause the war, and the state delegates who had voted to leave the Union would have to bear the responsibility. Still, Elizabeth had no reason to doubt that somehow the blame would shift to the people of her race, as it so often, so unfairly, did in other matters.

"I may come back to Washington in a few months, and live in the White House," Mrs. Davis mused, turning around to examine the drape of her dress in the mirror. "The Southern people talk of choosing Mr. Davis for their president. In fact, it may be considered settled that he *will* be their president. As soon as we go South and secede from the other states, we will raise an army and march on Washington, and then I shall live in the White House."

"Mrs. Davis," Elizabeth managed to say, "I'm very pleased that you've placed so much confidence in me. However, I —" She had to stop, to take a breath, to find a moment to think. "I have my business to consider. I have my church and my friends."

"We do have churches in the South, you may recall, as well as many colored women who would surely like to count you among their friends." A faint, amused smile turned up the corners of Mrs. Davis's mouth. "As for your business, it will surely thrive. I'll have plenty of work for you within my own household, but if that doesn't suffice, with my recommendation you'll have no trouble finding many eager new customers in Montgomery."

So the Davises were planning to remove to Alabama, not Mississippi. Elizabeth wondered why her patron had not mentioned this before. "I — I don't know what to say. Forgive me my uncertainty. I'm very grateful you think so highly of my work."

"Not only of your work, but also of you." Mrs. Davis caught her gaze in the mirror and held it. "Promise me you'll consider my proposal — although time is of the essence. I'll need your answer soon."

That much Elizabeth could do. "I promise."

31

Elizabeth kept her word, pondering Mrs. Davis's proposal, praying over it. She was tempted to accept. She liked the Davis family, and Mrs. Davis's reasoning seemed plausible. But to go so far south, so deep into the land of slavery — even as a freedwoman, life there would be difficult for her, far more difficult than in the slaveholding District of Columbia. But as much as she liked Mrs. Davis, she liked the Lewises more, and she would miss her friends in the congregation of Union Bethel Church. And though the Northerners might, as Mrs. Davis predicted, blame the colored race for the inevitable war and turn upon them in anger, weren't Southerners as likely to do the same?

After pondering the question alone, and with the deadline for her decision approaching, Elizabeth turned to her friends for guidance. One and all, freeborn and former slave, urged her to remain in Washington. They were astonished that Mrs. Davis would even presume to ask such a thing upon such a short acquaintance. Elizabeth had been in the family's employ less than three months, and Mrs. Davis expected her to leave her home and place herself in unimaginable risk in a land she herself expected soon to be torn by war? They did

not believe, as Elizabeth did, that Mrs. Davis's offer was generous, that it was a sign of respect. "Don't go," Virginia implored after one late-night talk in her parlor. "If you change your mind, you may not be able to come home."

Elizabeth knew her friends were right. She also knew that the North was far stronger than Mrs. Davis seemed to believe — in spirit as well as might. Mr. Lincoln's people were powerful and eager for victory, and Elizabeth could not believe that they would let the Southern states go without a fight or that they would give up as soon as the Southerners resisted. In the end, after all her questioning and pondering and prayer, her decision came down to one irrefutable fact: She was a colored woman, and she would be far wiser to cast her lot with the people of the North, many of whom supported abolition, than those of the South, most of whom believed she belonged in chains.

Elizabeth had not yet told Mrs. Davis of her decision when she arrived at the Davis residence a few days later to find that her patron had gone out earlier that morning to purchase several yards of floral chintzes, pretty but less fine than the fabrics she usu-

ally favored. "I'd like you to make me two wrappers," Mrs. Davis said, draping the fabrics upon the sofa.

"From chintz?"

"Yes, Elizabeth, from chintz." Mrs. Davis's smile twisted as if she were fighting back tears. "I must give up expensive dressing for a while. Now that war is imminent, I — and I daresay all Southern people — must learn to practice lessons of economy."

"Of course." Elizabeth gathered up the fabrics. "I'll get started right away."

"Thank you." After a moment, she added, "Elizabeth?"

"Yes, Mrs. Davis?"

"I think . . ." Her voice trailed off, and she inhaled deeply. "To be prudent, it would be best to finish the wrappers sooner rather than later."

Elizabeth understood.

The Davises' course was fixed, irrevocable. It was only a matter of time.

Elizabeth finished the wrappers a few days before the Davis family left Washington. When she presented the finished garments to Mrs. Davis, she admired them, set them aside, and handed Elizabeth a bundle of fine needlework, a difficult work-in-progress of her own that she wanted Elizabeth to finish. "You can send it to me by post when it is

done," she instructed, and then she paused to offer Elizabeth a hopeful smile. "Or perhaps you can call on me in the parlor of my new home and hand it to me yourself. Perhaps you won't have to walk very far. I'm sure that wherever we settle, we can arrange a room in our residence for you."

Elizabeth could delay no longer. "I'm very sorry, Mrs. Davis. I'm happy to finish your sewing, but I'll have to send it to you. I've decided to stay in Washington."

Mrs. Davis pressed her lips together and nodded as if she had expected Elizabeth to refuse, and yet she could not quite give up her cause for lost. "Aren't you tempted, even a little, by the prospect of being a First Lady's personal modiste?"

Elizabeth laughed shakily. "I am indeed, but not enough to leave my home. I promise, ma'am, if you return to Washington, I'd be pleased to sew for you again. More than pleased — I would be delighted."

"Oh, Elizabeth." Mrs. Davis regarded her with sad affection. "You betray yourself. You said *if* I return, not when."

On the twenty-first of January, Jefferson Davis and several other Southern senators resigned their seats and left Washington, casting their lots with their home states.

Later Elizabeth would read in the papers that Mr. Davis had expressed love for the Union and a desire for peace, but he had also asserted his right to own slaves and the right of states to secede. "I am sure I feel no hostility to you, senators from the North," he had told the assembly. "I am sure there is not one of you, whatever sharp discussion there may have been between us, to whom I cannot now say, in the presence of my God, I wish you well."

Soon thereafter, Mrs. Davis left Washington with her husband and children and slaves. The Southern states elected Jefferson Davis as their president, and Varina Davis became First Lady of the Confederacy.

CHAPTER TWO

February–March 1861

All of Washington City was abuzz with anticipation — and in certain quarters, apprehension — for the arrival of President-Elect Lincoln. He and his family were approaching the capital by a circuitous train route, both to greet as many supporters along the way as he could and to thwart anyone who might attempt to do him harm. "He hasn't even taken office yet and those secessionists are already threatening his life," said Walker Lewis one morning, offering Elizabeth his newspaper, which disgusted him too much for him to continue reading. "They won't bother to wait and see what he might do in office. They hate him on principle."

The ongoing, escalating conflict over Fort Sumter in Charleston Harbor also dominated conversation. Ever since December 26, when United States major Robert Anderson had moved his command from the vulnerable Fort Moultrie on Sullivan's Island to the stronger, more defensible fortifications controlling the harbor, the handful of federal troops there had been essentially under siege. In early January, on the same day Mississippi seceded from the Union, South Carolinian forces had fired upon the *Star of the West,* an unarmed merchant ship President Buchanan had sent to resupply and reinforce Major Anderson and his men. The ship had been forced to turn back, and reports from Fort Sumter had become increasingly dire as the men ran low on food, arms, and supplies. Although many Republicans called for an immediate military response, President Buchanan seemed inclined to wait out the last few remaining weeks of his presidency and let Abraham Lincoln worry about it when he took over.

A few officers' wives had been living on Sullivan's Island with their husbands, but when Major Anderson moved his troops from Fort Moultrie to Fort Sumter, the ladies had been sent over to Charleston for their safety. There they found every door closed to them. Not a single boardinghouse would offer them lodgings, and one landlady bluntly declared that if she offered the officers' wives a safe haven, she would lose all her other boarders. Discouraged and angry, the women had been obliged to leave their husbands to their defense of Fort Sumter and seek refuge in the North. When they arrived in Washington, bitter and defiant, they found themselves warmly welcomed by the Republicans and celebrated as the first martyrs of the war.

"I cannot imagine such a state of feeling," one of Elizabeth's patrons declared as Elizabeth dressed her for a levee at the White House one evening. Margaret Sumner McLean was the daughter of the Massachusetts-born Major General Edwin Vose Sumner and the wife of Captain Eugene McLean, a Maryland native with unabashed Southern sympathies. Her father's cousin was the abolitionist senator Charles Sumner, who had been savagely caned and nearly murdered on the Senate floor almost five years earlier by a colleague from South Carolina who had taken great offense to one of his antislavery speeches, which was not surprising considering that it had been full of personal insults. To say that Mrs. McLean's loyalties were probably divided in those troubled times was, in Elizabeth's opinion, a grave understatement. "To turn away helpless women, to leave them homeless and unprotected! I am quite indignant with so-called Southern chivalry."

"I hear a few Southern gentlemen offered the ladies rooms in their own homes," said Elizabeth, adjusting the fall of lace around Mrs. McLean's shoulders. "The ladies declined."

Mrs. McLean laughed in brusque dismissal. "They had no choice, and the gentlemen of Charleston must have known that. How could officers' wives accept the hospitality of men who had openly avowed enmity toward their husbands? I can imagine the turn the negotiations would have taken: 'Ho, there, Major Anderson! Still determined to hold Fort Sumter, are you? Did I mention that we have your men's wives?' "

"You think those Charleston men would have harmed the ladies?"

"Oh, probably not. They were gentlemen, not common ruffians. But even if their safety had been guaranteed and notarized, the ladies couldn't put their brave husbands under any obligation to their enemies. Nor should it have been necessary. Where were the kindly widows of Charleston, the dutiful landlords? How would they feel if their women were treated so contemptuously in Washington or New York?"

"I imagine they would not think well of it."

"No, indeed. They would consider it an act of war." Her gown and hair in order, Mrs. McLean dismissed Elizabeth with her thanks and a promise to send along Elizabeth's good wishes in her next letter to Varina Davis, a dear friend whom she missed terribly. Washington society wasn't the same without her, and the excitement of new acquaintances was a poor substitute for the company of longtime, loyal friends.

Elizabeth didn't see Mrs. McLean again until nearly two weeks later, when she unexpectedly called at the Lewis boardinghouse. Elizabeth was hard at work sewing in her rooms when she heard footsteps and the rustle of hoop skirts in the hallway. Glancing up from her work, she was astonished to discover Mrs. McLean standing there, regarding her imperiously over a muslin-wrapped bundle tied with twine. Elizabeth's heart sank, but she kept her face pleasantly expressionless. She did not like it when her patrons came to her rooms, especially without any notice whatsoever. It was more appropriate to their status — and more protective of her privacy — if she went to them.

"Elizabeth, I am invited to dine at Willard's next Sunday," Mrs. McLean declared by way of a greeting. "I positively have *not* a dress fit to wear on the occasion. I have just purchased material, and you must commence work on it right away."

Elizabeth did not allow even the smallest sigh of exasperation to escape her lips. "I have more work promised now than I can do," she replied evenly. "It is impossible for me to make a dress for you to wear on Sunday next."

"Pshaw! Nothing is impossible." Mrs. McLean swept the room with her gaze as if to confirm that no other lady stood waiting to assert her claim upon Elizabeth's time. "I must have the dress made by Sunday."

"I am sorry —"

"Now, don't say no again. I tell you that you must make the dress." Mrs. McLean raised a hand to forestall Elizabeth's objections. "I have often heard you say that you would like to work for the ladies of the White House. Well, I have it in my power to obtain you this privilege. I know Mrs. Lincoln well, and you shall make a dress for her provided you finish mine in time to wear at dinner on Sunday."

For a moment, Elizabeth wondered how a Massachusetts-born wife of a Southernsympathizing Marylander could have any acquaintance at all with the new First Lady, late of Illinois and not yet arrived in Washington. Then she remembered that Mrs. McLean's father was one of the cavalry officers who had volunteered to accompany the Lincolns from Springfield to the capital city. Perhaps the families were old friends from Mr. Lincoln's term in Congress years before. Perhaps Mrs. McLean could indeed bring about what she promised.

Elizabeth needed no further inducement. "Very well," she said, setting aside the dress she had been embroidering for another client, a kind, sweet-faced, grandmotherly woman who would never dream of complaining if Elizabeth finished her gown a day or two later than expected. Elizabeth felt a pang of guilt over the injustice, but she could not let such a rare and promising opportunity slip from her grasp. She resolved to make it up to her other patron somehow — but not before next Sunday.

Elizabeth persuaded Mrs. McLean to let her begin fitting the lining that very moment by assuring her that it was the only way she had any chance at all of finishing the dress in time. They met the next day at Mrs. McLean's residence across the street from Willard's Hotel, and the next, and then

Elizabeth had enough completed so that she could work on her own. But she was not entirely on her own; in order to meet the deadline, she hired two young ladies to assist her, skilled if inexperienced seamstresses she had hired for small tasks before. Even with their help, Elizabeth was obliged to work all day long and late into the night, barely pausing to eat and sleep and work the knots out of her neck, back, and fingers.

It took a small miracle, but somehow, after much worry and trouble, Elizabeth completed the dress by midmorning on the day of the dinner. She hurried to the McLean residence as soon as the last stitch was put into the hem; had her patron try it on; made a few last-minute, minuscule adjustments that likely no one else but another skilled mantua maker would notice; and then — at last and just in time — the dress was finished.

"Elizabeth, you are a marvel," Mrs. McLean declared, admiring herself in the full-length mirror. She had a lovely figure and the bodice fit as tightly as wallpaper, and the ashes of rose silk lent a warm elegance to her alabaster skin. "One glimpse of this dress is all the recommendation to Mrs. Lincoln you will need."

"All the same," said Elizabeth, "I would

be grateful if you would put in a good word for me too."

Mrs. McLean turned and peered over her shoulder at her own reflection, smiling with satisfaction at the snug lines of the bodice and the graceful drape of the flounce. "I'm tempted to keep you my little secret." She glimpsed Elizabeth's expression in the mirror and quickly added, "I'm only teasing. Of course I'll mention your name to the First Lady. You kept your part of our bargain and I'll keep mine."

Elizabeth murmured her thanks and hid her disappointment. Apparently she and Mrs. McLean remembered their arrangement quite differently. She had not toiled so long and so hard and with so little sleep for the mere mention of her name to the First Lady. "You shall make a dress for her" had been her patron's exact words. She had made it sound so certain. Now Elizabeth wondered if it had ever been within Mrs. McLean's power to grant her fondest wish.

Elizabeth cherished each precious letter George sent from Wilberforce University. She savored every word of his descriptions of his studies, his new friends, their merry antics, and his long hours bent over books in the library. He asked her as many questions about Washington as he answered about himself, eager for news of the election, the transition of power, and the famous personages she encountered. "Your observations make me the envy of my classmates," he told her. "They have to learn what little they can from the papers, while I receive your firsthand, eloquent dispatches at regular and frequent intervals. The fellows come to me with their questions about what is really going on in the capital (don't worry, Mother, I never pass on gossip about your patron ladies) and I am happy to oblige. I will never share the fine shirts you sew for me, Mother, but I am less selfish when it comes to the news."

George's gentle teasing made her smile, as did his generous praise. Her lack of formal schooling had always troubled her, although she knew she was fortunate to be literate at all. It was illegal for slaves to read and write, but none of Elizabeth's former owners had forbidden their slaves to learn if they were bright enough to pick it up on their own or if another slave taught them on their own time. Elizabeth did not think she was a very good writer, so she could not help but be flattered and charmed when her darling son called her eloquent.

She was laughing over George's comic

46

description of a recent snowball fight on the college's main quadrangle when a knock sounded on her door. It was an unexpectedly mild Sunday, a welcome glimpse of spring in early March, and she and Virginia had made plans to go walking later to watch the preparations for the next day's inauguration. Elizabeth hastened to the door, expecting her friend, but instead a young messenger stood outside in the hallway, a colored boy of about fourteen years, breathless from haste and clutching a letter. "I'm supposed to wait for a reply, ma'am," he said, panting.

Curious, Elizabeth unfolded the letter, skimmed the first line — and uttered a sound that fell somewhere between a groan and a laugh. "My dear Elizabeth," Mrs. McLean had written. "Do be so kind as to call on me at my home today at four o'clock P.M. With my best regards, etc., Mrs. Eugene McLean."

Shaking her head, Elizabeth read the brief letter again, as if she could make more words appear by sheer force of will. "Did she say anything else?" she asked the young messenger. "*Why* she wants me to come, perhaps?" And on such short notice, she almost added, but thought better of it.

"No, ma'am," he said, shaking his head.

"Just that I should bring this to Mrs. Elizabeth Keckley at the Lewis boardinghouse on Twelfth Street."

"Well, you've done as you were told." She folded the letter, slipped it into her pocket, and offered the messenger a coin. "Please return to Mrs. McLean and tell her that I thank her for her note, and I will call on her tomorrow morning at my earliest convenience."

He nodded and hurried off, and Elizabeth closed the door behind him. Sunday was supposed to be her day off, as her patrons ought to have known. She was a free woman, free to ignore unreasonable demands. Monday morning would be soon enough for whatever Mrs. McLean wanted, and if not, she could hire another modiste — although Elizabeth did not think it vain to doubt that her patron would find anyone as skilled and accommodating as herself.

The morning of Abraham Lincoln's inauguration dawned raw and overcast, the busy streets clouded with dust stirred up by a thin, intermittent wind. It was not yet nine o'clock when Elizabeth left her boardinghouse and joined the throngs of people already out and about, buzzing with anticipation for the day's events. She saw not one familiar face among the thousands as she walked the few blocks to Mrs. McLean's house. Along the way she spotted evidence of out-of-town visitors who had been unable to find room in the city's packed hotels and had instead spent the night on the streets — a makeshift bed on a pile of lumber, a line of people waiting to wash up at a public pump. An excited crowd was milling about Willard's Hotel when Elizabeth arrived, and she struggled to work her way through it to the McLeans' residence on the opposite side of the street. Breathless, she knocked loudly upon the front door, uncertain whether she would be heard at all, but before long the doorman answered. When she gave her name and explained her errand, she was told that Mrs. McLean was not at home. Just as she was wondering whether she should wait there or try to return home, one of Colonel McLean's aides appeared and told her she was wanted at Willard's.

Perplexed, Elizabeth again braved the throng, crossed the street, and somehow managed to push her way into the hotel through the crowded entrance. "There you are," someone exclaimed, and a hand seized her shoulder and whirled her about. It was Mrs. McLean, her gaze sharp and incredulous. "Why did you not come yesterday, as I requested?"

"Your note didn't say that it was urgent," Elizabeth reminded her.

"On the eve of the inauguration, how could it be otherwise?" Mrs. McLean's mouth thinned in disapproval. "Mrs. Lincoln wanted to see you, but I fear that now you are too late."

"Mrs. Lincoln wanted to see *me*?"

Mrs. McLean nodded impatiently. "A week ago, someone spilled coffee on the gown Mrs. Lincoln intended to wear today. She needed a dressmaker, so I recommended you. Lo and behold, she recognized your name. Apparently you've worked for some of her lady friends in St. Louis, not that it matters now."

"I'm sorry, Mrs. McLean," said Elizabeth, her heart sinking. If Mrs. Lincoln had requested a dressmaker, why on earth had Mrs. McLean waited a week to summon her? "You did not say what you wanted with me yesterday, so I judged that this morning would do as well."

"You should have come yesterday," Mrs. McLean scolded, but then she relented, if only a trifle. "Go on up to Mrs. Lincoln's room. She may find use for you yet."

As soon as Mrs. McLean gave her the

number of the suite, Elizabeth hurried off to find parlor number six. When she knocked upon the door, a cheerful voice invited her to enter, and when she stepped into the room, she found herself face-to-face with a dark-haired woman just over forty, inclined to stoutness but with a lovely complexion and clear blue eyes that boasted a quick, keen gaze. All about her were well-dressed ladies helping her prepare for the inauguration.

The dark-haired woman did not introduce herself, nor did she need to. "You are Elizabeth Keckley, I believe."

Elizabeth bowed her assent.

"The dressmaker that Mrs. McLean recommended?"

"Yes, madam."

"Very well." Mrs. Lincoln returned to her dressing table and examined her face in the mirror, touching the delicate skin beneath her eyes, frowning at what might have been newly discovered or newly imagined lines. "I have not time to talk to you now, but would like to have you call at the White House, at eight o'clock tomorrow morning." Turning in her seat, she caught Elizabeth's gaze and held it. "Where I shall then be."

The brief meeting was over. Elizabeth bowed herself out of the room and returned home, insensible to the ever-increasing crowds, the gathering of horses and men for the grand parade, the distant strains of martial music. Only a few years before, she had been a slave in St. Louis, working herself into a state of near collapse and wondering if she would ever earn enough money to purchase her freedom and her son's. Now she had an invitation to meet with the First Lady at the White House — and an extraordinary opportunity to win her as a patron.

Elizabeth wished George could be there to walk into the White House at her side. She would remember every detail and describe everything to him — every sight, every word of conversation, filling pages and pages if necessary so that it would be as if he had experienced it with her.

She spent the rest of the day alone in her rooms, sewing when she could keep her mind on her work, but more often letting her thoughts drift to her upcoming interview with Mary Lincoln.

Later her friends would tell her about the thrilling inauguration ceremony, about how the sky had finally cleared and how the proud cavalry had surrounded the president-elect's carriage as it rumbled at a stately pace up the cobblestones of Pennsylvania Avenue to the Capitol. They would tell her about Mrs. Lincoln, how she had glowed with pride as she observed the ceremony with her family from her seat on the platform erected on the Capitol steps. Elizabeth would smile when they described how the tall, gaunt president-elect had stepped forward, removed his hat, and then suddenly halted, realizing only then that he had no place to put it while he took his oath. His former opponent, the Illinois Democratic senator Stephen A. Douglas, had gallantly taken the hat and had held it for the new president until the last words were spoken. Elizabeth would be moved, later, when she read a transcription of President Lincoln's speech and learned how he had said, of the disagreeing citizens of North and South, "We are not enemies, but friends. We must not be enemies. Though passion may have strained, it must not break our bonds of affection. The mystic chords of memory, stretching from every battlefield and patriot grave to every living heart and hearth-stone all over this broad land, will yet swell the chorus of the Union when again touched, as surely they will be, by the better angels of our nature."

Knowledge of all this would come later. From the solitude of her rooms on Twelfth

Street, Elizabeth heard only the low booming of cannon fire that marked the moment Abraham Lincoln became the sixteenth president of the United States. More than thirty thousand people had packed the fenced grounds of the Capitol to witness the historic occasion, but Elizabeth, lost in her own thoughts and eagerly anticipating what could turn out to be the most important day of her life, was not among them.

CHAPTER THREE

March–April 1861
A few minutes before eight o'clock on the morning after the inauguration, Elizabeth walked one-third of a mile from her home to the White House, crossing Lafayette Square, passing the bronze statue of Thomas Jefferson in the semicircular drive. When she ascended the portico leading to the front entrance of the Executive Mansion, the short, burly, elderly Irish doorman admitted her into the vestibule, where moments later she spotted a familiar figure approaching from down a wide hall. "Good morning, Mrs. Keckley," the butler greeted her. "Welcome to the White House."

"Thank you, Mr. Brown," she replied, pleased and unexpectedly comforted to see a friendly face. Like her, Peter Brown was a former slave. He and his family lived only three blocks from Elizabeth, and they had become acquainted through the Lewises.

"I've come to meet with Mrs. Lincoln to see if she would care to hire me as her dressmaker. Any advice to smooth my way?"

Peter Brown chuckled and escorted her up a busy central staircase. Men of all types hurried by, both coming and going, almost certainly job seekers like herself, eager to secure a post within the new administration. "I haven't known the new First Lady long enough to be a good judge of her likes and dislikes," Peter confided in an undertone. He paused for a moment on the landing, allowing others to pass. "I'll say this much: Whatever you see, don't let it trouble you."

Mystified, Elizabeth wondered what he could possibly mean, but when he led her into a waiting room full of worn mahogany furniture, and three other well-dressed women looked up at their approach, she understood at once. She should have realized that the First Lady would have asked several of her acquaintances to recommend their favorite dressmakers, and naturally each lady would have been eager to curry favor by putting forth her favorite. As the women exchanged nods of greeting, Elizabeth felt their eyes upon her taking in every detail of her attire, just as she was assessing theirs. No one trusted a dressmaker who was not herself garbed in the most becoming costume she could afford. She was thankful she had worn her newest, most stylish dress, sewn from the finest blue, red, and tan plaid wool and perfectly tailored to her figure, with the colored lines so painstakingly matched that the pattern seemed unbroken from bodice to skirt.

"Mrs. Lincoln is still at breakfast," Peter told her, showing her to a chair. "She'll summon you presently. Chin up."

Elizabeth thanked him with a smile, but as she sank into her chair, her hopes plummeted. She had not expected to face any rivals that morning, and she doubted she would be chosen over these women, who were almost certainly better established in Washington City than she was. To make matters worse, each of them had the distinct advantage of being white. But she could do nothing to change those plain facts, so she sat straight in her chair, serene and patient, until at last one of the ladies Elizabeth had seen with Mrs. Lincoln at Willard's appeared and summoned the first mantua maker into an adjoining room.

Elizabeth was the last to be called.

She was taken into a family sitting room, oval shaped with a high ceiling and tall windows that looked out upon the White

57

House lawn, which sloped downhill to a tall iron fence and a marsh leading to the Potomac just beyond. Mrs. Lincoln stood beside one of the windows chatting animatedly with a companion Elizabeth did not recognize, but she glanced up as Elizabeth entered and came to greet her. "You have come at last," she said warmly.

"Thank you for seeing me, madam," said Elizabeth. She reached into her bag and withdrew several papers, which she had protected from creases and tears between two stiff pieces of cardboard. "I bring you several letters of recommendation from my customers in St. Louis."

"Yes, I know your reputation well." Mrs. Lincoln scanned the letters, nodded with satisfaction, and returned them. "For whom have you worked in Washington City?"

"Among others, Mrs. Senator Davis has been one of my best patrons."

Mrs. Lincoln's eyebrows rose. "Mrs. Davis! So you have worked for her, have you? Of course you gave great satisfaction?"

"Certainly, madam."

"So far, so good. Can you do my work?"

"Yes, Mrs. Lincoln," Elizabeth assured her emphatically. "Will you have much work for me to do?"

Mrs. Lincoln cupped her chin in her hand

as if considering the question. "That, Mrs. Keckley, will depend altogether upon your prices. I trust that your terms are reasonable. I can't afford to be extravagant." She threw a rueful glance to her companion, who shook her head in commiseration. "We are just from the West, and are poor. If you do not charge too much, I shall be able to give you all my work."

"I don't think there will be any difficulty about charges, Mrs. Lincoln." In Elizabeth's experience, white ladies of Mrs. Lincoln's status defined "poor" rather differently than she herself would. "My terms are reasonable."

"Well, if you will work cheap, you shall have plenty to do." A slight frown belied the breezy lightness of her tone. "I can't afford to pay big prices, and so I frankly tell you so in the beginning."

They quickly arranged satisfactory terms, and only then did Mrs. Lincoln mention that she wanted Elizabeth to begin immediately. She beckoned to her friend, who promptly produced a bright, rose-colored moiré-antique dress that Mrs. Lincoln wished to wear to the first levee of her husband's presidency, a grand public reception to be held on Friday evening. Mrs. Lincoln described the alterations she wanted, which were not at all daunting, so although Elizabeth would have only three days to work on it, she assured Mrs. Lincoln that the dress would be finished on time. After taking the First Lady's measurements, she carried the dress home, where she worked on it until late into the night. She knew that this garment, though not of her own design and inelegantly begun, was an audition of sorts. If she did well, Mrs. Lincoln would trust her with an original gown, and perhaps many more after that. If her alterations were judged unsatisfactory, she should expect no second chances.

The next day Elizabeth returned to the White House to fit the gown and found Mrs. Lincoln in excellent spirits, the center of a lively group of ladies, relations from Illinois, Kentucky, and elsewhere, all come to Washington City to enjoy the festivities. Mrs. Lincoln was dressed in a cashmere wrapper with fine quilting worked down the front and a simple headdress, while her companions wore morning robes. They chatted and teased one another cheerfully as Elizabeth helped Mrs. Lincoln into the dress and marked a few necessary adjustments. All the while Mrs. Lincoln was so merry and gracious that Elizabeth wondered what could have inspired the disparaging rumors about her temperament. Elizabeth had overheard some of her patrons — all Southerners, now that she thought about it — refer to the new First Lady as an ill-mannered, ignorant, and vulgar country bumpkin, but Mrs. Lincoln was certainly none of those things. Clearly Elizabeth would do well to trust the evidence of her own observations and dismiss such unkind remarks as the product of jealousy and politics.

Later, back in her own rooms, Elizabeth worked diligently upon the gown, adorning it with pearls and a point-lace cape with little time to spare. On Thursday afternoon, she was surprised to receive another summons to the White House, but having learned from the fiasco with Mrs. McLean, she quickly packed up the dress and her sewing basket and hurried off without a moment's delay. Upstairs in the oval sitting room once again, Mrs. Lincoln informed her that the levee was postponed until Tuesday, but before Elizabeth could breathe a sigh of relief, Mrs. Lincoln added that she had conceived of a few more improvements for the gown. Elizabeth hid her dismay as Mrs. Lincoln described what she wanted and it became evident that these were no simple adjustments but rather a significant alteration of the style. Still, she thought she could accomplish them in time and said so, and when Mrs. Lincoln added a waist of blue watered silk for her cousin Mrs. Grimsley to the order, she agreed.

"All will be ready in plenty of time for you to dress for the levee on Tuesday," Elizabeth promised, taking her leave as quickly as she could, knowing she had not a moment to spare.

For days she sewed and sewed, rising early and working late, barely pausing for meals and church and a newly arrived letter from George. She completed the last stitches early on Tuesday evening, just in time to fold it carefully with Mrs. Grimsley's completed blue silk waist and hurry the one-third of a mile to the White House. Peter Brown greeted her in the vestibule, but she knew the way well enough by then that he let her hasten upstairs on her own.

There she found Mrs. Lincoln in her dressing gown, in a terrible state of excitement despite her companions' attempts to soothe her. "I cannot go down," Mrs. Lincoln exclaimed, tearing herself from a cousin's embrace. "How could I possibly? I have absolutely nothing to wear. Imagine what people will say. Think of how they'll mock me."

"No one will mock you," said Mrs. Edwards, Mrs. Lincoln's patient elder sister, clad in a subdued gown of brown brocade.

"Wear the gray velvet," said Mrs. Grimsley, who wore a blue watered silk gown with a long train adorned with turquoises and pearls, and a headdress of white roses. "It's lovely and no one here has seen it yet."

Just then, the youngest of the ladies spotted Elizabeth lingering uncertainly in the doorway. "She's here," she cried out, gesturing, and everyone turned Elizabeth's way.

"There, now," said Mrs. Edwards, visibly relieved. "Didn't we tell you she would come?"

Her lips pressed together tightly, Mrs. Lincoln strode two paces toward Elizabeth before stopping short. "Mrs. Keckley, you have disappointed me — deceived me." Her face was pale with outrage, her eyes red rimmed. "Why do you bring my dress at this late hour?"

Elizabeth took a deep breath and carefully unfolded the gown, Mrs. Grimsley's smaller garment still draped over her arm. "Because I have just finished it, and I thought I should be in time."

"But you are not in time, Mrs. Keckley." Mrs. Lincoln shook her head, wrung her hands, and began pacing. "You have bitterly disappointed me. I have no time now to dress, and, what is more, I will *not* dress, and go downstairs."

Her ladies protested and reached out to her, but she brushed them off.

"I am sorry if I have disappointed you, Mrs. Lincoln, for I intended to be in time." Humiliated, Elizabeth took care to keep her voice calm, even, and firm. She saw no reason for such distress. She had plenty of time to get Mrs. Lincoln ready for the levee if the good woman would only consent to it. "Will you let me dress you? I can have you ready in a few minutes."

"No, I won't be dressed." Mrs. Lincoln halted, threw one glance at the window, another at the door, and flung her hands into the air, helpless. "I will stay in my room. Mr. Lincoln can go down with the other ladies."

"But there is plenty of time for you to dress, Mary," said Mrs. Grimsley.

"Let Mrs. Keckley assist you," implored Mrs. Edwards, "and she will soon have you ready."

Uncertain, Mary looked from her sister to her cousin and back. "Oh, very well," she said, subdued. "She may try."

Quickly Elizabeth helped Mrs. Lincoln out of her dressing gown and into the moiré antique before she could change her mind. She arranged Mrs. Lincoln's dark hair with red roses that complemented the hue of her gown. The dress was very becoming, and when Mrs. Lincoln examined herself in the mirror it was as if a freshening breeze blew away the storm clouds of only moments before, for she was all sunshine and smiles, very pleased with her appearance. She did indeed look very elegant in the rose moiré antique, accented beautifully by her pearl necklace, earrings, and bracelets.

A knock sounded on the door, and President Lincoln himself came in, with young Tad and Willie trailing after him. He greeted the ladies with smiles and compliments, and then threw himself on the sofa without any apparent fear of wrinkling his evening attire. His sons were immediately upon him, wrestling and laughing, and he made a great show of bravely fending them off, joking all the while. Amused, Elizabeth suppressed a smile. She never could have imagined the leader of the land roughhousing with his boys like any fond father.

Before long, Mrs. Lincoln said pointedly, "Perhaps the boys have had enough of that for now."

"No, Mother," said Willie. "We're not at all tired."

Mr. Lincoln laughed. "Maybe not, but your father is." He swung his long legs around and rose from the sofa as the boys darted off to play. Pulling on his gloves, he quoted a few lines from a poem about a barefoot boy's carefree play, and then another about a blacksmith whose hard work earned him a night's repose.

The other ladies were charmed, but his wife seemed barely able to contain her impatience. "You seem to be in a poetical mood tonight."

"Yes, Mother, these are poetical times." His smile deepened as he looked her over. "I declare, you look charming in that dress. Mrs. Keckley has met with great success." As he offered compliments to the other ladies — Mrs. Grimsley in the blue watered silk, Mrs. Edwards in an understated gown of brown and black, Miss Edwards in crimson, Mrs. Baker in ashes of rose, and Mrs. Kellogg in lemon-colored silk — Elizabeth flushed with pleasure and pride. The president himself had praised her handiwork and referred to her by name, although until that moment she had not realized that he even knew it.

"Shall we go downstairs, Mother?" the president asked his wife.

"In a moment," she said, frowning as she

searched her dressing table. "I cannot find my lace handkerchief."

Everyone swore that they had seen it on the table only moments before, but no one had any idea what had become of it. Elizabeth joined in the search with the others, but after a few minutes, Mr. Lincoln's laughter boomed again, and he raked a long-fingered hand through his hair and sent an aide after Tad and Willie. When the boys were brought back to face their parents — Willie, somber and good; Tad, bursting with mischievous smiles — it was easy enough to deduce what had become of the handkerchief. Eventually the playful thief was persuaded to relinquish his prize and the handkerchief was restored to its rightful owner. Only then did Mrs. Lincoln smile, take her husband's arm, and lead the other ladies downstairs to the levee, as elegant and regal as any queen.

For a long moment, Elizabeth stood watching after them, a bit confounded, marveling at all that she had seen. "George will never believe this," she murmured as she drew on her shawl and collected her satchel. Yet she had observed the scene with her own eyes.

That night, Elizabeth would later hear, a gracious and cordial President Lincoln had shaken hands with hundreds of well-wishers for more than two hours, welcoming strangers as warmly as friends and greeting many by name. Some of Elizabeth's longtime patrons had attended the event, but most Southern ladies of the established Washington social elite had stayed away, a calculated snub that could not have escaped the First Lady's notice. Those who did attend mingled freely, Northerners and Southerners alike, but their disagreements were surely never far from their thoughts, what with militias forming in their home states and Major Anderson's men languishing at Fort Sumter. While all eyes were fixed on the Lincolns — measuring, appraising — mischief had broken out in the unwatched cloakroom; when the guests departed, they discovered that their coats and wraps had been haphazardly mixed up and some had been stolen, inspiring one wag to remark that only one in ten guests left the gala clad in the same outer garments he had worn upon his arrival.

Mrs. Lincoln herself was well pleased with her first levee, having perhaps forgotten her distress and anger in the hours preceding it. She was less sanguine on the morning after the president's first state dinner held for members of his cabinet a few weeks later.

Elizabeth had dressed her in a striking blue silk gown, beautifully embroidered, and had watched her take her husband's arm happily and descend the grand staircase as if she expected to have a perfectly lovely time. The next day, however, when Elizabeth returned to the White House to sew and to present various ribbons for Mrs. Lincoln to consider for a new bonnet, she found her patron in a state of bewildered distress. The previous night, as the dinner guests were leaving, the secretary of the treasury's daughter, the twenty-year-old, auburn-haired beauty Miss Kate Chase, had slighted Mrs. Lincoln in front of all their guests.

"Including men from the papers," lamented Mrs. Lincoln. "Soon everyone will hear of it."

Elizabeth decided it would be kinder not to warn her that gossip would spread the tale swiftly enough without help from the press, if something deliciously shocking had indeed happened. Miss Chase was one of the most popular young ladies in Washington society, praised for her charm and wit as well as her beauty, and if she had affronted the First Lady, it would be quite a story. "What did she do?"

"Well . . ." Mrs. Lincoln hesitated. "It sounds silly when I describe it."

"Then perhaps it's really nothing after all."

"Oh, no, no, it's something." Mrs. Lincoln picked up a spool of ribbon, turned it over in her hands, and set it aside without really seeming to examine it. "I was bidding my guests good-bye, and when it came to be Miss Chase's turn, I said, 'I shall be glad to see you anytime, Miss Chase.' She replied, in a thoroughly lofty tone, 'Mrs. Lincoln, I shall be glad to have *you* call on *me* at anytime.' See how she puts herself above me? I will have to go to her. She does not intend to visit me."

Elizabeth frowned. Miss Chase's remark did possess a certain air of disrespect, but her reputation was that of a perfectly lovely and admirable, if ambitious, young woman. "That was not kind of her."

"Not kind? It was more than that. It was impertinent and unbecoming a young lady." Mrs. Lincoln rose and went to the window, looking out over the Potomac to the green hills of Virginia on the other side. "I suppose I should expect nothing better from the daughter of Secretary Chase. You know she and her father expected the Republican Party to nominate him instead of my husband."

"I did not know."

Mrs. Lincoln turned away from the window, nodding. "It's true, and since her mother is dead, if her father had been elected president, Miss Chase would have been his hostess. She believes that their rightful place is here in the White House, and that she should be First Lady now, not I."

"Well," said Elizabeth mildly, "he wasn't, and she isn't."

After a moment, Mrs. Lincoln laughed. "Yes, that's right. Still, I'm certain it remains her greatest ambition."

From that day forward, Mrs. Lincoln and Miss Chase were social rivals, each considering herself the highest lady in Washington society and resenting the other's attempts to demonstrate her superior rank. Miss Chase had the advantage of beauty, popularity, charm, and long-standing ties to the established elites, but Mrs. Lincoln had the president, the White House, and the title of First Lady. And, Elizabeth liked to flatter herself, Mrs. Lincoln had the advantage of a particularly skilled dressmaker who would make sure she always went out in public — or into battle, as it sometimes seemed — perfectly turned out.

For Elizabeth had become Mrs. Lincoln's regular modiste, and throughout the spring of 1861, she would sew more than fifteen gowns for the First Lady. She also often dressed Mrs. Lincoln in her finery and arranged her hair for balls, dinners, and levees. One evening, as the president observed how skillfully Elizabeth tended to his wife, he asked her if she were brave enough to attempt to subdue his own unruly locks.

"If you didn't make such a habit of running your hands through your hair, it wouldn't be such a tangle," Mrs. Lincoln admonished him.

The president merely smiled and sat down in his easy chair. "Well, Madam Elizabeth," he asked, "will you brush my bristles down tonight?"

"Yes, Mr. President," she replied, taking his comb and brush in hand. When she finished, he examined himself in the mirror and declared that his hair looked as if it had been taught a lesson. He was so pleased that it became his custom to ask Elizabeth to attend to his hair after she finished dressing his wife, and Elizabeth did what she could with it.

As the weeks went by, Elizabeth took on other duties within the White House, such as running errands for Mrs. Lincoln and tending to Willie and Tad when they fell ill with the usual mild childhood ailments, but modiste to the First Lady remained her most prominent role. Over time she would learn that Mrs. Lincoln preferred to wear white but that she was also fond of pink, crimson, bright yellow, deep purple, and royal blue. She loved to wear pearls against her skin and flowers in her hair, and she favored low, open necklines with short sleeves to show off her well-formed neck and shoulders, ignoring whispered criticism that such styles were more appropriate for younger women.

Elizabeth soon learned that scathing criticism of her newest and most important patron would be unrelenting, coming from all corners in copious amounts, much to the dismay and consternation of its unhappy subject, who could do nothing to staunch the flood.

On the morning of April 12, Washington was jolted awake by shocking and often contradictory reports from Charleston. Before sunrise that day, Confederate cannon had fired upon Fort Sumter. No, indeed — both parties were still engaged in serious negotiations. No, that was but wishful thinking — shots had been fired. No one knew what to believe. A furious battle was ongoing, or Major Anderson had surrendered. The fort was destroyed utterly and its defenders slaughtered, or the starving, exhausted Union troops had marched out under a flag of truce and were being held prisoner. The citizens of Washington crowded telegraph offices and hotels, demanding news and spreading rumors, but no one knew precisely what was happening, what might have already happened. Secessionists who had kept their opinions to themselves since Mr. Lincoln's administration took over the capital now cheered the start of war. Southern sympathizers openly sought recruits for the Confederate army, while loyal Union men rushed to join militias. In the streets, arguments turned into fistfights, and then the most alarming rumor of all swept through the city: Rebels were marching on Washington with an army twenty thousand strong.

Eventually the truth of Fort Sumter reached the capital: After his troops had exchanged fire with Confederate guns for thirty-four hours, Major Robert Anderson had been forced to surrender. On April 14, five additional Washington militia companies were called into active duty, for a total of about twenty-five hundred local soldiers serving throughout the district. Mounted soldiers were posted at all approaches to Washington City. Twenty cavalrymen guarded the White House, with hundreds more stationed in the immediate surroundings and at the Capitol, the Treasury, and the post office. The following day, President Lincoln issued a nationwide call for seventy-five thousand recruits, assigning a quota to each state. These troops, who would enlist to serve for ninety days, would surely be sufficient to put down the rebellion.

As Washington awaited reinforcements from the North and fears of an imminent Confederate invasion grew, the young colored men of Elizabeth's comfortable middle-class neighborhood as well as the less fortunate who lived along the alleyways were as eager as their white counterparts to take up arms in defense of their city. Even Peter Brown's eleven-year-old son, who worked as a shoeshine boy on the grounds of the Treasury Building, proudly told Elizabeth of his plans to enlist as a drummer boy as soon as he turned twelve. But every young man of color who tried to enlist, regardless of his age, strength, or status, was turned away.

"Either the need for soldiers is very small or the foolishness of Mr. Lincoln's recruiters is very great," Virginia Lewis remarked to Elizabeth one Sunday afternoon as they went on their customary stroll and discovered a few militia soldiers drilling on the grounds of the Capitol. The city had taken on the appearance of an armed camp, and everywhere, apprehensions were on the rise. Although it was the capital of the Union, Washington was essentially a Southern city, surrounded by the Union slaveholding state of Maryland on one side and Virginia, which had seceded after Mr. Lincoln issued the state quotas for recruits, on the other side, with only the Potomac separating them.

A few days earlier, the husband of one of Elizabeth's favorite patrons, Colonel Robert E. Lee, a Virginian, had been offered the command of the entire United States Army, but after careful consideration, he had declined and had gone home to his plantation in Arlington on the other side of the river. Elizabeth knew from conversations overheard in the White House that President Lincoln had fought valiantly to keep Virginia in the Union, and she knew from remarks Mrs. Lee had made in her presence that her husband had not wanted Virginia to secede. For every firebrand eager for war, there seemed to be two or more who had been drawn into the conflict reluctantly but were nonetheless resolved to do their duty with all their might. And with the conflict so obviously pivoting upon the point of slavery, was it any wonder that Negro men too wanted to do their part to help the Union triumph?

"The recruiters must think they'll have more than enough white volunteers to fill their quotas," Elizabeth said. "If the fighting goes on longer than they expect, maybe they'll let colored men enlist later."

Although the day was balmy, Virginia shivered. "I'd rather have the fighting over before that day could come. How terrible this rebellion would be if seventy-five thousand men weren't enough to finish it. Can you imagine the bloodshed?"

Elizabeth inhaled shakily, the acrid odors of camp refuse and coal smoke so heavy in the air that her eyes stung and watered. "I can imagine it all too well."

She tucked her arm through Virginia's and they turned toward home. Although she thought it was an outrage that men of color were forbidden to enlist, she was secretly relieved that her son would not be required to lay down his life for his country.

Elizabeth wondered if her husband, James, would try to enlist. As a young man he had been full of fight, and after John Brown's failed raid on Harpers Ferry, he had declared that if he had been there, he would have taken up arms and stirred up the slave revolt John Brown had intended. Suddenly James's visage appeared so clearly to her mind's eye that it was as if he stood before her, not rambling and drunk as he had been in their last years together but smiling, bold, and handsome as he had been when they first met.

Elizabeth gasped and stopped short, shaken by the vision. She had not thought of her husband in weeks, perhaps months. Why would he come unbidden to her thoughts now?

"Elizabeth?" Virginia had been brought to an abrupt halt when Elizabeth stopped. "What's the matter? You look as if you've seen a ghost."

Elizabeth managed a shaky laugh. "I haven't, not as far as I know. At least not recently."

Virginia smiled tentatively at her joke, but she looked uncertain. "What's troubling you, then?"

Elizabeth hesitated. Virginia knew she was married and that she and her husband were estranged, but Elizabeth disliked speaking ill of James, and as a consequence, she had told Virginia little about him. She wasn't sure why, but she was reluctant to admit that she had been thinking about him then.

So instead she nodded to the scenes of

preparation for the defense of the city — all around them, and all inadequate. "Aren't there reasons enough for all of us to be troubled these days?"

Virginia nodded. They watched a few moments more before continuing on home.

Soon, Elizabeth would wonder whether James's restless, wistful spirit had indeed visited her in that moment she had imagined him so vividly.

Not two days after her stroll with Virginia, a letter came from Missouri, written in a deliberate yet shaky hand, full of misspellings and apologies.

Dear Mrs Keckley

It greves me to writ and tell you that your husband James past on from this life in Feb of an alement of the liver. He did not suffer long and he was not alone at the end. Being as there was no money for a funerl he was layd to rest in the slaves field I hope this suits you. It was a gud Christian service there were prayers and hyms.

I know you and he livd apart but I thot you should be told because you are his wife and only kin. He was a gud man in his way as you know and his frens will miss him.

I am sorry I culd not tell you sooner but I did not know were you are. But your old landlady gave me this adres and I hope this letter will find you there and well.

                    Most Truly Yours I remain
                              Ephraim Johnson

Elizabeth held the letter for a long moment before folding it deliberately and returning it to the envelope. She was relieved to hear that James had not suffered long, but it pained her to think he had suffered at all.

She wondered who Ephraim Johnson was. She knew no one by that name.

No tears came to her eyes, and she wondered what that said about her, that she did not weep for her husband, a man she had once loved so dearly. The news of his death saddened her, but she did not feel grief stricken, perhaps because she found no small measure of relief in knowing that at last he was at peace. His earthly torment had ended.

"So," she said softly to the empty room, "I am now a widow."

Let James's faults be buried with him. She had no desire to think ill of him now that he was gone.

■ ■ ■

The residents of Washington City waited apprehensively to see which would arrive first, trained militia companies from the north or invaders from the south. Union troops traveling by train to the capital from Northern states would have to pass through Baltimore, about forty miles to the northeast. This should have been no concern; although Maryland was a slave state, it had remained in the Union. But rumors abounded that thousands of Marylanders with Southern sympathies were plotting to block the passage of Northern troops through the city, and since Baltimore had a history of street-mob violence, the rumors could not be ignored. Complicating matters was a quirk of Baltimore's railway system that meant Washington-bound trains would arrive at President Street Station, but would then have to be towed by teams of horses several blocks west through the city streets to Camden Station, from which they could resume their journey by rail. The system, merely inconvenient in peacetime, was potentially disastrous in war.

On the morning of April 19, the Sixth Massachusetts left Philadelphia on a train bound for Washington, arriving in Baltimore with weapons loaded. The wary men hoped for unimpeded passage through the city, but they had been warned that in the interim between stations they would likely receive insults, abuse, and possibly assault, all of which they had been ordered to ignore. Even if they were fired upon, they were not to fire back unless their officers gave the command.

The train carrying the Sixth Massachusetts arrived in Baltimore unannounced, and cars carrying seven of its companies were towed through the city unhindered. But word of the soldiers' presence spread quickly, and soon a crowd massed in the streets, shouting insults and threats. The mob tore up the train tracks and blocked the way with heavy anchors hauled over from the Pratt Street piers, forcing the last four companies of the Sixth to abandon their railcars and march through the city. Almost immediately, several thousand men and boys swarmed them, hurling bricks and paving stones, and dishes and bottles rained down upon them from upstairs windows. As the mob's rage grew, some few among them broke into a gun shop, and from somewhere, the soldiers heard pistol shots. The companies pushed onward at quick time, but when the furious mob blocked the streets ahead, the soldiers opened fire. The crowd dropped back and the soldiers managed to fight their way to the Camden Street Station, and after repairing other tracks sabotaged in the melee, the train sped off to Washington.

When the Sixth Massachusetts finally arrived, battered and bloodied, their appearance brought more alarm than relief to the citizens who had awaited them so anxiously. Four soldiers and at least nine civilians had been killed and scores more injured on the streets of Baltimore, and as reports came in of other railway lines destroyed, bridges burned, and telegraph lines severed, panic ignited as the people of Washington City realized they had been cut off from the North. As she walked to the White House, Elizabeth was shaken to observe citizens frantically piling their belongings onto wagons and into coaches and fleeing the city.

Within the Executive Mansion, Mrs. Lincoln worked valiantly to maintain a sense of calm, of normalcy. She fulfilled her role as hostess at official events the ladies of the entrenched Washington elite disdained, she enrolled Willie and Tad in the Fourth Presbyterian Sunday School, and she cajoled her husband out of his melancholy, which deepened as the crisis worsened. "I begin to believe there is no North," Elizabeth once heard the president say, and indeed, with no reinforcements arriving, no telegraph reports, no mail, she too felt the strange gloom of isolation, of being alone and surrounded by hostile, unseen enemies. It did not help that Southern newspapers managed to make their way into Washington with an ease that mocked their defenses. Time and again the *Richmond Examiner* proclaimed that Washington would make an excellent capital for the Confederacy, noting that most of the city's residents were from Virginia or Maryland anyway and would likely welcome the Confederate army as liberators, with cheers and flowers, rejoicing to be restored to the South.

Washington waited and prepared, until finally, at noon on April 25, the Seventh New York regiment arrived at the B & O Station. Relieved citizens cheered them as they marched to the White House to report to President Lincoln. Fears of an imminent Confederate invasion diminished as more troops arrived from Massachusetts, Rhode Island, and elsewhere, settling into the House chamber and the Capitol rotunda, while later arrivals quartered in the White House, the patent office, and the seminary at Georgetown, or pitched tents on the south lawn of the White House. Massachusetts masons built twenty brick ovens in the cellar of the Capitol to bake enough bread to feed the soldiers, and the noise of drums and bugles and musket-fire practice was so constant that Elizabeth could almost forget what Washington had sounded like before the soldiers came.

While the city transformed around her, Elizabeth sewed for Mary Lincoln, usually at the White House — which she preferred — but sometimes in her own rooms, where the First Lady enjoyed coming to have dresses fitted. One by one, most of Mrs. Lincoln's friends and family had returned to their own homes in Illinois and elsewhere, until only her loyal and sensible cousin Mrs. Grimsley remained, although she often dropped hints that she too missed her own home. As the Washington elite continued to snub Mrs. Lincoln, she found herself increasingly lonely and alone. Elizabeth, sympathetic and kind, became her confidante, and she soon discovered how unsettled Mrs. Lincoln felt in her new surroundings and in the elevated role she had so desired. Never before had she lived among strangers who were thoroughly unimpressed with her family name, which had always carried great influence back in Lexington, thanks to the prominent businessmen and politicians among her relations. Her husband surrounded himself with male colleagues who regarded her notes about policies and appointments as annoying and meddlesome, so that she had to struggle against his aides even for control over the very White House functions for which she played hostess. Excluded from her husband's inner circle, missing her departed sisters and cousins, disdained by the popular ladies of Washington, Mrs. Lincoln often told Elizabeth — sometimes sadly, sometimes in defiance — that Elizabeth was her only true friend within a hundred miles.

Elizabeth — who had been readily received into the elite of colored Washington society by virtue of her natural grace and dignity, her status as a White House intimate, and, ironically, the impressive bloodline she had inherited from Colonel Armistead Burwell, her father and former master — gently tried to steer Mrs. Lincoln down paths that might lead to her greater acceptance. While sewing for other clients, she had detected hopeful signs that the hearts of some of the ladies were softening toward the First Lady. "Nowadays the womenkind of Washington are united only in giving the cold shoulder to Mrs. Lincoln," Elizabeth Blair Lee, who had remained Varina Davis's friend despite their political differences, remarked to Elizabeth during a fitting. "We Republicans at least ought to rally around her."

But not even the friendship of the popular, imperious, and generous Mrs. Samuel Phillips Lee could redeem Mrs. Lincoln in the eyes of those who disparaged her for behaving as if the nation were not at war. When she discovered that Congress allotted twenty thousand dollars to each administration to refurbish the White House, Mrs. Lincoln promptly set about spending the allowance with unrestrained delight. Elizabeth would be among the first to agree that the White House had been sorely neglected; even upon her first visit, when the importance of her interview preoccupied her thoughts, she had not failed to notice the shabby state of the mansion's threadbare rugs, broken furniture, torn wallpaper, and ruined draperies, from which souvenir collectors had snipped pieces until they hung in tatters. But as necessary as the purchases were, it did not look well for the First Lady to be spending so much on carpets and china when some poor, brave soldiers went without tents and blankets.

Mrs. Lincoln's loyalty to the Union was also questioned — entirely without justification, as Elizabeth well knew. "Why should I sympathize with the rebels?" Mrs. Lincoln had once declared, angrily tossing aside a *Harper's* magazine that insinuated she might. "Are they not against me? They would hang my husband tomorrow if it was in their power, and perhaps gibbet me with him. How then can I sympathize with people at war with me and mine?"

While it was true that Mrs. Lincoln's brother, three half brothers, and three of her brothers-in-law were serving in the Confederate army, Mrs. Lincoln herself was a staunch Unionist, and despite growing up in a slaveholding family, she had stronger abolitionist leanings than her husband. This did not prevent Northern newspapers from printing entirely false tales that Mrs. Lincoln's youngest half sister, Emilie, whose husband was a general in the Confederate army, had used a presidential pass to smuggle supplies across Union lines to the rebels. Only Southerners correctly surmised where Mrs. Lincoln's loyalties truly resided, and they condemned her for it. They considered her a traitor whose repudiation of her Southern heritage disgraced her family's good name. Union and Confederate alike, each side believed her loyal to the other, and thus neither would claim her.

Although the immediate threat of invasion seemed to have passed for the moment, the Confederate army never felt very far away. Virginian militia companies drilled in Alexandria just across the river, and for every Union picket guarding the Washington side of bridges leading into the capital, there were Virginia militiamen posted on the other end. A Confederate flag flew boldly above an Alexandria hotel, easily visible from Washington City to anyone with a good vantage point and sharp eyes or a telescope. Elizabeth sometimes observed President Lincoln standing at a window in the White House, studying the flag in silence. Sometimes he sat back in his armchair, rested his feet on the windowsill, and watched ships on the Potomac through a telescope, occasionally letting his gaze drift upward to the rebel flag whipping in the wind. If it seemed an especial taunt, he never said so in Elizabeth's presence.

The war was very close, and it would come closer still.

Telegraph and mail service resumed, and in early May, Elizabeth received a letter that had been delayed in the crisis.

April 24, 1861

Dearest Mother,

I hope this letter finds you safe and well. The news from Washington has been so alarming of late that I can only pray that the papers are following their usual custom of exaggeration.

I write in haste, and yet I write reluctantly, for I fear that you will not welcome what I must tell you. Mother, I am a soldier. You may well ask how this can be, since colored men are not welcome in the ranks of the Union Army. This I discovered firsthand when I and some of my fellows went to enlist at Columbus and were rejected, with the jeers and insults of the white recruits burning in our ears. My friends had no choice but to return to school, but I was too restless to remain, so instead I went home to St. Louis. There, alone, without my duskier-skinned friends, no one had cause to think me other than a white man, and so I signed my name.

Mother, I know you will not be pleased that I have left school without finishing the term, and I am sorry for grieving you, but I am confident I will be allowed to resume my studies when my service is done. It is only a three-month enlistment, but everyone says it will be over well before then, and I could not miss my chance to strike a blow for the Union. I am ever mindful that if not for you I would still be a slave, and thus I have a special obligation to help deliver others from bondage into freedom. I am willing to give this noble cause the three months they ask, and my life if necessary.

Please write to me often, and pray for me always. I am and will always be

Your Devoted Son,
George W. D. Kirkland
Private
First Missouri Volunteers, Company D

Elizabeth was in tears well before she reached his closing lines. He thought she would be upset because he left college before the end of the term? *That* was what he believed would grieve her the most — not his deception, not his youthful, impetuous enlistment, not the possibility of his death on the battlefield?

Blinded by tears, dizzy with anguish, she groped for a chair and sank into it, crumpling the letter in her hand. She pressed her lips together to still her weeping, before

91

Virginia or Walker or one of the other tenants heard her distress and came running to see what was wrong. She trembled in silence until she calmed herself, desperately chasing from her mind's eye visions of her precious only child lying wounded or dying in some distant Southern meadow.

But even in the midst of her fear, she was proud of her son — deeply, profoundly proud. He was right. God had blessed them with the means to free themselves from the misery of enslavement, and therefore they both were obliged to help the many others of their race still held in bondage — George in his way, and she in hers.

She prayed the Lord would reward his noble willingness to sacrifice his life by sparing it.

CHAPTER FOUR

May–August 1861

During the winter of secession, Elizabeth's dressmaking business had declined as many of her best patrons departed for the South, but as spring flourished, so did her fortunes. By that time Mrs. Lincoln had proudly displayed Elizabeth's handiwork at many a White House gathering, and suddenly she found herself the best-known and most coveted mantua maker among the loyal Union women of Washington. With more work than she could handle on her own, she rented a workroom across the street from her boardinghouse and hired assistants. Her patrons understood that Elizabeth must always give the First Lady preference, so whenever Mrs. Lincoln traveled, other ladies rushed to place their orders.

Mrs. Lincoln could scarcely stroll down Pennsylvania Avenue without reporters setting telegraph lines abuzz with the news, so when she and her cousin Mrs. Grimsley traveled to New York on a shopping expedition in early May, newspapermen hounded their every step. Stories of their attending the theater, inspecting carriages at a manufacturer, dining, enjoying soirees, and visiting local luminaries filled newspaper columns and invited spiteful commentary. When Elizabeth read of Mrs. Lincoln's expenditures upon carpets, china, mantel ornaments, and other furnishings for the White House, she winced in sympathy, wishing it were possible for her patron to be more discreet. She also worried at the amount Mrs. Lincoln seemed to be spending, not only because the papers depicted her as wasteful, but also because Elizabeth could not imagine how the congressional allowance could stretch far enough to cover it all.

But it was impossible not to be caught up in her patron's delight when she returned to Washington, flush with excitement, eagerly anticipating the delivery of her goods. "I am determined to transform the White House into a showplace worthy of our nation," she told Elizabeth as she led her and Mrs. Grimsley room to room, describing her purchases and where she intended to arrange them. Repairs and restoration would have to be completed first, of course, but Mrs. Lincoln planned to escape the noise and dust, as well as the heat and disease of summertime Washington, by taking Tad and Willie north as frequently as she could.

"I'd like to take Mr. Lincoln as well," she confided, "if only I could pry him away from his cabinet."

No one in Washington could forget the Confederate threat looming ever nearer. For weeks the Confederate flag had waved and snapped in the breeze above Alexandria, taunting them with the threat of invasion, which set their nerves on edge and sent prices for flour, coffee, and other groceries soaring. One morning in late May, Elizabeth woke to the tolling of firehouse bells and went down to breakfast to learn from the Lewises that shortly after dawn, ten Union regiments had quietly crossed the Potomac and had captured Alexandria — but the leader of the New York Zouaves, Colonel Elmer Ellsworth, had been shot and killed, the only casualty of the mission.

Elizabeth's heart sank. "Are you certain?" She had seen Colonel Ellsworth often in the White House and knew him to be a particular favorite of the president. She knew that sometime before the election, Mr.

Lincoln had met the young man in Chicago and had urged him to move to Springfield to study the law. He had been part of the honor guard that had accompanied the president-elect on the train to Washington, and after secession, Mr. Lincoln had used his influence to obtain him a good position in the military. He was only a few years older than Mr. and Mrs. Lincoln's eldest son, Robert.

"There's no mistake," Walker told her, shaking his head grimly. "His is the first blood shed on rebel soil."

"The first drops of many," said Virginia quietly.

Elizabeth's thoughts flew to George — so near in age to the colonel, so eager to join in the fight — and then to the Lincolns. Mrs. Lincoln had liked Colonel Ellsworth nearly as much as her husband did. She would be heartbroken.

Although she was not expected that day, Elizabeth quickly made her way through the muddy streets to the White House, determined to offer Mrs. Lincoln whatever comfort she could. At the door, a somber Mr. McManus told her that the household had plunged into mourning. "Mr. Lincoln was in his library with visitors when word came of the colonel's death," the elderly doorman confided. "Peter Brown says he was so overcome by emotion that he could not speak."

"I'd best see to the First Lady," Elizabeth said, hurrying off.

She found the First Lady in her boudoir, clad in a cheerful floral day dress and sitting at her dressing table, staring straight ahead at nothing. She looked up when Elizabeth entered, a faint light of surprise cutting through her grief. "Ah, Elizabeth," she said. "How did you know I needed you?"

"I heard the bells tolling for the colonel and thought you might." Elizabeth went straight to the wardrobe and began sorting through the First Lady's dresses for a more suitable garment. Suddenly she was seized by the cold realization that she would likely be asked to sew many black dresses in the months ahead as her patrons lost husbands, sons, and brothers, and donned the somber colors of mourning that custom demanded. Shaking off the thought, she spied a black silk dress Mrs. Lincoln must have brought with her from Illinois and held it up. "What do you think of this?"

"It will be fine, I'm sure." Mrs. Lincoln barely glanced at the dress. "We're going out this afternoon, Mr. Lincoln and I, to the navy yard to view the body and pay our respects. After that I believe — I believe the colonel will be removed here, to lie in state in the East Room."

Elizabeth nodded and began unbuttoning Mrs. Lincoln's bodice.

"That dreadful flag provoked him so," said Mrs. Lincoln, her voice distant. "He promised my husband he would tear it down. That's exactly what he did, and he was killed for it."

"Killed for a flag?" asked Elizabeth, without thinking. It seemed like such a waste.

"It should never have happened." Mrs. Lincoln knotted her handkerchief in her lap. "Before a single shot was fired, a lieutenant was sent into Alexandria under a flag of truce, to warn the Confederate commander that they faced an overwhelming force, and he had until nine o'clock to evacuate or surrender."

The commander must have chosen one or the other rather than fight; surely Elizabeth would have heard some distant sounds of battle in Washington if the rebels had resisted. "Which did they choose?"

"They chose to retreat. The lieutenant reported to Colonel Ellsworth that the rebels said they would not resist because the town was full of women and children. Most of the rebel troops boarded a train and left Alexandria well before the deadline, but a few stayed behind. I don't know why. They were captured and imprisoned in a slaver's pen." Mrs. Lincoln sighed as Elizabeth helped her out of her day dress. "I should tell you, Elizabeth, this is only what I've gathered here and there, not an official report of any kind." A trace of anger made her voice tremble. "My husband confides in me less and less."

"Tell me anyway," Elizabeth prompted gently as she straightened Mrs. Lincoln's chemise. She wanted to know what had become of the young officer, and the effort of telling the story seemed to keep Mrs. Lincoln calm.

"Well, from what I've heard, Colonel Ellsworth set off with some of his men to capture the telegraph office, but then he happened to pass the hotel where that flag was flying as bold as brass. He knew how it vexed my husband, what an eyesore it had become."

"For everyone in Washington," Elizabeth agreed, assisting Mrs. Lincoln into the black silk dress. Mrs. Lincoln moved as Elizabeth willed, as compliant as a doll.

"Perhaps he thought the president was watching the hotel that very moment, and perhaps he wanted to signal that the town had been captured. We'll never know. But in any case, Colonel Ellsworth marched into the hotel and up to the roof, and he took hold of that flag and tore it down. He returned downstairs to his men —" Mrs. Lincoln pressed her handkerchief to her lips, steeled herself, and continued. "As he carried the captured banner downstairs, the owner of the hotel stepped out of nowhere and shot him in the chest, from just a few feet away."

Elizabeth's hands froze in the midst of buttoning Mrs. Lincoln's bodice. "Lord have mercy."

"One of Colonel Ellsworth's soldiers promptly avenged him — he killed the man with a musket round to the head." Mrs. Lincoln looked over her shoulder at Elizabeth, her expression full of pain. "But he was too late, you know. Too late to save him."

Elizabeth pressed her lips together, shaking her head. "I am truly very sorry, Mrs. Lincoln. I know you and the president were very fond of him."

"We were indeed." Mrs. Lincoln fell silent as Elizabeth finished dressing her. "I believe he was like another son to Mr. Lincoln. And to both of us, he was a bit of home, do you understand? With all the promise of youth, all the vigor and courage —" A sharp intake of breath. "I shall have to write to his mother. Mr. Lincoln will, of course, but I should too. Although I can't imagine what I will say." Her voice broke, and she sank back down into her chair.

"Mrs. Lincoln," said Elizabeth steadily, "is there anything I can do for you, anything at all, for you or for Mr. Lincoln?"

"You've done what I needed most, Elizabeth, as you always do." Mrs. Lincoln offered her a sad, tight smile. "Sometimes I don't know how I'd endure living in this —" She waved a hand as if to indicate all of Washington City. "Well. You know how it is, and how I rely upon you."

A small glow of pride warmed Elizabeth's heart. She did indeed know. "It is my great pleasure, Mrs. Lincoln."

A few days later, when Mrs. Lincoln next summoned her to the White House, Elizabeth learned that thousands of mourners had come to pay their respects to the young colonel as he lay in state in the East Room. Among them was Robert Lincoln, who had traveled all the way from Harvard to mourn and to comfort his parents. They seemed shaken, not only by their personal loss, but also by the sense that this early, violent, and sudden death heralded the sacrifice of many young, valiant men who would perish in the months ahead.

Afterward, the flag that Colonel Ellsworth had given his life for was presented to the First Lady. Mrs. Lincoln was honored and deeply moved, and kept it always.

The death of this soldier she had barely known made Elizabeth ever more fearful for the one she loved most of all.

George wrote often, at least twice a week, entertaining her with tales of camp life and his humorous early mishaps as a novice soldier. Elizabeth had seen enough of soldiering in Washington to realize that he gave her only the most optimistic, uncomplaining version of his new life, and that it was certainly more difficult than he let on. As far as he could tell, he was the only man of color in the regiment, which was comprised nearly entirely of German immigrants, with some Irish and native-born Americans mixed among them. "I am whiter than most of my comrades," he said in an early letter, "so you need not worry that I will be found out." Many civilian Missourians disliked the Germans, but George admired their industry and stoicism, and he shared their abolitionist views.

The slave state of Missouri was a curious case, having voted in March to remain in the Union but not to supply men or weapons to either side. That decision had not prevented Unionists and secessionists alike from forming militia units on their own and jostling for control over the various federal armories located throughout the state. Within weeks of George's enlistment, the First Missouri under the command of Captain Nathaniel Lyon marched on Camp Jackson, where secessionist Missouri Volunteer Militia troops were holding captured Union heavy artillery and munitions, which had been given to them by the Confederates so they could attack the St. Louis Arsenal. Nearly seven hundred militiamen were forced to surrender, but when they refused to take an oath of allegiance to the United States, Captain Lyon decided to arrest them and march them through the streets of St. Louis to the arsenal, where he intended to parole the humiliated men and order them to disperse.

George's account of how Captain Lyon's plans went terribly wrong, though rendered in a son's carefully selective prose, reminded Elizabeth alarmingly of the altercation in Baltimore. As the First Missouri marched the captured secessionists through the city, indignant residents shouted insults and hurled rocks and paving stones upon the

103

soldiers. "The refrain 'Damn the Dutch!' was shouted at our German comrades so often and with such anger that I thought, at last there is someone hated more than the Negro," George wrote. Next, some accounts claimed, a drunken civilian stumbled into the path of the marching troops, fired a pistol at them, and fatally wounded a captain in the Third Missouri. The soldiers responded by opening fire, first above the heads of the civilians and then into the crowd. Twenty-eight people were killed, including women and children, and some fifty more were injured. Several days of rioting broke out, during which anti-German hatred ran rampant throughout St. Louis, civilians shot at soldiers from the windows of their businesses and homes, and troops once again fired upon crowds in the streets. Although George described the events lightly, with a young man's bravado, Elizabeth could tell he was shaken.

In the middle of June, George told her in a later letter, the First Missouri and other federal regiments marched on Jefferson City to find that the secessionist governor had abandoned the state capital. The Union forces easily captured the city and pursued the governor and his Missouri State Guard to the town of Boonville, about fifty miles

104

to the northwest. "It was a minor skirmish, short and sweet," George wrote, "but we whipped the State Guard, drove the secesh away, and secured the Missouri River Valley for the Union. Not a bad day's work if I do say so myself."

They were encamped at the time he wrote his letter, and he did not know when they would march again or to where. He urged her not to worry, and asked her to pray for him, and promised he would write again soon. "I am ever mindful of my special obligation," he wrote in closing. "Nothing I suffer on the battlefield is of any consequence if it brings freedom to all our race. I only wish my friends from college would be allowed to take up arms as I have done. Sometimes when I hear my comrades talk about the cowardice and inferiority of the Negro I am tempted to do more than speak up in 'their' defense. I want to leap to my feet and shout, 'Haven't I fought as bravely as you? Haven't I marched as far and endured as much? If my blood is shed, will it not be as red as yours? Well, I too am a Negro, and I defy you to explain how I am not as good a soldier as you!' But of course I cannot say it — not yet. When the war is over the truth will be known, and then let no man call me his inferior."

Elizabeth was too proud of him to burden him with her worries and misgivings. George had enlisted to prove himself, to preserve the Union, to deliver others of their race from bondage. She, who had lived nearly forty years a slave, knew all too well that his purpose was noble and necessary.

To think that when she first discovered she was carrying him, more than twenty-four years ago, she had been despondent. She had not wanted to have relations with Alexander Kirkland, and she had dreaded bearing a child into slavery. But after George was born, her greatest fear had been that he would be taken away from her.

By midsummer, the newspapers were filled with stories of battles here, skirmishes there, advances and retreats upon towns Elizabeth had never heard of. Prisoners were taken on both sides, but Mr. Lincoln and his advisers did not know what to do with the men in their custody. As rebels, they had committed treason and should by law have been hanged, but that would be abhorrent on such a large scale — and would almost certainly result in retaliation against captured Union soldiers. An exchange of prisoners, a well-established practice between nations at war, would be construed as recognizing the Confederacy as a legitimate, sovereign government, which the president was disinclined to do. So captured rebels were held indefinitely, sometimes moved from slave pens to navy brigs to civilian Washington prisons, while Mr. Lincoln and his advisers debated what to do with them — and with rebel property the Union Army had seized on the other side of the Potomac. Robert E. Lee's captured Arlington plantation was perhaps the most valuable estate in Virginia, and some of Mr. Lincoln's advisers urged him to sell it to help fund the war and to act as a warning to other planters. Elizabeth understood that the gentleman who had once smiled at her as he pressed one hundred dollars into her hand and told her to spare no expense on his wife's gown was now a rebel, not only a rebel but their general, but she could not help feeling sorry for his wife, her former patron. The plantation had come to the Lees from her side of the family, descendants of Martha Washington. It pained Elizabeth to think that Mrs. Lee might never see her ancestral home again.

Elizabeth had not forgotten other former patrons who had fled Washington for their seceded states. In June she completed the fine needlework Varina Davis had left in her care, but she was confounded by the puzzle of how to get it to her. The postal service had stopped delivery to the Confederacy on the first of June, and although Elizabeth heard tales of smugglers who carried goods freely between North and South, she had no idea how to make such arrangements nor would she feel comfortable trusting anyone who engaged in the practice. In the end she entrusted the embroidery to Mrs. Davis's friend Matilda Emory, the wife of Major William Emory. A Marylander serving alternately in Indian Territory and the capital, he had quit the Union Army in May against his wife's wishes. Not content merely to protest, Mrs. Emory had had her husband reinstated by retrieving his letter of resignation herself. Despite Mrs. Emory's strong Union sentiments, she had remained close to Mrs. Davis, and, without explaining how she would accomplish the task, she assured Elizabeth that she would get the embroidery safely to her friend.

Since leaving Washington City barely six months before, Mr. Davis had been elected president of the Confederacy and Mrs. Davis had become their First Lady. Sometimes Elizabeth thought back to her months working in the Davis household and marveled at the changes time had wrought. Mrs. Davis and her husband had moved from Alabama to Virginia, or so the papers claimed, and they now resided in another White House in Richmond, the new Confederate capital. Elizabeth wondered if her former patron still entertained hopes that the Confederates would capture Washington City and that she would take her place in the first grand residence to bear that title. Observing the new Union defenses all around the district, Elizabeth suspected that conquering the city would not be as easy as Mrs. Davis had once believed.

The First Lady presently occupying the White House would certainly have something to say about Mrs. Davis's confident declarations, if Elizabeth were foolhardy enough to stir up her temper by telling her about them. Mrs. Lincoln was, as she had ever been, a patriotic Unionist, and although the president's cabinet repeatedly thwarted her efforts to influence her husband on policy matters, she used her position to support the Union cause in other ways. She hosted dinners for dignitaries and, hoping to raise people's spirits, she arranged for the Marine Band to perform concerts every Wednesday and Saturday when the White House grounds were open to the public. She toured regimental encampments and visited soldiers in the hospital, often distributing delicacies from the White House kitchen and gardens with her own hands. She obtained weapons from the War Department and had them sent to a Union colonel in her home state of Kentucky along with a sincere, heartfelt letter professing her admiration for him as well as her loyalty and love for the nation. She reviewed troops with her husband and was charmed when an army colonel broke a bottle of champagne over a carriage to christen the field where his men were bivouacked as "Camp Mary" in her honor.

Elizabeth wished Mrs. Lincoln's sincere and helpful efforts received more than an occasional complimentary aside in the press. Unfortunately, reporters and gossips alike were far more fascinated by stories of her secessionist relatives and her lavish expenditures on fringed satin bed curtains and a purple-and-gold dinner service emblazoned with the seal of the United States on each piece — as well as a second set adorned with her own initials. The press hounded her so that she could not escape them, not even on her trips away from Washington to escape the heat, the disease, and the swarms of flies and mosquitoes that plagued the city throughout those oppressive summer days.

Mrs. Lincoln was at home at the end of July when word began to spread that troops were gathering near Manassas Junction, Virginia. Thousands of citizens eager for diversion packed picnic hampers and hired carriages to take them out to watch the spectacle. Politicians determined to witness history, reporters chasing the story, curious workmen, ladies with parasols thrilled by the prospect of danger and heroism — all wanted to watch Brigadier General Irvin McDowell and his mighty Army of Northeastern Virginia soundly defeat the rebels before marching on to take Richmond and bring a quick and decisive end to the conflict.

Several of Elizabeth's young assistant seamstresses had been invited to accompany a few young men in their wagon. "Come with us, Mrs. Keckley," urged Emma Stevens, a former slave from Maryland who rented a small attic room in the Lewises' boardinghouse. As a very young child, she and her mother had been granted their freedom when their old mistress passed away, but the woman's heirs had contested the will. Emma and her mother had been kept in slavery for ten long years more while the lawsuit Emma's mother brought against the heirs dragged out in court. Upon miraculously winning their case, and their freedom, Emma and her mother had adopted the last name of the lawyer who had courageously represented them in a hostile courtroom.

Elizabeth smiled and shook her head. "Thank you, no."

"Oh, do join us," Emma said persistently. "There will be plenty of room in the wagon. And it's a Sunday. You shouldn't work on a Sunday."

"I must," Elizabeth said. "Mrs. Lincoln needs the white day dress finished before her trip to the seaside. You young people go and have a good time, but do take care."

She breathed a sigh of relief when Emma gave her a small disappointed pout and set off on her own, immediately brightening at the thought of her friends and the charming escorts awaiting them. Elizabeth didn't want to admit to the younger woman, her favorite of her assistants, that she could not bear to watch the scenes of battle and to be painfully, vividly reminded of what George might be facing at that very moment somewhere in Missouri.

She sewed all day in her rooms with the windows and doors open to stir the stifling air, breaking only for lunch and for a walk with Virginia along the river, where the stench diminished the pleasure of the cooling breeze. They heard the rumble of gunfire to the west, and they wondered how the battle was faring. "We may be sorry later that we missed all the excitement," Virginia remarked.

"I'm certain I won't," Elizabeth replied.

As they walked back to Twelfth Street, they passed a telegraph office, where men and boys lingered, waiting for news of the battle. The Confederates were on the run, from the sound of it, and they overheard two men say that the Union Army was expected to be in Richmond within a week. Gladdened by the remarkably good report, they returned home to tell Walker what they had learned. Back in her rooms again, Elizabeth took up Mrs. Lincoln's dress, threaded a needle, and allowed herself to hope that the war could be over by the autumn, in time for George to muster out of the army and resume his classes at the start of the term.

Her hopes were dashed before morning.

Sometime after nightfall, noises outside roused her from sleep — carriage wheels, horses' hooves, voices raised in alarm. She hurried to the windows, but they looked out over the garden and she could see nothing but the backs of other houses and the glow of a few lighted lamps visible through the windows. As the commotion continued, more lights joined them. Elizabeth dressed quickly and went outside to the front sidewalk, where she found Virginia, Walker, and a few of their neighbors watching in stunned amazement as carriages and wagons and men on horseback came streaming through the city as fast as their tired horses could carry them, their expressions stricken and terrified.

"What happened?" Elizabeth asked Virginia, who only shook her head, pressed her lips together, and clutched her arm. They held on to one another as the ominous parade went by, realization dawning that these were the spectators who had so enthusiastically set out for Centreville to observe the battlefield earlier that day.

Finally Walker waved down a colored man on a dray, who slowed his team but would not stop. "It was a rout," he called down from the driver's seat. "Hundreds dead. Whole companies lost. McDowell's army's retreating back to the city if they haven't been caught or killed yet, and the rebels are right behind them."

Virginia gasped, and Elizabeth felt a chill. Emma and two of her other young protégées were in the midst of all that chaos.

"Were any civilians hurt?" she called out to the driver, but he had already hastened away.

All through the night the civilians made their way back to the capital, shaken and exhausted, with wild tales of their narrow escape from certain death. They had been at some distance from the fighting, closer to the river, so they were the first to return. Elizabeth had almost given up hope when Emma appeared, escorted by a young man who solicitously entrusted her to the care of Walker, Elizabeth, and Virginia. "It was a nightmare," Emma told them, wide-eyed and trembling. "I've never seen anything like it. If we hadn't been near the back of the crowd, close to the wagon —" She shook her head and fell silent as Virginia led her into the house.

Not until dawn did the first soldiers reach the city, their expressions stunned and haggard, their uniforms torn and disheveled, their ranks diminished. Gone were the waving of regimental colors and the stirring martial music of fife and drum. Famished and exhausted, some of the troops dropped their kits in doorways, on sidewalks, on empty lots, and lay down to sleep where they were. Some observers cast off their shock and hurried back into their homes, quickly returning with bread, cheese, apples, and other food to distribute to the passing soldiers. Elizabeth and Virginia joined in, offering water from pitchers and pails as quickly as one man could pass the dipper to the next.

The wounded came too, brought into the city by the wagonload. There were not enough beds for all the soldiers who needed them, nor enough bandages, nurses, food — nor hospitals for that matter. A few gray-clad rebel prisoners were marched in on foot and under guard. Some citizens shouted curses and threw stones at the captives, but a few bold Confederate sympathizers among them called out encouragement as they were led off to the Old Capitol on First and A streets Northeast, which had been turned into a federal military prison.

For hours the people of Washington waited in terror for the Confederate army to press their advantage and take the city, but the invasion never came.

In the days that followed, the people of the North wanted revenge and President Lincoln wanted answers. Even as volunteers filled recruiting offices, the president closeted himself with his advisers, determined to ascertain how the battle had gone so terribly wrong and how they could ensure it would never happen again. Already the press had taken to calling the Union's disorderly retreat from the battlefield "the Great Skedaddle," shaming the Union soldiers and heartening their enemies.

"They were green troops," Mrs. Lincoln told Elizabeth, staunchly defending the soldiers — and by extension her husband, who had sent them into battle. "They aren't green anymore. They will never again suffer such an embarrassing rout."

Elizabeth hoped she was right, and her thoughts flew to her son. In his last letter, George had written that the First Missouri was preparing to march on Springfield, Missouri, but he did not know when they would set out. She wished she knew whether they had departed yet, whether they had arrived, whether the battle had been fought, and who had emerged victorious. George was still green himself, she thought, despite his regiment's involvement in the conflict in the streets of St. Louis and the minor skirmish at Boonville. He had yet to face the kind of warfare McDowell's men had faced at the creek called Bull Run, and she felt sick at heart when she imagined him facing rebel guns and cannon.

The days between George's letters elapsed in a ceaseless misery of waiting and worry.

The arrival of each letter brought only momentary joy and relief, because although she savored each word, she knew that the letters offered no assurances of his safety any longer, only proof that he had been alive and unhurt at the time he had written them.

But that was something, at least. She kept his letters safely tucked away in a rosewood box her former mistress had given her as a farewell gift when she departed St. Louis. Every Sunday evening she read the letters in the order he had written them, a ritual that grew lengthier every week. They were talismans that closed the distance between them and, she hoped, would bring him back to her someday.

The first days of August were oppressively hot and humid, with no relief on the horizon. After hosting a state dinner for Prince Napoléon III, Mrs. Lincoln took Willie and Tad and her cousin Mrs. Grimsley on a vacation to Long Branch, Manhattan, and upstate New York, but her absence left Elizabeth busier than ever as other ladies rushed in with their dressmaking demands. She sewed for Mary Jane Welles, the wife of the secretary of the navy; Margaret Cameron, the wife of the secretary of war; and Adele Douglas, the young widow of the late Senator Stephen A. Douglas from Illinois. Recently widowed, the lovely Mrs. Douglas dressed in deep mourning but with excellent taste, so that even in her sorrow other ladies were jealous of her beauty and grace.

In the middle of the month, with summer storms worsening the humidity and bringing no relief from the heat, Elizabeth received a letter sent from Missouri but addressed in an unfamiliar hand. It could not be from George, she thought, quickly opening the envelope, or from her former mistress Anne Garland, whose writing she knew well. Heart pounding with sudden apprehension, she unfolded the letter and read it slowly, word by word, afraid to reach the end.

Near Springfield, Missouri
August 11, 1861
To Mrs. Elizabeth Keckley, Washington, DC:

Dear Madam,

It is with great pain that I write to inform you of the death of your son, George Kirkland. By his good conduct and bravery while with me, he had won the respect of myself and his fellow soldiers, and should he have lived I would have promoted him soon. He was shot through the body at the Battle of Wilson's Creek, where his last words were of our noble struggle and how we must see it through. He is buried here beside his brothers in arms who also fell that day. His effects I shall send home at the earliest opportunity.

Yours truly,
Charles W. Anderson
Captain, Commanding Company D
First Missouri Volunteers

Elizabeth felt the room shift and turn around her before all went dark.

CHAPTER FIVE

August 1861–March 1862

When George's personal effects arrived a week later, Elizabeth kept them on her bureau for two days before mustering up the courage to examine them. They included all of her letters, neatly bound with a ribbon; a book of psalms; a sewing kit that could be rolled up and tied, commonly called a housewife; a rosewood ink bottle; a tin cup; a small tobacco box, also of tin; and a pair of bone dice. She touched the items one by one, imagining them in his hands. She was glad that he had found solace and inspiration in Holy Scripture while at war, but she did not like to think that he had taken up smoking and gambling.

It no longer mattered.

In the midst of her bereavement, Elizabeth found comfort in a heartfelt, compassionate letter from Mrs. Lincoln and from the gentle kindness of Virginia, Walker, and

Emma, whose eyes brimmed with tears when she told Elizabeth she wished she would have known her fine, heroic soldier. For a brief moment, Elizabeth allowed herself to imagine George and Emma meeting, falling in love, marrying, raising children — but then she banished such thoughts forever.

He had died a free man. That much, at least, she had done for her son.

In autumn Mrs. Lincoln returned to Washington, and duty again called Elizabeth to the White House. The battlefront had moved off from the outskirts of Washington, but every day brought new reports of intense fighting and grisly scenes of death and destruction. War raged in several states, and the Union Army endured one demoralizing defeat after another. In Washington, a stretch of rainy weather flooded the Potomac, washing corpses of Union soldiers killed weeks before at the Battle of Ball's Bluff downstream until they were fished out between the bridges at Fourteenth Street. Near the river and canals, sewers overflowed into the streets, spreading a miasma of stench and sickness for blocks. Soldiers camped in the surrounding hills, bunked close together in soggy tents where smallpox and typhoid fever struck them down in great numbers.

Union soldiers fought Confederate, doctors and nurses struggled against disease, police and volunteers alike battled the fires that broke out with alarming regularity, and Mr. Lincoln struggled with his cabinet and with General McClellan, who seemed incapable of pressing his advantage on the battlefield or even recognizing when he had it. All the while, Mrs. Lincoln engaged in a very different sort of battle. Her renovations to the White House had garnered her much criticism in the press and had run well over budget, and to Elizabeth's dismay, the gardener, James Watt, had taught her how to pad bills and hide expenses in his account. Ignoring the commissioner of public buildings' warnings that she had no money left to spend, Mrs. Lincoln continued running up debts until it became impossible to conceal them from her husband anymore. They argued furiously on her forty-third birthday, and afterward Mrs. Lincoln begged the commissioner to intercede with the president on her behalf. Reluctantly he did so, and although Elizabeth did not witness Mr. Lincoln's explosive reply — "I swear I will never approve the bills for flub dubs for this damned old house!" — everyone heard of it later.

Mrs. Lincoln's reputation suffered further damage thanks to the questionable characters who populated her evening salons — a coterie of favorites, almost exclusively men, who flattered her vanity and may have betrayed her confidences. It was said that one of her regular callers provided a copy of the president's annual message to Congress to the *New York Herald,* which published the speech before he could deliver it. After that, Mr. Lincoln warned his wife against idle talk, banished the man blamed for the leak from the White House, fired the gardener, and to Mary's sorrow, ceased confiding in her altogether where the work of his government was concerned.

Elizabeth soon learned firsthand what Mrs. Lincoln's troubles had already demonstrated: Unscrupulous people were eager and determined to wriggle their way into the White House for their own wicked purposes. As soon as Elizabeth became well-known throughout Washington as Mrs. Lincoln's modiste, strangers crowded around her affecting friendship, hoping that she could use her influence to obtain them a job, secure them a favor, or provide gossip they could use to their own benefit.

One day, a woman Elizabeth had never

met called on her at her rooms, placed an order for a dress, and insisted upon paying her partly in advance. For quite some time she came daily to see Elizabeth for fittings and adjustments, never failing to be gracious and kind. On the day the dress was complete and she came to pick it up, she hesitated before saying, "Mrs. Keckley, you know Mrs. Lincoln?"

"Yes," said Elizabeth, folding the dress carefully for her new patron to take home.

"You are her modiste, are you not?"

"Yes."

"You know her very well, do you not?"

Elizabeth kept her expression smooth and pleasant, wondering where the questions would lead. "I am with her every day or two."

"Don't you think you would have some influence with her?"

So at last, there it was. "I cannot say. Mrs. Lincoln, I presume, would listen to anything I should suggest, but whether she would be influenced by a suggestion of mine is another question."

"I am sure that you could influence her." The woman offered her an ingratiating smile. "Now, Mrs. Keckley, I have a proposition to make. I have a great desire to become an inmate of the White House. I have heard so much of Mr. Lincoln's goodness that I should like to be near him, and if I can enter the White House no other way, I am willing to go as a menial." At this Elizabeth tried to speak, but the woman hurried on as if she hadn't noticed. "My dear Mrs. Keckley, will you not recommend me to Mrs. Lincoln as a friend of yours out of employment, and ask her to take me as a chambermaid? If you will do this you shall be well rewarded. It may be worth several thousand dollars to you in time."

Elizabeth regarded her with amazement. "Madam, you are mistaken in regard to my character. Sooner than betray the trust of a friend, I would throw myself into the Potomac. I am not so base as that. Pardon me, but there is the door, and I trust that you will never enter my room again."

The woman sprang to her feet, her expression utterly astonished and outraged. "Very well," she snapped as she strode from the room. "You will live to regret your action today."

"Never, never," Elizabeth exclaimed, slamming the door shut behind her. A moment later, she heard a rap upon it and tore it open only to find Emma standing in the hallway.

Emma inclined her head down the hallway. "Why is she leaving in such a huff?"

"Oh, it's nothing," said Elizabeth shortly, beckoning Emma inside. "Just another opportunity hunter. She claims it's her heart's desire to work as Mrs. Lincoln's chambermaid."

"She doesn't look like a chambermaid," observed Emma. "But she does look somewhat familiar."

"I'd never seen her before she ordered that dress, and I hope never to see her again."

She wanted nothing more than to forget the incident, but Emma's curiosity had been piqued, and she promptly launched her own investigation. Before long she discovered that the woman was an actress, who had confided to several friends her determination to enter the White House as a servant, learn the secrets of its inhabitants, and publish a scandalous account to the world. "She underestimated your principles, and your loyalty," said Emma, clearly relishing her triumph at discovering the scheme.

"Let that be a lesson to us both." Elizabeth never would have accepted a bribe, but she knew others would have had no qualms about doing so. When she thought of how long and how hard she had worked to raise the twelve hundred dollars to purchase her freedom and George's, she could well understand how someone else in her place would have given in to temptation. But Mrs. Lincoln was no longer only a patron, or even just the First Lady. She had become a friend, and Elizabeth would rather die than betray her.

For Mrs. Lincoln, the autumn was marked by changes in the White House staff, some she desired and others that were forced upon her. After all the schools in the district were shut down due to the wartime emergency, the First Lady decided to open a classroom in the White House rather than send Willie and Tad off to boarding school. She hired a tutor, arranged desks and a chalkboard, and brought in her sons' best friends, Bud and Halsey Taft, as classmates. Until then, the youngest Lincoln boys' education had been sorely neglected by their indulgent parents. Willie had a scholarly bent and often read and composed poetry on his own, but Tad was barely literate, something Mrs. Lincoln resolved to remedy. Both Mr. and Mrs. Lincoln valued education and hoped their younger sons would come to love learning as much as they did, and perhaps in time follow their eldest brother, Robert, on to Harvard. Privately, Elizabeth heartily approved of the new plan, which she hoped would give the mischievous boys some much-needed discipline along with the usual lessons. She had long regretted that she had been given no formal education, and she disliked seeing any opportunity for learning squandered.

Some new members of the White House staff should have been reassuring, but instead their presence made Elizabeth uncomfortably aware of the dangers confronting the president in those perilous times. New doormen — some of them officers from the new Metropolitan Police, dressed in civilian attire and carrying concealed weapons — could be found in the public rooms, and uniformed sentries were posted on the grounds. In the year since his election, the president had received so many threatening letters that it was impossible to keep track of them all, although their frequency and virulence had increased since Bull Run. Mrs. Lincoln worried more about her husband's safety than he seemed to, and she urged him to travel unannounced and accompanied by guards whenever he moved about the city. He considered such precautions unnecessary and consequently ignored his wife's requests, which made her fret all the more.

Mrs. Lincoln was also concerned about

threats from within. She and the president often discussed his cabinet members in Elizabeth's presence, and Elizabeth had observed that the First Lady was a shrewd judge of character, and her intuition about other people's sincerity was usually more accurate than her husband's. Elizabeth had learned early on that Mrs. Lincoln despised Secretary of the Treasury Salmon Chase, whom she called a selfish politician instead of a true patriot, but Elizabeth attributed some of her dislike to the fact that he was the father of her most bitter social rival, the lovely Miss Kate Chase.

Mrs. Lincoln thought no better of Secretary of State William Seward. One morning, Elizabeth arrived at the White House earlier than usual to find Mr. Lincoln sitting in a chair, holding the newspaper in one hand and stroking little Tad's head with the other. While Elizabeth was basting a dress, a servant entered with a letter for Mr. Lincoln that had just arrived by messenger. He broke the seal and read the letter in silence.

"Who is the letter from, Father?" asked Mrs. Lincoln.

"Seward." Mr. Lincoln tucked the letter into his pocket. "I must go over and see him today."

"Seward! I wish you had nothing to do

with that man. He cannot be trusted."

Mr. Lincoln regarded her mildly, but Elizabeth thought she saw the corner of his mouth twitch as if he were trying not to smile. "You say the same about Chase. If I listened to you, I should soon be without a cabinet."

Mrs. Lincoln looked as if she thought that would be a significant improvement. "Better to be without it than to confide in some of the men that you do. Seward is worse than Chase. He has no principle."

"Mother, you are mistaken." The brief glint of humor had turned sober. "Your prejudices are so violent that you do not stop to reason. Seward is an able man, and the country as well as myself can trust him."

"Father, you are too honest for this world! You should have been born a saint." The president scoffed at that, but Mrs. Lincoln persisted. "You will generally find it a safe rule to distrust a disappointed, ambitious politician. It makes me mad to see you sit still and let that hypocrite Seward twine you around his finger as if you were a skein of thread."

"It is useless to argue the question, Mother." Mr. Lincoln returned his gaze to the newspaper. "You cannot change my opinion."

That did not dissuade her from trying. She called Andrew Johnson a demagogue and warned her husband that if he placed him in a position of power, he would regret it one day. When the popular General McClellan was promoted, she declared that he was a humbug, because he talked so much and did so little. When Mr. Lincoln protested that he was a patriot and an able soldier, Mrs. Lincoln retorted, "You will have to find some man to take his place — that is, if you wish to conquer the South."

General Ulysses S. Grant was definitely not the officer she would have chosen to replace McClellan. "He is a butcher," she often said, "and is not fit to be at the head of an army." When Mr. Lincoln pointed out that he had been very successful in the field, she replied, "Yes, he generally manages to claim a victory, but such a victory! He loses two men to the enemy's one. He has no management, no regard for life. If the war should continue four years longer, and he should remain in power, he would depopulate the North." She shook her head, indignant and angry. "I could fight an army as well myself. According to his tactics, there is nothing under the heavens to do but march a new line of men up in front of the rebel breastworks to be shot down as fast as they take their position, and keep marching until the enemy grows tired of the slaughter. Grant, I repeat, is an obstinate fool and a butcher."

"Well, Mother, supposing that we give you command of the army," said Mr. Lincoln, a merry gleam in his eye and a ring of irony in his voice. "No doubt you would do much better than any general that has been tried."

If the offer had been made in earnest, Elizabeth would not have been surprised if Mrs. Lincoln had accepted. Then her husband would have had to listen to her counsels.

The war cast a somber mood over the holidays, but Mrs. Lincoln was determined to celebrate. Elizabeth made her a blue velvet gown to wear to a performance at the National Theatre, as well as other dresses for her afternoon receptions and the president's formal levees. The two youngest Lincoln boys were merry, but Mr. Lincoln seemed always melancholy, his cares weighing heavily upon him. Mrs. Lincoln endeavored to cheer him out of his gloomy spells, but the reliable tactics of the past were losing their power to affect him.

Robert Lincoln came home from college for the holidays, and his presence added joy to what already had turned out to be a surprisingly triumphant season for the First Lady. Her much-maligned renovations had transformed the reception areas of the White House into elegant showplaces, earning rave reviews in the papers and grudging praise from even her most persistent detractors.

As for Elizabeth, she celebrated Christmas quietly, with church services on Christmas Eve and the morning of Christmas Day. As they had the year before, the Lewises invited her to join their family for a midday feast, and this time Emma too was a welcome guest. Her friends were so gracious and easy that it wasn't until later that Elizabeth realized that they were each taking care to amuse and divert her, knowing that her first Christmas without her son was bound to be mournful. She was so touched by their kindness that she endeavored to be of good cheer. She reminded herself that thanks to the Savior whose birth they celebrated that day, her son would have eternal life. Surrounded by friends, comforted by the certainty that she and George — and her father and mother too — would be reunited in heaven someday, she could not grieve, if only for that day, if only on Christmas.

The social success Mrs. Lincoln enjoyed

during the Christmas season extended into the New Year. Thousands visited the White House for the traditional New Year's Day reception, and although some guests continued to criticize Mrs. Lincoln's decorating expenses and others gossiped about corruption scandals within the administration, many more visitors praised the refurbished Executive Mansion as tastefully and elegantly done, befitting a glorious nation.

A brilliant levee followed shortly after the New Year's Day reception, and the next morning, Mrs. Lincoln spoke of it in glowing terms while Elizabeth fitted her for a dress. "I have an idea," she mused. Although she spoke as if suddenly inspired, Elizabeth had the distinct impression that she had been pondering whatever she was about to say for quite some time. "These are war times, and we must be as economical as possible. You know the president is expected to give a series of state dinners every winter."

"Yes, of course." Elizabeth had dressed Mrs. Lincoln for almost every one of them.

"These dinners are very costly." Mrs. Lincoln shook her head and sighed as if no words would suffice to describe the outrageous expense. "I thought that if I gave three large receptions, the state dinners could be scratched from the program. What do you think?"

Elizabeth considered. A large reception would allow the Lincolns to entertain a far greater number of guests for the cost, but what Washington society would think of abandoning tradition was another matter. In any event, Mrs. Lincoln had surely already made up her mind, in which case it was simply best to agree with her. "I think you're right, Mrs. Lincoln."

Mrs. Lincoln brightened. "I am glad to hear you say so. If I can persuade Mr. Lincoln, I shall not fail to put the idea into practice."

Before Elizabeth finished her work for the day, Mr. Lincoln joined them, his expression clouded with frustration. "I've just come from the sickbed of my recalcitrant general," he said, sighing gloomily as he settled into a chair. "At least today he can blame typhoid fever for his reluctance to budge."

Mrs. Lincoln murmured sympathetically for a moment, and then, either to distract him from his gloom or because she simply couldn't wait, she proposed her changes to their social calendar. The president mulled it over, then frowned and said, "Mother, I am afraid your plan will not work."

"But it *will* work, if you will only determine that it *shall* work."

"It is breaking in on the regular custom," he noted mildly. The protocol was indeed complex, with the rules of etiquette and the ranking of guests carefully noted. The president and the secretary of state alternated hosting evening receptions from the last week of January through March, and the White House also gave weekly dinners for various members of the government as well as receptions for military officers, diplomats, and Supreme Court justices. Breaking these well-established Washington traditions had the potential to offend.

"But you forget, Father, that these are war times, and old, impractical customs can and should be set aside," Mrs. Lincoln said. "The idea is economical, you must admit."

"Yes, Mother, but we must think of something besides economy."

Elizabeth hid a smile. Matters of economy plagued both Lincolns, due in no small part to Mrs. Lincoln's notorious spending habits, but frugality had become a tool each employed when it served them and dispensed with when it did not. Mrs. Lincoln was usually the spendthrift and her husband the more cautious, and it was amusing to see them trade roles.

"I do think of something else," Mrs. Lincoln retorted. "Public receptions are more democratic than stupid state dinners — are more in keeping with the institutions of our country, as you would say if called upon to make a stump speech. There are a great many strangers in the city, foreigners and others, whom we can entertain at our receptions, but whom we cannot invite to our dinners."

Mr. Lincoln pondered this. "I believe you are right, Mother," he finally said. "You argue the point well. I think that we shall have to decide on the receptions."

When her husband's gaze was turned elsewhere, Mrs. Lincoln shot Elizabeth a look of triumph. She had won the day.

For all her talk of economy, for the first of these receptions, Mrs. Lincoln decided to host a grand ball in the East Room. As word of her lavish plans spread, she once again invited criticism — not only from the usual suspects in the press and the popular circles, but also from her husband's cabinet secretaries, who took to calling her Hellcat behind her back, though not behind Elizabeth's. She wouldn't carry hurtful tales of their bold hostility to her patron, but she knew cruel remarks usually managed to make their way from the offices, through the servant's quarters, and on to the subject of their derision.

If the men's sniping troubled Mrs. Lincoln, she feigned indifference and threw herself into her preparations. She collaborated on a new dress with Elizabeth, an off-the-shoulder white satin gown with a low neckline, flounces of black lace, black and white bows, and a long, elegant train. She planned an elaborate menu of roast turkey, foie gras, oysters, beef, duck, quail, partridge, and aspic, complemented by an assortment of fruits, cakes, and ices, and fanciful creations of spun sugar. She sent out seven hundred invitations to prominent men in government and their wives, as well as to certain favorite friends, important Washington personages, and visiting dignitaries. "Half the city is jubilant at being invited," Elizabeth overheard Mr. Lincoln's personal secretary remark, "while the other half is furious at being left out in the cold." Expectations soared after the *New York Herald* predicted that the ball would be "the most magnificent affair ever witnessed in America."

But such raptures in the press were not enough to entice everyone. The usual detractors, and many more besides, expressed astonishment and disgust for the vain spectacle of the ball and its hostess. A great many of the invitations were brusquely declined, and nearly one hundred were returned with indignant notes protesting such excessive frivolity when the nation was distracted, mournful, and impoverished by the war. "I am astonished by such impertinence from a gentleman," Mrs. Lincoln exclaimed to Elizabeth one afternoon as she read her mail. "Listen to what Senator Benjamin Wade writes: 'Are the President and Mrs. Lincoln aware that there is a civil war? If they are not, Mr. and Mrs. Wade are, and for that reason decline to participate in dancing and feasting.' " Mrs. Lincoln slapped the letter down on the table. "Are we aware there is a war? We are scarcely aware of anything else!"

"I cannot imagine that anyone is more mindful of the war than Mr. Lincoln," said Elizabeth.

Outraged, Mrs. Lincoln bolted from her seat and stalked to the window. "If canceling the ball would bring a swift end to the war, or even a single hour of respite to a weary soldier, then I would be the first to propose it."

Elizabeth murmured soothing words until Mrs. Lincoln calmed herself. If only the war could be ended so easily. At the moment,

Elizabeth would have settled for an end to the tempests that sprang up whenever someone affronted Mrs. Lincoln. Her critics judged her actions without understanding the motives behind them, which meant they would never be fair and only rarely accurate. As they were unlikely to change, it would serve Mrs. Lincoln well to cultivate a sense of calm and learn to ignore them. A dignified silence was often the best response to spiteful gossip — but that was not Mrs. Lincoln's way.

Soon thereafter, Mrs. Lincoln was distracted from her frenzy of planning when Willie caught a severe cold while riding his pony in foul weather. A few days before the ball, his condition worsened into a fever. Elizabeth had nursed both children through measles and a host of other illnesses, and this time too Mrs. Lincoln summoned her to his bedside. With tender efficiency, Elizabeth cared for Willie — a kind, gentle, thoughtful boy, everyone's favorite — and tried to comfort his mother, who fretted and worried incessantly, as she always did when any of her children fell ill. She had lost her second-born, Eddie, to chronic consumption when he was not quite four years old, and she lived in terror of losing another son.

Soon it was evident that Willie was becoming steadily weaker. One afternoon, Elizabeth was at his bedside pressing a cooling cloth to his brow while Mrs. Lincoln hovered nearby, telling Willie cheerful stories of his pets, although he was too drowsy to pay much attention. Mr. Lincoln entered to check on his son, as he often did throughout the day. "How is my boy?" he asked.

"He seems to be unchanged since this morning," Elizabeth replied. "No worse, but no better either."

"Perhaps he'll turn the corner soon," said Mr. Lincoln, but his eyes did not brighten as they would have had he felt true hope.

Elizabeth managed what she hoped was an encouraging smile. "I've seen sick little boys recover from much worse."

"I should cancel the ball," Mrs. Lincoln fretted. "It's ridiculous to think of hosting such an event with our boy in his sickbed. I can recall the invitations, postpone it until after he recovers."

"No, the reception should go on," said Mr. Lincoln. "You've already gone to too much trouble and expense to cancel now."

"I don't mind the trouble." Mrs. Lincoln's voice carried an edge. "Surely our guests will understand, and if I send word to the caterers immediately, they shouldn't have any difficulty accommodating a delay of a week or two."

The president fell into a thoughtful silence for a moment and then said, "Why don't we consult Dr. Stone first?"

His wife agreed, so the Lincoln family physician was sent for, and in due time he arrived to examine his patient. "Your son is much improved," Dr. Stone announced after checking the boy's pulse, listening to his breathing, and questioning him about his symptoms. "There is every reason to expect a full recovery soon."

"Oh, thank heavens," said Mrs. Lincoln fervently. "And — what do you think about the reception?"

"I see no reason why it shouldn't go on as planned," the doctor replied, packing his instruments into his bag. "I assure you, Mr. President, madam, your son is in no immediate danger."

Mrs. Lincoln clasped her hands together as if in prayer and thanked Dr. Stone profusely, but after he left, her momentary brightness faded. "As glad as I am with this good news, I don't feel like dancing with Willie suffering so."

"If you don't feel like dancing, we won't have dancing," Mr. Lincoln replied. "Come now, Mother. We won't be far away. We can come upstairs and look in on him as much as you like, and I'm sure we can rely upon Madam Keckley to nurse him in our absence, can we not?"

"Certainly," said Elizabeth. "I'll stay the night too, if you like."

Thus reassured, Mrs. Lincoln agreed to the arrangements, and so plans for the reception continued. Even after Tad too fell ill, the Lincolns reminded themselves of Dr. Stone's diagnosis and carried on, hopeful that their boys would be up and around soon.

On the evening of the reception, Elizabeth arrived early to dress Mrs. Lincoln and found her sitting at Willie's bedside, drawn and pensive, holding his small hand in hers. "His fever worsened overnight," she told Elizabeth softly. "The doctor insists he is in no danger, but I believe he's taken a turn for the worse."

The boy's sweet face did appear more flushed than Elizabeth had yet seen it, and his breathing seemed labored. "How is Tad?"

"Not well, but he's faring better than his brother." Mrs. Lincoln sighed and rose, pressing the back of her hand to her forehead. "I'd better dress for the ball. To think, at one time I had been so looking forward to it."

Mrs. Lincoln summoned a servant to sit with Willie until Elizabeth could return after helping her prepare for the evening. In the boudoir, Elizabeth helped the First Lady don the white satin gown with its long train and black and white embellishments, and then arranged her hair in a headdress of black and white flowers. Mrs. Lincoln wore more flowers on her bosom, a half-mourning bouquet of crepe myrtle in honor of the recently widowed Queen Victoria.

Mr. Lincoln came in to escort his wife downstairs to the reception before she was quite ready, and while he waited for them to finish, he stood with his back to the fireplace, his hands clasped behind him. His expression was solemn, and although his gaze was fixed on the carpet, his thoughts seemed very far away.

When Mrs. Lincoln was dressed, she admired herself in the mirror, her long train sweeping the floor. The rustle of satin roused Mr. Lincoln from his reverie, and he regarded his wife for a moment before the barest of smiles touched his lips. "Whew! Our cat has a long tail tonight."

Mrs. Lincoln raised her eyebrows at him but otherwise made no reply.

"Mother," he said, taking in her bare arms and neck, "it is my opinion that, if some of that tail was nearer the head, it would be in better style."

Elizabeth did not often disagree with the president, but in this case, she did not share his opinion in the slightest. Mrs. Lincoln's beautifully formed shoulders and neck were her best features, and the gown's low neckline set them off to great advantage. Mrs. Lincoln turned away from her husband with a look of offended dignity, but before long she consented to take his arm, and together they went downstairs to welcome their guests.

Elizabeth returned to the sickroom, where Willie languished in a fitful, sweaty doze. Before long she heard the Marine Band begin to play in the reception halls below, their music drifting through the ceiling and down the halls like the low, muted whispers of grieving spirits.

Throughout the evening, Mrs. Lincoln frequently left the party to come upstairs and look in on her darling boy, sometimes with her husband by her side. Anxiously she would ask Elizabeth if there had been any change, but each time Elizabeth could only shake her head. Shortly before the ball ended, Willie seemed to struggle for breath, but after a worrisome hour, his breathing eased. The moment her guests departed,

Mrs. Lincoln joined Elizabeth at Willie's bedside, and together they kept vigil until the first light of dawn crept above the horizon.

"You should rest, Elizabeth," Mrs. Lincoln told her in a voice raspy from exhaustion and worry.

"I'm fine, Mrs. Lincoln," she replied gently. "Why don't you go to bed instead?"

"It would be no use. I couldn't sleep. No, Elizabeth; you've been keeping watch over Willie longer than I. I must insist that you rest."

Elizabeth knew that it would do her no good to argue. "Very well, Mrs. Lincoln." She rose wearily, arching her back to relieve the stiffness. "I'll sleep for a time, but I'll be back down as soon as I wake so you can take a turn."

Mrs. Lincoln nodded distractedly, her gaze fixed on her suffering child.

Elizabeth found the bed that had been made up for her in the servants' quarters, undressed to her chemise, and lay down with the quilt pulled up to her chin. She slept restlessly and woke shortly before noon with vague memories of foreboding dreams. Someone had kindly left a full pitcher beside the washbasin, and after making a quick toilet she hurried downstairs to relieve Mrs. Lincoln, only to discover that Willie had not rallied during her absence.

Over the next few days, Willie declined, steadily and inexorably, while his parents watched and waited and prayed. The president canceled a cabinet meeting and Mrs. Lincoln a levee rather than stray too far from their son's sickbed. Willie's best friend, Bud Taft, visited, and fell asleep on the floor, so determined was he not to leave his favorite companion's side. Elizabeth attended them all, not neglecting little Tad, who was not as seriously ill as his brother and had been confined to a separate bedroom. She stayed overnight at the White House when she was needed, and hurried away to her own home for rest and a change of clothes when she could be spared. All the while, Mrs. Lincoln kept vigil at Willie's bedside, surely haunted by memories of the long, sorrowful days more than a dozen years earlier when she had watched her son Eddie slip away.

On February 20, a mild, sunny day, Willie finally breathed his last. For all the long hours Elizabeth had spent at his sickbed, when he passed away she happened to be at home, where a messenger immediately summoned her. She hurried to the White House, and once there she asked to see Mrs. Lincoln, but the First Lady had been taken to her bed, inconsolable and keening. Elizabeth paused to check in on Tad — the poor child was feverish, grief stricken, and terrified — before she went to assist in washing and dressing Willie, laying him out upon the bed in the Green Room, and covering his face gently with a white cloth.

Elizabeth was keeping vigil alone when Mr. Lincoln entered the room, his face ashen and haggard, his eyes red and tormented. Elizabeth was too shocked and sorrowful to address him, so she nodded respectfully and stepped aside to the foot of the bed as he approached. She had never seen a man so bowed with grief, and she had seen many, far more than she could ever bring herself to count.

He lifted the sheet from his son's face and gazed at him long and tenderly. "My poor boy, he was too good for this earth," he murmured. "God has called him home. I know that he is much better off in heaven, but then we loved him so. It is hard, hard to have him die!"

Great, heaving sobs choked off his words. Tears filled Elizabeth's eyes as she watched the anguished father bury his head in his hands, his angular frame shaking with grief. She wanted more than anything to offer words of comfort, but she knew none would suffice, and she found herself unable to speak.

Later Elizabeth sat with Mrs. Lincoln in her rooms, where the curtains were drawn and the mirrors covered. She came again the next day and found Mrs. Lincoln wild with lamentations and sorrow. She was inconsolable, shattered by loss, unable to rise from her bed even to care for Tad, who was still struggling to recover from his illness. As the White House was draped in the black crepe of mourning, she collapsed in paroxysms of grief, shrieking and wailing, frightening Tad and worrying Elizabeth, who could do nothing to help her. Dr. Stone prescribed laudanum, but whenever the stupor of a dose lifted, Mrs. Lincoln seemed worse off than before. Elizabeth had nursed many people through illnesses, but she had never faced anything like Mrs. Lincoln's hysteria and felt powerless to help her. To her relief, Mr. Lincoln quickly understood that she was out of her depth and arranged for Rebecca Pomroy, a nurse who had been working in a military hospital, to be reassigned to the White House so she could look after Mrs. Lincoln and Tad.

Under Nurse Pomroy's care, Mrs. Lincoln regained the presence of mind to write to

Mrs. Taft, begging her to keep her boys at home during the funeral because the sight of the children with whom her son had passed so many happy hours would devastate her. Elizabeth never told Mrs. Lincoln that her husband had secretly allowed Bud to come to the White House to see Willie one last time before he was placed in his casket. Shortly thereafter, Mrs. Lincoln managed to leave her bed for a final, private farewell with her husband and two surviving sons in the East Room, where the public services would be held later that day. Mrs. Lincoln was too distressed to endure the rituals of grief, so she retreated to her rooms while members of Congress, cabinet secretaries, diplomats, generals, and dignitaries filed in to pay their respects and offer condolences.

On the one-week anniversary of Willie's death, the president locked himself in the Green Room for a time — Elizabeth did not know but could well imagine — to be alone with his thoughts, to remember his beloved son, to pray. He observed the private mourning ritual every Thursday for several weeks thereafter, and it seemed to offer him solace. Tad improved day by day under the watchful eye of Nurse Pomroy, but as he would take his medicine from no one but his father, the president was frequently called out of meetings to administer the dose. Robert grieved the loss of his young brother, but he endeavored to maintain a brave, manly front, and the effort seemed to sustain him. Of the survivors, Mrs. Lincoln alone found no lessening of her grief. She was alternately paralyzed by sorrow or frantic with despair, and her sudden bouts of keening frightened Tad and alarmed the entire household.

Elizabeth was present the day Mr. Lincoln inadvertently revealed that he feared his wife's nerves would never recover. Once, when Mrs. Lincoln was caught up in one of her spells of unmitigated anguish, Mr. Lincoln took her gently by the arm, led her to the window, and solemnly pointed to St. Elizabeths Hospital in the distance.

"Mother," he said, "do you see that large white building on the hill yonder?"

Mrs. Lincoln nodded, her eyes widening. Everyone in Washington recognized the lunatic asylum, an imposing landmark on the city skyline.

"Try and control your grief," the president continued steadily, "or it will drive you mad, and we may have to send you there."

Elizabeth muffled a gasp of horror. That this might be Mrs. Lincoln's fate was an idea too terrible to contemplate, and she was shocked that Mr. Lincoln would speak so to his grieving wife. And yet, in the days that followed, it seemed that the warning alone had compelled her to try to regain control of her nerves. Even so, Robert was so concerned by his mother's slow progress that he implored for his aunt Elizabeth Edwards to return to the White House, hoping that she would be able to comfort his mother even though the sisters had had a falling out the previous autumn. When she arrived, she discovered her younger sister bedridden with grief and her nephew Tad sobbing that he would never see his brother again. But Elizabeth observed that Mrs. Edwards' presence brought an immediate sense of relief to the family. It was she who was able to persuade Mrs. Lincoln to leave her bed and dress, and later, to venture out to attend church services.

But despite these incremental improvements, Mrs. Lincoln was often overcome and overwhelmed by sorrow and spent most of the next month in seclusion within the White House. Elizabeth was often with her, sewing her mourning wardrobe, offering whatever comfort she could. Once, when Mrs. Edwards was not with them, Mrs. Lincoln suddenly said, "If Willie had lived, he would have been the hope and stay of my old age." Her voice was quiet, her thoughts faraway. "But Providence did not spare him."

Elizabeth understood, perhaps as only another grieving mother could. She had hoped that George would go far in life and that she would be able to rely upon him in her later years, but Providence had not spared her son either.

In the same distant voice, Mrs. Lincoln added, "I believe Willie's death is God's punishment for my sins, for my vanity and self-indulgence."

"What?" exclaimed Elizabeth. "You cannot mean that."

"His decline began on the night of my lavish reception," she said bitterly. "What clearer sign do I need of God's judgment than that?"

"Oh, Mrs. Lincoln, no." Elizabeth shook her head. "No. God is not so cruel."

"Isn't He?" Mrs. Lincoln's gaze drifted to the window, but Elizabeth could not tell what it rested upon. The church steeple? The hospitals filled with wounded soldiers? St. Elizabeths across the Anacostia River? "If His punishment is just, who are we to call it cruelty?"

CHAPTER SIX

March–April 1862

In the weeks following Willie's death, Mrs. Lincoln struggled to get through each day. She avoided public appearances and clung to her sister Mrs. Edwards, who often stood in for her when she did not feel up to receiving visitors. She shunned the Green Room, where her dear son had been laid out, and she never again invited the little Taft boys to the White House. She saved the casket flowers from Willie's funeral and a poignant eulogy written by the poet Nathaniel Parker Willis, but she gave away all his toys and games. She could not bear to be reminded of him, and yet he was always in her thoughts.

Mr. Lincoln mourned also, but he did not have the luxury of secluding himself away from the world. Squabbles in Congress continued, the profound question of what to do about the slaves persisted, and the war went on.

The Confederates had salvaged the steam frigate *Merrimack* from the Norfolk navy yard, cut off its upper hull, armored it with iron, and rechristened it the *Virginia* before sending it out upon the James River to decimate the Union fleet. The next day the Union navy retaliated with its own ironclad ship, the *Monitor,* whose unconventional deck design and revolving gun turret astonished all who witnessed the battle from other Union and Confederate ships on the water and the riverbanks on both sides. Neither warship was able to inflict much damage upon the other, but the North was able to maintain its blockade of Norfolk and Richmond, and thus claim victory.

A few weeks later in early April, the Union defeated the Confederates at Shiloh in Tennessee, but it was the bloodiest battle of the war so far, with more than thirteen thousand killed, wounded, or missing on the Union side and nearly eleven thousand for the South. Among those killed was Mrs. Lincoln's half brother Samuel B. Todd, an officer serving with the Twenty-fourth Louisiana. His death reminded Mrs. Lincoln's critics of her family ties to secessionists and stirred up the old, groundless questions about her loyalties — a monstrous thing to do at such a time, Elizabeth thought, showing utter disregard for Mrs. Lincoln's grief. After the costly victory, General Ulysses S. Grant was vilified in the press and many called for his removal, but President Lincoln replied, "I can't spare this man; he fights."

President Lincoln too fought, on other fronts. Recent antislavery lectures at the Smithsonian Institution had inspired a rising chorus of voices among abolitionists and radical Republican factions in Congress calling for emancipation. Some of his military officers had taken the lead in emancipating slaves under certain circumstances, but not always with the president's sanction. For more than a year, abolitionists had been arguing that the Union could not hope to win the war unless it deprived the Confederates of their labor force by emancipating their slaves. Frederick Douglass, a former slave and tireless advocate for the colored race — and someone Elizabeth greatly admired — concurred, writing in his newspaper, "Arrest that hoe in the hands of the Negro, and you smite the rebellion in the very seat of its life." In July 1861, General Benjamin Butler had put three escaped slaves to work at Fort Monroe, declaring that they were "contraband of war" and that he was not obliged to return them to their masters under the Fugitive Slave Law because they had come from a state that had left the Union. Congress upheld the legality of General Butler's policy, and thereafter, other "contraband" were offered work to help the war effort, and their numbers rapidly grew. At the end of August, and without any authorization from the president whatsoever, Major General John C. Frémont, commander of the army's Department of the West, issued a proclamation freeing the slaves of Confederates within the state of Missouri. The president was furious when he learned what Frémont had done and commanded him to rescind the proclamation; when Frémont refused, Lincoln revoked it himself, angering Northern abolitionists and bringing a storm of criticism down upon himself.

President Lincoln's ostensible reluctance to free the slaves puzzled and disappointed Elizabeth, but the longer she worked in the White House and the better she knew him, the more she understood that he indeed wished to abolish slavery, but on his own terms and on his own timetable. She knew he worried that immediate and total emancipation would drive the slaveholding border states out of the Union and into the Confederacy, and she did not envy him his burdens. But by early spring of 1862, attitudes had shifted and opportunities had manifested. Perhaps encouraged by the increasing demands from the public, and perhaps inspired by reports from his field commanders who employed "contraband" as laborers, cooks, and nurses, President Lincoln must have decided the time was right to nudge the idea of abolition forward. One morning in early March, he called Massachusetts senator Charles Sumner to the White House to read him the draft of a bill that would grant individual states the right to establish emancipation within their borders. Slave owners would be compensated with federal funds for the loss of their property, and freed slaves would be given the opportunity to immigrate to proposed colonies in Africa or Central America. In the past, the abolitionist senator had decried such incremental, compensatory measures, but recognizing the opportunity for great and lasting change the bill offered, he resolved to support it. Within hours, he and his fellow Massachusetts senator Henry Wilson began to push through Congress a bill calling for emancipation in the District of Columbia.

On the Senate floor, Henry Wilson spoke eloquently of the contributions the free colored population had made to the district — how they strove for self-improvement and had created schools, churches, businesses, and benevolent societies. All their accomplishments had come about despite the unfair "black codes" that constricted their lives and freedoms. They paid taxes for schools that their own children were not permitted to attend, a grievous injustice. It was time for them to become truly, fully free, and no honest citizen had any reason to doubt that emancipated slaves would follow their fine example and become industrious members of society upon gaining their liberty.

Not everyone agreed with Senator Wilson, of course, or with another important supporter of the bill, Thaddeus Stevens, the leader of the radical Republican faction and the lawyer who had represented Emma and her mother in the legal suit that had granted them their long-deferred freedom. Strong opposition to the bill was led by Peace Democrat Clement Vallandigham of Ohio, and the debate played out over several days. Walker Lewis and several other respected colored men of Washington City came to the Senate gallery day after day to observe the speeches, evoking displeasure and alarm from some senators, especially Garret Davis of Kentucky, who interrupted a bitter speech against the bill to snarl, "I suppose in a few months they will be crowding white ladies out of the galleries!" Undeterred, Walker and his companions continued to attend the debates and report on the progress of the bill to the colored community, who awaited the vote for passage with great anticipation and hope.

Newspaper reporters covered the story in a more official capacity; the *National Republican* praised Senator Wilson, but the Washington *Evening Star* warned that the aim of the Emancipation Bill was to enforce Negro equality upon white men. In New York, Horace Greeley, who for years had lambasted President Lincoln in the pages of his *Tribune,* was so elated by the proposal that he thanked the Lord Almighty that Lincoln had become so wise a ruler. Mr. Lincoln showed no reaction to Mr. Greeley's endorsement in Elizabeth's presence, but Mrs. Lincoln made no effort to hide that she was unimpressed. "Today he showers my husband in praise," she said, waving a hand dismissively. "Tomorrow it may well be criticism again."

It seemed to Elizabeth that most white Washingtonians did not share Mr. Greeley's opinion of the president. In letters and petitions to congressmen, editors, and anyone else with any degree of influence, they demanded that the bill be voted down. Those who owned slaves were against the bill for reasons they hardly needed to explain, but some citizens who had never owned a slave denounced the measure also. Emancipation would open the floodgates to a tide of free Negroes who would compete with white citizens for jobs, they warned. Runaway slaves would flee to Washington and become a burden to the public. With the war on, the government couldn't afford to compensate district slave owners up to three hundred dollars per slave as the bill called for; it would be more prudent, more frugal, and all over better to let them keep their slaves for now and be responsible for their upkeep than to have the government shoulder that burden.

The bill's opponents could complain and they could protest, but the federal government did not need their approval to bring the measure to a vote. On April 3, the Senate passed the Emancipation Bill twenty-nine to fourteen, and a few days later, the House voted in favor by a margin of ninety-three to twenty-nine. After that, President Lincoln waited four days, a time in which he listened respectfully to impassioned arguments on both sides of the issue, and then, on April 16, a beautiful spring day, he signed the bill into law.

With a few strokes of his pen, he had abolished slavery forever in the capital of the United States.

The colored residents of Washington responded with unrestrained jubilation. Voices rose in joyful cheers and reverent hymns throughout colored neighborhoods, where community leaders, well aware that their every action was being watched and judged, urged them to respond with quiet dignity. Such self-possession came naturally to Elizabeth, but even she laughed and cheered and danced a little jig with Virginia in the parlor when they heard the news. "If I had known this was coming, I would have saved my money," remarked another boarder, an elderly shoemaker who had recently bought his freedom. He said it so comically that all who heard him burst out laughing, the sound of it ringing out with exultation and joy, echoing other happy celebrations throughout the city. Their faith in the president had been renewed, as was their resolve to see slavery abolished everywhere, for everyone, for all time.

On Sunday, Elizabeth joined her fellow believers at Union Bethel Church, where freeborn, freedmen, and the newly, suddenly free rejoiced and gave thanks. She gloried in the minister's sermon, heartfelt words of rejoicing and thankfulness and praise to God, who had delivered them from bondage. And yet there was a somber undercurrent to their worship, for they were ever mindful of the great many people of their race who had not benefitted from the new law, and they understood that freedom brought with it great responsibility. "We must resolve," the minister declared, as surely other ministers were also doing in the sixteen other colored churches throughout Washington, "that by our industry, character, and moral righteousness we will prove ourselves worthy of the glorious privilege that has been conferred upon us. We have always been an orderly and law-abiding people, and so in the future we must strive to live so morally and industriously that anyone who is today disappointed with the passage of this law will forget why they ever opposed it."

Elizabeth's hopes for those outraged white citizens of Washington were less ambitious. She wouldn't ask for them to forget their objections altogether, but she would gladly settle for their acceptance of the fact that emancipation was the new law of the land

— and for their greater tolerance for the colored folks who had also made the city their home.

The day after Mr. Lincoln signed the bill into law, Elizabeth was sewing in her rooms, her windows wide open to the faintly pungent spring breeze and the chirping of songbirds, when a knock sounded upon her door. In the hallway stood a dark-haired white woman of about thirty years, sensibly attired in a brown wool dress. "Good afternoon," Elizabeth greeted her. "May I help you?"

The woman's brown eyes lit up with expectation. "You are Elizabeth Keckley, the mantua maker?"

"Yes, I am."

"How do you do?" The younger woman extended a hand, and Elizabeth shook it. "My name is Mary Ames. I'm a Washington correspondent."

"Oh, dear," said Elizabeth without thinking, surprise driving away her usual composure. "That is — I beg your pardon, Mrs. Ames. How do you do?"

"I'm quite fine, thank you." She glanced past Elizabeth's shoulder into her rooms, and Elizabeth was profoundly grateful that Mrs. Lincoln had not chosen that day of all days to surprise her with a visit to discuss a new dress design. "I wondered if we might chat for a bit?"

"I'm terribly sorry, but if you're seeking information about the president and Mrs. Lincoln —"

"Oh, no, no, that's not my purpose at all," Mrs. Ames interrupted. "I am pursuing a story, but you are my intended subject, not the Lincolns."

"Why would you want to write about me?" Curiosity compelled Elizabeth to open the door wider. "For that matter, why would anyone want to read about me?"

"Because of the new emancipation law, of course. Everyone wonders what the consequences will be, for Washington itself as well as all the new freedmen. I would like to write a piece describing the accomplishments of several former slaves who have done well for themselves since coming to the city." She smiled winningly. "And who has accomplished more than the celebrated dressmaker Elizabeth Keckley? From slave cabin to White House — quite a remarkable rise."

"That's very kind." Elizabeth managed a small, uncertain smile. "I've always tried to be industrious, and I've been blessed by generous patrons who have graciously recommended me to their acquaintances."

"Oh, you're too modest," protested Mrs. Ames. "You've succeeded thanks to your talent and your unmatched reputation. Surely you know how highly the ladies of Washington regard you. When I asked around for recommendations for successful late slaves to interview, your name came up more than any other."

Elizabeth firmly warned herself not to succumb to flattery, but she felt herself wavering. "If I agree to an interview, it is with the understanding that I never gossip about my patrons."

"Of course." A shadow of disappointment darkened Mrs. Ames's amiable expression for a moment, but it quickly lifted. "Discretion is essential between a dressmaker and her customer, whether she lives in the White House or the house around the corner."

"I'm glad you understand."

"I don't intend to publish a scandal, Mrs. Keckley." Mrs. Ames paused for a moment, considering. "No matter how much my editor might prefer one. After all, scandalous tales sell papers. But so do newsworthy and inspirational pieces, which is what I intend this to be. Your story will inspire these newly emancipated slaves to practice economy, industry, and morality so that they might achieve as you have done." Almost as an aside, she added, "It might also serve to reassure the white citizens of Washington that they have nothing to fear. Sudden change can be frightening, you know, and emancipation has brought dramatic change."

Elizabeth hesitated. "I suppose it would do no harm if I spoke to you. The story might even do some good."

"There's no question that it shall," Mrs. Ames declared as Elizabeth beckoned her inside.

Elizabeth prepared tea, and they chatted in her front room. At first Elizabeth spoke cautiously, with great reserve, mindful of how her patrons — Mrs. Lincoln in particular — would react to her words. Then, halfway through her second cup of tea, she lost herself in reminiscing about her slavery days, about George, about her astonishing new life in Washington, and she revealed more about her past sorrows than she had intended. It was only after the teapot had cooled and Mrs. Ames had filled up several pages with notes that Elizabeth, too late, wondered if she had said too much.

"When will your story be printed?" Elizabeth asked after the interview concluded and she had shown Mrs. Ames to the door.

"Perhaps as early as tomorrow, if I apply

myself," Mrs. Ames replied cheerfully.

Elizabeth's heart thumped anxiously as they exchanged good-byes. She had expected to have more time to — not to *warn* Mrs. Lincoln, exactly, but to inform her that the article was forthcoming, and to reassure her that Elizabeth had not carried any tales from the White House. She didn't think she had said anything that could possibly offend, but with the First Lady, that was sometimes difficult to anticipate. With any luck, she would be able to read the piece before Mrs. Lincoln did — and perhaps Mrs. Lincoln wouldn't see it at all.

The very next day, one of Elizabeth's neighbors in the Lewis boardinghouse rapped on her door and handed her the newest edition of the *Evening Post.* "I know you must be the 'Lizzie' in this story," Miss Brown said, her dark eyes shining with excitement. "Congratulations, my dear."

"Thank you," said Elizabeth, taking the paper. They chatted for a few minutes, but as soon as Miss Brown departed, Elizabeth closed the door, sank into a chair, and held the paper in her lap, eager and yet apprehensive to see what Mrs. Ames had written. She took a deep breath and began to read, her eyes lighting on the title, "Lives of the Late Slaves," and the first subtitle, "A

Slave-girl's Story." Elizabeth skimmed the tale of a nine-year-old girl from the Congo and stopped when the column was broken by another subtitle, "A Stylish Black Woman." Then she steeled herself and read on.

Lizzie —— is a stately, stylish woman. Her cheek is tawny, but her features are perfectly regular, her eyes dark and winning; hair straight, black, shining. A smile half sorrowful and wholly sweet makes you love her face as soon as you look on it. It is a face strong with intellect and heart, with enough of beauty left to tell you that it was more beautiful still before wrong and grief had shadowed it.

That was not such a bad beginning, Elizabeth thought. Her name was spelled differently than she wrote it, but the editor had also removed her last name to shield her privacy, so perhaps the alternate spelling was meant to do the same. And it was good to hear that she had "enough of beauty" remaining at her age, she thought wryly before returning her gaze to the newspaper.

Lizzie's father was a gentleman of "the chivalry," and in her mother's veins ran some of the best blood of the Old Dominion.

I cannot tell the wrongs of her childhood and early youth; if I were to try my hand would stiffen with horror, my heart, in its strong indignation, would stifle the words I might utter.

In her girlhood she was sold to a family who took her to a great city of the Northwest. For years the "gentleman," the "lady," and their large family of children were supported by the labors of this young slave. Lizzie's great skill and taste made her the fashionable dressmaker of this metropolis. She earned thousands of dollars, and it all went to the support of her master's family. The young ladies went in fashionable society and enjoyed their fine costumes none the less that they were first earned and then made by the young slave, who, thrice as intelligent and quite as handsome as themselves, sat through the weeks and months in a chamber at home, spending her life for them.

Elizabeth felt her first stirrings of dismay. She had never called Armistead Burwell her father; that honorific she reserved for George Hobbs, her mother's devoted husband, whom Elizabeth had loved dearly. She had also never referred to Colonel Burwell as a member of "the chivalry"; that turn of phrase was entirely Mrs. Ames's. But that was not the worst of it. She had never claimed to be "thrice as intelligent" as her former young mistresses. They could not sew as well as she, but to be fair, few people could. They were as bright and clever as any young ladies Elizabeth had ever known, and Elizabeth cared for them very much, despite the regrettable tension ever present in the bonds of their affection that prevented them from being true friends. What on earth would they think of her if they believed that she had boasted of her superior intelligence? She could only pray that the fracture in the nation would prevent the newspaper from falling into their hands, or if it did, that they would know that Elizabeth never would have said such a thing and that the reporter must have misunderstood her.

The article went on to describe how Elizabeth had earned fame as a skilled dressmaker in that "great city of the Northwest," how she had purchased her freedom, how her son had died on the battlefield wearing Union blue and taking with him "the last earthly hope and consolations of his mother's heart," and how she had "turned her face from the West, and came here, sorrowfully, wearily, to begin life anew." She winced at a few factual and chronological errors, but overall, Mrs. Ames had described her experiences nearly as Elizabeth had shared them. A few mistakes could be forgiven.

The article went on to praise her accomplishments since arriving in Washington City:

It is Lizzie who fashioned those splendid costumes of Mrs. Lincoln, whose artistic elegance has been so praised during the past winter. It was she who "dressed" Mrs. Lincoln for "the party," and for every grand occasion. Stately carriages stand before her door, whose haughty owners sit before Lizzie docile as lambs while she tells them what to wear. Lizzie is an artist, and has such a genius for making women look pretty, that not one thinks of disputing her decrees. Thus she forgets her sorrows, interesting herself to serve each one who comes, as if to dress *her* was the chief business of her existence. But to the woman who stretched out her hand to her as a sister, she broke into passionate tears, saying, "I am alone in the world. I have nothing to live for any longer. I try to interest myself in these things, but cannot."

"Oh, dear," Elizabeth murmured to the empty room. She did not mind being called an artist, or a genius, but she doubted very much that any of her patrons would be pleased to know that they had been described as haughty in one sentence and docile as lambs and subject to her commands in the next. But the conclusion of the paragraph utterly bewildered her. At first she did not know who the "woman who stretched out her hand to her as a sister" was meant to be — Mrs. Le Bourgois, who had organized the ladies of St. Louis to help her attain her freedom? Mrs. Lincoln? — until it came to her that the reporter was speaking of herself, a rather strange claim to make based upon their short acquaintance. It was also astonishing to read how she had wept during their interview, for Elizabeth had not shed a single tear. She might have said that she lived alone, but she had never lamented that she was alone in the world, nor would she ever say that she had nothing to live for any longer. She had her work, her friends, her freedom, her faith — she would never succumb to despair. How embarrassing it was to think that now her friends and patrons would believe she did, because of course they would recognize her as quickly as Miss Brown had done. What had possessed Mrs. Ames to invent such sentimental phrases, and to place them in Elizabeth's mouth?

The article went on to describe where Elizabeth lived, although thankfully Mrs. Ames had not provided her address or named the Lewises as her landlords. She concluded with a dramatic final assessment of Elizabeth, saying, "A woman of thought and refinement, a woman of deep affection and high aspiration, she stands alone in her womanhood, alone in the universe."

Why did Mrs. Ames emphasize Elizabeth's solitude? Elizabeth was not friendless, helpless, and forsaken. She had lost her son, but in this she was not unlike many other mothers in those perilous days of war. She had many friends. She had the patronage of Mrs. Lincoln and many other ladies of quality in Washington. Elizabeth did not understand what she had said or done to make such an impression of loneliness upon the reporter.

"If one is going to write the life of another," Elizabeth said aloud, rising from her chair with the newspaper still clutched in her hand, "one should always, always write the truth. Anything else is a waste of paper and ink and words."

She should have thrown the paper away and forgotten it, and yet some faint pride or vanity compelled her to fold it neatly and tuck it away for safekeeping in the same trunk in which she saved fabric from Mrs. Lincoln's gowns, leftover scraps too small for dressmaking that Mrs. Lincoln generously allowed her to keep.

Suddenly Elizabeth realized that the article could have been much worse. For all her mistakes and fictions, Mrs. Ames had said nothing unflattering about Mrs. Lincoln and had written several things that could be construed as praise for the First Lady's style and elegance. That was no small blessing, and as Elizabeth latched the trunk shut, she breathed a sigh of relief and resolved to avoid speaking to reporters in the future. She would not tempt fate by risking embarrassment and scandal in the press a second time.

CHAPTER SEVEN

May–October 1862

In May, although Mrs. Lincoln still grieved deeply, she made an effort to resume her usual routines and former duties. She forced herself to stroll the White House grounds with visiting friends and to take carriage rides. She sent bouquets from the conservatory to acquaintances and important dignitaries, and she gave Nurse Pomroy delicacies from the White House kitchen and garden to distribute at military hospital wards. Her remaining sons, Tad and Robert, the latter of whom had come home from college for the summer, provided her with the most compelling distraction from her sorrow.

For weeks she had mentioned idly in conversation that she believed fresh air and a change of scenery would do her good, so Elizabeth was not surprised when Mrs. Lincoln announced that in the middle of June, the Lincoln family would relocate to their summer residence. Anderson Cottage, she told Elizabeth, was a charming two-story dwelling of stucco and gables on the 240-acre grounds of the Soldiers' Home, an asylum established as a place for wounded veterans to convalesce. It was about two miles north of the city, a cool, wooded, secluded haven on a hilltop, far enough away from the Capitol and the White House to act as a restful retreat, but near enough for Mr. Lincoln to travel back and forth as needed.

Although Mr. Lincoln returned to the city almost daily, Mrs. Lincoln and her sons did not, so Elizabeth saw the First Lady very little throughout the late spring and summer. Although many other ladies left Washington to escape the heat, the insects, the pervasive illnesses, and the sights, sounds, and smells of a city given over to the care of thousands of ill and wounded soldiers, enough of Elizabeth's patrons remained to keep her sewing busily during Mrs. Lincoln's absence.

At times Elizabeth wished she too could ride off to a cool summer retreat, but she made the most of the early mornings and temperate evenings to go for walks, attend lectures, or enjoy outings with the Lewises.

One evening, she and Virginia were coming home from a choir concert at the Fifteenth Street Presbyterian Church when they heard a band playing merry music a few blocks away. Curious, they both instinctively slowed their pace to listen. They exchanged a glance, and Elizabeth asked what they were both thinking: "Shall we see what that's about?"

Virginia eagerly agreed, and so they followed the enchanting melody to the home of Mrs. Farnham. The yard was brilliantly illuminated with lanterns, and white ladies and gentlemen were strolling about, enjoying conversation in the night air, glasses of punch, and lovely music.

Virginia tucked her arm through Elizabeth's and, with a nod, indicated the colored butler standing sentinel at the gate. By unspoken agreement, they crossed the street and approached him. "Good evening," Elizabeth greeted him pleasantly. "Would you kindly satisfy our curiosity? What happy occasion is Mrs. Farnham celebrating?"

"It's a festival, ma'am," he said. "A benefit for the sick and wounded soldiers."

"A benefit?" echoed Virginia.

The sentinel nodded. "Yes, ma'am. The guests pay twenty-five cents to enter, and then they can buy tickets to exchange for punch and delicacies. For a few tickets more, they can request a special tune from the band. All the money will go to help the suffering soldiers get the things they need — medicine, bandages, blankets, good food — everything that's in short supply."

"What a marvelous idea," said Elizabeth. "I hope it's a complete success."

The sentinel thanked them politely as they moved on.

As she and Virginia made their way home, Elizabeth mulled over what they had seen. "Virginia," she said thoughtfully as they turned onto Twelfth Street, "something occurs to me."

"And what is that?"

"If white people can give festivals to raise funds for the relief of suffering soldiers, why shouldn't the well-to-do colored people work for the benefit of the suffering of our race?"

"I don't see any reason why we should not," said Virginia. "Heaven knows we have suffering colored folks all around us in abundance, and more coming every day."

It was a sobering truth. Just as the opponents of the president's bill had warned, Washington after emancipation had become the refuge of contraband, runaways, and freedmen emigrating from slave states.

Before the law abolished slavery in the district, the contraband population had numbered only a few hundred. Newcomers found places to live in the town houses along Duff Green's Row on East Capitol Street and were taken up into the ebb and flow of the city with little difficulty. After emancipation became law, however, their numbers had swelled into the thousands. They arrived in the city alone or with their families in tow, footsore, hungry, exhausted, most of them field hands with no trade or training except farm labor, almost all of them illiterate. Very few contraband could find or afford rooms in colored homes or boardinghouses, and even fewer had set out for the capital with any thought of what they would do once they arrived. At first they were accommodated in Camp Barker, a complex of empty soldiers' barracks, stables, and tents, but when these places filled to overflowing, the refugees built themselves shacks of blankets, mud, and scraps of wood in camps that sprouted up near military hospitals, beside the forts on the outskirts of the city, or tucked away in alleys. Sometimes the government administrators failed to distribute rations efficiently, and entire families went hungry. Diseases like dysentery, smallpox, and typhoid flourished in the overcrowded, filthy camps, and the dead were buried in makeshift cemeteries not far away.

White Washingtonians, even some of those who had supported emancipation, had become increasingly alarmed by the rising tide of impoverished refugees. They were not alone in their worries. Some among the colored elite and middle class, whose loftier status within the city social hierarchy seemed tenuous even at its best, were determined to distinguish themselves from their uneducated, destitute, darker-skinned brethren. In Washington's colored community, rank was determined according to one's wealth, distance from slavery, and lightness of skin tone. Thus freeborn Negroes of means were at the pinnacle, with light-skinned former slaves a rung below, darker-skinned freedmen beneath them, and slaves lowest of all, with barely a toehold on the ladder. It was an order not unlike what Elizabeth had known as a slave, wherein light-skinned house slaves — often the children, grandchildren, or siblings of their masters — held themselves above the darker field hands. The unspoken rules were strictly observed even within the White House, and even the president was powerless to enforce equality. Mrs. Lincoln had told Elizabeth regretfully of William Johnson, Mr. Lincoln's dark-skinned personal valet, who had come with them to Washington from Springfield but had left soon thereafter, before Elizabeth came into her service. The lighter-skinned White House servants had snubbed William and subjected him to such adamant scorn that after enduring two days of it, he resigned and asked the president to help him find employment elsewhere.

Thankfully, most middle-class colored Washingtonians overcame these class prejudices to assist the contraband. They acted out of compassion, and they acted out of self-interest, understanding well that many white people saw no difference between the prosperous colored merchant whose wife and daughters dressed in silk and the shoe-less, whip-scarred contraband who had been a slave only weeks before. As the lowest among them fared, so everyone of their race would be perceived, and thus for their own sakes it was essential to forgo snobbery and raise up all colored people. Elizabeth wished no one needed to be reminded that it was also simply the right thing to do, to be charitable to those in need.

The following Sunday, with encouragement from Virginia, Walker, and Emma, Elizabeth received permission from her minister to address the congregation after his sermon. She was not accustomed to speaking before so great a crowd, but she summoned up her courage, stepped up to the pulpit, and reminded herself that the need was too great to allow nerves to get the better of her.

"We have all observed the great migration of newly freed slaves to Washington," she began. "They come with great hope in their hearts and all their worldly goods on their backs. Fresh from the bonds of slavery, from the benighted regions of the plantation, they come to the capital looking for liberty, but many of them don't know it when they find it. Many good friends have reached out to them in the spirit of charity and compassion, but for each kind word spoken, two harsh ones have been uttered."

A few women nodded as they fanned themselves, their hats bobbing emphatically.

"The newly liberated have not been welcomed, but repelled," said Elizabeth, "and their bright, joyous dreams of freedom are fading in the presence of that stern, practical mistress, reality."

Murmurs of agreement went up from the pews.

"Instead of flowery paths, days of perpetual sunshine, and bowers hanging with golden fruit, the road has been rugged and the garden full of thorns," Elizabeth continued. "Appeals for help too often are answered by cold neglect. Poor children of slavery, men and women of our race — the transition from slavery to freedom has been too sudden for them! They are not prepared for the new life that has opened before them, and now the great masses of the North look upon their helplessness with indifference. Our white neighbors, observing those who have come to us as refugees, have learned to speak of our entire race as idle and dependent."

A more emphatic response followed these words — grim nods of assent, a scattering of amens, and encouraging calls for her to speak on.

"It is our sacred duty to help our own," said Elizabeth, "and these poor unfortunates are indeed our own. Our Lord Jesus Christ instructed us to love our neighbor. He told us that whatever we do unto the least of His brethren, that we have also done unto Him. Brothers and sisters, I ask you to look toward the contraband camps and see your neighbors, and to join me in creating a society of colored people to work for the benefit of the suffering freedmen."

A loud crash of applause greeted her

proposal, and as Elizabeth nodded her thanks and returned to her pew, the minister took the pulpit and invited anyone who would be interested in founding a relief association to stay after services for its inaugural meeting.

Two weeks later, the Contraband Relief Association officially commenced, with forty women members and Elizabeth as its elected president. They planned benefit concerts and festivals, and they organized volunteers to work in the contraband camps. Their most prominent members solicited donations from well-to-do Northerners, white and colored alike. With the funds they raised, they purchased essential supplies for the camps — shoes, clothing, bedding, food, tools — and helped the contraband settle into permanent homes.

Elizabeth often visited the camps to teach sewing, reading, and simple housekeeping to the colored women struggling to care for their families in the squalid conditions. Because of her dignified, well-spoken manner and status as the president of a relief organization, officials often asked her to escort visiting dignitaries who came to inspect the camps. On one such occasion, she guided a Miss Harriet Jacobs, a former runaway slave from North Carolina a few years older than herself and a prominent, influential abolitionist. Miss Jacobs's knowing, compassionate gaze took in every detail as Elizabeth showed her around and described the contrabands' plight. "They're willing and ready to work, but they've never worked for wages," Elizabeth noted as they passed a group of young men listening intently to a well-dressed colored man in spectacles who addressed them from atop an overturned crate. Suddenly one of the young men folded his arms over his chest, lifted his chin, and frowned thoughtfully up at the speaker in a manner so reminiscent of her lost son, George, that Elizabeth had to look away, pained. "We have to teach them how to seek work for pay, how to settle on fair wages, and how to leave an employer who treats them unfairly."

Miss Jacobs nodded, studying the young men as she followed Elizabeth past. "And is there work to be found?"

"Oh, indeed, yes. The war has created ample quantities of that." Elizabeth guided Miss Jacobs around a tent where a soldier was distributing loaves of bread to a cluster of gaunt, silently determined women, some of whom clutched young children dressed in tatters. "Do you know about President Lincoln's new law, the one that allows him to employ 'persons of African descent' to help put down the rebellion?" Miss Jacobs nodded. "Then perhaps you already know that soon after the law was passed, the government set about registering contrabands and distributing rations, clothing, and wages in exchange for their labor in support of the Union. The men of the camps cut firewood, haul water, dig ditches, police hospital grounds, construct roads, build whatever needs to be built, and repair whatever needs fixing."

"And the women?"

"They work as laundresses and cooks, and they take turns watching one another's children. For wages, men receive ten dollars a month. Single women hire at four dollars a month, while a woman with one child earns two and a half, perhaps three." Suddenly Elizabeth halted and placed a hand on Miss Jacobs's arm, bringing her to a stop. "Make no mistake, the most unpleasant tasks always fall to the contraband, the work no one else wants to do — cleaning privies, burying dead horses and mules, removing the human refuse of the hospital wards. It's important, necessary work, but it's also hard, exhausting toil, and not what they had expected of freedom."

"Their dreams have failed to live up to

their expectations," Miss Jacobs remarked as she resumed walking.

"That's true," said Elizabeth, hurrying to catch up with her, "but until I spent more time among them, I did not realize how extravagant their dreams had once been — and how thoroughly demoralized the dreamers have become."

Something, some embarrassment or uncertainty, restrained Elizabeth from confiding that whenever she visited the camps, refugees would crowd around her, lamenting in their distress and pleading for relief. For some, the bitterness of their disappointment cast their memories of slavery in a false, rosy glow, so that they pined for their old lives. Elizabeth had been dismayed the first time she had heard one old woman declare that she would prefer to return to slavery in the South, where everything was familiar and her master had provided for her, rather than suffer the miserable freedom of the North. Elizabeth told herself that the old woman and others who felt as she did were not to blame for their despair, and she did not hold their words against them. After a lifetime of dependence, they knew nothing else, and the worries and cares of poverty had given them a harsh introduction to freedom.

"Are all the camps in such a state?" Miss Jacobs asked. "Everything seems to be in short supply except for disease, misery, hunger — and the will to triumph over them, which is heartening to see."

"The need for the simple necessities of life and comfort is great everywhere," Elizabeth said, "but I have heard that conditions are somewhat better across the river."

"Across the river, in Virginia?"

"Oh, yes. Part of General Lee's estate at Arlington has been transformed into a settlement called Freedman's Village. I haven't visited it myself, but you certainly should, to make your report complete. I've heard that all of the men and most of the women are gainfully employed. They also have the benefit of plenty of exercise in the open air, something that is denied the people here."

Miss Jacobs nodded thoughtfully. "I'd certainly like to see that for myself."

When the tour was over, Elizabeth accompanied Miss Jacobs to the street where her carriage waited. She waved farewell as the driver assisted Miss Jacobs inside, but she paused, bewildered, when the driver addressed her as Miss Brent, and she answered to the name.

"You mean you didn't know?" one of her

fellow volunteers exclaimed later, when Elizabeth told her about the curious exchange. "Miss Harriet Ann Jacobs is also known as Miss Linda Brent."

"You don't mean the author?"

"Is there any other Miss Linda Brent? When she writes, she uses a nom de plume for her own protection, but I assure you they are one and the same."

Elizabeth was so astonished she had to laugh. She had read *Incidents in the Life of a Slave Girl* soon after its publication, and she had been greatly moved by the author's courageous escape to freedom in the North and her tireless efforts to see her two children freed as well. So many anecdotes from Miss Brent's — Miss Jacobs's — life were painfully familiar to Elizabeth, and the story had lingered in her thoughts long after she finished the book. She had even been inspired to compose a few memory sketches of her own, describing her childhood as a slave and the harrowing years of her young womanhood, when she had been preyed upon by Alexander Kirkland and a cruel mistress to whom she had been "lent" had tried to break her spirit with regular beatings. She had thought one day to share her writings with her son, but after his death, her interest in the project had waned.

Perhaps she should take pen in hand again someday. Even if she never published a memoir, as Miss Jacobs had done, she might share her story with her closest friends.

In the weeks that followed, she heard that Miss Jacobs had indeed visited Freedman's Village in Alexandria, and that she had been so moved by their plight and impressed by their progress that she had decided to stay and work. For her part, Elizabeth continued her efforts in the camps in the capital, teaching necessary skills and offering guidance. It was heartening to see that while some disillusioned freedmen and women yearned for a past that had never really existed, others set themselves to the work of rising above their humble beginnings. They built sturdy cabins for their families and cultivated gardens. They saved their earnings and bought chickens and pigs. They joined churches and sent their children to the camp schools, where their teachers marveled at their swift and steady advancement. Clear-eyed, proud, and determined, they planned carefully for the future and strove forward to meet it. As the months passed, the more hesitant and anxious among them started to follow the others' example, and Elizabeth and her fellow volunteers rejoiced as their labors began to bear fruit.

The work of the Contraband Relief Association was worthwhile, never-ending — and expensive. Elizabeth contributed all that she could afford from her own earnings, but she knew the organization needed to find other sources of funds if it were to thrive.

Although Elizabeth had gone to the White House only rarely that summer since Mrs. Lincoln spent most of her time at the Soldiers' Home or traveling with Robert and Tad, she had seen enough of the inner workings of President Lincoln's administration to know that he was surely embattled and struggling. The war was going badly. General Stonewall Jackson's outnumbered Confederate forces had stymied the Union Army in the Shenandoah Valley, forcing it to draw back to the Potomac. In the Seven Days' Battles in Virginia, General McClellan had again retreated despite defeating the Confederates on three consecutive days. A Union attack on Vicksburg failed, thwarting their attempt to gain control of the Mississippi River. In Richmond, Kentucky, Confederate troops soundly defeated a smaller band of Union soldiers, taking most of them prisoner. And at a second battle at the stream called Bull Run, General John Pope suffered a disastrous loss, with more than fifteen thousand troops reported killed, wounded, missing, or captured and the rest of his army driven back across the river toward Washington by General Robert E. Lee.

Elizabeth's heart went out to the president, knowing full well that each defeat would weigh heavily upon him, but she was less sympathetic and utterly bewildered by another battle he fought. In July, President Lincoln had tried valiantly to persuade congressmen from the border states to enact a plan for gradual, compensated emancipation, and although the effort failed, it had assured Elizabeth that his heart was in the right place. Within weeks, however, he made statements in the press that forced her to question whether she truly understood anything about his position on abolition. On August 14, the president received a delegation of Negro leaders at the White House and made his case for the colonization of freed slaves in Africa or Central America. The presence of the colored race on the American continent had caused the war, the president asserted, and enmity between races was certain to persist after the conflict was resolved. Even when they ceased to be slaves, the colored race would never be equal to the white, and thus it would be better for both if they were separated.

The delegation left the White House unconvinced and angry, and they immediately shared the disappointing outcome of their historic meeting with sympathetic members of the press. A few days later, in a *New York Tribune* editorial titled "The Prayer of Twenty Millions," Horace Greeley furiously censured the president for failing to execute the laws of the land by not demanding that his generals immediately obey the emancipating provisions of the new Confiscation Act. He accused the president of "being unduly influenced by the counsels, the representations, the menaces, of certain fossil politicians hailing from the Border Slave States," appeasing them to the detriment of the nation. No champion of the Union cause on earth believed that the rebellion could be put down unless slavery, its cause, was ended as well, Mr. Greeley insisted, warning that "every hour of deference to Slavery is an hour of added and deepened peril to the Union."

Three days later, President Lincoln responded to the editorial with a terse letter, which Mr. Greeley published on August 25 along with his own lengthy rebuttal. Excusing Mr. Greeley's "impatient and dictatorial tone" out of deference to their friendship, the president emphatically stated that his goal was to save the Union, and nothing else. "My paramount object in this struggle is to save the Union," he wrote, "and is not either to save or to destroy slavery. If I could save the Union without freeing any slave I would do it, and if I could save it by freeing all the slaves I would do it; and if I could save it by freeing some and leaving others alone I would also do that. What I do about slavery, and the colored race, I do because I believe it helps to save the Union; and what I forbear, I forbear because I do not believe it would help to save the Union."

Everyone in Washington either read the heated exchange in the papers or heard about it from friends and neighbors. Unionists ambivalent about emancipation were satisfied by the president's stated priorities, but Elizabeth knew of no one else who was. Outraged abolitionists insisted that the president seemed incapable of understanding that the surest and swiftest way to win the war and save the Union was to emancipate all slaves everywhere and to allow them to don Union blue and take up arms in service to the nation. As for Elizabeth, she certainly wanted slavery abolished everywhere. She wanted colored men to be allowed to enlist as her son, George, had done. But she also wanted the contraband to be healthy, well fed, educated, employed, and prosperous, and she knew that no amount of wishing could make it so — only hard work and careful planning. She wanted to believe that the president too had to work hard and plan carefully to bring about what he desired, and that there were good reasons for his delay, and that that was why he did not yet free the suffering slaves, although he could with a few strokes of a pen.

She wanted to have faith in him, but she hoped he would not delay much longer.

In mid-September, in a costly battle along Antietam Creek in Maryland, General McClellan managed to repulse General Lee's advance into the North. Although the president was displeased that General McClellan had allowed the battered Confederate army to withdraw to Virginia without pursuit, the stalemate was victory enough to hearten him.

Less than a week later, newspapers across the North published a proclamation in which the president declared that "on the first day of January in the year of our Lord, one thousand eight hundred and sixty-three, all persons held as slaves within any State, or designated part of a State, the people whereof shall then be in rebellion against the United States shall be then, thenceforward, and forever free."

When Elizabeth read the entire preliminary Emancipation Proclamation in the *National Republican* on September 23, her spirits soared, and she felt her faith in Mr. Lincoln renewed. Now, at last, details that had been kept secret leaked out, and the president's tactical delays made sense. Mr. Lincoln had wanted to free the slaves all along, his supporters insisted, despite his earlier statements that the war was being fought only to preserve the Union. He had written his Emancipation Proclamation weeks or perhaps months earlier and had presented it to his cabinet, but he had been obliged to wait until after a decisive Union victory before he could announce the proclamation to the American people or it would appear an act of desperation. Mr. Lincoln had also wanted to determine whether freeing the slaves was constitutional, and he had come to believe that it was indeed legal for him, by virtue of his war powers as commander in chief, to free the slaves in areas under rebellion.

The colored community and abolitionists of all races rejoiced, but in the days that followed, as the president's words were discussed and debated, their celebration was tempered by concerns that it did not go far enough. The proclamation called for the abolition of slavery only in states that were in rebellion as of January 1, 1863, so in theory, if a state agreed to return to the Union before that date, slavery would be permitted to continue there. The proclamation did nothing to free the enslaved people living within the loyal Union border states of Delaware, Kentucky, Maryland, and Missouri, as well as Tennessee and parts of Louisiana, Confederate territory that had come under Union control. What practical good did it do to declare slaves free in regions where the people did not respect Mr. Lincoln's authority and therefore were highly unlikely to obey his laws? It seemed to Elizabeth that Mr. Lincoln had emancipated slaves where the Union could not free them and kept them enslaved in places where the Union did enjoy the power to give them liberty.

And yet, despite its weaknesses, the proclamation was worth celebrating as proof that the nation was moving forward with single-minded determination toward greater freedom for all. The old Union was gone forever. When the nation was restored, it would be a new United States.

The day after the proclamation was published, a large crowd complete with a band gathered outside the White House to serenade the president and offer speeches of praise. The president stepped outside to thank them, saying, "I have not been distinctly informed why it is this occasion you appear to do me this honor, though I suppose it is because of the proclamation." The crowd applauded and shouted back that he indeed had it right. The president went on to say, with his characteristic humility, "What I did, I did after very full deliberation, and under a very heavy and solemn sense of responsibility. I can only trust in God I have made no mistake." The crowd roared back their assurances that he had not.

Elizabeth too believed he had made no mistake, and that greater freedoms would be forthcoming.

She also believed that very soon, her Contraband Relief Association would be more necessary than ever.

Earlier in September, the First Lady had left Washington to visit New York with Tad. In October, plagued by severe headaches, buffeted by storms of grief, and desiring a sympathetic companion, she asked Elizabeth to join her at the Metropolitan Hotel in Manhattan. Elizabeth eagerly agreed, not only because she had never visited New York and desired very much to see it, but also because the trip would enable her to promote her cause to a new audience. Armed with credentials and letters of recommendation, Elizabeth took the train to Manhattan, settled into the accommodations Mrs. Lincoln had arranged, and, the following morning, told the First Lady about her work.

"This is truly a noble effort," Mrs. Lincoln declared. She was swathed in mourning black from head to toe and had suffered unpleasant symptoms throughout her travels, but for a moment she seemed restored to her former self, energetic and bustling with plans. "I insist upon joining your list of subscribers. Will a contribution of two hundred dollars suffice?"

"Why, yes, Mrs. Lincoln," said Elizabeth, delighted by her generosity. "Thank you very much."

"It is the very least I can do for all you've done for me," Mrs. Lincoln said, and set about writing to her husband to secure the funds.

During her time in New York, Elizabeth circulated among the colored community, soliciting and acquiring donations to purchase much-needed supplies for the contraband camps. She was introduced to the Reverend Henry Highland Garnet, who led a meeting on behalf of her association at his Shiloh Presbyterian Church. After Elizabeth told the steward of the Metropolitan Hotel about her mission, he promptly raised an impressive sum from among the colored dining room waiters.

When Mrs. Lincoln decided to take a side trip to visit Robert at Harvard, she asked Elizabeth to accompany her, and again she seized the opportunity. In Boston she was introduced to Mr. Wendell Phillips, a lawyer, orator, and abolitionist of such devotion that for years he had refused to taste cane sugar or wear cotton because both were produced by slave labor. He and other Boston philanthropists contributed generously and pledged her their support for her cause. She also met Reverend Leonard A. Grimes, who presided over a mass meeting at the Twelfth Street Baptist Church, where his wife established a Boston branch of the Contraband Relief Association. Reverend Grimes happened to be a friend of Mr. Frederick Douglass, whom Elizabeth had long admired, and he offered to write to the renowned abolitionist and orator on her behalf. From his lecture tour in England, Mr. Douglass not only made a sizable contribution to the association, but he also raised money for them from several English antislavery societies.

Throughout her autumn travels, and with the encouragement and support of Mrs. Lincoln, Elizabeth worked tirelessly to gather donations for contraband relief, ever mindful of her son George's belief that as freed slaves, they had a special obligation to help deliver others of their race from bondage. Elizabeth agreed wholeheartedly, but she also believed that their obligation to help those in need endured even after their chains and shackles were removed. They who had already crossed the river into the land of freedom were obliged to turn and offer a hand to those who were taking their first tentative steps upon the shore, and Elizabeth resolved to do exactly that.

CHAPTER EIGHT

December 1862–May 1863

On the evening of December 31, Elizabeth and Emma went to Union Bethel Church to attend a freedom vigil, just like thousands of other colored folks in hundreds of colored churches all across the North. By sundown every pew was full, and while they waited for the minister to begin, the worshippers prayed, sang, and testified about their experiences as enslaved people. At ten o'clock, the minister stood before the congregation, opened his well-worn Bible, and led them in prayer before preaching a sermon about God, Satan, Mr. Lincoln, and the coming day of eternal freedom. He asked the Lord to bless the New Year's morning only a few hours away, and to bless the hand of President Lincoln when he held the pen to sign the Emancipation Proclamation. As he celebrated the imminent glorious event, he also spoke of what freedom meant for the people of their race and reminded them of the new responsibilities they must now willingly and cheerfully shoulder. Then, almost as if he believed their white neighbors and leaders of government were among them, he began to address them directly. "Your destiny as white men and ours as black men are one and the same," he declared. "We are all marching toward the same goal. Give us therefore the same guarantee of life, liberty, and the pursuit of happiness that you have enjoyed since the founding of our great nation, and make the very same demands of us to support the government as you make of yourselves."

A chorus of amens went up from the congregation.

"Give us the vote and give us arms to fight," the minister said, his voice rising to a shout. "Let us don Union blue and shoulder our rifles. Do not put vulgar prejudice before necessity and national preservation. Do not refuse to receive the very men who have a deeper interest in the defeat of the rebels than any others. Cannot black men wield a sword, fire a gun, march and countermarch, and obey orders like any man?"

The congregation called out that yes, they could, of course they could.

"A man who wants to win a fight doesn't approach his enemy with one hand tied behind his back," the minister said. "If your house is on fire, and a black man offers you a bucket of water, do you refuse it? If you are drowning, and a black man reaches out to haul you to shore, do you tread water and hope a white man happens by before you go under, or do you seize that dusky limb and live?"

A roar of approval greeted his words. Elizabeth applauded until her palms stung, the minister's stirring words lifting her to her feet and sending righteous determination pumping through her veins, as warm and strong as life.

Just before midnight, the minister's tone changed again. "At this time I want no one to pray standing up with bowed head," he intoned. "No sister sitting down, with bended neck praying, and no brother kneeling on one knee, because his pants are too tight for him. I want all of us to get down on both knees to thank Almighty God for our freedom and for President Lincoln too."

Side by side, Elizabeth and Emma knelt. From the corner of her eye, Elizabeth saw Emma's lips moving in silent prayer. Silence fell over the church, broken from time to time by a worshipper calling out to the Lord for guidance when freedom dawned, just as He had guided them through the dark night of slavery. People called out for the Lord to guide President Lincoln as well.

In reverent silence, Elizabeth echoed those prayers with all her heart.

Despite her late night, Elizabeth rose at her usual hour the next morning and went to the White House to dress Mrs. Lincoln for the annual New Year's Day reception at eleven o'clock. The First Lady, pale and drawn, had already chosen a black dress and bonnet and was awaiting Elizabeth in her boudoir. "I cannot help but think of all we have passed through since we last welcomed a New Year," she murmured as Elizabeth buttoned her dress up the back. "Every day from now until spring will mark an unhappy anniversary."

Elizabeth knew she was thinking in particular of Willie's death. "When the first anniversary of my son's passing came, I made sure to keep busy." In truth, the day that she suffered the worst was not the anniversary of the date he had fallen on the field but rather the day she had received the letter announcing his death. "There's always so much to do at the contraband camps that I had no trouble finding work enough to occupy my thoughts so I couldn't dwell upon my grief."

"Perhaps I should do something of that sort," said Mrs. Lincoln. "The soldiers always need care and attention, especially those languishing in the military hospitals. They do so seem to like it when I write letters home for them when they cannot write themselves." She managed a tremulous smile, and she seemed relieved to have a plan. "I shall do as you suggest, Elizabeth, and distract myself with the needs of others. Even if it does not ease my pain, it will at least accomplish some good for the soldiers."

"I hope it does both," said Elizabeth.

When Mrs. Lincoln finished dressing, she asked a servant if the president was ready to go downstairs, and she was told that he was in his office, writing. "Still?" she asked, and to Elizabeth she added, "He's been working on the final draft of that proclamation since last night."

"The Emancipation Proclamation?" Elizabeth asked, suddenly uneasy. What else could Mrs. Lincoln mean? From the moment the newspapers had published the preliminary decree, President Lincoln had been bombarded by criticism. Northern Peace Democrats declared that they were not going to fight a war to free slaves, and in the midterm elections, opponents of emancipation made their displeasure known by electing Democratic governors and congressmen. The Democrats worried that despite this apparent rejection of Mr. Lincoln's policies by the voting populace, he would go ahead regardless and sign the proclamation into law, while abolitionists and radical Republicans worried that he would not. Rumor had it that the president's cabinet had been urging him to make changes to the document up to the last minute, and that rumor appeared to be true.

Elizabeth could only pray that the changes the president was making — even at that very moment, not very far away — would not cut the heart out of the new law.

Elizabeth left the White House before Mr. Lincoln appeared, passing guests arriving for the reception on her way out. She wished she could have seen the president — not to question him about the proclamation, because he had enough burdens without bearing her inquiries too, but to see if she could discern from his expression whether his revisions meant good or ill for her race.

Instead of turning toward home, she walked to Union Bethel Church, where the vigil continued. Along the way she observed a crowd gathered outside the telegraph office, where the moment a messenger arrived from the White House to confirm that the deed was done, the news would be sent with electric speed to newspaper offices throughout the North. Other men, white and colored alike, clustered near the doorway of a printer's, where clerks waited to typeset the proclamation as soon as the official phrasing was known. Elizabeth suspected they would be waiting quite a long time. The New Year's Day reception was by custom a three-hour affair. Mr. Lincoln would stand in the East Room shaking hands and welcoming visitors — foreign diplomats first, then ranking officials, and lastly the public, anyone who wished to come. After shaking all those thousands of hands, it would be a wonder if his own hand was not too worn out to hold a pen.

When Elizabeth arrived at Union Bethel Church, the minister and several of the nearly two dozen members of the congregation keeping vigil broke off their prayers and hurried over to question her. She told them what she knew, which amounted to little more than the expectation that they were in for a lengthy wait. They nodded resignedly and resumed their prayers or hushed conversations, listening to the bells toll the passing hours, glancing up quickly at the sound of the door, settling back down to wait again.

And then, in the late afternoon, a deacon burst into the chapel, breathless, sweat on his brow, a paper clutched in his right hand, the smell of ink still fresh upon it. "It's done!" he shouted. He was too winded from his run to read the proclamation aloud, so he handed it to the minister, who stepped up to the pulpit and read it slowly and emphatically, each word ringing through the church. Elizabeth felt relief and joy wash over her as with every line it became more evident that the president had made only a few changes to the preliminary proclamation she had read so often that she had learned it by heart. The list of territories under Union control had been revised due to the advances the army had made in the interim — but far more significant were two new paragraphs that had not appeared in the preliminary version released the previous autumn. In the first of these, President Lincoln enjoined the people newly freed by the proclamation "to abstain from all violence, unless in necessary self-defense." A murmur arose from the congregation as the meaning of the words sank in. Never before had they been permitted to defend themselves physically, to fight off a vicious beating by a cruel white master or mistress. Now they could stand their ground and fight to preserve their lives, if confronted by such a choice. It was a revelation.

The second addition was more astonishing yet. "And I further declare and make known that such persons" — the newly emancipated — "of suitable condition, will be received into the armed service of the United States to garrison forts, positions, stations, and other places, and to man vessels of all sorts in said service."

Cheers rang out, and shouts of astonishment. In the rebellious territories, slaves were free and men of color would be allowed to fight for the Union.

The day many among them thought would never come had arrived at last.

The congregation broke into prayers of thanksgiving and songs of rejoicing, and together they paraded to the White House, where hundreds of other jubilant citizens both white and black sang and shouted praise to the president, who briefly appeared at a window to acknowledge them with a humble, solemn bow.

Later Elizabeth went to the contraband camps, where the struggling freedmen forgot their cares for a while and celebrated the dawn of a new day of liberty, the first day of their new lives when they would not fear the whip, live in terror of the auction block, or dread having their children and husbands and wives sold away from them, never to be seen again.

In the evening, a hush fell over the throng as the Reverend Danforth B. Nichols, superintendent of freedmen, read the Emancipation Proclamation aloud, intoning each word with careful clarity. When he finished, and after the applause and cheers faded, he raised his hands for their attention and cautioned them that the law did not apply everywhere — not in neighboring Maryland, for one. But not even that sobering counsel could diminish their joy.

At long last, freedom was at hand.

As the anniversary of Willie's death approached, Mrs. Lincoln became almost feverishly restless, and she poured her excess energies into her social obligations as First Lady. She resumed receiving callers on Saturday afternoons, and although she still dressed in deep mourning, she and the president began to venture out in the evenings again, attending recitations or going to the theater, which was Mr. Lincoln's favorite entertainment.

Mrs. Lincoln continued to find her greatest comfort in her two surviving sons. She brightened considerably every few months when Robert visited, and although Elizabeth privately found the young man severe and prickly, she was always happy when he came home from school for the joy his company brought his parents. His visits were not entirely cheerful, however, for he was very eager to quit Harvard and join the army, and he would always use his few days at home to press his case.

Mrs. Lincoln adamantly opposed his enlistment, as she often told her husband when they were alone — alone except for Elizabeth, sewing nearby and quietly listening. "We have lost two sons, and their loss is as much as I can bear, without being called upon to make another sacrifice," Mrs. Lincoln declared one day in mid-February when the subject resurfaced yet again.

"But many a poor mother has given up all her sons," Mr. Lincoln replied mildly. At that, Elizabeth half expected them both to glance sympathetically her way, but they did not. It stung to think that they might have forgotten her loss, or forgotten that she was there. "Our son is not more dear to us than the sons of other people are to their mothers."

"That may be, but I cannot bear to have Robert exposed to danger. His services are not required in the field, and the sacrifice would be a needless one."

"The services of every man who loves his country are required in this war," Mr. Lincoln replied. "You should take a liberal instead of a selfish view of the question, Mother."

Mrs. Lincoln was firmly resolved that Robert should stay in school, and since neither could persuade the other they let the matter drop for a while, perhaps wearily certain that it would not be long before Robert again implored them to permit him to enlist.

Although the argument had ended for the moment, Mr. Lincoln's words lingered in Elizabeth's thoughts. The services of every man were required, he had said. Perhaps she was still hurt that it had not occurred to Mr. and Mrs. Lincoln that one of those mothers who had given up all her sons to the Union cause sat among them, because she felt a strange, unfamiliar desire to rebuke the president. Every man who loved his country, he had said. She was tempted to inquire whether he included men of color in that calculation.

Why did he *not* include men of color —
every man of color, not only the newly
emancipated slaves living in captured Southern territories — if every man who loved
his country was needed so desperately?

Elizabeth's prediction that the Contraband
Relief Association would be more essential
than ever after emancipation proved true.
The needs of the men, women, and children
in the camps were so great that even the
generous contributions of concerned friends
were insufficient to supply everyone with
the basic necessities of health and comfort.
Throughout the winter, Elizabeth gave
increasingly more of herself to the association — more of her time, and more, too
much more, of her money. For the first time
since she had established herself comfortably in Washington, she found herself struggling to make ends meet, and she could not
endure the worry and uncertainty. For most
of her life, she had served masters and
mistresses who badly managed their finances, incurring debt and moving from
one town to another in a futile pursuit of a
better living. While a slave, she had promised
herself that if she ever gained her freedom,
she would never be so careless with money.

Now it seemed that she was following her old masters down the same road of precarious economy. It made no difference that her debts sprang from altruism rather than reckless pursuit of a loftier style of living than she could afford; she would end up at the same miserable destination.

She would have confessed her troubles to her friends, but she didn't want to worry Emma needlessly about the state of the dressmaking business, and she was reluctant to upset Virginia, who was with child. Instead she brooded silently and secretly, or so she believed, until one day at the White House. She was sorting trims for Mrs. Lincoln to consider for a new dress and mulling over her worries when Mrs. Lincoln suddenly said, "Good heavens, Lizzie, why are you scowling at those ribbons? If you dislike them so much, we'll send you to the shops for something else, although I don't know what else they'll have in black that we haven't seen already."

"Forgive me," said Elizabeth, embarrassed. "The ribbons are fine. I confess my thoughts were elsewhere."

"I knew something was wrong." Mrs. Lincoln sat beside her and patted her hand. "Tell me. You've been sighing and frowning for days. Are you unhappy? Indisposed?"

"Merely worried." Elizabeth hesitated, but she felt cornered, and she had to offer some explanation. "I find that I am living beyond my means."

"You?" said Mrs. Lincoln, astonished. "I don't believe it. You've never been a spendthrift. You are always reliably sensible."

Elizabeth managed a small, wan smile. "I don't live lavishly, if that is what you mean, but lately I've been spending much of my earnings — whatever does not go to food and rent — on the contraband camps."

"Well, then . . ." Mrs. Lincoln thought for a moment as if tallying the ways Elizabeth might economize. "You must simply stop doing that."

"But the need is so great." Elizabeth steeled herself and said aloud what she had been dreading to acknowledge, even to herself. "I must earn more money."

Mrs. Lincoln looked taken aback. "Lizzie, dear, as much as I would love to assist you, I cannot possibly pay more for my dresses than I already do. Mr. Lincoln already believes I spend too much — not on dresses, mind you, but on other things."

Elizabeth tended to agree with the president on that count. "Oh, no, Mrs. Lincoln. I didn't mean to suggest that I intend to raise my prices. I wouldn't dream of asking any of my patrons to pay more than is fair, especially not you." She hesitated. "However, I do think I need to find some way to increase my income."

"Could you take on new customers, sew more dresses?"

Elizabeth thought back to those hard, long years in St. Louis when she had worked herself almost to collapse from exhaustion and injury trying to earn the money to buy her freedom and George's. She nearly shuddered from the memory of pain, of constant headaches and backaches and eye strain and sore fingers. "I don't think I could possibly sew more than I already do."

"Well, there must be another way you could earn a little extra," said Mrs. Lincoln confidently. "And there are surely other sources of funding for your association other than your wages. We simply haven't given it enough thought. We'll think of something."

Elizabeth thanked her, her spirits lifting even though she wasn't truly any closer to a solution. It was good to see Mrs. Lincoln more like her old self again, briskly efficacious and intent on a new scheme.

A few days later, Mrs. Lincoln rose to meet her when she arrived and clasped Elizabeth's hands in her own. "Elizabeth, I think I have a solution."

"It would be very welcome news if you do," Elizabeth replied, as surprised as she was relieved.

Mrs. Lincoln explained that the Treasury Department needed employees for the cutting room, workers who trimmed the printed sheets of currency into bills. Seamstresses were highly desirable for these posts due to their proficiency with scissors. "The work is not arduous, and the pay is reasonable," said Mrs. Lincoln, clearly delighted with herself. "Best of all, it should not take away time from your dressmaking business."

"I — I hardly know what to say," stammered Elizabeth, overwhelmed. "It sounds ideal."

"Good! You'll need to apply, of course, but I'm confident that with my recommendation you'll have no trouble." Mrs. Lincoln hesitated for a moment and seemed to steel herself. "There's one small hurdle that you'll have to overcome first — an ugly, unpleasant, dishonest hurdle."

The choice of adjectives was so bewildering that for a moment Elizabeth could only look at her. "What do you mean?"

"I think it would ease your way if you were introduced to Mr. Chase before you apply."

She meant Salmon P. Chase, the secretary of the treasury and the father of Mrs. Lincoln's biggest social rival, the lovely and charming Miss Kate Chase. "But you despise Secretary Chase."

Mrs. Lincoln lifted her chin and inhaled deeply. "I shall put aside my revulsion long enough to arrange the interview."

And so she did. Later that afternoon, when Mr. Chase came to the White House to confer with the president, Mrs. Lincoln managed to be outside her husband's office as he departed. Expressing delight at the chance encounter, Mrs. Lincoln told him there was someone she would very much like him to meet, and she led him to the Lincolns' private sitting room, where Elizabeth waited.

Elizabeth had seen Mr. Chase in passing often, but they had never been formally introduced. She set aside her sewing and rose when Mrs. Lincoln escorted him in, keeping her features carefully composed even though the obvious annoyance and impatience in his expression disconcerted her. To his credit, he did his best to be gracious when Mrs. Lincoln introduced them. "Mrs. Keckley, of course," he said, shaking her hand. "The renowned dressmaker. My daughter speaks very highly of you."

"Thank you, sir," she replied. "I think very highly of her as well." She ignored Mrs. Lincoln's raised eyebrows, which, fortunately, Mr. Chase did not observe.

Mrs. Lincoln got right to the point, and when she finished explaining the purpose of the meeting, Mr. Chase gave Elizabeth an appraising look and said, "So, Mrs. Keckley, you'd like to give up sewing for a job in the cutting room? From what I've heard, that would distress a great many ladies throughout Washington."

"I would not give up my sewing, sir," she said. "I simply wish to supplement the income from my business."

"There is no one in the district more qualified to wield a pair of shears than Elizabeth," Mrs. Lincoln broke in. "The Treasury Department can certainly entrust the task of cutting paper in straight lines to her. She does far more complicated work than that every day."

"I have no doubt she does." Mr. Chase studied Elizabeth for a moment. "Very well, Mrs. Keckley. If this is what you desire, you should apply to the Treasury Department. I shall tell the assistant secretary that we spoke, and after that, I'm sure your qualifications will speak for themselves."

"Thank you very much, Mr. Secretary," Elizabeth said. He gave her a nod and strode from the room, with Mrs. Lincoln hurrying after as if to thank him with the courtesy of an escort. When Mrs. Lincoln returned, she told Elizabeth that she would write to Mr. George Harrington too, to add her own recommendation to Mr. Chase's.

Mrs. Lincoln immediately sat down with pen and paper, and before long she was blotting the ink on her composition. "I've assured him that you are industrious and will perform your duties faithfully," she said, well satisfied with her work. "I also informed him that you will not be able to begin working for him until the middle of April, after the busy social season, when I will need you less frequently. I hope that suits you."

"The timing would be perfect," said Elizabeth. "Thank you very much, Mrs. Lincoln."

Beaming, Mrs. Lincoln summoned a servant to take the letter. "Now we await their reply."

It would only be a matter of time, Mrs. Lincoln assured her the next day, and again the day after that. Perhaps Mr. Chase had not yet found a moment to broach the subject with Mr. Harrington. Every department was managing the best it could with the war on, but sometimes even important matters were delayed.

A week went by, and another. Elizabeth's

hopes diminished, but she did not complain. Mrs. Lincoln had shown her a great kindness in recommending her to Mr. Chase and Mr. Harrington, and Elizabeth did not wish to appear ungrateful. Mrs. Lincoln, however, had no reservations about complaining when she thought complaints were warranted. Indignant that the department had shown neither Elizabeth nor herself the courtesy of a reply, she declared that she would discover the reason why even if she had to go to the Treasury Department herself.

Elizabeth knew she had found her answer when she arrived at the White House one morning to find Mrs. Lincoln waiting pensively by the window, her expression vexed and faintly embarrassed.

"You've heard from the Treasury Department," Elizabeth said flatly. "I didn't get the job."

"I'm very sorry, Elizabeth," said Mrs. Lincoln. "All agreed that your qualifications are exemplary, but I'm told the cutting-room supervisor had some . . . reservations. He had his current employees' feelings to consider."

Immediately Elizabeth understood, and she felt humiliated for ever entertaining the slightest expectation of being offered the position. "His other employees don't wish to work side-by-side with a woman of color."

Mrs. Lincoln crossed the room and placed her hands on Elizabeth's shoulders. "It's wrong, I know it, and I'm so very sorry. If it were up to me, you should have the post and anyone who does not care for your company would be free to resign."

"Regrettably, it is not up to you."

"No." Mrs. Lincoln frowned. "It is not — although I believe it *should* be up to me, as I am the First Lady."

Nodding, Elizabeth turned away and sank wearily into a chair. She had not felt so hurt and discouraged and outraged all at once since her slavery days.

"We'll think of something else," Mrs. Lincoln said, offering her an encouraging smile. "Don't give up, Elizabeth."

"I am not in the habit of giving up," she replied, but she had no idea what to do next.

To celebrate Tad's tenth birthday, Mrs. Lincoln proposed a family outing to visit the Army of the Potomac encampment near Falmouth, Virginia, on the north bank of the Rappahannock. At sunset on Saturday, April 4, in the midst of an unexpected spring snowstorm, the president, Mrs. Lincoln, Tad, and a small entourage of friends, administration officials, and trusted members of the press boarded the steamer *Carrie Martin*. They set off south down the river, passing Alexandria and Mount Vernon, where the ship's bells tolled a salute to George Washington in keeping with the time-honored custom of the river. Blinding, swirling snow forced the captain to put in to a sheltered cove for the night, and although the storm worsened overnight, the next morning they continued on to the crowded supply port of Aquia Creek, arriving on Easter Sunday. The party transferred to a flag-adorned train and chugged through fierce winds past huge snowdrifts to Falmouth Station, where General Hooker welcomed them.

The weather delayed their official plans for a day, but in the week that followed, the president and First Lady reviewed the troops, enjoyed a grand parade of cavalry, visited patients and staff in field hospitals, and ventured down to the shore of the Rappahannock, close enough to see Confederate troops waving to them from the other side. The family returned to Washington on April 11, their spirits much improved by the time away from the city. When Elizabeth came to the White House the next day, she observed that Mr. Lincoln seemed heartened by the readiness, strength, and spirit of the troops he had met, while Mrs. Lincoln appeared much more relaxed and contented — despite one irritating incident in a receiving line in which a vivacious, flame-haired equestrienne who had married a Prussian prince and acquired the title Princess Salm-Salm had ardently kissed the president rather than shaking his hand. Delighted, several other ladies had been emboldened to kiss him too, until he had been all but undone by an assault of kisses. Princess Salm-Salm had laughingly explained that General Sickles had put the ladies up to it, in hopes that their kisses would cheer the gloomy president. Mrs. Lincoln had been greatly affronted, but she refused to let those silly women ruin the excursion for her. What she always wanted above all else was time in the company of her husband and children, and the brief trip with Mr. Lincoln and Tad had clearly done her a world of good.

Mrs. Lincoln had returned to Washington with a new plan to help Elizabeth out of her troubling circumstances. In conversation with the staff at a field hospital, she had been informed about a new law that entitled Elizabeth, as a widow whose only son had been killed in action, to a government pension. "All you need to do is apply at the United States Pension Office," Mrs. Lincoln assured her. "In my opinion, it is the very least the nation can do to express our gratitude for your sacrifice."

Elizabeth thanked her, and as soon as she could, she went to the appropriate office and collected the necessary forms. The clerk looked askance at her as he explained the various signatures and affidavits she would need to collect, but she was used to such looks from white men who found her in places where they did not expect to see a woman of color, and so she ignored him. It was not until later, when she spoke with several of the men whom she asked to testify on her behalf, that she realized she was again suspended in that strange middle ground between the white world and the black, and that circumstances not of her making would prevent her from obtaining the pension she so desperately needed.

Even though a few scattered contraband regiments existed and it seemed likely that someday soon colored men would be welcomed into their own army regiments, George had enlisted nearly two years before by passing himself off as white. He had been able to do that, but one glance at Elizabeth would reveal that she was not a white woman. It would be difficult enough to explain how a black woman had given birth to a white man, but it was not even the most painful problem: Her son was, in the eyes of the law, illegitimate. George was the product of rape, the offspring of a liaison she had never desired, and yet, due to the curious morality surrounding race and marriage and the "peculiar institution" of slavery, Elizabeth would suffer for what would be perceived as her sexual indiscretion.

Discouraged, Elizabeth feared that would be the end of it, but just when her prospects were at their bleakest, Miss Mary Welch, a longtime patron whom she had first met in St. Louis, drew the story out of her. "I believe I know someone who can help you," the kind woman said, indignant that Elizabeth should be caught in such a tangle of bureaucratic unfairness. "Leave it to me."

A few days later, Miss Welch introduced Elizabeth to her friend Illinois congressman Owen Lovejoy, a staunch abolitionist with a great deal of experience unsnarling the knots of racially biased laws. He gladly agreed to help her prepare her application, and when he was obliged to return to Illinois before the task was done, his younger brother, Joseph, took over. A third brother, Elijah, the eldest, had been shot and killed about twenty-five years earlier while trying to defend the printing press of his abolitionist newspaper from an angry pro-slavery mob.

Both surviving brothers were present when Owen Lovejoy summoned her to his office to discuss his solution to her dilemma. "The crux of the matter is that the Union Army believes your son is a white man," said Owen Lovejoy. He had strong, intelligent features, a keen gaze, and dark hair receding from a bold brow. "We need to show that George was, in fact, the legitimate mulatto son of you and Mr. Alexander Kirkland."

Elizabeth felt a sudden stir of apprehension. "How will we do that?"

The brothers exchanged a look, and then Joseph Lovejoy spoke. "You will testify that you and Mr. Kirkland were married."

"But . . . we never were," she said faintly. The very thought of it made her sick to her stomach. "Even if the idea were not wholly, utterly repugnant to me, I could never place my hand on the Holy Bible and swear to something that was not true."

The brothers exchanged another glance, and Elizabeth knew at once that they had anticipated her reaction. "Mrs. Keckley," said Owen Lovejoy gently, "we have studied

230

the matter backward and forward, and it is our professional opinion that this is the only way you will be able to obtain the pension."

"You *are* the widowed mother of a soldier killed in the line of duty, are you not?" asked Joseph Lovejoy.

"Of course," Elizabeth replied, taken aback.

"And does not the law declare that widowed mothers who have suffered this loss are entitled to the pension?"

"Yes."

"Then I hope you agree that it would be an injustice to deny you that pension simply because other, lesser laws weigh against you."

"Your son did not claim to be a white man," said Owen Lovejoy. "He stood in line to enlist, and when he put his signature to paper, the recruiters assumed he was a white man. They not only accepted him, they were glad and eager to have him."

"Your son did not lie to enlist," his brother added, as if to reassure her. Indeed, it did comfort her to have her son's honesty confirmed.

"As for the other complication . . ." Owen Lovejoy hesitated. "Forgive me for addressing a subject that I can only assume must bring you great pain. The circumstances of

231

your son's conception are not your fault. It was not your choice to bear Mr. Kirkland a child out of wedlock."

It was not her choice to bear him a child at all, Elizabeth almost retorted, but she could not utter the words that would sound, to anyone who did not know her, like a rejection of her son, like an admission that she had not loved him. The greatest truth of her life was that she *had* loved George, fiercely and proudly, loved him as strongly and passionately as she had hated his father.

"It would be a grave injustice, therefore," Owen Lovejoy continued, "to hold the letter of the law above that which is truly right — and it is most certainly right for you to receive the pension that your son's patriotic sacrifice earned for you."

"And if you *are* denied the pension," his brother added, with a defiant edge to his voice, "it will only help our political cause."

Elizabeth wasn't quite sure what cause he meant — abolition? Equality? Republicanism? — but what she needed at the moment was something that would do her immediate, practical good, not intangible political victories that might benefit her in years to come. "You both speak like lawyers," she said shakily. "You don't need to coax me along with sweet words that poorly conceal what it is you want me to do. I know you want to help me, so please, let's speak plainly with one another. Your recommendation is that I should lie in order to secure my pension, isn't that right?"

"Well . . ." Joseph Lovejoy hesitated. "Yes. It is wrong to lie, but in this case, a small lie would serve the greater truth of justice."

"And you believe that only by lying will my application succeed?"

"I know it," said Owen Lovejoy in a voice that allowed no room for doubt.

"Then that is what I shall do."

The Lovejoy brothers nodded, satisfied that they had persuaded her. She wondered if they understood precisely which of their carefully measured phrases had ultimately convinced her. Owen Lovejoy had said — and the law maintained — that her son had earned that pension for his mother by giving his life for the Union. That was what did it. She would not cast aside George's last gift to her out of deference to foolish laws governing race and marriage that had not been designed with colored people in mind and that had never helped a single slave, not one, not ever. Why should those laws apply to her now when they had never applied before, during the long, difficult years when they might have eased her suffering?

She trusted that the Lord would forgive her for the lies she intended to tell, freely and without reservation.

In the middle of April, Elizabeth stood before Justice of the Peace William S. Clary and two respected witnesses to offer her sworn testimony. She was the widowed mother of George W. D. Kirkland, private, First Missouri Volunteers, Company D, killed on August 10, 1861, in the Battle of Wilson's Creek. George's father was her first husband, Mr. Alexander Kirkland, a white man, who died when George was only eighteen months old. The Garland family later took mother and son to St. Louis, where Elizabeth married James Keckley, but for the past three years they had lived apart and Elizabeth received no support from him. She had purchased her freedom and her son's for twelve hundred dollars and infinite toil and labor, and she had relied upon her son's contributions from his wages to help pay back the debts she had incurred by doing so. She still owed two hundred dollars upon that debt, as well as one hundred more yet unpaid for George's education. George had left no widow or minor child under the age of sixteen. Elizabeth had not,

234

in any way, been engaged in, or aided or abetted, the rebellion in the United States, and she had willingly laid her son's life upon the altar of her country.

Any lingering guilt she might have felt about lying was dispelled when two respected ministers, Daniel A. Payne, bishop of the African Methodist Episcopal Church, and John M. Brown, clergyman, separately swore that they had known her for ten years and that every word of her testimony was true. Elizabeth wondered how anyone could possibly be fooled by that, when she had never denied — and it could be easily proven — that she had not come to Washington City until 1860.

But Elizabeth did so solemnly swear, and the documents were signed and the seals affixed, and within a few weeks her application was approved. From that day forward, and for the rest of her life, she received a pension from the federal government. As compensation for her loss it was hopelessly inadequate — eight dollars a month, later raised to twelve, for the life of her son — but it often made the difference between contentment and worry, so she was grateful.

The fair weather of spring helped to lift

spirits a trifle throughout the beleaguered city, but to Elizabeth it seemed as if Mr. Lincoln was becoming gaunt and aged beyond his years by the cares of war. The Union Army was in such great need of soldiers that Congress had been obliged to pass a draft law applying to married white men between the ages of twenty and thirty-five, and single white men up to the age of forty-five. Black men were exempt because they were not considered citizens, and anyone who could afford to hire a substitute could avoid service. The unfairness of a system that sent poor men to war and let rich men buy their way out created great anger and resentment throughout the North.

At the end of April and into May, Union and Confederate forces met at Chancellorsville, a crossroads town west of Fredericksburg in Spotsylvania County, Virginia. Although the Confederates lost their celebrated general Stonewall Jackson to friendly fire, General Lee won a decisive victory in what became the bloodiest battle the war had yet manifested, with over seventeen thousand casualties for the North and nearly thirteen thousand for the South. Devastating news and thousands of wounded flooded Washington City, turning it again into one expansive, sprawling field hospital, with the stench of death and decay pervading the air so that Elizabeth kept her windows closed day and night in a futile attempt to block out the smell and the images of battlefield horror it evoked.

A few weeks later, in mid-May, General Grant led his troops across the Big Black River in Mississippi and on to Vicksburg, but two direct assaults on the city were repulsed, and the Union forces settled back to the dispiriting, tedious business of the siege.

Although Mrs. Lincoln did not like her husband to walk about Washington City without a military escort because of the frequent letters he received threatening assassination, the president often went alone back and forth between the White House and telegraph office in the War Department to collect the most recent bulletins from the field. Once, when Elizabeth was with Mrs. Lincoln in the family's sitting room fitting a dress, the president returned from one of those solitary walks, his step slow and heavy, his expression careworn and unhappy. Like an exhausted boy he flung himself upon a sofa and shaded his eyes with his long, bony hands, a complete picture of dejection.

Mrs. Lincoln exchanged a quick, worried

look with Elizabeth and asked, "Where have you been, Father?"

"To the War Department," he replied shortly.

Mrs. Lincoln did not let his tone discourage her. "Any news?"

"Yes, plenty of news, but no good news. It is dark, dark everywhere."

Mrs. Lincoln sighed softly, and Elizabeth's heart went out to the president. When she tried to imagine what it must be like to bear his burdens, she did not know how one man could carry so much upon his shoulders.

She continued adjusting the fit of Mrs. Lincoln's bodice, watching from the corner of her eye as Mr. Lincoln stretched out one of his long arms, took a small Bible from a stand near the head of the sofa, opened it, and leafed through the pages almost idly until a passage caught his eye. Soon he was engrossed in reading, and after about fifteen minutes had passed in near silence, Elizabeth glanced his way and observed that his expression seemed greatly changed, almost cheerful. The dejected frown had vanished, and a new resolution and hope lit up his countenance. Curious, Elizabeth wondered what he had read to have discovered so much comfort so quickly. Murmuring an excuse about a misplaced pincushion, Elizabeth quietly walked around the sofa pretending to search for it, but really stealing a glimpse of the open Bible, and she discovered that the president was reading from the Book of Job. Greatly moved, Elizabeth could almost imagine hearing the Lord speaking to him in a thunderous voice from the whirlwind of battle: "Gird up thy loins now like a man: I will demand of thee, and declare thou unto me." The sublimity of witnessing the ruler of a mighty nation turning to Holy Scripture for comfort and courage, and finding both in his darkest hour, brought tears to her eyes, and she was obliged to quickly compose herself before returning to Mrs. Lincoln's side.

Mrs. Lincoln too looked to the Bible for solace and guidance, but after Willie's death, she delved more and more often into the mysteries of spiritualism. She consulted mediums and invited them to hold séances in the White House, hoping to communicate with the spirits of her dead children. Not only did the most gifted spiritualists help her to see and speak with Willie and Eddie, Mrs. Lincoln affirmed, but they also warned her about daring new offensives General Lee was planning and treachery within her husband's cabinet. "I have been warned that there is not one man among them except the postmaster general who would not stab my husband in the back if the opportunity arose," Mrs. Lincoln told Elizabeth one morning after a séance. While Elizabeth believed that some of the spiritualists certainly did possess unexplained powers, she knew that long before any message from the beyond told her so, Mrs. Lincoln already had been convinced that the cabinet secretaries were motivated by avarice and the lust for power rather than love of country and loyalty to her husband.

In matters of spiritualism, Elizabeth also encouraged the First Lady to develop a little healthy skepticism. Unscrupulous frauds were known to prey upon widows and bereaved parents, interpreting the ringing of an unseen bell or mysterious tappings as messages from their departed loved ones, coded messages of undying love and reassurance, when in fact the mediums themselves made the noises with devices concealed beneath the table. The previous summer, Mrs. Lincoln had been taken in by just such a scoundrel, a stout, debonair British gentleman who called himself Lord Colchester and claimed to be the illegitimate son of an English duke. He earned quite a reputation in Washington for his prowess, so Mrs. Lincoln invited him to the

White House for a demonstration. Sometime after that, gossip about the alleged nobleman raised Mr. Lincoln's suspicions, so he asked Dr. Joseph Henry, head of the Smithsonian Institution, to investigate. Dr. Henry in turn enlisted the aid of Noah Brooks, a correspondent for *The Sacramento Union* and President Lincoln's closest friend within the press. Mr. Brooks attended one of Lord Colchester's séances in a darkened room at the residence of a true believer, but just when the unseen spirits were at their most loquacious, Mr. Brooks reached beneath the table, seized a hand that was rapping upon a drum with a bell, and shouted, "Strike a match!" Before any of the astonished participants could comply, the drum struck Mr. Brooks a strong blow across the head. When someone finally lit a lamp, it illuminated a startling scene — Mr. Brooks, blood trickling down his face, grasping the arm of Lord Colchester.

In the uproar that followed, the Englishman slipped away, but a few days later, Mrs. Lincoln summoned Mr. Brooks to the White House. She had received a note from Lord Colchester demanding that she arrange a War Department pass for him and hinting at blackmail if she did not obey. Together Mrs. Lincoln and Mr. Brooks arranged for the false clairvoyant to come to the White House, ostensibly to collect his pass, and when he arrived Mr. Brooks confronted him as a swindler and a humbug, and ordered him to leave Washington immediately or be thrown into the Old Capitol Prison. Lord Colchester promptly fled the city and did not trouble Mrs. Lincoln again. When Mrs. Lincoln later told Elizabeth the entire story, she laughed so merrily that one would almost think she had been amused by a farce rather than deceived by a charlatan. But even though Lord Colchester had been discredited, Mrs. Lincoln retained her faith in other spiritualists and clung to her belief that her dear sons Willie and Eddie did indeed appear to her, not only in the midst of a séance, but beside her bed at night, waking her from sleep to assure her they were together and happy in heaven.

Not all of Mrs. Lincoln's messages from the spirit realm offered comfort. Sometimes when Elizabeth arrived at the White House, she found Mrs. Lincoln shaken and pale, with dark shadows beneath her eyes. Those were the mornings Mrs. Lincoln had been visited the night before by terrifying premonitions that her husband would be murdered. They were only nightmares, Elizabeth tried in vain to assure her, terrible to endure but still nothing more than unpleasant dreams. Mrs. Lincoln was not convinced, and even Elizabeth had to admit she had good reason. It was wartime. President Lincoln moved freely about in a city full of strangers and secessionists. He regularly received anonymous letters full of wild threats and promises that he did not have long to live. Sometimes his friends became so worried on his behalf that they took turns sleeping in the White House to watch over him. For his part, although he too sometimes endured sleepless nights and suffered foreboding dreams, Mr. Lincoln ignored the dangers, or laughed off the threats, and only reluctantly conceded to the guards assigned to escort him when he traveled longer distances from the mansion.

Elizabeth was bent over her sewing in the Lincolns' sitting room one afternoon when Mrs. Lincoln broke off their conversation at the sight of Mr. Lincoln putting on his overshoes and shawl. "Where are you going now, Father?" she asked.

"I am going over to the War Department, Mother," he said resignedly as he stood and adjusted his collar, "to try and learn some news."

"But, Father, you should not go out alone. You know you are surrounded with danger."

"All imagination," he said. "What does anyone want to harm me for? Don't worry about me as if I were a little child, for no one is going to molest me." Utterly unconcerned, or perhaps simply fatalistic, he departed for his solitary walk, closing the door behind him.

Mrs. Lincoln could not emulate his studious confidence. She seemed to read impending danger in every rustling leaf, in every whisper of the wind, and Elizabeth could not honestly say that she was wrong to do so.

CHAPTER NINE

June–December 1863

For months, President Lincoln had rejected appeals to allow freed slaves and freeborn black men to enlist as combat soldiers, but over time, Elizabeth observed, his resistance appeared to be weakening. Perhaps the rising pressure of demands from radical Republicans, appeals from respected black leaders like Frederick Douglass, and, most of all, the army's overwhelming need for more troops had forced him to take a more pragmatic — and less prejudiced — view of the matter. One of the White House doormen once told Elizabeth that he had witnessed an occasion when Vice President Hamlin introduced the president to his son and several other white officers who had volunteered to command black soldiers in combat. "The president seemed deeply moved," the doorman confided, "and then he said, 'I suppose the time has come.'"

"If you ask me, 'the time' arrived months ago and has been sitting idle outside the president's office ever since," said Elizabeth dryly. It was unlike her to say anything critical of the president, whom she admired and respected greatly, but on this subject, like emancipation, she found herself made impatient by his inexplicable, unhelpful delays. But as always, she told herself he likely had good reason and that he would take action when the time seemed right.

Then, in late May, the War Department issued General Order Number 143, which established the Bureau of Colored Troops to recruit and train black soldiers. By the middle of June, the First Regiment United States Colored Troops was organized in Washington and began training on Analostan Island in the Potomac River near the Virginia shore, a ferry ride away from Georgetown. Their presence brought a great swell of pride to Washington's Negro community, and to the refugees still living in the contraband camps. Whenever Elizabeth went there to teach and to distribute necessities, she heard men and women referring to them as "*our* soldiers." They had become every colored family's sons and brothers.

As the June weather grew sultry, Mrs. Lincoln traveled north, as she had in summers

246

past, to escape the heat and the other afflictions of summer. She and Tad spent a week visiting her friend Sally Orne in Philadelphia before returning to Washington to prepare for the family's annual retreat to the cool, quiet haven of the Soldiers' Home. While Mrs. Lincoln was away, Virginia gave birth to a beautiful baby girl, whom she and Walker named Alberta Elizabeth. The delivery was blessedly easy, and both mother and child were in good health and spirits. Elizabeth was proud and honored when the Lewises asked her to be Alberta's godmother, a role she gladly accepted.

It was an unexpected stroke of good fortune that the birth coincided with Mrs. Lincoln's absence, freeing Elizabeth to care for Virginia as she recovered and to help Walker look after the older children. Elizabeth did not expect to see the First Lady again until later summer or perhaps early autumn, but on July 2, as Washington stirred anxiously with rumors that General Lee was on the move toward the Potomac, Elizabeth was shocked by news that Mrs. Lincoln had been badly injured in a carriage accident.

Elizabeth immediately raced to the White House, where she found Mrs. Lincoln in bed with her head bandaged, the able Nurse

Pomroy nearby. "Mrs. Lincoln," she exclaimed, hastening to her side. "What happened? Are you all right?"

"Oh, Elizabeth, you're so good to come to me. I'm somewhat bruised but I'm really quite fine." Even so, Mrs. Lincoln looked pale and anxious. She waited for Nurse Pomroy to step out of the room before adding, "Mr. Lincoln and I were at the Soldiers' Home. He was going to take the carriage into the city, but at the last minute he decided to depart earlier on horseback instead, so I came along in the carriage later, alone."

"And Tad?" prompted Elizabeth, worried. "Was he riding with you?"

"No, thank heavens. He remained behind with friends." Mrs. Lincoln took a deep, shaky breath. "I was riding along as pleasantly as always when suddenly, without warning, the horses bolted. The carriage absolutely broke apart. I had to jump to safety or I would have — well, I hardly dare to think of what could have happened."

"Did you injure yourself in the carriage or in the jump?"

"Neither," said Mrs. Lincoln with a wry twist to her mouth. "In my clumsy landing. I stumbled and fell, and I hit my head on a rock. It bled a frightening amount and I confess I was a bit dazed afterward, but thankfully, I happened to fall almost directly in front of an army hospital, of all things, and some dutiful soldiers serving there ran to my aid."

"Thank heavens they were nearby."

"Thank heavens, indeed." Mrs. Lincoln reached for her hand and pulled her to a seat on the edge of the bed. "Elizabeth, I'm frightened. It was no accident."

Elizabeth felt a chill of dread. "What do you mean?"

Mrs. Lincoln's voice trembled, and her hand tightened around Elizabeth's. "After the horses were brought under control, it was discovered that someone had unscrewed the bolts holding down the driver's seat of the carriage. When the seat came loose, it frightened the horses. That's why they jumped and ran."

"How terrible," Elizabeth exclaimed. "Someone deliberately tried to injure you?"

"Not me — Mr. Lincoln. He was supposed to be riding in the carriage, remember?"

"Oh, my goodness." Elizabeth felt faint with alarm. "Do you have any idea who's responsible?"

Mrs. Lincoln shook her head. "My husband has entire states full of enemies. It could have been one of the authors of any of those dreadful letters he's received. We should have been keeping a list of their names. It could have been a Southern spy chosen by Jefferson Davis himself."

Elizabeth could not imagine Mr. Davis arranging for Mr. Lincoln's murder, but she had known him in peacetime, not at war. He could have changed.

"After this, Mr. Lincoln simply must agree to increase his guards." Mrs. Lincoln settled back weakly against her pillow. "I simply must insist upon it and he must agree. You can imagine how terrible and guilty he feels knowing that I was injured in his stead."

Elizabeth managed a helpless laugh. "Then I suppose now is the time to press your advantage."

Mrs. Lincoln joined in, her laughter weaker than Elizabeth's and bearing a slight note of hysteria. "I hadn't considered that. Perhaps today I should also confess my debts."

"Oh, dear me, no. The shock would injure him far worse than any carriage accident."

Mrs. Lincoln smiled, too fatigued to laugh anymore. She closed her eyes, and Elizabeth held her hand until she drifted off to sleep.

By the next morning, Mrs. Lincoln felt

much improved, and so she continued to prepare for a glorious Independence Day celebration. She had agreed to a grander, more elaborate event than she had allowed since Willie's death, with the Marine Band scheduled to perform on the White House grounds, a large viewing stand erected on the Mall, firecrackers, and a parade of regiments to march alongside twelve councils of the Masons, Odd Fellows, and Union League. The spectacle was meant to inspire patriotism and boost morale, but with increasing ire over Congress's new draft measures and worries about the Confederate army's bold advances, some administration officials wanted to cancel the celebration. All of Washington was in a state of nervous agitation as General Lee led his army across the Potomac and into Pennsylvania, and as military engagements in that state seemed increasingly likely, fears that Washington sat helpless and undefended soared. Nevertheless, when the president's private secretary shared these worries with Mrs. Lincoln, she told him stoutly that her husband was confident that the Union forces would halt Lee's advance and that they should not let their resolve crumble or it would dishearten the entire city.

So the celebration went on as planned —

but Mrs. Lincoln did not join in. On the morning of July 4, while her husband anxiously awaited reports from Vicksburg, where Grant was attempting a new assault on the city, and from a small farm town in Pennsylvania called Gettysburg, where Union and Confederate forces had finally met, Mrs. Lincoln's injury took a sudden turn for the worse. A messenger came for Elizabeth while she was out with Emma enjoying the festive day, so it was not until midafternoon that she realized she was needed and she hurried off to the White House.

She found Mrs. Lincoln in bed, fretful and feverish. Earlier that day, Nurse Pomroy had discovered that her wound was badly infected, and she had been obliged to reopen it to drain the laudable pus. The injury became inflamed, and Mrs. Lincoln was in significant distress.

Elizabeth sat with her that day and the next, and at times her fever became so dangerously high that Mr. Lincoln sent a telegram to Robert to urge him to return home at once. The president paced from his wife's sickroom to the telegraph office and back, but the welcome news of the Union victory at Gettysburg and promising but unconfirmed reports of Grant's success at

Vicksburg distracted him only momentarily from his wife's decline.

Elizabeth assisted Nurse Pomroy as best she could, but she could do frustratingly little more than bathe Mrs. Lincoln's brow, read to her, assure her that all would be well, and pray. Within days General Grant's success in Vicksburg was confirmed and it seemed that the momentum of the war had finally shifted in favor of the Union, but Mrs. Lincoln was no better and Robert had still not arrived, nor had he sent word of when he might be expected. Worried anew when no one could confirm his eldest son's whereabouts, Mr. Lincoln telegraphed Robert again and urged him to make haste to Washington. Then draft riots broke out in New York, where Robert was last known to have been; over the course of several terrifying days, mobs of white men, most of them Irish immigrants, attacked draft offices, looted shops, destroyed black-owned businesses, burned to the ground an orphanage for colored children, and violently attacked people of color in the streets, brutally murdering more than one hundred. Finally the New York State Militia and other troops were sent in to restore order, but the death and destruction sent waves of shock throughout the North and sparked fears that the draft would evoke similar violence in other cities.

Two weeks after Mrs. Lincoln's accident, Mr. Lincoln seemed so overwhelmed by worry and strain that Elizabeth began to fear for his health as much as for his wife's. While most of the North celebrated the recent military victories, Mr. Lincoln was preoccupied with calamities — New York City was in a shambles, General Meade had failed to pursue General Lee and had allowed him to escape, Robert Lincoln was unaccounted for, and Mrs. Lincoln was fading away, struck down by a blow meant for himself.

Finally, days later, Robert arrived home, greatly easing his father's worries. If the young man offered an explanation for his lengthy absence and his silence, Elizabeth never learned what it was. Under Nurse Pomroy's attentive care, Mrs. Lincoln gradually improved. Her fever relented; her wound closed. To Elizabeth's relief, every day she seemed a little stronger, but the midsummer heat and humidity impeded her recovery. When malaria began to spread through the city, it was decided that Mrs. Lincoln could not endure the climate of Washington in her condition and should relocate to the north until she regained her health. Mr. Lincoln quickly made the necessary arrangements: As soon as she was strong enough, Robert would escort his mother and brother to a resort in Manchester, Vermont, nestled in the sublimely beautiful Green Mountains and famed for the healing properties of its natural mineral waters. It sounded to Elizabeth like a cool, restful haven, the ideal place for Mrs. Lincoln to convalesce.

Elizabeth packed Mrs. Lincoln's trunks for her, and on the day of her departure, Elizabeth came to the White House to see her off. "You should come with me," Mrs. Lincoln urged again, as she had several times before. "I feel so much better in your company."

Elizabeth was tempted, but she had accepted too much work from her other clients to pack a bag and quit the city on such short notice. "I wish I could," she said, "but my commitments oblige me to stay behind."

Mrs. Lincoln sighed her acceptance, and soon the carriage departed with her and her sons to meet the train that would speed them northward.

As Elizabeth walked along the curved path in front of the White House on her way home, she heard a man behind her remark to a companion, "The Hellcat gave the Tycoon quite a scare, didn't she?"

Stung, Elizabeth halted, drew herself up, and turned to face them. "If you please," she said crisply, looking up at the men, quietly furious, "do not ever again use that loathsome word to describe Mrs. Lincoln in my presence."

She recognized the stupefied men gaping back at her as two very junior secretaries within two obscure departments. She did not even know their names, but she would bet they knew hers.

"I beg your pardon, ma'am," the younger of the two managed to reply. The men quickly tipped their hats and shamefacedly hurried past her down the sidewalk.

Her anger spent, Elizabeth watched them scurry off, and the ridiculousness of the scene obliged her to smother a laugh. Perhaps no woman of color had ever addressed them like that before. They had better learn to mind their manners or they would be hearing from her again.

Suddenly she realized that she had objected to "Hellcat" but not the equally disrespectful, if less spiteful, "Tycoon," and then she truly did laugh.

Mrs. Lincoln stayed away from Washington

for nearly two months. In all that time, Elizabeth sewed for other ladies and dedicated the rest of her hours to the Contraband Relief Association, raising funds from abolitionists and well-to-do people of color from throughout the North and teaching sewing and other practical skills to the women and girls residing in the camps. She took on a few promising young freedwomen as apprentice seamstresses, and with their earnings they were able to afford rooms in pleasant boardinghouses and escape the camps, which seemed perpetually squalid despite the bedding and other small comforts Elizabeth and the other volunteers provided for them. Her young assistants bloomed in their new lives, mentored by Elizabeth and Emma, their eager guides to all things a young woman of color needed to know in order to successfully navigate Washington City.

During Mrs. Lincoln's absence, the president was preoccupied with the hard business of war. The Union victories at Gettysburg and Vicksburg seemed, to him, to mark a turning point, but the weeks following those costly triumphs were not without setbacks. The valiant but ultimately bloody and unsuccessful attack of the Fifty-fourth Massachusetts upon the Confederate stronghold Fort Wagner near Charleston was especially heart wrenching for the Negro community, for the Fifty-fourth Massachusetts was one of the first official colored regiments and a great source of pride for their race. Their casualties in the fierce assault were shockingly high, so reports of their courage and heroism were bittersweet. Elizabeth was proud that the men of her race had acquitted themselves so nobly and had inspired more colored men to enlist, but she mourned for them, and prayed for their wives and mothers.

Shortly before Mrs. Lincoln returned to the capital, Elizabeth heard other sad news from the battlefield — sad for the Lincolns personally, at any rate, although not for the Union. Mrs. Lincoln's brother-in-law, the Confederate general Ben Helm, husband of her beloved half sister Emilie, had been killed at the Battle of Chickamauga in Georgia. Years before, on the advent of war, Mr. Lincoln had offered his favorite sister-in-law's husband a generous commission as paymaster of the Union Army, but Mr. Helm had declined and had enlisted with the Confederates instead. After Shiloh, he had been promoted to brigadier general and had gone on to lead the famed "Orphan Brigade," Kentucky's most celebrated infantry unit. Now he was gone, and their darling "Little Sister" was in mourning, but the Lincolns could not publicly grieve for a rebel.

Soon thereafter, only a day or two after Mrs. Lincoln returned home, word spread that her youngest half brother, Captain Alexander Todd, had been killed the day before his brother-in-law General Helm while serving as his aide-de-camp at the Battle of Baton Rouge. Aleck had been only an infant when Mrs. Lincoln had left home, but the red-haired, cheerful boy had been everyone's favorite, and Elizabeth knew Mrs. Lincoln was very fond of him.

When Elizabeth next received a summons to the White House, she departed at once, eager to see her best patron again after so many weeks apart. Mrs. Lincoln greeted her warmly, clasping her hands and smiling, and declared theirs the happiest of reunions. Elizabeth was relieved to see that Mrs. Lincoln's health seemed almost entirely restored to her, but an air of sadness lingered about her that Elizabeth could only assume sprang from her recent losses.

They had been discussing new dresses for the upcoming social season for only a few minutes when Mrs. Lincoln suddenly said, "Elizabeth, I have just heard that one of my brothers has been killed in the war."

Elizabeth was taken aback by the lack of emotion in her words. "I also heard the same, but I hesitated to speak of it, for fear the subject would be a painful one to you."

"You need not hesitate." Mrs. Lincoln attempted a matter-of-fact smile, but her lips trembled. "Of course, it is but natural that I should feel for one so nearly related to me, but not to the extent that you suppose."

Elizabeth did not know what to say. "Indeed?"

Mrs. Lincoln clasped her hands in her lap and studied them. "Aleck made his choice long ago. He decided against my husband, and through him against me. He has been fighting against us, and since he chose to be our deadly enemy, I see no special reason why I should bitterly mourn his death."

"I suppose not," Elizabeth replied slowly, torn between relief and regret. She was thankful that Mrs. Lincoln did not appear possessed by the same madness of despair that had seized her after Willie's death, but she knew Mrs. Lincoln felt deep sorrow over the loss of her kin, rebel or otherwise, all the same. To feign indifference was an act for her critics, for the spiteful masses who eagerly snatched up any crumb of proof, however tenuous, of the First Lady's disloyalty. It was not a pretense she needed to maintain in front of Elizabeth, and Elizabeth was very sorry that her patron and friend could not be perfectly honest with her so that she could offer her the comfort her broken heart surely needed.

Months earlier, in springtime, Mrs. Lincoln's longtime social rival Miss Kate Chase had become engaged to the wealthy former Rhode Island governor and current United States senator William Sprague IV, and their November wedding in the parlor of the Chase mansion was anticipated to be the social event of the season. Fifty guests, including President and Mrs. Lincoln, the cabinet secretaries and their wives, and certain senators, congressmen, and generals had been invited to the ceremony, and five hundred more would join them at the reception. When Elizabeth mentioned to Mrs. Lincoln that she would be sure to keep that afternoon open so she would be available to dress her for the occasion, Mrs. Lincoln told her that would not be necessary. "I believe I will have a terrible headache that day," she said lightly.

"But, Mrs. Lincoln," protested Elizabeth, "aren't you worried about how it will look if you don't attend? Everyone of quality in

Washington will be there."

"I rather worry what it would say if I did attend," Mrs. Lincoln retorted. "You know those Chases, father and daughter alike, have always believed that they belong in the White House rather than us. Mr. Chase has spent the last three years in the high office my husband bestowed upon him making friends and setting himself up as an alternative candidate, and he would be all too delighted to snatch the Republican nomination away from Mr. Lincoln. I absolutely refuse to promote the daughter through any political favor to the father, nor will I promote the father by offering social preference to the daughter. They are my husband's rivals, Elizabeth, and therefore also mine."

Elizabeth understood Mrs. Lincoln's point of view, and yet it filled her with misgivings. Although Mrs. Lincoln was frequently indisposed, surely no one would believe her excuse of illness if she failed to appear at the wedding, and her critics would concoct their own wild theories that would invariably cast her in an unflattering light. Mr. Lincoln must have concurred, for when his entreaties for her to accompany him failed, he attended the wedding alone and lingered at the reception for two hours as if to compensate for his wife's absence.

Elizabeth wished she could have attended the wedding reception, if only to observe the guests in their finery. Several of the ladies had been attired in gowns of her creation — Mrs. Mary Jane Welles's lovely rose moiré antique and Mrs. Elizabeth Blair Lee's stunning off-the-shoulder crimson silk were especially fine examples of her handiwork, she thought — and she would have taken both pride and pleasure in comparing her handiwork to that of other mantua makers. Like many other Washingtonians who had not been invited, Elizabeth eagerly read descriptions of the wedding in the papers the next day. The new Mrs. Sprague was said to have been resplendent in a bridal gown of white velvet with a needlepoint lace veil, a diamond solitaire ring worth four thousand dollars sparkling on her graceful hand. As she had entered the room, the Marine Band had played "The Kate Chase March," composed by Mr. Thomas Mark Clark especially for the occasion. Most of the papers listed the most prominent guests, among whom President Lincoln ranked highest. A few reporters pointedly noted that Mrs. Lincoln was not present, but only one cattily mentioned her "sudden and curious" illness and added a wholly insincere wish for a swift recovery from her "uncannily timely affliction."

But it was Tad Lincoln who truly did fall ill only a few days after the wedding. His symptoms were frighteningly reminiscent of the illness he had suffered in the winter of 1862, the same illness that had claimed his brother's life. His parents became increasingly worried as he began a familiar decline. Elizabeth tended him as she had his brother, and Nurse Pomroy was always on call. Mr. Lincoln had agreed to offer a few appropriate remarks at the dedication of a new national cemetery in Gettysburg, but the day before he was scheduled to depart, Mrs. Lincoln begged him not to go. "Mother, it is my duty," Elizabeth heard him tell his wife, and when she burst into tears and declared that he was a better bureaucrat than a father, the wounded, dispirited look in his eyes pained Elizabeth so much that she had to look away. She had never known another man with such nobility of soul and greatness of heart, and she wondered why Mrs. Lincoln sometimes seemed blind to her husband's exemplary qualities. Over time, Elizabeth had come to believe that Mr. Lincoln was unselfish in every respect and that he loved his children and their mother very tenderly. He asked for nothing but affection from his wife, but he did not always receive it. When one of her wayward, impulsive moods seized her, she often said and did things that wounded him deeply. If he had not loved her so much, she would have been powerless to hurt him, but he did care about her and about her opinion of him. She often hurt him in unguarded moments, but afterward, in times of calm reflection, she would not fail to regret her cruel words.

This, Elizabeth thought, would surely be one of those occasions.

The next day, Elizabeth arrived at the White House to find Tad bedridden, Mrs. Lincoln hysterical, and President Lincoln deeply melancholy as he prepared to leave for the train station. "Tad was too ill to eat his breakfast this morning," Mrs. Lincoln told her, wringing her hands as she turned back to her husband. "Please, Father, don't go. Mr. Everett will be offering the oration. You said yourself that your remarks are secondary. You would not be missed."

"I flatter myself that I would be," he said, wearily putting on his coat and hat. Mrs. Lincoln stopped pacing long enough to submit to his kiss good-bye, but as soon as he departed, she burst into tears. Elizabeth hurried to offer her a handkerchief, led her to the sofa, and tried to calm her with soothing words, but Mrs. Lincoln had worked herself into a frenzy and would not be comforted. Eventually Elizabeth persuaded her to sit quietly, and she sent for a soothing cup of tea, and by noon, the hour Mr. Lincoln's presidential train was scheduled to depart, she had managed to compose herself. Reminding Mrs. Lincoln that she must remain calm or she would frighten her son, Elizabeth accompanied her to Tad's sickroom, where he promptly sat up in bed and asked for something to eat.

Relief illuminated Mrs. Lincoln so vividly that it was as if a shaft of sunlight had broken through storm clouds. She immediately sent word to the kitchen to prepare her son's favorites, and when they were brought up to him on a tray, he ate slowly, but with a steady appetite. When he lay down again, Mrs. Lincoln and Elizabeth left the room to let him rest under Nurse Pomroy's watchful eye. "Mr. Lincoln was not feeling well himself this morning," Mrs. Lincoln remarked in an undertone as they returned to the sitting room. "I do hope he won't exhaust himself on this trip."

Elizabeth nodded, carefully keeping her expression mild. Just as she had predicted, now that the crisis had passed, Mrs. Lincoln regretted the harsh words she had hurled at her husband before his departure. "Mr. Hay and Mr. Nicolay will look after the president," she reminded the First Lady. "They are traveling with him, aren't they?"

"Oh, yes. They've made up quite a party." There was a slight edge to Mrs. Lincoln's voice. "Although it's smaller than it could have been."

"Tad was too ill to travel," Elizabeth protested, "and you were needed here to look after him."

"Oh, dear me, I wasn't speaking of us, Elizabeth. Certain others, who were invited to come, declined the president's invitation."

"Who?" asked Elizabeth, surprised. "And why? I should think it would be quite an honor to travel with the president for such an important occasion."

"One *would* think so, unless one were Secretary Chase — not that his refusal surprises me — or Secretary Stanton, or Senator Stevens, who used to be a reliable friend." Mrs. Lincoln lowered her voice. "They do not believe my husband will win reelection, and they wish to put some distance between themselves and him so that none of his so-called failures will reflect upon them."

"Of course he'll win," said Elizabeth, indignant. "As for those men — I'm astonished by their disloyalty after all he's done for them."

"With few exceptions — very few — his cabinet secretaries are loyal to no one but themselves," Mrs. Lincoln replied darkly, and then she felt silent for a moment, thinking. "I believe I'll send my husband a telegram to let him know that our Tad is feeling better. That will ease his mind, I have no doubt."

Elizabeth agreed, pleased that Mrs. Lincoln was thinking of her husband's feelings and the difficulties he struggled with as a matter of course and not merely her own.

Tad continued to improve, but two days later, Mr. Lincoln returned from Gettysburg with a fever, which soon turned into varioloid, a mild form of smallpox. He was quarantined in the White House for three weeks, but Mrs. Lincoln confided to Elizabeth that he was rather cheerful about it. Since he had been president, he had noted, people had been crowding about him, always asking for something. "Now let the office-seekers come," he joked weakly from his sickbed, "for at last I have something I can give all of them."

■ ■ ■ ■

In the first week of October, not long after Mrs. Lincoln's return to Washington City, President Lincoln had issued the Proclamation of Thanksgiving. Despite the destruction of the war, he noted, the year 1863 had been bountiful, with fruitful fields, steady industry, widening national borders, increasing population, and plenteous mines. Even in the midst of a civil war of unprecedented magnitude and severity, peace had been preserved with foreign nations, order had been maintained everywhere except the theater of war, and laws had been made, respected, and obeyed. "It has seemed to me fit and proper," the president declared, that these gifts of a merciful Lord "should be solemnly, reverently and gratefully acknowledged as with one heart and one voice by the whole American People. I do therefore invite my fellow citizens in every part of the United States, and also those who are at sea and those who are sojourning in foreign lands, to set apart and observe the last Thursday of November next, as a day of Thanksgiving and Praise to our beneficent Father who dwelleth in the Heavens."

After the president's proclamation was

released, Mrs. Lincoln and Elizabeth agreed that it was a wonderful idea, but when the day Mr. Lincoln had selected for the National Day of Thanksgiving finally arrived, it found the president still confined to his sickbed. Elizabeth imagined that he gave thanks nonetheless — for his son Tad's improving health, for recent military victories that offered a glimmer of hope that the Union would ultimately triumph, and for loyal friends and wise counselors, and that most precious rarity of all, loyal friends who offered wise counsel.

On that Thursday of Thanksgiving, Elizabeth attended a special service at her church. Among the many blessings for which she gave thanks, she included President Abraham Lincoln. She could not imagine a better man to lead the nation through those dark years than he.

One blustery December day soon thereafter, Elizabeth was making her way to the White House sitting room where she usually sewed when a servant took her aside and cautioned her that Mrs. Lincoln was with a visitor, and sounds of intermittent weeping had been heard through the door all morning. Thanking him for the warning, Elizabeth prepared herself before opening the door.

Inside, Elizabeth found Mrs. Lincoln seated on the sofa, her hands clasped in those of a small figure swathed in black crepe — a dark-haired, sweet-faced woman who looked to be nearly two decades younger than Mrs. Lincoln, with pale cheeks and large, tragic, red-rimmed eyes. The ladies were engaged in impassioned conversation, but at the sound of the door, they fell abruptly silent and two tear-streaked faces turned her way. "Ah, Elizabeth," said Mrs. Lincoln, rising, her hand still in the younger woman's. "Allow me to present my dear sister Mrs. Emilie Helm."

"How do you do, Mrs. Helm," said Elizabeth cordially, with a polite bow of the head, but Mrs. Helm was too distraught to do more than press her lips together in a pained semblance of a smile and nod.

Mrs. Lincoln crossed the room, placed a hand on Elizabeth's elbow, and guided her back toward the door. "My sister and her daughter arrived only yesterday, and we have so much to discuss. Would you come back tomorrow — no, the day after? And would you please —" Her voice dropped to a murmur. "What I mean is, we would not like it whispered about that Little Sister is staying with us."

Elizabeth agreed, somewhat bemused, and

made her way home. She had worked in the presence of Mrs. Lincoln's guests many times before, but then again, Mrs. Helm was a most unusual visitor, being the widow of a Confederate general. Elizabeth wondered what the press would make of her finding sanctuary within the White House.

Two days later, Elizabeth resumed sewing for Mrs. Lincoln, and before long she was able to piece together the story of Mrs. Helm's arrival at the White House. The young widow and her daughter had been traveling to Mrs. Lincoln's stepmother's home in Kentucky when they were detained at the border because Mrs. Helm refused to take the oath of allegiance to the United States. To do so would dishonor the memory of her beloved husband, Mrs. Helm insisted, and since the stymied border guards did not know what else to do with her, they held her at Fort Monroe, hoping she would change her mind and swear the oath so they could send her on her way. When her resolve did not falter, they telegraphed President Lincoln to ask him what they should do. He promptly telegraphed back, "Send her to me."

Mr. and Mrs. Lincoln adored the young widow they both called Little Sister, and both found comfort in her presence. Each was anxious to hear her opinion regarding the health of the other; to Mary, Mrs. Helm said that she thought the president looked well, only thinner, but when Mr. Lincoln confided that he thought Mrs. Lincoln's nerves had gone to pieces, she replied that Mrs. Lincoln seemed very nervous and excitable, and her rapturous insistence that she saw Willie's and Eddie's spirits at the foot of her bed at night was frightening, abnormal.

As the days passed, Elizabeth overheard Mr. Lincoln imploring Mrs. Helm to extend her visit, because Mrs. Lincoln seemed better in her sympathetic company. Elizabeth too had noticed a marked improvement in her manner with Little Sister there, but she observed that for all the good she did, Mrs. Helm also introduced an uncomfortable tension into the household. Word had spread throughout Washington that the Lincolns were harboring an unrepentant rebel beneath their roof, stirring up displeasure and contempt and more aspersions about Mrs. Lincoln's suspect loyalties. One morning, Tad and his cousin got into a shouting match over who was the real president, Tad's father or Jefferson Davis. Worst of all was a confrontation that took place in the Blue Room one evening, which a distressed

Mrs. Lincoln described to Elizabeth the next day. Senator Ira Harris, father of a colonel in the Army Ordnance Department and stepfather of an officer in the regular army Twelfth Infantry Regiment, and General Daniel Sickles, who had lost a leg at Gettysburg, had come to the White House to meet Mrs. Helm, ostensibly to inquire about mutual acquaintances. The conversation took a disconcerting turn when Senator Harris, perhaps influenced by an excess of alcohol, began taunting the young widow with praise for the Union's recent victories in the West, where her husband had been killed.

"And, madam," he had said, fixing his glare upon her, "if I had twenty sons they should all be fighting rebels."

"And if I had twenty sons, Senator Harris," she had tearfully retorted, "they should all be opposing yours."

"And then," Mrs. Lincoln told Elizabeth, indignant and outraged, "Senator Harris turned his bleary eye upon me and demanded to know why Robert wasn't in the army!"

"Oh, dear," said Elizabeth. "What did you reply?"

"I told him that Robert was not a shirker and that he is preparing even now to enter the army. I declared that if fault there be it is mine, as I have insisted that he should stay in college a little longer since I believe an educated man can serve his country with more intelligent purpose than an ignoramus. The senator merely harrumphed at me. I wish I had thought of something more clever, but I was too upset. Robert knows he is criticized for not enlisting, and he would do so this very day if I permitted it." Mrs. Lincoln frowned and wrung her hands. "I fear that someday soon, my husband will overrule me and let him do it."

"Perhaps Mr. Lincoln could use his influence to find Robert a safe post."

"I don't believe there is any such thing. Oh — but then, after Senator Harris flung that question in my face, General Sickles hobbled out of the room to go harass my husband on his sickbed."

"No!"

"Yes! Can you believe the nerve? Honestly, the general asked my husband, lying ill in his private chamber, how he could have a rebel in the house. My husband gave him all the courtesy due him as a wounded veteran, and then he said very solemnly, 'Excuse me, General Sickles, my wife and I are in the habit of choosing our own guests.'"

"Mrs. Helm is family," said Elizabeth. "Union or Confederate, family must come first."

"Oh, Elizabeth" — Mrs. Lincoln shook her head ruefully — "if everyone felt as you do, we might not have had any war at all. I could fill pages and pages if I listed all the families I know that have been divided by this war. I would start with my own and go on and on until it broke my heart."

Before the month was out, the strain in the household indeed became too much, and Mrs. Helm returned to Kentucky. Before she departed, she consented to take the loyalty oath, and so the president granted her amnesty.

After Little Sister was gone, Mrs. Lincoln sighed wistfully to Elizabeth that it would have been lovely if she could have remained at the White House throughout the holidays, to help them reclaim some joy from the season, but it was not to be.

But as Christmas approached, and as Mr. Lincoln recovered from his illness, and after the ordeal of Willie's birthday with its painful memories of all they had lost was behind them for another year, something of the spirit of the season must have shone a little brighter for Mrs. Lincoln. One morning, she announced that she would put off her mourning weeds on the first day of January and begin the New Year afresh. Delighted, Elizabeth immediately began working on a new gown for Mrs. Lincoln to wear to the annual New Year's Day reception. What a pleasure it would be to attire her most visible patron in something other than black silk and crepe after such a long time.

The gown would be magnificent, rich purple velvet adorned with Valenciennes lace and white satin fluting, with a sweeping train, finished with a headdress boasting a large white plume. "It will be good luck to begin the New Year finely attired in new clothes," Elizabeth told Mrs. Lincoln as she cheerfully fit the muslin lining to her form.

Mrs. Lincoln sighed. "We will need more than good luck if my husband is to win the war and keep his high office in the year to come."

"That's certainly true," Elizabeth replied, pinching two folds of fabric with her thumb and forefinger as she slid a pin into place. The Lincolns would also need perseverance, hard work, faith, and courage. Without those, all the luck in the world wouldn't make any difference.

Chapter Ten

January–November 1864

Guests who met the president and his wife at the New Year's Day reception that year took note of Mrs. Lincoln's emergence from official mourning, which some believed was long overdue. Elizabeth knew that although Mrs. Lincoln still felt the pain of Willie's death acutely, she realized that the demands of the upcoming election obliged her to put aside the solace of ritual for the sake of her husband's political future — and her own.

Mr. Lincoln's nomination and reelection was by no means certain. History and custom were against him; no sitting president had been reelected in more than three decades, when Andrew Jackson had won his second term in 1832. The people's approval of President Lincoln reflected the outcomes on the battlefield, soaring in the aftermath of victory and plummeting after defeat. With an eventual Union victory seeming ever more possible, political discourse had begun to address the question of how to bring the South back into the Union after the war was over. Plans were under way for the reconstruction of Tennessee, Louisiana, and Arkansas, which were already largely under federal military control, but not everyone agreed with the president's approach. As the incumbent, he could not avoid receiving the blame for every wartime failure, and for every partial success that wasn't succeeding quickly enough. Most Democrats declared his entire presidency a massive failure — an inaccurate but hardly unexpected assessment, given the source — but even his own party was divided in its opinions about his performance in office. Radical Republicans complained that he was too lenient with vanquished Confederates and that his plans for postwar reconstruction were insufficiently harsh. To secure the nomination, Mr. Lincoln would somehow have to convince the Republicans to unite around him, but this would be no easy task.

Mrs. Lincoln was determined to do all she could to help. In the cold, gray days of early January, she mustered up her will and resumed her Sunday receptions, taking care to invite anyone who would be well placed to support her husband. The first presidential levee of the year came on January 9, followed by the round of balls and dinners that ushered in the winter social season. Mrs. Lincoln accepted as many invitations as was proper, and entertained her own guests in fine style, and afterward wrote gracious letters and sent gifts of bouquets from the White House greenhouses to prominent figures in government and business.

It was inevitable, perhaps, that Mrs. Lincoln's schemes would set her at odds with members of her husband's cabinet, who had their own ideas for the president's social calendar. The worst conflict, and the most upsetting for Mrs. Lincoln, was with John George Nicolay, the president's personal secretary, who was charged with the responsibility of arranging state dinners. Single-minded in her resolve to do nothing to promote the ambitious Secretary Chase, Mrs. Lincoln told Mr. Nicolay not to invite him, his daughter, or his son-in-law to a cabinet dinner scheduled for the end of January. Mr. Nicolay balked and told the First Lady he could not possibly exclude one of the secretaries, not only because it went against custom, but also because it would make the president appear spiteful and overly wary of a potential rival. Mrs. Lincoln insisted, and Elizabeth had the dubious privilege of witnessing more than one argument between her and the adamant Mr. Nicolay, who — never within the First Lady's presence but often within earshot of the White House staff — began referring to Mrs. Lincoln as Her Satanic Majesty. When Mr. Lincoln became aware of the conflict, he put an abrupt end to it by ordering Mr. Nicolay to invite Mr. Chase and the Spragues, and by telling his wife to let the matter drop.

"You see how little power I have in this house of men," Mrs. Lincoln lamented to Elizabeth, bitter and humiliated in defeat. "Everything I do is for the benefit of my husband, but if I am not overruled, I am ignored entirely."

Elizabeth consoled her as best she could — although privately she thought Mrs. Lincoln had exercised poor judgment in attempting to exclude Mr. Chase and his family — but Mrs. Lincoln worried so much that she hardly slept for two days following the incident. To her credit, on the afternoon of the dinner, she sent Mr. Nicolay a contrite note of apology through the White House doorman. If Mr. Nicolay responded in kind, or at all, Mrs. Lincoln never mentioned it in Elizabeth's presence.

As much as Mrs. Lincoln regretted the

dispute with Mr. Nicolay, she remained as full of antipathy and mistrust for Mr. Chase as ever, and she urged her husband to investigate his loyalties. "If he thought he could make anything by it, he would betray you tomorrow," she insisted. "I am not the only one who has warned you."

That was true enough, for there were a great many witnesses to Mr. Chase's political ambitions. For months he had been traveling throughout the North, making speeches and shoring up support, expressing his personal hopes that Mr. Lincoln would be reelected while coyly avoiding going on the record about his own potential candidacy. Mr. Chase was a particular favorite among the abolitionists and radical Republicans who believed that the Proclamation of Amnesty and Reconstruction that President Lincoln had issued the previous December was too mild and cautious.

Even to Elizabeth it was evident that Mr. Lincoln disapproved of Mr. Chase's forays into campaigning, but it seemed that he merely observed the secretary's activities with mild, watchful tolerance, waiting to see if they would get out of hand. Mrs. Lincoln believed they already had. "Why do you not ask for his resignation?" she demanded in one especially heated moment. It upset her greatly that Mr. Chase showed her husband such disrespect, and she could not comprehend why Mr. Lincoln allowed a rival to remain in a lucrative, influential post where he acquired more power day by day.

"Fire him, and openly acknowledge that he is my opponent for the nomination?" replied Mr. Lincoln. "I am not ready to declare that I am so doubtful that I retain the confidence of the people."

The heated subject came up again one day while Elizabeth was dressing the First Lady for a levee. "Even Dr. Henry believes that the secretary's behavior has been so disgraceful that he ought to be dismissed from the cabinet," the First Lady told her husband heatedly as Elizabeth tied her satin sash into an attractive bow. Dr. Anson Henry was a longtime family friend from Illinois and Mr. Lincoln's trusted personal physician. "He himself discovered that Mr. Chase's people have been spreading unkind rumors about me, so you can't say I'm merely making that up."

"I would never say that to you, Mother," said Mr. Lincoln mildly.

"You might not say it to me, Father, but you might say it to others, and you might think it," she retorted. "You must promise me to get rid of Secretary Chase once and for all."

"I cannot and will not do that, Mother."

None of her appeals would persuade him, so finally she threw her hands in the air in frustration and strode to the other side of the room, fuming. She yanked the chair back from the desk, sat down stiffly, and began scratching out a furious letter to someone — but with her in such a temper, Elizabeth dared not peek over her shoulder to see whom.

After a moment, the president sighed and settled down wearily in his easy chair. "Well, Madam Elizabeth," he asked, his voice hoarse and tired, "will you brush my bristles down today?"

"Certainly, Mr. President."

Taking up his comb and brush, Elizabeth dressed his hair, arranging it as neatly as she could. Mr. Lincoln sat in glum, brooding silence while she worked, until suddenly his mouth curved in a faint smile and he said, "Madam Elizabeth, you have lived on a farm, have you not?"

"Yes, Mr. President," she said. "When I was a child in Virginia."

"Then you know what a chin-fly is."

Elizabeth smiled. "Sadly, sir, I am acquainted with the pesky species."

"When I was a boy, my brother and I were once plowing corn, I driving the horse and he holding the plow," Mr. Lincoln reminisced. "The horse was lazy, but on one occasion, he rushed across the field so that I could scarcely keep pace with him running as fast as I could. On reaching the end of the furrow, I found an enormous chin-fly fastened upon him, and so I swatted it off. My brother asked me why I did it. I told him I didn't want the poor old horse bitten in that way. 'But Abe,' said my brother, 'that's all that made him go!' "

Elizabeth laughed.

"Now, Madam Elizabeth," said Mr. Lincoln, more cheerful than she had yet seen him that day, "if Mr. Chase has a presidential chin-fly biting him, I'm not going to swat it off, just in case that is what makes the Department of the Treasury go."

Elizabeth considered. "Sometimes a chin-fly can become such a nuisance that the horse flicks its tail and cranes its neck trying to bite it and is so busy trying to get at it that he forgets to plow."

Mr. Lincoln frowned thoughtfully. "I suppose in that case, it would be right to swat that chin-fly without delay. The trick is knowing when the chin-fly goes from being a help to a hindrance."

"It's good that you know how to properly deal with chin-flies," said Elizabeth pertly, and she was rewarded with the president's laugh. On the other side of the room, Mrs. Lincoln gave a loud, drawn-out, exasperated sigh.

As the dreary, muddy winter dragged on, it began to appear that "presidential chin-flies" were not the only pests driving the Department of the Treasury. For months, Washington gossip hinted at irregularities in business and immorality among the Treasury staff. One outraged citizen wrote to President Lincoln accusing Secretary Chase of speculation in stocks, gold, and cotton. Women employees were reportedly hired for their personal attractions rather than their skills, and several young ladies claimed that they were refused employment until they yielded to the passionate embraces of the superintendent of the Bureau of Engraving and Printing. (When Elizabeth heard that particular rumor, she was greatly relieved that she had not been hired to work in the cutting room the year before.) More shocking yet, dozens of the department's young, unmarried, female employees were said to be with child.

Alarmed, Mr. Chase brought in a detective from the War Department to investigate the allegations, and when the detective found outrage and scandal everywhere he looked, a special congressional committee began a formal inquiry. After hearing the testimony of a series of witnesses, including two young clerks who swore that they had been coerced into intimate encounters with their employer, the committee could not unanimously conclude whether the charges were true or false. The public preferred to believe the most scandalous, salacious version of events, and so even if the Department of the Treasury was not the "most extensive Whorehouse in the nation," as one critic claimed, its reputation was tarnished — as was Mr. Chase's, at a time he most wanted to appear to be a responsible, trustworthy leader.

A more cautious man might have reined in his presidential ambitions at that point, at least until someone else's more shocking story distracted the public, but Mr. Chase did not — nor did his most ardent supporters wish him to. His friends in Congress organized a committee to promote his candidacy, and Mr. Chase encouraged his supporters even if he did not directly participate in their activities, which they sometimes undertook without his knowledge. In February, his campaign supporters drafted and circulated two documents: one that criticized President Lincoln's first term in office without mentioning Mr. Chase, and another, which became known as "the Pomeroy Circular" after its author, Mr. Chase's campaign chairman, Kansas senator Samuel C. Pomeroy. The Pomeroy Circular denounced President Lincoln and put forth Mr. Chase as "a statesman of rare ability and an administrator of the highest order" who possessed "more of the qualities needed in a President, during the next four years, than are combined in any other available candidate." It asserted that reelecting Mr. Lincoln would be next to impossible, and that to avoid the disaster of a Peace Democrat victory in November, all loyal Republicans had to rally to Mr. Chase to ensure that he won the nomination.

If Mr. Chase's supporters had hoped to keep the widely distributed documents confidential, they were sadly disappointed. The Pomeroy Circular was leaked to the press and was soon reprinted in the *National Intelligencer* and other papers. Outraged Union loyalists who received copies of the memo by mail in envelopes marked with the congressional frank of Mr. Chase's supporters forwarded their copies to Mr. Lincoln at the White House, often including personal notes expressing their disgust with Mr. Chase and their steadfast allegiance to the president.

Elizabeth heard whispers that the intrigue greatly embarrassed Mr. Chase, and she learned from snatches of conversation she had overheard in the Lincoln family sitting room that Mr. Chase had written to Mr. Lincoln disavowing any knowledge of the Pomeroy Circular until it was published in the press. She also knew that upon receiving Chase's chagrined letter, the president had replied with a brief note acknowledging that he had received it and promising a longer reply when he had time to compose one. That longer letter went out almost a week later, Elizabeth believed, but what it said she did not know, and of course she was in no position to ask. Almost every secret she knew about the inner workings of the White House she had learned by accident, by happening to be present at moments when important words were spoken.

Whatever it was that Mr. Lincoln had written to Mr. Chase, the outcome of the embarrassing scandal was less than Mrs. Lincoln had hoped, for he remained secretary of the treasury. "I don't know how my husband can bear being in the same room with such a traitor," Mrs. Lincoln muttered irritably to Elizabeth one day at the end of February when she realized he wasn't going anywhere. Nevertheless, Mr. Chase appeared greatly subdued, and on March 5, he publicly announced that he was not a candidate for the Republican nomination. "I suppose that's something," said Mrs. Lincoln, remarkably more cheerful.

The incident had inspired Mr. Lincoln's staunchest supporters to rally around him and go politicking within their home states on his behalf, but even with Mr. Chase out of contention, the way was by no means clear. A small group of Republicans urged Vice President Hannibal Hamlin to declare his candidacy, but he quickly put a stop to that, declaring that he stood by the president. A few radical Republicans championed General Benjamin Butler, the Union military commander of New Orleans, who they believed could unite prowar Democrats and the radical and moderate wings of the Republican Party. The general had won admirers for his strong opposition to slavery and his uncompromising occupation of Baltimore and New Orleans, but when he failed to garner widespread popularity, he eventually dismissed the faction's overtures.

In February, the *New York Herald* had called for the nomination of General Ulysses S. Grant, but the very idea seemed to horrify the Union commander, who publicly and adamantly insisted that Mr. Lincoln's reelection was essential to the Union cause. That suited Mrs. Lincoln very well; she often disparaged General Grant as a butcher who did not care how many troops were slaughtered so long as he could claim victory in the end. Elizabeth had often heard Mrs. Lincoln declare that if General Grant should ever be elected president of the United States, she would desire to leave the country and remain absent throughout his term of office.

John C. Frémont, who had been the fledgling Republican Party's first presidential nominee in 1856, was strongly popular among abolitionists like the German-American population of St. Louis. Unlike General Grant, General Frémont was willing and eager to supplant his commander in chief. For years he had been harboring resentment against the president, who had revoked his 1861 proclamation freeing the slaves of Confederates within the state of Missouri and had subsequently fired him as commander of the Union Army's Department of the West. General Frémont alone seemed unlikely to follow the course of President Lincoln's other potential challengers and remove himself from consideration.

Mrs. Lincoln refused to sit idly by and hope everything worked out in her husband's favor. She campaigned for him in her own way, cultivating friendships with politicians and businessmen of dubious character but with ample wealth, influence, or, ideally, both. Gossip swirled about her yet again, scathingly impugning her for surrounding herself with a certain class of men. When Elizabeth, ever attuned to appearances, delicately ventured that Mrs. Lincoln's new friends and correspondents did not seem to be the sort of gentlemen Mr. Lincoln would choose as friends, Mrs. Lincoln replied, "I have an object in view, Elizabeth. In a political canvass it is policy to cultivate every element of strength."

Dubious, Elizabeth asked, "And you consider these gentlemen from New York to be a strength, despite the unpleasant chatter your friendship with them inspires?"

"These men have influence, and we require influence to reelect Mr. Lincoln," the First Lady explained. "I will be clever to them until after the election, and then, if we remain at the White House, I will drop every one of them, and let them know very plainly that I only made tools of them. They are an unprincipled set, and I don't mind a little double-dealing with them."

Elizabeth was shocked that Mrs. Lincoln could so blithely plan to use unscrupulous, possibly dangerous men to her own advantage, dismiss them when they had served their purpose, and then mock them by announcing what she had done. "Does Mr. Lincoln know what your purpose is?"

"God, no! He would never sanction such a proceeding."

"Perhaps that should be enough to recommend against it."

"Oh, Elizabeth." Mrs. Lincoln shook her head as if she should have known that Elizabeth would understand no better than her husband. "I keep him in the dark, and will tell him when all is over. He is too honest to take the proper care of his own interests, so I feel it to be my duty to electioneer for him."

As always, Mrs. Lincoln professed the best of intentions and truly seemed to believe she was doing what was good and necessary — and once again, Elizabeth found herself dismayed. She wished Mrs. Lincoln would be more prudent. The First Lady was quite a schemer, but she was surely out of her depth among such shrewd, experienced New York politicians, for whom double-dealing and electioneering were a way of life. Elizabeth feared that it was far more likely that the crafty, flattering gentlemen were using Mrs. Lincoln than that she was using them. She did not see any way the First Lady's alliances with such men would end well.

Elizabeth had another reason for disliking the First Lady's trips to New York. Whenever Mrs. Lincoln was worried or upset, she found comfort in shopping. Whenever she traveled to the North, the newspapers were full of snide reports about how she had ransacked the treasures of Broadway stores, filling her carriage with shawls, boas, capes, handkerchiefs, parasols, fans, bonnets, boots, and gloves. Elizabeth fought to conceal her astonishment if she happened to be present when Mrs. Lincoln's purchases were delivered, but one eighty-dollar handkerchief made her jaw drop, and a two-thousand-dollar shawl caused her to gasp aloud, hand to her heart. Estimating the bills, Elizabeth could not see how Mrs. Lincoln could possibly afford all that she acquired, not when her rough calculations strongly suggested that Mrs. Lincoln's personal expenses that spring surpassed her entire budget for the White House refurbishing during the first year of her husband's presidency.

A member of the White House staff was charged with the thankless task of approving all of Mrs. Lincoln's official expenditures, but no one monitored her personal spending. Perhaps everyone assumed it would be constrained by her husband's salary, but that, of course, was not so. If the First Lady ordered luxurious goods from a fine shop on Broadway or Pennsylvania Avenue, every shopkeeper therein would be all too delighted to extend her credit — but eventually, the bills would come due, and payment in full would be expected, and later demanded.

As soon as the spring sunshine dried the muddy roads of Virginia enough to make them passable, the armies would be on the move, and for the first time, General Grant would face General Lee. Everyone in the North realized that defeating General Lee was crucial to ending the rebellion, not only because General Lee was a brilliant strategist, but also because his army protected the Confederate capital of Richmond.

On April 25, at midday, Elizabeth, Emma, Virginia, and the Lewis girls joined the crowds lining Fourteenth Street to watch General Burnside's thirty thousand troops march out to reinforce the Army of the Potomac. In the early months of the war, every parade of soldiers had drawn throngs of cheering onlookers, but since then the sight of passing regiments had become so commonplace that they attracted little notice. But this was no ordinary procession. This time the column included seven regiments of United States Colored Troops, three of them recruited in nearby Maryland, and it seemed that every person of color in Washington and many more besides had come to see them set out to confront General Lee.

Pride surged through Elizabeth's veins as she waited, listening as the stirring sounds of fife and drums heralded the column's approach. Down New York Avenue they came, smart and polished, turning south onto Fourteenth Street past cheering crowds. Virginia lifted toddler Alberta up to her shoulder while the older Lewis girls, Jane and Lucy, rose up high on tiptoe, craning their necks to see over the heads of the crowd. "There they are," Virginia cried, gesturing for her children to look. "Do you see how well they march? Do you see? Those are *our* soldiers, our brave colored soldiers."

As the girls, eyes shining, assured their mother that they did indeed see, Elizabeth gazed at the dark, proud, eager faces of the colored soldiers and felt her throat constricting with emotion. Their splendid uniforms, the rousing music, the bold and steady marching, the cheering crowd — in that glorious moment it seemed to Elizabeth that there might be no limit to what the people of her race could accomplish in the years to come, unhindered by slavery, when peace reigned over a nation united once again. It was the most sublime spectacle she had ever witnessed, and she prayed that the men would acquit themselves bravely. Everyone would be watching them, she knew, and many would maliciously hope for them to fail. They must succeed, and they would succeed, and in so doing they would disprove every false, slanderous word uttered about the folly of allowing men of color to enlist.

The marching corps approached Willard's Hotel, where President Lincoln and General Burnside stood on the eastern portico to review the parade. When the colored troops passed the president, they waved their hats in the air and cheered for the Great Emancipator, the man who had set their people free. Mr. Lincoln stood with his hat off, bowing and nodding, showing them the same respect and courtesy he had shown every white soldier.

The column needed more than four hours to cross Pennsylvania Avenue. After the soldiers came ambulances, then thousands of cattle to feed the troops, all heading across the river to Virginia. A renewed sense of purpose and determination filled the city, from the marching soldiers to the people lining the streets shouting blessings and good wishes upon them. And then they were gone, leaving hope and fear and anticipation and apprehension in their wake.

The crowds dispersed, and the people went home. Now, all knew, they had to brace themselves for the inevitable onslaught of casualties.

They did not have long to wait.

While the Union and Confederate armies clashed in the Wilderness, the dead and wounded came flooding into Washington from field hospitals, just as they had after the battles at Bull Run, the Peninsula, Antietam, and Gettysburg. The wounded arrived in ambulances, one train a day, but the trains were miles long and had jolted and jerked their suffering passengers over great distances, without food and comforts, filthy and fainting, limbs gone, wounds untended. Injured, sick, and dying soldiers, corpses, prisoners, officials — the choked docks and stations and roadways could not be cleared swiftly enough to make room for new transports. The noxious odor of bodies in the summer heat hung sickly sweet over every street and alley, and the remains of the dead piled up faster than the embalmers could attend to them. One Washington undertaker fell so far behind as he raced to work through his backlog of deceased that he was briefly arrested and cited for causing a public nuisance. All of Washington seemed to be one great, terrible hospital, and no corner of it was spared the miasma of death.

From the Wilderness the fighting moved on to the Spotsylvania Court House, and from there to the North Anna River, and then on to Cold Harbor. Casualties were massive on both sides, disproportionately so for the Union, but the outcomes of the battles were tactically inconclusive. More revealing was what General Grant did each time he failed to destroy General Lee's army: In circumstances where his predecessors had always chosen to retreat, General Grant regrouped and moved his army forward, again and again, keeping General Lee on the defensive and inching ever closer to Richmond. The people of the North realized then that General Grant possessed a very different military mind than they had witnessed thus far in the war.

In the last major battle of the campaign, General Grant surprised General Lee by directing his engineers to construct a pontoon bridge 2,100 feet across the James, stealthily crossing the river, and threatening Petersburg, the most important supply base and railway depot for the entire region, including the Confederate capital of Richmond. If General Grant could capture Petersburg, Richmond would inevitably fall. The Union troops settled in for the siege.

The split within the Republican Party widened throughout the spring. At the end of May, the radical Republican faction convened in Cleveland to select their own candidate for the general election, determined that he should win enough delegates to make Mr. Lincoln's nomination irrelevant. Styling themselves as the Radical Democracy Party, they were expected to choose General Frémont as their nominee, although rumors floated about that some among them held out hope for General Grant, who could not have made his disinterest in the office more clear. He had enough to do fighting the war, Elizabeth thought, without taking on all the additional fighting that went on in Washington.

Soon after the convention closed, Elizabeth was dressing Mrs. Lincoln for an evening at the opera with Postmaster General Blair and his daughter when Mr. Lincoln entered carrying a newspaper. "Nicolay brought me the *Herald,* so I can examine the news from Cleveland at my leisure," he told his wife, his expression nonchalant but his eyes shining with suppressed amusement.

Mrs. Lincoln's brows drew together. "Didn't you read the report at the telegraph office yesterday?"

"I did," he said, settling down on the sofa and stretching out his long legs in front of him, "but Nicolay must have believed I wanted it."

"Has the news changed?" inquired Mrs. Lincoln, in an ironical tone that implied she knew it had not.

"No, every word is the same. Frémont is their man — the man, anyway, of the four hundred people who showed up for the convention."

"Was that all?" exclaimed Elizabeth, forgetting herself. "Only four hundred?"

Mr. Lincoln's mouth quirked in a smile. "That's right, Madam Elizabeth. A mere four hundred." Suddenly inspired, he sat upright and reached for the Bible on the wooden stand nearby. "That reminds me," he said, turning pages. "First Samuel, chapter twenty-two, verse two." He found the passage, cleared his throat, and began to read the scripture. " 'And every one that was in distress, and every one that was in debt, and every one that was discontented, gathered themselves unto him; and he became a captain over them; and there were with him about four hundred men.' " He replaced the open Bible on the stand. "Four hundred again. An interesting number, it seems to me."

In this way, Elizabeth discovered that Mr. Lincoln was not terribly concerned about Mr. Frémont being put up against him.

A few days later, at their convention in Baltimore, Republicans loyal to Abraham Lincoln renamed themselves the National Union Party to distinguish themselves from the gentlemen who had met in Cleveland. They also hoped the new name would appeal to War Democrats, with whom they wanted to forge a coalition. Like themselves, the War Democrats were in favor of the war, and they wanted to break away from the antiwar Peace Democrats to support a candidate who reflected their views — but they could not bring themselves to vote for a Republican. A candidate from the new

National Union Party, on the other hand, might be tolerable.

In the proceedings, Republicans and War Democrats united to nominate Mr. Lincoln as their candidate. The nomination would have been unopposed but for a delegation of twenty-two radical Republicans from Missouri, who first nominated General Grant before changing their votes so Mr. Lincoln's nomination would be unanimous. The delegates also established their party platform, which praised the president for his management of the war and called for, among other critical issues, the pursuit of the war until the Confederacy surrendered unconditionally, a constitutional amendment to abolish slavery, assistance for disabled Union veterans, and the construction of a transcontinental railroad.

Next the agenda turned to the selection of a vice president. Previously Mr. Lincoln had expressed his desire not to interfere and to let the convention decide, and once the debate began, he stuck to his resolution. Vice President Hannibal Hamlin wanted to be renominated, but much had changed since the election of 1860, and this time his candidacy stirred up little enthusiasm. Many delegates believed that they should select a War Democrat from a border state to broaden the appeal of the ticket. After some wrangling, they eventually chose Andrew Johnson, the Union military governor of Tennessee, a War Democrat and Southern Unionist who was nominated overwhelmingly on the first ballot.

Later that same month, the assistant secretary of the treasury resigned. Mr. Lincoln made his criteria for selecting a successor quite clear, but Secretary Chase disregarded the president's wishes. In the ensuing disagreement, Secretary Chase loftily submitted his resignation as a matter of principle, as he had many times before — but this time, the president astounded him by promptly accepting.

Elizabeth expected Mrs. Lincoln to be overjoyed. At last, two things she had greatly desired had come to pass: Mr. Lincoln would be on the ballot in the November presidential election, and Mr. Chase was out of the cabinet. Mrs. Lincoln's worries should have eased, at least a little, but instead she seemed more agitated and anxious than ever. "What do you think about the election?" she asked Elizabeth one sultry morning at the end of June as she gazed out the open window upon the Potomac.

Elizabeth looked up from her work, fabric

on her lap, needle in hand. "I think that Mr. Lincoln will remain in the White House four years longer."

Mrs. Lincoln turned away from the window, her face a curious mixture of hope and apprehension. "What makes you think so? Somehow I have learned to fear that he will be defeated."

"Because he has been tried, and has proved faithful to the best interests of the country," replied Elizabeth. "The people of the North recognize in him an honest man, and they are willing to confide in him, at least until the war has been brought to a close. The Southern people made his election a pretext for rebellion, and now to replace him by someone else, after years of sanguinary war, would look too much like a surrender of the North."

Mrs. Lincoln looked as if she wanted very much to believe her. "So you believe Mr. Lincoln is likely to be reelected?"

"Mr. Lincoln is certain to be reelected," said Elizabeth emphatically. "He represents a principle, and to maintain this principle the loyal people of the loyal states will vote for him, even if he had no merits to commend him."

Mrs. Lincoln pondered this for a long moment in silence. "Your view is a plausible one, Elizabeth, and your confidence gives me new hope." Her expression suddenly clouded over with worry again, belying her words. "If he should be defeated, I do not know what would become of us all. To me, to him, there is more at stake in this election than he dreams of."

Elizabeth studied her, wary and wondering. "What do you mean, Mrs. Lincoln?"

Mrs. Lincoln hesitated, took a deep breath, and said, all in a rush, "I have contracted large debts, of which he knows nothing, and which he will be unable to pay if he is defeated."

Elizabeth's heart sank. She had suspected as much for ages. Steeling herself, she asked, as perhaps she should have asked months before, "What are your debts?"

Mrs. Lincoln began to pace in front of the open window, wringing her hands. "They consist chiefly of store bills. I owe altogether about twenty-seven thousand dollars, the principal portion at Stewart's, in New York."

Elizabeth dropped her threaded needle and fell back against her chair. It was a shockingly enormous sum, more than Mr. Lincoln's entire annual salary.

"You understand, Elizabeth, that Mr. Lincoln has but little idea of the expense of a woman's wardrobe. He glances at my rich dresses, and is happy in the belief that the few hundred dollars that I obtain from him supply all my wants." She stopped pacing and threw Elizabeth a beseeching look. "I must dress in costly materials. The people scrutinize every article that I wear with critical curiosity. The very fact of having grown up in the West subjects me to more searching observation. To keep up appearances, I must have money — more than Mr. Lincoln can spare for me. He is too honest to make a penny outside of his salary; consequently I had, and still have, no alternative but to run in debt."

Shaking her head in disbelief, Elizabeth tried to sort out Mrs. Lincoln's rationalizations. "And Mr. Lincoln does not even suspect how much you owe?"

"God, no!" she exclaimed. "And I would not have him suspect. If he knew that his wife was involved to the extent that she is, the knowledge would drive him mad. He is so sincere and straightforward himself that he is shocked by the duplicity of others. He does not know a thing about any debts — and I value his happiness, not to speak of my own, too much to allow him to know anything. This is what troubles me so much. If he is reelected, I can keep him in ignorance of my affairs, but if he is defeated, then the bills will be sent in, and he will know all."

A hysterical sob escaped her then, and Elizabeth was compelled to assure her that Mr. Lincoln would be reelected, of course he would. She was also tempted to warn her that Mr. Lincoln's reelection would only delay the inevitable, but the First Lady was already in such a dreadful state that Elizabeth couldn't bear to make matters worse with more harsh truths. Instead she murmured words of comfort and platitudes about frugality that she resignedly expected Mrs. Lincoln to ignore.

The subject resurfaced from time to time throughout those oppressive summer days, for anxiety seized Mrs. Lincoln with every bill that arrived in the mail or political setback that caused President Lincoln's popularity to sag. Sometimes Mrs. Lincoln feared that her husband's enemies would discover the particulars about her debts and use them against him in the campaign. Whenever this thought occurred to her, she became almost wild with agitation and fear.

Sometimes too she seized upon a way out of her troubles that seemed, to Elizabeth, a vain hope. "The Republican politicians must pay my debts," she would declare. "Hundreds of them are getting immensely rich off the patronage of my husband, and it is but fair that they should help me out of my embarrassment. I will make a demand of them, and when I tell them the facts they cannot refuse to advance whatever money I require."

Elizabeth thought that they certainly *could* refuse, and very likely *would,* and that all Mrs. Lincoln would accomplish with this scheme would be to place herself in the way of malicious gossip yet again. She gently discouraged her from confessing her debts to anyone but her husband and her trusted sisters, but she could not compel Mrs. Lincoln to heed her counsel — on this, or on practicing frugality, or on any other matter. What frustrated Elizabeth most was that all the while the First Lady fretted about her debts, she continued to spend, buying shawls and gloves and expensive trinkets she did not really need. The pleasure of buying pretty things seemed to help her forget her misery for a brief moment, but all the while, she was really only making matters worse.

Never in her life had Elizabeth known a more peculiarly constituted woman.

In the first week of July, General Sherman was making little headway in his offensive maneuvers upon Atlanta, and in the Shenandoah Valley, Confederate lieutenant general Jubal Early halted the Union major general David Hunter's thrust south and then turned his rebel army north toward the Potomac. Most Northerners assumed this was yet another summer raid and paid it little attention, but General Early's Army of the Valley kept advancing, skirting Harpers Ferry to cross the Potomac at Shepherdstown and moving on into Maryland. State officials in New York and Pennsylvania were worried enough to call out more than twenty-four thousand militia to provide defense, but most people of Washington City had such confidence in General Grant that they could not believe the rumors that their city might soon be in danger.

General Early captured Hagerstown and then Frederick, demanding cash, clothing, food, and other necessary supplies from the citizens. Rebel soldiers fanned out into the countryside, claiming cattle and horses and harvesting at will from local orchards. This seemed to prove that they were indeed on a simple plundering expedition, especially since the War Department released no information to the contrary.

Then worrisome rumors began to circulate that General Early had crossed the Potomac with nearly twenty thousand troops and was advancing upon Washington. The newspapers printed the alarming stories, retracted them, and printed them again: General Lee had sent General Early north to menace Washington and Baltimore in the hopes of forcing General Grant to divert troops from Richmond to defend them. General Early intended to kidnap President Lincoln and hold him hostage, forcing the Union to capitulate. General Early planned to invade the Union capital in order to convince foreign nations that they must recognize the Confederates as a legitimate government. Mrs. Lincoln was with her family at the Soldiers' Home, so Elizabeth could not hope to overhear anything that might dispel or confirm the talk on the streets. Like everyone else, she could only gather whatever useful news she could, and wait.

On July 9, the governor of Maryland and the mayor of Baltimore declared an emergency and called their citizens to arms. "It may without exaggeration be said today that we are having something of an excitement," the Baltimore correspondent of *The New York Times* breathlessly reported. Union major general Lew Wallace, commander of the Middle Department and Eighth Army

Corps, moved his meager forces — about 6,300 troops, mostly Hundred Day Men — in place to resist General Early's advance, not knowing whether he intended to move toward Baltimore or Washington. The two armies met on the banks of the Monocacy about forty miles northwest of the capital, but General Wallace's army was badly outnumbered.

Almost immediately, refugees from the countryside of Frederick and upper Montgomery counties began streaming into Washington on wagons piled high with their household goods, babes in arms, livestock trailing along behind. They told harrowing stories of advancing armies and narrow escapes, and it soon became evident that General Early's forces had pushed forward to Rockville, a mere twenty miles away. The War Department had withheld information from the public to avoid causing a panic, but now there could be no more pretense. General Early was coming, and the city was not prepared to withstand him.

Although miles of trenches and earthworks surrounded Washington, the most experienced soldiers had been gathered into the Army of the Potomac for General Grant's march on Richmond, and the soldiers left behind, mostly National Guardsmen from Ohio, had not been trained to use their forts' heavy artillery. Every able-bodied citizen was called to defend the city. The Pennsylvania Bucktails who guarded the White House left their customary posts for the front lines. Quartermaster clerks took up arms and formed ranks. Eighteen hundred men from the convalescent camps and thirty-two hundred more from the Invalid Corps were put on active duty. Nearly one thousand marines and mechanics from the navy yard traded their tools for rifles. Civilians were quickly recruited into a Loyal League militia, and dozens of colored men were compelled to serve as teamsters.

President Lincoln was at Fort Stevens when the defenders began firing upon the Confederate advance; later it was said that he had stood on a parapet, a perfect target amid the flying bullets, until a nearby soldier roughly ordered him to get down unless he wanted his head knocked off. In a potential disaster worthy of Bull Run three years before, thousands of eager civilians — men, women, and children — rushed to the fort to watch the spectacle, and when soldiers forced them away, they scaled fences, trees, and hills to get a better look at the fight.

But even as General Early's forces reached

the breastworks at Fort Stevens and he began gathering his troops for a full-scale attack, Union reinforcements from the Sixth and the Nineteenth Corps under Major General Horatio G. Wright began arriving in southwest Washington by steamer. The numbers of these desperately needed veteran fighters were few, but General Early must not have known that, because after two days of skirmishing — during which time additional Union troops arrived, further strengthening their defenses — he withdrew before dawn on the morning of July 13, so stealthily and unexpectedly that the Union defenders did not realize the Confederates had gone until it grew light enough to look out from the fort and see that they had disappeared.

Exultant, the civilian defenders left the battlements and resumed their ordinary lives, but President Lincoln was greatly displeased that yet another Confederate army had gotten away. Elizabeth was simply grateful, and enormously relieved, that they had gone.

August waned, oppressively hot and sultry, with little good news from the battlefield and even less from the presidential campaign. At the end of the month, the Democratic National Convention met in Chicago and nominated President Lincoln's disgruntled former general in chief of the Union Army, George B. McClellan, on a peace platform that called for a cease-fire and negotiated settlement with the Confederacy. With General Grant unable to advance upon Richmond and General Sherman stalled near Atlanta, the war seemed to have ground to a dispiriting halt.

Mrs. Lincoln, too, was noticeably discouraged. She took to visiting Elizabeth in her rooms, ostensibly to discuss necklines and trims and trains, but the election loomed ever larger in her thoughts. "Elizabeth," Mrs. Lincoln said forlornly, "where do you think I will be this time next summer?"

"Why, in the White House, of course."

"I can't believe so." Tears appeared in her eyes. "I have no hope of the reelection of Mr. Lincoln. The canvass is a heated one, the people begin to murmur at the war, and every vile charge is brought against my husband."

"No matter," Elizabeth replied firmly. "Mr. Lincoln will be reelected. I am so confident of it, that I am tempted to ask a favor of you."

Mrs. Lincoln's eyebrows rose. "A favor. Well, if we remain in the White House I shall be able to do you many favors. What is this special favor?"

"I should like for you to make me a present of the right-hand glove that the president wears at the first public reception after his second inaugural."

Mrs. Lincoln laughed, astonished. "It will be so filthy when he pulls it off that I shall be tempted to take the tongs and put it in the fire. I cannot imagine what you want with such a glove."

Smiling, Elizabeth lifted her chin, refusing to be dissuaded. "I shall cherish it as a precious memento of the second inauguration of the man who has done so much for my race. He has been a Jehovah to my people — he has lifted them out of bondage, and directed their footsteps from darkness into light. I shall keep the glove, and hand it down to posterity."

Mrs. Lincoln shook her head. "You have some strange ideas, Elizabeth," she remarked. "Never mind, you shall have the glove; that is, if Mr. Lincoln continues as president after the fourth of March next."

"It is a certainty," said Elizabeth, as she had many times before throughout that long, hot summer. Mrs. Lincoln only smiled, wistful and worried.

■ ■ ■ ■

A few days later, General Sherman captured Atlanta.

The news came to Mr. Lincoln by telegram on September 2. Exultant, the president commanded every arsenal and navy yard to fire a one-hundred-gun salute in General Sherman's honor, and at Petersburg, General Grant saluted his brother in arms by ordering all of his batteries to fire live rounds at the enemy, which they did within the hour, with much rejoicing.

The people of the North were jubilant. After a dismal summer full of stalemate, discouragement, and defeat, the Union Army suddenly surged toward victory — and so too did Mr. Lincoln. Overnight he had become a victorious commander in chief, and in the transformed political environment, the radical Republican effort to replace him seemed dangerously unwise. The possibility that the Republican electorate would divide their votes between Mr. Lincoln and General Frémont, and thereby allow the Democrats to seize the presidency, began to worry members of the new National Union and Radical Democracy parties. In September, President Lincoln asked for the resignation of Postmaster General Blair, who among all the members of his cabinet particularly infuriated the radical Republican faction. In the meantime, though no one would claim or could prove a connection, General Frémont withdrew from the race.

The political distinction between the two remaining candidates could not have been more clear — President Lincoln, leader of a victorious army and savior of the Union, and General McClellan, a once-popular and perpetually hesitant military leader whose party insisted upon a peace platform he himself did not advocate.

In the weeks leading up to Election Day, Secretary of War Edwin Stanton made sure that soldiers were given absentee ballots, if the laws of their states permitted, or furloughs so they could travel home to vote. President Lincoln himself wrote to several of his generals asking them to grant leave to soldiers from states where the election would likely be a close call — Indiana, Pennsylvania, Missouri, and New York — assuming that the Union soldiers would overwhelmingly support the Republican ticket as they had in the off-year elections. Even the former secretary Salmon Chase, still stinging from his abrupt dismissal from the Department of the Treasury, began praising President Lincoln in public and then campaigning for him in crucial Midwestern states. His support was no less beneficial for all that he was obviously angling for the newly vacated position of chief justice of the Supreme Court.

Although the outcome of the election had never looked brighter for Mr. Lincoln, Mrs. Lincoln had her own campaigns to wage to help ensure his victory. She had come to trust Elizabeth's taste and judgment, so she had asked Elizabeth to accompany her to New York for one last autumn shopping trip. When Mrs. Lincoln needed to return to Washington in time for the election, Elizabeth remained in New York to attend to her business there — making purchases on her behalf, obtaining estimates for fabrics, placing or canceling orders, paying or deferring bills, and carrying on the First Lady's business affairs as directed, sending telegrams back and forth, often several times a day.

Elizabeth remained in New York for all of November, which meant that she spent Election Day not at home in the nation's capital as she had four years before, but in the fraught, anxious city where memories of violent draft riots still evoked pain and anger, and where Mr. Lincoln had never been popular.

It was there too that Elizabeth heard the glorious news that Mr. Lincoln had been reelected — not only elected but decisively so, receiving fifty-five percent of the popular vote and an enormous margin in the Electoral College, two hundred and twelve votes to General McClellan's twenty-one.

Alone in her rented room, suddenly overwhelmingly homesick, Elizabeth nevertheless rejoiced.

All of her predictions had proven true. The good people of the loyal states had wisely decided that Mr. Lincoln should continue at the nation's helm.

CHAPTER ELEVEN

December 1864–April 1865

"The war continues," Mr. Lincoln began his annual presidential message to Congress in December, but after that somber opening, it took a more optimistic turn, certainly more so than his previous three State of the Union addresses. The Union Army was steadily advancing, and the results of the November elections proved that the people of the North were resolved to see the war through to victory. Despite their significant losses, the North still had more men and resources than the South. As if he expected his address to be read in the Confederate capital — and indeed it likely would be printed in the Richmond papers within days — Mr. Lincoln noted that the overmatched South could have peace the moment they decided to lay down their arms and submit to federal authority. His administration would not, however, compromise in any way on the matter of slavery; in fact, the president called on the House to approve the constitutional amendment abolishing slavery that the Senate had already passed. The end of slavery throughout the nation was only a matter of time, he asserted, and "the sooner the better."

A few days later, while Salmon P. Chase was being sworn in as the new chief justice of the Supreme Court, word arrived in the capital that General Sherman had reached the Atlantic, the terminus of his march across Georgia. On Sunday, December 25, the general sent the president a telegram bearing most unusual but nonetheless heartening holiday greetings: "I beg to present to you, as a Christmas gift, the city of Savannah, with 150 heavy guns and plenty of ammunition, and also about 25,000 bales of cotton."

That year Washingtonians celebrated Christmas with patriotic jubilance, and a week later they welcomed the New Year with reinvigorated hopes. Nearly four thousand citizens attended the annual New Year's reception at the White House, filling the public rooms to overflowing so that when they were ready to depart, some of the more agile guests had to exit through a first-floor window in the East Room and clamber down a long ramp of wooden planks to the ground.

For Elizabeth, the last day of January was a greater, more joyful harbinger of new beginnings than the first, for it was on January 31 that the House voted to approve the Thirteenth Amendment, abolishing slavery throughout the United States. For the first time, people of color were allowed into the congressional galleries, where they watched the final speeches and heard the vote taken in breathless quiet, breaking into cheers and joyful weeping when the measure passed. Although three-fourths of the states still had to ratify the amendment before it would become the law of the land, the colored residents of Washington rejoiced, certain that slavery had been dealt a fatal blow.

Despite the ongoing war, there was much to be thankful for in the first months of 1865, but Mrs. Lincoln found herself caught up in a frenzy of discontent. After Mr. Lincoln was reelected and various resignations and appointments were made, Mrs. Lincoln made some staffing changes of her own, beginning with firing the longtime White House doorman Edward McManus. Elizabeth wasn't sure why; apparently he had failed to deliver some documents on time or he had divulged a secret Mrs. Lincoln had entrusted to him — the other servants were not sure and Mrs. Lincoln would not say. When Mr. Lincoln heard about the dismissal, he and Mrs. Lincoln had a terrible quarrel in front of a member of her New York coterie, embarrassing her greatly. Worse yet, a disgruntled Mr. McManus carried tales of her overspending, duplicities, and ill tempers to Thurlow Weed, a New York newspaper editor and political organizer whom Mrs. Lincoln particularly despised. Scandalous stories began to make the rounds, compelling Mrs. Lincoln to frantically write a flurry of letters in her own defense to the New York elite in an attempt to salvage her reputation.

While Mrs. Lincoln waged war for her social status, her husband and eldest son embarked on a secret campaign of their own. After graduating from Harvard College in July 1864, Robert had again sought his parents' blessing to enlist in the army, and Mrs. Lincoln had again adamantly refused. Angered, Robert declared that if he could not live as he wanted he would at least escape the "glass house" of Washington, so he returned to Cambridge and enrolled in Harvard Law School. Six months later, with the Union Army sweeping relentlessly through the South, Mr. Lincoln decided to grant his son's longtime wish. Without consulting his wife, he wrote to General Grant and asked him to find a post for Robert that would neither place him on the front lines nor bestow upon him a coveted position that ought to go to a more deserving veteran soldier. The general wrote back that he would gladly welcome Robert into his "military family," and so it was that on February 17, Robert Todd Lincoln entered the army as a captain and began serving as an assistant adjutant general on General Grant's own staff. Mrs. Lincoln kept up a brave, tremulous front, assuring the nation that she was very proud of her son, but she confided to Elizabeth that she was nervous and afraid, even though Robert was so well placed that he would likely never see a single battle.

On the night before Mr. Lincoln's second inauguration, a terrible storm struck Washington City. Elizabeth was jolted awake by the crash of thunder and the scour of hail upon the roof, and she sat up in bed, her quilt gathered around her, heart pounding, until it subsided enough for her to lie back down and try to fall asleep. It was not an ill omen, she told herself firmly. It was only a storm, perhaps more severe than others they had seen in that damp early spring, but still, only a storm.

The next morning, she woke to a gray day. She had planned to attend the parade with Emma and two of her other assistant seamstresses, and later to join Virginia and Walker on the grounds of the Capitol to witness Mr. Lincoln take the oath of office and give his second inaugural address, but the torrential rain had turned the streets of Washington to canals of mud ten inches thick, and she had no desire to wade through them, fighting the crowds for the rare dry patches of earth. She would have to go out later, first to the White House to dress Mrs. Lincoln for the White House reception, and then to an inaugural party with the Lewises and other friends, but with any luck the streets would be drier by then.

"Oh, do come," Emma protested when she knocked upon Elizabeth's door and she apologetically explained her change of heart. "How can you think of staying away the first time colored folks are allowed on the Capitol grounds for an inauguration? The streets aren't so bad everywhere, and the little boys are out in full force."

Enterprising youngsters relished muddy days, because they would carry wooden planks around the streets and charge ladies a few pennies to have an improvised boardwalk placed before them to walk upon. "You go," said Elizabeth. "You go and tell me all about it later."

"I won't tell you a thing," Emma retorted. "It's your own choice to stay home, and you'll have to suffer the consequences."

"If you tell me about the president's address," Elizabeth said, "I promise to describe for you every detail of the gown Mrs. Lincoln will wear to the inaugural ball — and I'll show you how I fashioned the train."

Emma hesitated, tempted, but when she turned to go she merely lifted her chin airily and said, "I'll think about it."

Emma's desire to learn a new dressmaking skill won out, and so when she returned to the boardinghouse in the early afternoon, she came to Elizabeth's rooms straightaway, eyes shining, features bright and animated. The parade had been splendid despite the mud, with horses and men marching proudly and bands playing as merrily as music was ever heard. A team pulled a model ironclad gunboat, complete with a revolving turret that startled and delighted onlookers by firing blanks as it made its way down Pennsylvania Avenue. Smartly attired representatives from fire departments of Washington and Philadelphia, civic organizations, and fraternal lodges from across the

North had marched proudly, carrying banners and flags. A local printers' society had mounted a hand press on a wagon, and as they processed along, they cheerfully printed broadsides and distributed them to spectators they passed along the way. Most gratifying of all, for the first time people of color had marched in the parade too, a battalion of colored soldiers as well as distinguished leaders of several Negro civic associations. People of their race were at last included in the inauguration, fully part of the celebration and ceremony, not merely onlookers in the crowd or the unseen workers who cooked the food and cleaned up afterward.

Later, on the muddy Capitol grounds, Emma and her friends had stood in the crowd beneath overcast skies threatening rain, waiting with thousands of others for President Lincoln to emerge from within and take his place on the East Portico with the newly completed Capitol dome above. "And then he stepped out, a sheet of paper in his hand," Emma said, glowing with remembered awe. "As soon as the people recognized him, they let out a great roar of welcome and gladness, and just then — oh, you should have seen it, Elizabeth! — at the moment he took his place, the clouds parted and the sun broke through, and a bright shaft of sunlight shone down upon him like a blessing from heaven."

Elizabeth leaned forward eagerly, captivated. "And what did he say?"

"I don't recall," Emma said lightly, with an indifferent shrug. "You can read about it in the papers tomorrow."

"Emma!"

She laughed. "I'm only teasing, but you deserved it. Oh, it was a marvelous speech. Brief, but all the better for it in my opinion."

Elizabeth nodded. "Brevity is his custom in daily speech too, unless he's telling a story or reading aloud from one of his favorite authors." As soon as she spoke, she could have kicked herself for how puffed up and pompous she sounded, boasting about her familiarity with the president.

If Emma thought she was showing off, she gave no sign of it. "It was a lovely address, clear and sad and warm, full of forgiveness and reconciliation," she said. "He talked about the war, and how slavery was the cause of it, and how four years ago everyone, North and South alike, had wanted to avoid war, but one side would make war rather than let the nation survive, and the other would accept war rather than let it perish. He talked about the Lord too, and how strange it is that each side prays to the same

God and invokes His aid against the other."

Elizabeth nodded. It was something she had often thought in the months since George was killed. She had prayed for her son every day and every night he was at war, and somewhere, the mother of the young man who had killed George had been praying for her son too.

Suddenly Elizabeth was struck by the realization that after so many years of war, the rebel who had killed George could very well have fallen as well, cut down by a Minié ball or disease or dreadful accident. Another woman might have felt a surge of righteous satisfaction at the thought, but Elizabeth felt only sorrow.

"Mr. Lincoln suggested that the Lord sent us this terrible war as punishment for the offense of slavery," Emma went on, "and that the war may be a mighty scourge to rid us of it."

"Perhaps it is," said Elizabeth softly.

"He ended with words so profound that I wrote them down as soon as he finished." Emma withdrew a scrap of paper from her pocket and unfolded it. "These were the last lines as best I could remember them: 'With malice toward none, with charity for all, with firmness in the right as God gives us to see the right, let us strive on to finish the work we are in, to bind up the nation's wounds, to care for him who shall have borne the battle and for his widow and his orphan, to do all which may achieve and cherish a just and lasting peace among ourselves and with all nations.' " Emma smiled self-consciously, folded the paper, and tucked it into her pocket with a shrug. "I probably didn't do it justice. The whole speech will likely be in the paper tomorrow, so you'll be able to read it properly then."

"I'm sure you captured the spirit of it, if not every word." Elizabeth's throat tightened with emotion, and she blinked away tears. "I'm glad I didn't have to wait for the morning to hear those words." So compassionate, so true, just like the man who had spoken them.

"You should have been there," Emma scolded her fondly, shaking her head.

"I wish I had been, despite the ankle-deep mud and the crowds. And now, Emma," said Elizabeth, lowering her voice conspiratorially, "how would you like to be the only person in Washington — the entire United States, rather — besides Mrs. Lincoln and myself who knows what she will be wearing to the inaugural ball?"

Emma's pretty face lit up with joy as Elizabeth described the rich, pure white satin, the needlepoint lace shawl, the elegant draping and exquisite trims. Emma hung on every word as intently as if she thought she might be required to re-create the gown from memory later. She already knew how to sew the narrow vertical pleats in the back of a mantua bodice so it would fit the body like wallpaper; Elizabeth herself had taught her to make the tiny, interlocking stitches that could withstand the strain across the figure and avoid unattractive gaping. She had also shown Emma how to use longer, looser stitches for the skirts so the seams would not pucker and ruin the lines of the gown, and after much practice Emma could do so flawlessly.

Emma was becoming quite a skilled seamstress, but Elizabeth had so much more to teach her. With her natural talent, bright mind, and deft fingers, Emma would surely master every technique, and in time she could become as accomplished as Elizabeth herself — perhaps even more so.

Elizabeth believed that a student who surpassed her would indeed be a fine legacy — more precious and enduring and gratifying than all the beautiful gowns she had made for the ladies of Washington City, even those she had made for the First Lady of the land.

Later that evening she picked her way through the muddy streets to the White House, where she found Mrs. Lincoln in a state of nervous excitement. "I'm sure I'm not the first to offer you congratulations on this momentous day," Elizabeth told her warmly, "but I offer them all the same, and I hope you'll find them among the most sincere."

"Thank you, Elizabeth," Mrs. Lincoln said, sighing, "but now that we have won the position, I almost wish it were otherwise. Poor Mr. Lincoln is looking so broken-hearted, so completely worn out. I fear he will not get through the next four years."

"Of course he will," said Elizabeth stoutly. "The campaign taxed him, but that's over now, and spring is here, and news from the front has never been more cheering."

"Well, that's certainly true," admitted Mrs. Lincoln, without looking at all heartened. "If only this terrible war would be over! I confess that I live in dread of the inauguration ending, because when it does, Robert must return to the war."

"I thought his post was safe."

"He isn't marching out with the infantry if that's what you mean, but he goes wherever General Grant goes, and the general is at the front."

Her voice broke with fear and worry, and Elizabeth's heart went out to her. The war must end soon, she almost said, but people had been saying that for so long that the words had ceased to have any meaning. But surely now, even after so many false hopes and disappointments, the phrase finally rang with truth. On every side the Confederates were losing ground and the lines of Union blue advanced in triumph. Almost every day, Elizabeth could look out her window and see artillery going past on the way to fire a salute in honor of some new victory. Even so, she understood why Mrs. Lincoln would worry incessantly until the war was over and Robert was entirely out of danger.

When it seemed as if Mrs. Lincoln might sink into a brood, Elizabeth endeavored to draw her out by asking for her impressions of the inauguration. "Mr. Lincoln spoke brilliantly," Mrs. Lincoln replied, brightening a trifle. "Did you know he missed the entire procession?"

"I didn't."

"It's true! He had so much business to attend to that he went to the Capitol ahead of time in his barouche, and he was there signing bills until the last minute." She uttered a small laugh, an encouraging sign. "So all the people lining the streets later and cheering him as his carriage passed at the head of the parade — why, they were cheering only me. I doubt they would have carried on so had they known."

Elizabeth smiled. "I'm sure many would have."

Mrs. Lincoln laughed again, scoffing and yet pleased. "Oh, Elizabeth, that small deception was not even the greatest scandal of the hour." She paused dramatically. "When the vice-president–elect arrived to take his oath of office, he was drunk."

"No!"

"Indeed he was, and he downed nearly two tumblers of brandy right there in the Senate chamber." Mrs. Lincoln had become more animated as she warmed to her subject. "Mr. Hamlin made some perfectly lovely, gracious remarks to introduce his successor, and then Mr. Johnson came up and began spouting the most astonishing, rambling harangue I've ever had the misfortune to witness."

"How shocking," exclaimed Elizabeth. "What on earth was he thinking?"

"I don't know that he was thinking at all. He was red-faced and barely coherent, and when the secretary of the Senate tried to bring the appalling performance to a close, Mr. Johnson persisted as if he were quite deranged." Mrs. Lincoln shook her head. "My poor husband entered in the middle of this disaster and stood with his head bowed, enduring the embarrassment in dignified silence and waiting patiently until Mr. Johnson finished and took his oath of office."

"It was not the president's embarrassment, but Mr. Johnson's," said Elizabeth.

"Why, certainly, but it spoiled the occasion all the same." Mrs. Lincoln pursed her lips and shook her head. "What a dreadful debut. I doubt he will ever live this down. None of us who were there will ever forget it."

Elizabeth could tell by her sharp frown of disapproval that Mrs. Lincoln would never forgive him either.

Elizabeth was arranging Mrs. Lincoln's hair when the president entered, so Elizabeth went to him, extended her hand, and offered her sincere congratulations. "Thank you," he said, grasping her outstretched hand warmly and holding it. "Well, Madam Elizabeth, I don't know whether I should feel thankful or not. The position brings with it many trials. We do not know what we are destined to pass through. But God will be with us all. I put my trust in God." He released her hand and crossed the room to sit down upon the sofa, his expression solemn.

Elizabeth felt painful sympathy for both wife and husband, First Lady and president. From every region of the fractured nation came glorious news of the Union Army's successes, and yet, alone in their private chambers, the Lincolns looked careworn, sad, and anxious on a day that should have been their triumph. In her quiet way, she tried to cheer them with pleasant conversation, and by the time she finished dressing Mrs. Lincoln, it did seem that their spirits had risen at least a little. Mrs. Lincoln took the president's arm, and as he led her off downstairs where thousands of citizens waited to meet them, Mrs. Lincoln called over her shoulder, "I'll have that glove for you Monday night, Elizabeth, when you come to dress me for the Inaugural Ball."

Elizabeth smiled, pleased that she had remembered.

While the Lincolns welcomed the public and graciously accepted their congratulations, hiding their weariness and worry rather than spoil the occasion for their many well-wishers, Elizabeth attended a smaller but not less joyful gathering of Washington's colored elite. With an effort, Elizabeth put aside her concerns for the dispirited Lincolns for the moment and joined her friends and acquaintances in celebrating Mr. Lincoln's victory, certain that he would accomplish great things for the nation and its people of color in his second term. Mr. Frederick Douglass was in attendance, and as a longtime admirer Elizabeth was very pleased to have the chance to speak with him. He captivated all within earshot by relating an incident that had occurred at the White House scarcely two hours before. Many people of color had come to Washington for the inauguration, and dozens of them had desired to attend the levee, but they had not been permitted to enter. Mr. Douglass had stood on the edge of the crowd, already mentally composing a righteously indignant letter of protest, when a member of Congress spied him, remarked about the press of the immense crowd, and asked, "You are going in, of course?" When Mr. Douglass told him, regretfully, that he would not, the congressman exclaimed, "Not going in to shake the president by the hand! Why, pray?"

"The best reason in the world," Mr. Douglass had said, his tone dignified but ironic. "Strict orders have been issued not to admit people of color."

Elizabeth could not imagine Mr. Lincoln

issuing such a command on such a day, and she wondered which of the secretaries had been responsible for it, or if some misunderstanding had occurred between the crowd and the doormen. Just as she was about to suggest that Mr. Douglass return to the White House and try again, Mr. Douglass continued his tale, explaining that the congressman had been quite perturbed that he had been "placed under ban." He had taken the famed orator inside, led him through the crowd to the president, and asked permission to introduce them. Mr. Lincoln readily agreed, and soon Mr. Douglass stood face-to-face with the president, who shook his hand and said, "Mr. Douglass, I am glad to meet you. I have long admired your course, and I value your opinions highly."

Mr. Douglass was obviously proud of the manner in which the president had welcomed him, and all who heard him tell his story were proud too, and pleased that the president had treated one of their leaders with such respect and interest. Elizabeth was not at all surprised, not only because she had observed the president receiving guests often enough to know that he never failed to be courteous, but also because she herself had granted a friend's request to arrange a meeting between the president and the former slave and abolitionist Sojourner Truth the previous October. She had not witnessed their conversation, but afterward she learned that Sojourner Truth had spoken well of the president and had been honored and pleased by his attention. Mr. Lincoln did not have a perfect record of dealing with the colored race, as Elizabeth would be among the first to admit, but he was learning, and she was confident that his abundant compassion for his fellow man would guide him to an even greater understanding of their unique concerns and hopes for the future.

Although she would never exaggerate her position by claiming the title of adviser, Elizabeth liked to think that she too had played some small part in helping President Lincoln know the desires and worries of colored people better. She hoped she had used, and would always use, her acquaintance with the president and her time in the White House for the good of her race.

The crowds who had come to the capital to mark President Lincoln's second inauguration departed soon after the ceremonies, but the city remained full of strangers, with more arriving every day. Confederate soldiers were abandoning General Lee's army in droves, and while most simply went home, others crossed into Union lines and surrendered. Some straggled into Washington on foot, the tatters of their gray or butternut uniforms hanging from their emaciated frames, but most arrived around four o'clock every afternoon on the "deserters' transport," disembarking on railway platforms one or two hundred at a time. Once in the Union capital, they took the oath of allegiance and were assigned to work on farms, in factories, or upon the western frontier. Until they shipped out to their new posts, they were permitted to wander the city as they pleased, striking up conversations and sharing tobacco with Union soldiers who had been their mortal enemies not long before, their Confederate uniforms drawing curious, suspicious glances until they became commonplace. Indeed, the sight of the thin, ragged former rebels became so typical throughout Washington that at least one newspaper reporter worried that they might in fact represent a devious invasion by the enemy, massing their numbers and awaiting the order to strike at the heart of the Union from within. But the truth seemed to be far simpler. The Confederate soldiers were starving, and they had

341

realized that an army that could not feed its soldiers could not withstand its opponents much longer. They were hungry and tired and sick of war, and many resented futilely persisting in what they called a "rich man's war but a poor man's fight." So they had withdrawn, trusting that they would not be captured, and that if they were, they would not be shot for their crime. Indeed, it seemed to Elizabeth that there could not be enough soldiers left in the rebel army to shoot all the deserters.

Later, Elizabeth would wonder if the Confederate government's new measure to increase their army had compelled some of their soldiers to desert. Soon after the inauguration, Northern newspapers announced that the Confederate congress had voted to allow slaves to enlist in the rebel army, and thereby earn their freedom. Elizabeth and every other person of color she knew, from her friends in the boardinghouse to her fellow churchgoers at Union Bethel to the former slaves she assisted in the freedmen's camps, wondered how anyone of their race could agree to fight to preserve the institution that had kept them and their families in bondage and degradation. They were shocked by reports that, a mere nine days after Jefferson Davis signed the measure into law, three companies of Confederate Negro soldiers were drilling in Richmond's Capitol Square. Elizabeth felt the sharp sting of betrayal whenever she thought of colored men in rebel gray, but she felt profoundly sorry for them too. They surely did not understand what was happening in the wider country around them, or they never would have made such a bewildering choice or, as Virginia grimly called it, a deal with the devil.

The inauguration brought newcomers not only to Washington but also into the most intimate circles of the White House, for between the November election and the commencement of President Lincoln's second term, several members of his cabinet resigned, and others were named to replace them. Iowa senator James F. Harlan assumed the post of secretary of the interior, a staffing change that seemed to please Robert Lincoln, who was — not as secretly as he seemed to believe — courting Mr. Harlan's daughter, Mary. Elizabeth too was glad to see Mr. Harlan elevated to such an important post, because his wife, a kind, gracious woman, was one of her favorite patrons, and Elizabeth was very happy for her.

On April 3, a Monday, Mrs. Harlan had

come to Elizabeth's reception room at the boardinghouse with material for a new dress, a lovely green-and-white striped silk. "I'm not certain about the color," Mrs. Harlan mused as Elizabeth examined the fine fabric. "I fear it will make me appear sallow."

"Oh, I don't think it shall." Elizabeth beckoned Mrs. Harlan to step closer to the window, where she draped the fabric over Mrs. Harlan's shoulder and bosom and stepped back to study the effect. "I think it's very becoming to your complexion and it suits your hair and eyes well."

"Mr. Harlan likes me in green." Mrs. Harlan had to raise her voice to be heard over a sudden clamor in the streets, a cacophony of passing artillery.

"All the more reason to wear it often," Elizabeth replied, nearly shouting as whistles and cheers joined the din.

"What is going on out there?" Mrs. Harlan wondered aloud, peering out the window.

"They must be on their way to fire off a salute. We've become quite accustomed to the show around here." Then, frowning thoughtfully, she added, "I admit this does seem more exuberant than usual."

Mrs. Harlan's eyebrows rose. "This must mean good news, then."

"It surely must."

A look of understanding passed between them, and together they hurried outside. "Excuse me, sir," Elizabeth called to a man whistling cheerfully as he strode after the artillery. "What's happened? What's the news?"

"What's the news, you ask?" The man whooped and threw his hat into the air. "Richmond's fallen, that's the news!"

As the man hurried off to retrieve his hat and rejoin the impromptu parade, Elizabeth gasped, Mrs. Harlan cried out, and then they joined hands and twirled about in a circle, laughing and cheering. "I must tell the girls," Elizabeth exclaimed, and dropping Mrs. Harlan's hands, she ran across the street to her workrooms. "Emma, girls," she called out as she burst into the room where her assistant seamstresses sewed. "Richmond has fallen!"

"We heard! We know!" Elated, Emma threw her arms around her, and only then did Elizabeth notice her young assistants were laughing and crying and embracing all around her. "Did you hear the best part? It was colored soldiers that took the city. *Our* soldiers!"

Elizabeth's spirits soared. Speechless with happiness, she clasped her hands to her heart and laughed aloud.

"That's not the best part," another seamstress called out joyfully. "The best part is that you promised us a day off when Richmond fell."

Everyone burst out laughing, and Elizabeth joined in, helpless to do otherwise, until, catching her breath, she shook her head and waved them to silence. "I can't send you all home," she protested. "Mrs. Harlan is waiting across the way with silk for a new dress."

A chorus of dismay greeted her words. "Mrs. Harlan can't want to stay and fit the lining for a dress now," Emma protested. "Surely she wants to celebrate too."

When the other seamstresses chimed in, urging her to at least go and ask, Elizabeth wavered. "Don't leave yet," she said, but her irrepressible smile undercut whatever sternness she might otherwise have mustered. She dashed back across the street, where she found Mrs. Harlan in her reception room, gathering up the silk they had let fall to the floor in their excitement.

"Mrs. Harlan," Elizabeth exclaimed, hurrying to help. "I'm terribly sorry. I had to share the good news with my assistants, and as it happened they already knew, and they reminded me of a promise I had made them months ago, that when Richmond fell I would give them the day off, although I realize it's terribly inconvenient —"

"Not at all," Mrs. Harlan assured her, smiling. "For such good tidings, I would gladly wait another day or two for my dress. You must keep your promise. Give your girls a holiday and a treat, by all means."

Elizabeth thanked her profusely and promised to begin fitting her lining the next day. Mrs. Harlan agreed, and as she departed for her home, Elizabeth put the green-and-white striped silk in a safe place, snatched up her bonnet, and hurried back to her workrooms. "More good news, girls," she called out, but she didn't need to say any more, because they had guessed that their long-promised holiday had come at last. They implored Elizabeth to join them, and this time she agreed. Arm in arm, they joined the celebration already spilling over into the streets, their hearts overflowing with joy, their happiness reflected in the faces of the people they passed, clerks and shopkeepers and housemaids and waiters whose businesses had also declared a holiday. Residents draped patriotic banners and bunting from their windows, and bands quickly formed up on street corners and in parks to play spirited marches and merry jigs. Crowds gathered outside the homes and offices of various dignitaries and called for them to come out and address them, but of the many who complied, only the few loudest could be heard over the din. An eight-hundred-gun salute shook the city, three hundred booms for the fall of Petersburg, five hundred for Richmond. As the afternoon passed, Elizabeth observed many young men — and many more without the excuse of the foolishness of youth — celebrating by indulging in too much liquor, and she was alternately scandalized and amused to observe neighbors she knew to be sober, responsible folk tottering down the streets, singing and proclaiming the glory of President Lincoln, General Grant, and the Union Army in loud, slurring voices. Tomorrow they would regret their overindulgence, but for the moment, nothing could diminish their rejoicing, or Elizabeth's.

President Lincoln had been in Virginia since the last week in March, and he was meeting with General Grant in Petersburg when Richmond fell. He decided to tour the captured Southern capital the next day, and when Mrs. Lincoln heard of his plans, she proposed to meet him at City Point on the

James River and accompany him into the conquered city.

This would be Mrs. Lincoln's second trip to General Grant's City Point headquarters within two weeks. She and Tad had traveled there with the president and a small party the week before, but Mrs. Lincoln had returned early, and alone, leaving Tad behind with his father. Mrs. Lincoln had not explained why she had cut her visit short, and although she had been abrupt with Elizabeth when asked about her travels, she had revealed enough for Elizabeth to conclude that the tour had been something of a disaster. When the party had gone out to review the troops, the president had ridden ahead on horseback accompanied by General Grant and two officers' wives, but Mrs. Lincoln and Mrs. Grant had been obliged to trail after them in an ambulance slowed to a crawl by shin-deep mud. Mrs. Lincoln finally arrived to find that the review had already begun and that the beautiful wife of Major General Ord was riding alongside Mr. Lincoln in a place of honor that properly belonged to herself. Seized by one of her jealous fits, she gave the young Mrs. Ord a terrible tongue-lashing, hurled abuse upon the astonished Mrs. Grant, and ferociously attacked her husband in front of everyone, demanding that he fire Major General Ord immediately, a command her husband quite reasonably ignored. Elizabeth did not know whether Mrs. Lincoln had fled back to Washington in shame or if Mr. Lincoln had ordered her away, but apparently, time to reflect and knowing that the incident had cost her a chance to see her son Robert had chastened her. When she mentioned that she was determined to try again to see Richmond, Elizabeth asked if she might accompany her. Years before, Petersburg had been her home, and she was curious to see it again, to stroll along its familiar streets as a free woman.

On April 5, at eleven o'clock in the morning, Mrs. Lincoln, Tad, Elizabeth, and the rest of their party, which included Senator Charles Sumner; Secretary of the Interior James Harlan; Mrs. Harlan, whose green-and-white striped silk dress Elizabeth had belatedly begun; Miss Mary Harlan, the young lady Robert Lincoln was courting; and several other gentlemen departed Washington on the steamer *Monohasset*. When they arrived at Fort Monroe the following morning, Mrs. Lincoln learned that President Lincoln had entered Richmond two days before.

"Are you sure you meant to say Richmond?" the First Lady queried the aide-de-camp, crestfallen. Elizabeth knew she had strongly hinted to her husband that she wanted him to wait for her so they might tour the fallen capital together. "In his telegram he said he went to Petersburg."

He had done that first, Mrs. Lincoln was promptly assured. It was the following morning that he had entered Richmond, scarcely a day after the Confederate army had evacuated, while flames still licked at the ruins. The aide-de-camp, apparently oblivious to Mrs. Lincoln's deepening frown, went on to tell them that a group of colored workmen had recognized the president from a distance and, to his embarrassment, had shouted, "Glory, hallelujah!" at his approach and had fallen to their knees to kiss his feet. "Please don't kneel to me," President Lincoln had told them. "You must kneel only to God and thank Him for your freedom." Escorted by the German-born general Godfrey Weitzel, Mr. Lincoln had toured the Confederate White House and had sat at Jefferson Davis's desk. Later he and his escort had passed the infamous Libby Prison, where thousands of captured Union soldiers had suffered starvation, disease, and unimaginably cruel treatment

— and where Mr. Lincoln's own brother-in-law, Confederate captain David Humphreys Todd, had served as a warden.

"I see," said Mrs. Lincoln flatly when the aide-de-camp finished his report. Immediately she stormed to the telegraph office and sent her husband several urgent messages imploring him to wait and to allow her party to join him on his boat, since theirs was dreadfully uncomfortable and she much desired to see Richmond by his side. After some back-and-forth, the arrangements were made, and soon the First Lady's party joined the president's aboard the *River Queen,* steaming up the James River, traveling with swift ease along a route that not long before had been impassable even to Union gunboats. Elizabeth spent hours on deck, holding on to the railing and lifting her face to the sun, savoring the breeze and the pure, balmy air. The river flowed along majestically, and its banks were lovely and fragrant with the first sweet blossoms of spring. Beyond them stretched fair fields, the very image of peacetime bounty — but all too often, the illusion of prosperity was broken by glimpses of deserted army camps and ruined forts, the ugly detritus of war.

Elizabeth had not glimpsed the fertile fields and green hills of her birthplace for years, and she had long yearned to see them again. Virginia would forever remind her of her mother, and her father, her aunts and uncles and cousins, her son, George, as a babe in her arms, her mother's warm kisses, the hours spent in the company of those she loved best. Her childhood had been difficult, full of pain and fear and loss, and yet she treasured a few precious, golden memories of those years. When she had embarked for City Point, a part of her so deep she was unaware of it had expected the journey to reunite her somehow with all she had lost. As the *River Queen* carried her along, the sad, unsettling truth of her own expectations dawned upon her, and she felt the first stirrings of regret.

Perhaps she should not have come.

At long last the *River Queen* arrived in Richmond, and, brimming over with curiosity, Mrs. Lincoln's party entered the smoldering city. Elizabeth would not admit it aloud, but she also felt the smallest stirring of apprehension. The streets were unnaturally subdued, save for a few citizens who averted their eyes as they hurried past on business of their own, and occasional patrols of Union soldiers. The Virginia statehouse where the Confederate congress had met was in a state of disarray that spoke of fear and haste — desks broken, papers scattered, chairs overturned as if their last occupants had fled in alarm. While her companions walked ahead, marveling at the desolation the Confederate congress had left in the wake of their flight, Elizabeth gathered her skirts in one hand and bent to pick up a handful of documents. She skimmed the first page, and her abrupt, ironic laugh when she realized what she held caused Mrs. Lincoln and Mrs. Harlan to glance over their shoulders at her, curious. "It's a resolution," Elizabeth said, indicating the papers. "It prohibits all free colored people from entering the State of Virginia."

Senator Sumner shook his head and snorted, but another gentleman in the party, the Marquis de Chambrun, smiled and said, "My dear madam, I think you need not fear that anyone will come to arrest you on that account."

"Thank you, sir," Elizabeth replied. "I confess that had not even occurred to me."

"Are you going to save those papers as a keepsake?" Mrs. Lincoln inquired. She often teased Elizabeth about her attachment to objects that evoked fond memories.

"I think not," said Elizabeth shortly, and let the papers fall to the floor.

They moved on to the senate chamber,

where Elizabeth sat in President Jefferson Davis's chair and gazed around the room, imagining it filled with rebel senators and contemplating the many decisions he must have made from that very place, and what they had cost him, what they had cost them all. When she moved on to the vice president's chair to give the others a chance to try the president's, her thoughts flew to Mrs. Davis and her children. She imagined them in flight or in hiding, hastening south to the imperfect sanctuary of their Mississippi home or cowering beneath the sheltering roof of a brave and loyal friend. Wherever they were, Elizabeth hoped Mrs. Davis and the children were safe. They were blameless, and she prayed no harm would come to them. As for Mr. Davis, before the war she had liked him and had considered him a gentleman, but he had made his choices and would have to live with the consequences. She would never wish suffering upon him, but she thought it unlikely that he would survive the war unscathed.

Later the party visited the Confederate executive mansion on K Street, which had also been called the White House, although it was gray stucco. The Richmond ladies in charge of its safekeeping glared at them darkly as they toured the elegant three-story residence, but they were in no position to bar any of them from exploring wherever they pleased. Elizabeth could not help but search each room for signs of her former patron — a forgotten quilt in the second-floor nursery, a dress that could not be stuffed into an overfull satchel — but she found nothing, and the absence made her feel oddly despondent.

With a will, she endeavored to cease brooding and to adopt her companions' cheerful curiosity. Eventually their lively spirits elevated hers, and by the time they returned to the *River Queen,* she too felt a flush of triumph and renewed hope that the end of the war could not be long in coming.

It was a merry party that gathered around the dining table in the ship's cabin that evening. For Elizabeth it was a special pleasure to dress Mrs. Lincoln for an event to which she herself was invited. Introductions were made all around, and they were chatting pleasantly about their impression of Richmond when one guest, a young captain attached to the Sanitary Commission, turned to the First Lady and said, "Mrs. Lincoln, you should have seen the president the other day, on his triumphal entry into Richmond. He was the cynosure of all eyes. The ladies kissed their hands to him, and greeted him with the waving of handkerchiefs. He is quite a hero when surrounded by pretty young ladies."

"Is he, indeed," said Mrs. Lincoln, her voice brittle with frost.

The young officer's pleasant smile faltered. "Why, yes, Mrs. Lincoln. Quite a hero."

Elizabeth's heart sank, but before she could think of a way to gracefully change the subject, Mrs. Lincoln fixed him with a steely glare and said, "And do you find him that way often? Surrounded by pretty young ladies, I mean?"

The captain flushed. "Why, no, Mrs. Lincoln, that is to say —" He glanced frantically down the length of the table, but his friends were too startled to come to his rescue.

"That is to say what, precisely?" Mrs. Lincoln prompted him sharply.

Elizabeth muffled a sigh and resisted the urge to slouch in her chair and stare at her plate as Mrs. Lincoln needled the poor young man, who would surely never forget his wretched evening aboard the president's steamer. Mrs. Lincoln made quite a scene before she wore herself out, and Elizabeth felt both indignant and embarrassed as she observed the other guests exchanging knowing looks and regarding the president with sympathy. They did not understand what Mrs. Lincoln had been through those past few days, how overtired she was from her travels, or they would have shown her more compassion and understanding.

Even so, Elizabeth found herself wishing that Mrs. Lincoln could learn to rein in her tempers, so it would not always fall to others to accommodate them.

The next morning, the entire party decided to visit Petersburg, and Elizabeth was only too eager to accompany them. As the president's special train sped them ever closer to the city where Elizabeth had been a slave twenty years before, her heart pounded with excitement and dread. She did not know what she would find there, what, if anything, would remain of the life she had once known — what, if anything, she wanted to remain.

When they disembarked at the station, Elizabeth parted company with the others; while they headed out to inspect forts and hospital camps and to confer with generals, she wandered off on her own in search of people she had known in days gone by. The city was at once both unsettlingly familiar and greatly changed. Many houses she had once admired had suffered neglect or damage from artillery; some shops that she had often visited on errands for her mistresses had shuttered their windows or displayed different names in their windows or upon their doors. She glimpsed familiar faces among the people she passed, but they walked by her without a glimmer of recognition in their eyes. Almost unwillingly, she made her way down to the riverfront where she and James had once strolled, sharing conversation and hopes and dreams — and in James's case, lies. Her heart sank deeper into sorrow with every step, and she was just about to turn and hasten back to the train station when she heard a woman behind her call, "Elizabeth? Lizzie Hobbs?"

With a start, Elizabeth whirled around and spotted a face she knew well — twenty years older, much thinner, with silver in her black hair and lines around her mouth, but still as dear to her as ever. "Martha? Can it truly be you?"

The woman nodded, tears filling her eyes. "It is."

"Oh, my dear friend," Elizabeth gasped as she hurried to close the distance between them and embrace her. "I never thought to see you again."

"I never thought to see you." Martha held her out at arm's length, and when she smiled, Elizabeth saw that her bottom front teeth were missing. "What on earth are you doing here? I thought you'd bought your freedom and disappeared up north."

"I didn't disappear," Elizabeth replied, laughing tearfully, hiding her shock. Martha was thin, so very thin, and her dress was worn and patched. Martha was a talented seamstress, a freeborn colored woman who had worked at Mrs. Miller's dry goods store. Though she was five years older than Elizabeth, they had become fast friends thanks to Elizabeth's frequent visits to purchase fabric, thread, needles, and other notions for her mistresses. "I've been living in Washington City since before the war. I've set myself up as a dressmaker there."

"How wonderful!" Martha shook her head in admiration. "You always did work marvels with fabric."

"How is your husband? Did he ever buy that land north of the river he liked so well?"

"No, no, he never did." Martha's smile faded. "He passed on ten years ago from smallpox, but my girls are doing well. My eldest is married now and has two little ones. How is your George?"

Elizabeth dug her fingernails into the palm of her hand to hold back the grief that suddenly welled up within her. "He's gone. He was killed in the war, in the Battle of Wilson's Creek in Missouri."

"Oh, my goodness. He was a soldier, you mean. I'm so sorry he's gone."

"I'm sorry for your loss too."

"But you must be so proud."

"Yes," Elizabeth forced herself to say. "Yes, very proud."

They walked along together for a while, and Martha reunited her with several mutual friends who remained in the city. Throughout the war years, every one of them had endured hardships and deprivations Elizabeth could not have imagined while she dwelled comfortably in her boardinghouse on Washington's pleasant Twelfth Street, but none of them complained or said more than was necessary about their suffering. They all admired her dress, which was only her second best but was well made and whole, and expressed joy without even the smallest taint of envy that she had done well for herself. Her heart went out to them, and she wished with all her strength that she could help them. She had a few Union dollars in her pocket, which they first refused and then gratefully accepted when she reminded them of debts she owed them from her Petersburg years, debts they did not recall because she had invented them on the spot. When she bade her old friends good-bye, she urged them to write to her if ever she could do anything for them.

She said good-bye to Martha last of all, and remembering her skill with needle and thread and cloth, she urged her to make her way to Washington City if she could. "I have too many dresses to make and not enough hands," she said. "You could earn a good living, working with me."

Martha looked as if she wished with all her heart she could accept, but she shook her head. "My girls need me," she said, "and Richmond is my home. I can't leave."

"But it will be so hard for colored folks in the South when the war is done."

Martha managed a smile. "It's always been hard, and we've always gotten by."

Before they parted ways, Elizabeth made Martha promise that she would at least keep the offer in mind, and then, heavyhearted, she made her way back to the place where the presidential party had agreed to meet. The sad sights of the day mingled with distant memories so painfully that she was eager to board the train and depart, but the president did not wish to set out right away. On an earlier visit, he had seen a large, peculiarly shaped oak tree that he was quite keen to show them, so they willingly accompanied him to the outskirts of the city, where it grew in stately solitude. Only after admiring it — and even Elizabeth, in her melancholy, had to admit that it was indeed a magnificent specimen — did they return to the train station and leave Petersburg.

Elizabeth was not sorry to put the city behind her, but as if to jeer at her eagerness to go, the train moved along at a crawl back to City Point, for what reason, Elizabeth could not fathom. Their pace was so slow that President Lincoln was able to observe a terrapin basking in the warm sunshine on the wayside. He called for the conductor to stop the train and had one of the brakemen bring the creature to him, and he and Tad amused themselves with it all the way to the James River, where their steamer waited. The president's obvious delight in the terrapin's lethargic, ungainly movements — and the ridiculous similarity between the train's pace and the reptile's — lifted Elizabeth out of her gloom, and so by the time they boarded the *River Queen,* she was feeling somewhat restored, although her wistfulness lingered.

For a week the *River Queen* remained on the James River, usually anchored at City Point, offering a pleasant, comfortable respite to all on board. General Grant and his wife visited the steamer several times, as did other officers and dignitaries, and whenever the president was not off on an excursion, he lounged about with the rest of the party, as comfortably at his ease as if they were all old friends.

On the day before they were to return to Washington, Mr. Lincoln went out for one last review of the troops, and in the evening he returned to the steamer thoroughly exhausted. "Mother," he told his wife wearily, "I have shaken so many hands today that my arms ache tonight. I almost wish that I could go to bed now."

Mrs. Lincoln murmured sympathetically and urged him to excuse himself and retire, but the president hated to disappoint his companions, so as the twilight shadows lengthened and the lamps were lit, he remained among them. When all was brilliantly illuminated, Elizabeth found herself utterly entranced by the lovely vision of the ship shining on the waters like a floating palace. A military band was on board, and as the night deepened, an air of enchantment enveloped the scene. Several officers came aboard to bid the president farewell, and around ten o'clock, they called upon him to make a speech. With some effort, the president rose and said, "You must excuse me, ladies and gentlemen. I am too tired to speak tonight. On next Tuesday night I will make a speech in Washington, at which time you will learn all I have to say. And now, by way of parting from the brave soldiers of our gallant army, I call upon the band to play 'Dixie.' It has always been a favorite of mine, and since we have captured it, we have a perfect right to enjoy it."

The moment he sat down, the band struck up the tune, and when the last sweet notes faded away, the listeners applauded, and to Elizabeth they seemed almost reverential, as if each understood that the great, solemn duty that had occupied them for so long was almost accomplished, but the great task of rebuilding the Union yet awaited them.

At eleven o'clock, the last farewells were spoken, those who were to remain behind disembarked, the festive lights were taken down, and the *River Queen* set out for Washington.

All the next day the steamer slowly traveled up the bay and the Potomac. To avoid debating reconstruction with Senator Sumner, the president read aloud from *Macbeth,* dwelling somberly on the Scottish king's torment. When the *River Queen* passed Mount Vernon, the marquis declared that in years to come, Mr. Lincoln's home in Illinois would be honored as reverently as President Washington's in Virginia. "Springfield," Mr. Lincoln said, and to Elizabeth his voice seemed full of quiet longing. "How happy I shall be four years hence to return there in peace and tranquility!"

The steamer arrived at the capital at six o'clock on Sunday evening, where the travelers disembarked one last time and went their separate ways. It was not quite sunset, so Elizabeth walked home alone, enjoying her solitude after so much time in the company of others. The trip had been wonderful, enlightening, but she was looking forward to crossing the threshold of her own rooms and sleeping in her own bed. As she strolled along, she observed that the streets were rather full of people for a Sunday evening, especially a Palm Sunday evening, and that bonfires were burning as if to illuminate her way home. "What's happening?" Elizabeth asked a neighbor as she turned onto Twelfth Street and spotted him taking in the scene from his front steps. "Is all this to welcome the president and First Lady home?"

"It's a celebration," he called back, "and a vigil. We're all just waiting. It won't be long now!"

Elizabeth felt a thrill of excitement and

gladness, and she almost thought she could guess his reply when she asked, "Won't be long until what?"

"Until it's over," her neighbor shouted gleefully. "General Grant cut off Lee's retreat at Appomattox Court House. The rebels are surrounded!"

CHAPTER TWELVE

April 1865

At daybreak, Elizabeth woke to a five-hundred-gun salute that shook her bed and rattled the windows. Through the walls of the boardinghouse, she heard other residents respond with sleepy cheers, and she knew at once that General Lee must have surrendered.

Quickly she dressed and went downstairs to the foyer, where Virginia, Walker, Miss Brown, Emma, and a few other neighbors were gathering to share what little news they had. "Does this mean the war is over?" Elizabeth asked, but no one could say for certain. No one knew precisely what was happening in North Carolina between General Sherman and his Confederate counterpart, General Johnston. Walker proposed heading to the telegraph office for official word, but thunderclaps had picked up where the cannons had left off, and a heavy rain was falling. Elizabeth and Virginia had no desire to venture out in the downpour, but nothing would keep Walker and Emma from satisfying their curiosity, and so they set out together.

Watching from the windows, Elizabeth estimated that thousands of others had headed out into the streets despite the storm, laughing and embracing and cheering. Elizabeth felt so lighthearted that she thought she might burst out in laughter or song, so as soon as the rain tapered off, she and Virginia gathered the Lewis girls and joined the celebration. Impromptu parades formed as civilians linked arms with soldiers and sang "Rally Round the Flag" and cheered as they followed bands marching through the muddy streets. Steam fire engines adorned with flags and bunting shrilled their whistles. Soldiers and mechanics towed a battery of six howitzers in from the navy yard and fired off salutes at whim. Elizabeth felt herself carried along with the crowd as it made its way to the White House, where she added her voice to the exultant, thankful chorus singing "The Star-Spangled Banner." Shouts rang out for the president to come and make a speech. A cheer went up when Tad poked his head out of a window, and a louder cheer followed when he waved a captured rebel flag for the crowd's amusement. Before long Mr. Lincoln himself appeared, and a great roar went up, and hundreds of hats were flung into the air. When the din subsided enough for the president to be heard, he said, "I am very greatly rejoiced to find that an occasion has occurred so pleasurable that the people cannot restrain themselves."

Elizabeth laughed and applauded along with the crowd.

"I suppose that arrangements are being made for some sort of a formal demonstration," Mr. Lincoln mused aloud, "this, or perhaps tomorrow night."

"We can't wait," someone called out.

"We want it now," another cried, and soon hundreds of other voices chimed in with their agreement.

"If there should be such a demonstration, I, of course, will be called upon to respond," Mr. Lincoln protested, "and I shall have nothing to say if you dribble it all out of me before."

His eager listeners responded with laughter and applause.

Mr. Lincoln looked out upon the crowd. "I see you have a band of music with you."

"We have two or three," a man called back.

"I propose closing up this interview by

the band performing a particular tune which I will name," Mr. Lincoln said. "Before this is done, however, I wish to mention one or two little circumstances connected with it. I have always thought 'Dixie' one of the best tunes I have ever heard. Our adversaries over the way attempted to appropriate it, but I insisted yesterday that we fairly captured it." A great shout of assent met his words. "I presented the question to the attorney general, and he gave it as his legal opinion that it is our lawful prize." As laughter and applause again rang out, the president raised his hand to the musicians. "I now request the band to favor me with its performance."

Never had Elizabeth heard the tune played more merrily. Afterward the band immediately struck up "Yankee Doodle," and the crowd clapped along.

As the last notes faded, Mr. Lincoln said, "Now give three good hearty cheers for General Grant and all under his command." The crowd did so eagerly, and Elizabeth joined in as loudly as anyone there. "Three more cheers for our gallant navy." This command too was promptly obeyed.

Then, with a modest bow, the president disappeared from the window, to the applause and whoops and shouts of the people

371

below. Shortly thereafter, word spread through the crowd that they ought to march to the Department of War next and call for Secretary Stanton to address them too, but Elizabeth, Virginia, and Emma decided to leave the throng and take the children home.

That evening, Elizabeth reflected upon Mr. Lincoln's impromptu speech at the window, and she considered that for all the years she had known him, and for all the many times they had chatted while she worked at the White House, she had never heard him make a public speech. On their last night aboard the *River Queen,* and again that day at the White House window, he had promised a formal speech for the following day. Perhaps because she regretted missing his inaugural address, she became very anxious to hear his speech, the first after General Lee's surrender.

The next morning, Mrs. Lincoln called on Elizabeth at the boardinghouse to discuss her ideas for a new gown. As she was leaving, Elizabeth asked her if she might come to the White House that night and attend the president's speech.

"Certainly, Lizzie," said Mrs. Lincoln. "If you take any interest in political speeches, come and listen in welcome."

"Thank you, Mrs. Lincoln." After a moment's hesitation, she added, "May I trespass further on your kindness by asking permission to bring a friend with me?"

"Yes, bring your friend also," Mrs. Lincoln said graciously, and then, as if she had almost forgotten, "and do come in time to dress me before the speaking commences."

"I will," Elizabeth promised. "You may rely upon that."

Mrs. Lincoln nodded and swept from the room. Moments later, through the window, Elizabeth watched her step from the house to the street, where she ascended into her carriage and drove away.

Elizabeth thought of Virginia, and she thought of Emma, and she wished that she had asked Mrs. Lincoln if two friends could accompany her. But since it was too late to amend her request, she decided to invite Emma. Her young assistant attended every speech of Mr. Lincoln's that she could, including the second inaugural address, which she had described so well for Elizabeth. Since she admired the president so much, it seemed only right to offer her the opportunity to hear him speak from a place of honor within the White House.

Thrilled, Emma immediately accepted the invitation, and so at seven o'clock, they entered the White House through the front door, as Elizabeth had done alone countless times before. On the way upstairs to Mrs. Lincoln's chamber, Elizabeth touched Emma's arm, a silent signal that they should tread softly. As they passed Mr. Lincoln's room, they slowed their pace and glanced through the half-open door. The president was seated at his desk, looking over his notes and muttering to himself, his expression thoughtful, his manner abstracted. Elizabeth paused for a moment to watch him, knowing that he was rehearsing and refining the words he would soon speak not only to the crowd gathering outside, but to the entire nation and beyond, for everyone would read his remarks in the papers in the days to come. When the president spoke, his words traveled around the world, so each one had to be selected with care.

When they reached Mrs. Lincoln's rooms, Emma waited outside while Elizabeth swiftly dressed Mrs. Lincoln in yellow silk and arranged her hair with early spring blossoms. Mr. Lincoln appeared just as Elizabeth was finishing, and they both graciously agreed to allow Elizabeth to introduce Emma to them. Elizabeth hid a smile as the young woman shook their hands and managed to chat politely with them for a brief moment, even though the unexpected honor left her quite tongue-tied.

Great crowds had gathered in front of the White House, and over the music of the Marine Band, loud, eager calls were made for the president to appear. When he finally advanced to the center window above the door, a thrilling roar went up from the throng assembled in the darkness below. Looking out from another second-story window nearby, where she and Emma stood as equals among many distinguished ladies and gentlemen, Elizabeth could scarcely breathe from amazement. She had never seen such a mass of people before, like a black, gently swelling sea in the night, the motion of the crowd like the ebb and flow of the tide upon the stranded shore of the ocean. The faces near the front were clearly discernible, but they faded into ghostly outlines farther away. Lending the scene a weird, spectral beauty was the indistinct hum of voices that rose above them all, reminiscent of the subdued, sullen roar of an ocean storm or the wind sighing through a dark, lonely forest. It was a grand, imposing scene, and when the president regarded it all with a piercing, soulful gaze as he waited for the cheers to subside, he seemed to Elizabeth more like a demigod than a mortal man.

Every window of the White House was illuminated by hundreds of tiny candles arranged in tiers on slender strips of wood, but the flickering candlelight must have seemed insufficient, for at once a cry went up for someone to fetch a lamp. When it was brought, Elizabeth heard little Tad cry, "Let me hold the light, Papa! Let me hold the light!"

Mrs. Lincoln gestured and said something that Elizabeth could not make out, but she must have asked for her son's wish to be granted, for the lamp was passed to him.

"We meet this evening, not in sorrow, but in gladness of heart," the president began, and a hush fell over his listeners. "The evacuation of Petersburg and Richmond, and the surrender of the principal insurgent army, give hope of a righteous and speedy peace whose joyous expression cannot be restrained."

Yes, Elizabeth thought, yes, and the compassion and thankfulness in his voice filled her heart until it seemed to lift her upward. Emma drew in a breath and touched Elizabeth on the arm, and Elizabeth knew that her young friend was as moved by the striking tableau as she was — father and son standing together in the presence of thousands of free citizens, the elder pronouncing eloquent ideas for the fate of a nation, the younger looking up at him with proud admiration.

Elizabeth stood not far from the president, and after he praised the military and turned to the fraught subject of reconstruction, the light from Tad's lamp fell fully upon him, so that he stood out boldly against the night. A sudden, chilling thought struck Elizabeth then, and drawing closer to Emma, she murmured, "What an easy matter it would be to kill the president, as he stands there! He could be shot down from the crowd, and no one would be able to tell who fired upon him."

Bleakly, Emma nodded. Elizabeth could hardly pay attention to the rest of the speech, so afraid was she that one of the many vicious men who had sent him violent, threatening letters lurked within the shadowed throng below. Only a few days before, Elizabeth had overheard Mrs. Lincoln requesting additional protection for her husband, and soon thereafter officers from the Metropolitan Police had been posted at the White House to handle new threats of arson, kidnapping, and other terrors. But since then, General Lee's surrender seemed to have eased Mrs. Lincoln's perpetual worries, at least a little. Even so, Elizabeth found herself seized by an intense, foreboding dread that the president's enemies had not abandoned their hatred when General Lee conceded defeat at Appomattox.

Suddenly Emma clutched her arm, and a smile lit up her face. Pulled from her dark reverie, Elizabeth quickly picked up the threads of the president's speech. "It is also unsatisfactory to some that the elective franchise is not given to the colored man," Mr. Lincoln said, referring to criticism of the new Louisiana state constitution. "I would myself prefer that it were now conferred on the very intelligent, and on those who serve our cause as soldiers."

Elizabeth managed just in time to muffle a gasp. Unless her ears were deceiving her, the president had just told the world that he approved of enfranchisement for black Union soldiers and certain other men of color.

"Can he mean it?" Emma asked in a whisper. "Will our men be permitted to vote?"

"I think they will be," Elizabeth whispered in reply, a thrill of excitement putting a tremble in her voice. Perhaps that would be only the beginning. Perhaps the lady suffragists would finally have their way too. Elizabeth could imagine the obstacles tumbling over one after the other like books on a too-crowded shelf: First colored soldiers would be allowed to vote, and then prominent black men, and then all black men, and then white women, and last of all but finally, women of color like her and Emma and Virginia. It could happen. Some people had said that slavery would be with them forever, and yet it had been abolished. Good people with strong convictions could overturn any injustice if they simply refused to quit. But even as she took heart, Elizabeth could not forget that the march to justice had ever been arduous and long, and the changes she yearned for might not come within her lifetime.

But she had already witnessed so many remarkable events since coming to Washington City. Why might not universal suffrage be another?

Elizabeth's thoughts were still full of the night's splendors when she went to the White House the following Saturday, and yet, after thanking Mrs. Lincoln for allowing her and Emma to attend, something compelled her to mention the sudden apprehension she had felt when Mr. Lincoln stood dangerously illuminated and vulnerable before the crowd.

"Yes, yes, Mr. Lincoln's life is always exposed," Mrs. Lincoln agreed, sighing. "Ah, no one knows what it is to live in constant dread of some fearful tragedy. The president has been warned so often that I tremble for him on every public occasion. I have a presentiment that he will meet with a sudden and violent end."

"I suppose it is only natural that you should worry," said Elizabeth, thinking again of the dreadful letters Mr. Lincoln received nearly every day. Mrs. Lincoln received her fair share too, though not as many as her husband.

Mrs. Lincoln shook her head. "I said *presentiment.* I'm not speaking of ordinary worries and fears that might plague anyone in my circumstances, any wife whose husband has made enemies. The sensation is much too powerful for that."

Mrs. Lincoln seemed so certain, so despondent, that Elizabeth wished she had never encouraged her when she had consulted spiritualists after Willie's death. Surely one of them had planted this sepulchral notion in her head when she was tormented with grief.

She was quiet too long, for Mrs. Lincoln frowned and said, "I know that look. You think I'm being foolish, but you're too polite to say so. Well, what would you think if I told you Mr. Lincoln shares my beliefs?"

"I — would not know what to think," said Elizabeth, taken aback.

"He has had several premonitions himself." Mrs. Lincoln pressed her lips together and inhaled deeply, and a furrow appeared between her brows. "The first came to him a few days after the election in 1860, when we were still in Springfield. The weight of his new responsibilities was settling upon him, and he was having trouble sleeping. He was in his office chamber reclining on a lounge, when his gaze fell upon the mirror and he saw his image reflected with two faces, one much paler than the other. He was very unsettled by the sight, and little wonder. I believe the vision meant that he would be elected twice, but not live out his second term."

Shaken, Elizabeth nonetheless mustered up enough skepticism to ask, "Mr. Lincoln himself believes this was a vision, not merely a trick of the light upon a poor glass and weary eyes?"

"Well, if he did not say so, it was evident from his manner. But there have been others. He has a strange recurring dream preceding events of great significance. He describes himself as aboard a ship — he

381

cannot describe it but he knows it always to be the same vessel — moving swiftly toward a dark and indefinite shore. He had this dream before Antietam, Murfreesboro, Gettysburg, and Vicksburg."

"Goodness." Elizabeth shivered as if Mrs. Lincoln's very words carried a chill. "But if this dream is somehow prophetic, it seems to presage victory, not death."

"I suppose that's true." Suddenly tears sprang into Mrs. Lincoln's eyes. "But I have not yet told you the worst of his dreams. I truly wish he had never told me."

"Why, Mrs. Lincoln." Alarmed, Elizabeth took her by the elbow and guided her to a seat on the sofa. "Perhaps we've dwelt too long on this subject —"

"No. No. I've begun and I must tell you the rest." Mrs. Lincoln took out her handkerchief, dabbed at her eyes, and distractedly twisted the fine white cloth into a rope on her lap. "Only a few days ago, Mr. Lincoln and I were chatting with his guard Mr. Lamon and a few others when the conversation turned to the abundance of dreams in the Bible. 'If we believe the Bible,' my husband said, 'we must accept the fact that in the old days God and His angels came to men in their sleep and made themselves known in dreams.' When I asked what had

382

prompted the remark, he first asserted that he did not believe in dreams, and then he went on to describe a dream that he'd had a few nights before, and which has strangely annoyed him ever since."

"What was this dream?" asked Elizabeth uneasily, though she almost didn't want to know.

"He told us that about ten days before, he had retired very late because he had been up waiting for important dispatches from the front. He was not long in bed when he fell into a weary slumber and began to dream. He said there seemed to be a death-like stillness about him, and then he heard subdued sobs, as if a number of people were weeping. In the dream he left his bed and wandered downstairs, where the silence was broken by the same pitiful sobbing, but the mourners were invisible. Though he searched from room to room, and saw no one, the same mournful sounds of distress met him everywhere he went. The rooms were lit, and every object was familiar, but where were all the people who were grieving as if their hearts would break? He became puzzled and alarmed, wondering what could be the meaning of all this. Determined to find the cause of circumstances so mysterious and so shocking, he

kept on until he arrived at the East Room
— where he met with a sickening surprise.
Before him was a catafalque, on which
rested a corpse wrapped in funeral vest-
ments. Soldiers were standing guard all
around while throngs of people gazed
mournfully upon the deceased, whose face
was covered, and some wept pitifully. 'Who
is dead in the White House?' my husband
demanded of one of the soldiers. 'The
president,' came the answer. 'He was killed
by an assassin.' Then a loud, terrible wail of
grief went up from the mourners and woke
him."

"How dreadful," exclaimed Elizabeth. No
wonder the president had grown so gaunt
and weary, if such terrible imaginings
plagued him at night. "But, Mrs. Lincoln,
you must not fear that this nightmare will
come to pass."

Mrs. Lincoln regarded her flatly. "You said
yourself that it would have been an easy
matter for an assassin to kill him as he stood
at that window last night."

And how Elizabeth regretted saying so.
"What I mean is that you should not believe
that these are anything more than troubled
dreams. They are not glimpses into the
future. It would be astonishing if Mr. Lincoln did *not* have nightmares prompted by

the threats made against him — in fact, it is a testament to his strength that he does not have more of them."

Mrs. Lincoln looked as if she wished she could believe her. "I've ordered the guards increased, but I don't know what else I could —"

She broke off abruptly as the door opened and Mr. Lincoln entered. Mrs. Lincoln quickly composed herself, but something in Mr. Lincoln's expression told Elizabeth that he had detected her mood in that brief interval before she concealed it. He greeted them, peered curiously at them for a moment, and went to the window, where he gazed out upon the yard, smiling. "Madam Elizabeth," he said suddenly, turning to her. "You are fond of pets, are you not?"

"Oh, yes, sir," she answered.

"Well, come here and look at my two goats."

Elizabeth caught Mrs. Lincoln's eye; she discreetly nodded and gestured for Elizabeth to go ahead. When she stood beside him at the window, he nodded to the goats frolicking on the grass below. "I believe they are the kindest and best goats in the world," he declared, his eyes twinkling with good humor. "See how they sniff the clear air, and skip and play in the sunshine. Whew!

What a jump," he exclaimed as one of the goats bounded high over a stony patch. "Madam Elizabeth, did you ever before see such an active goat?"

She smiled. "Not that I can recall, sir."

"He feeds on my bounty, and jumps for joy," Mr. Lincoln mused. "Do you think we should call him a bounty-jumper?"

Elizabeth laughed at his play on words. "If you'd like to, Mr. President, I don't see why not."

"But I flatter the bounty-jumper," he said. "My goat is far above him. I would rather wear his horns and hairy coat through life, than demean myself to the level of the man who plunders the National Treasury in the name of patriotism." A sudden shadow fell over his face. "The man who enlists into the service for a consideration, and deserts the moment he receives his money but to repeat the play, is bad enough, but the men who manipulate the grand machine and who simply make the bounty-jumper their agent in an outrageous fraud are far worse. They are beneath the worms that crawl in the dark hidden places of earth."

Before Elizabeth could reply that with the national draft ended, the bounty hunters would no longer be able to profit as they had, both goats looked up at the window and shook their heads in a friendly sort of way. "See, Madam Elizabeth?" said the president, brightening. "My pets recognize me. How earnestly they look. There they go again; what jolly fun!" He laughed out loud as the goats bounded swiftly to the other side of the yard.

"Come, Lizzie," Mrs. Lincoln called out sharply. "If I want to get ready to go down this evening I must finish dressing myself, or you must stop staring at those silly goats."

Elizabeth exchanged a quick look of understanding with the president before hurrying back to Mrs. Lincoln. The First Lady was not overly fond of pets, and she could not understand why Mr. Lincoln took such delight in his goats. Elizabeth would never say so, but she thought Mrs. Lincoln ought to be glad for any pleasant distraction Mr. Lincoln found from his cares. His goats, his favorite authors, conversations with intelligent friends, and the occasional night at the theater were rare respites from the unrelenting pressures of his high office.

Elizabeth finished dressing Mrs. Lincoln quickly, unconcerned with her patron's frown of annoyance. It would fade soon enough, and in the meantime, Elizabeth would rather have Mrs. Lincoln irritable than anxious and brooding over dark,

387

imagined omens, the cruel offspring of a mind weary from strain and sorrow and too much toil.

A few days later, early on the morning of Good Friday, Elizabeth walked to the White House with the bodice, skirt, and sleeves of a new spring frock to fit for Mrs. Lincoln, an embroidered French muslin with cap sleeves and a delicate lace trim around the neckline. Already the First Lady was looking forward to moving to the Soldiers' Home for the summer, where she hoped her husband would rest and regain his vigorous good health. The war had demanded much of him, and reconstruction would likely demand more, but as General Sherman advanced in North Carolina, it seemed that the war would soon end, at long last. The worst was certainly behind them.

Elizabeth turned onto Fifteenth Street just as colored soldiers marched past flanking columns of captured rebel troops. Onlookers did not mock them, but instead offered them sympathetic glances or pretended not to notice them rather than add to their disgrace. They could have hurled insults — or bricks, if they were truly vengeful — but most Washingtonians seemed to feel as Elizabeth did, that these unfortunate captives surely wanted only to go home, just as Northern fathers, sons, brothers, and sweethearts wanted more than anything else to return to their families. With the war so near its conclusion, and the outcome certain, everyone wanted nothing more than for it to end before any more blood was shed.

The sight of colored soldiers guarding white Confederate prisoners was no longer uncommon, and yet Elizabeth halted and watched the columns and guards pass, marveling. How the city had changed during the past four years — and even just in the past week. The exuberant rejoicing of the first days after General Lee's surrender had settled into a calm sense of hope, gratitude, and peace, despite the ever-present concerns about what yet lay ahead. In all but the most radical, punitive hearts, Mr. Lincoln's recent speech had inspired a mood of forgiveness and clemency. Elizabeth thought of the old friends she had seen in Petersburg the previous week, and all those she had known in Virginia and Missouri and even North Carolina, where she had been subjected to such torment, and she hoped the president's plans for reconstruction would treat them gently.

At the White House, she was pleased to find Mrs. Lincoln in a cheerful mood.

Captain Robert Lincoln and General Grant had arrived that morning from Virginia, and over breakfast Robert had given his parents his firsthand account of General Lee's surrender at Appomattox. "What a momentous occasion it was," Mrs. Lincoln remarked as Elizabeth helped her into the skirt and bodice, "and how fitting that the son of the president was there to witness it."

Mrs. Lincoln was in especially good spirits, not only because Robert was home and safe, and not only because the previous night Mr. Lincoln had again dreamed of the ship carrying him swiftly toward a distant shore, a dream that he believed foretold General Sherman's imminent victory against General Johnston in North Carolina. "My husband sent me a note this morning," she confided, "inviting me to go for a drive this afternoon."

Elizabeth had to smile. "He sent you a note? Wouldn't it have been faster simply to ask you as you went in to breakfast together?"

"Faster, but not half so charming," rejoined Mrs. Lincoln. "It reminds me of the days of our courtship back in Springfield. We've endured so much since then that it's often difficult to recall what it felt like to be young sweethearts."

Smiling, Elizabeth adjusted the neckline of the dress, slipping one pin and then another in place. "Perhaps a pleasant day together will help you remember."

"We both need a pleasant, restful day for other reasons besides, but I fear that my husband is not likely to see one today."

"Why not? Isn't he entitled to a little holiday on Good Friday?"

"If you could persuade him of that, you would have my undying gratitude. Since breakfast he has been sitting through conferences with legislators and petitioners, and after that his cabinet will be meeting. I may not see him at all until this afternoon — at which point I will insist that he have a proper luncheon before our ride instead of merely munching an apple at his desk. He grows gaunt and gray and people blame me for not feeding him enough."

"They should blame the White House cook before you," remarked Elizabeth, "but even that is unfair."

Mrs. Lincoln heartily agreed, but at that moment her disappointment that she might not see her husband until later vanished, because Mr. Lincoln strode into the room. "I've been to the War Department," he told his wife after greeting them both. "I saw General Eckert there, and told him of our plans to attend the theater tonight, and I invited him to come along."

Mrs. Lincoln's eyebrows rose. "Did you? Well, I suppose there's room in the box for him and us and General and Mrs. Grant too."

Mr. Lincoln flung himself onto the sofa. "There is, Mother, but we won't need it, because General Eckert cannot join us."

Mrs. Lincoln's laughter carried the slightest hint of amused exasperation. "Then why mention it at all?"

"I thought you liked me to tell you every detail of my day."

Mr. Lincoln looked as if he might tease her more, but just then Robert entered carrying a small portrait. "Here it is, Father," Robert said, handing him the object. "General Robert E. Lee, as promised."

"Yes, thank you, son." Mr. Lincoln set the picture on the table before him and studied the general's visage thoughtfully. "It is a good face; it is the face of a noble, brave man."

"I think it's a fine likeness," said Robert, clearly pleased with himself.

Mr. Lincoln nodded appreciatively and then looked up at him from beneath raised brows. "Well, my son, you have returned safely from the front. The war is now closed, and we will soon live in peace with the brave men that have been fighting against us. I trust that the era of good feeling has returned with the end of the war, and that henceforth we shall live in peace."

"Amen," Elizabeth murmured, so softly that not even Mrs. Lincoln heard her.

"Now listen to me, Robert," the president continued. "You must lay aside your uniform and return to college. I wish you to read law for three years, and at the end of that time I hope that we will be able to tell whether you will make a lawyer or not."

"Yes, sir," said Robert solemnly, and his father rose and shook his hand, looking more cheerful than Elizabeth had seen him in a long time.

Elizabeth was happy to see the family enjoying a moment of domestic harmony after so much strife and worry. It *was* scarcely a moment, though; Mr. Lincoln hurried off soon thereafter to attend the meeting of his cabinet, and Robert left too, perhaps to rejoin General Grant. Alone again, Elizabeth and Mrs. Lincoln resumed fitting the dress, and they were not quite finished when a servant came in with a message from General and Mrs. Grant, explaining that they had decided to visit their children in New Jersey and would be unable to accompany the Lincolns to the theater. "How disappointing that they would cancel on such short notice," said Mrs. Lincoln, flinging the letter on the table. "Lately Mrs. Grant seems to seize upon any excuse to avoid spending time in my company."

Elizabeth could hardly blame the general's wife for that, considering how Mrs. Lincoln had unfairly castigated her in the carriage at City Point. "Could you invite another couple instead?"

"It would be a waste of paper and ink to try. Who would be free at this late hour?"

"Who would not eagerly abandon other plans for the honor of sharing the presidential box with Mr. and Mrs. Lincoln?"

"General and Mrs. Grant, evidently," Mrs. Lincoln retorted, but as Elizabeth continued to adjust and pin her dress, she reconsidered. "I suppose we could find other guests, and if not, I wouldn't mind keeping my husband all to myself for a change."

"To yourself, and hundreds of other theatergoers," Elizabeth reminded her, and was pleased to see Mrs. Lincoln smile.

Later, as Elizabeth packed up her things, she asked, "Do you want me to come back later to dress you for the theater?"

"Well —" Mrs. Lincoln hesitated. "I think

not. I'm not altogether certain we shall go after all. I feel a headache coming on, and Mr. Lincoln has been worn out from unrelenting toil. I suppose we shall decide after our ride, but I don't want to oblige you in the meantime."

"If you decide you need me," Elizabeth reminded her, "you know you can always send for me."

Mrs. Lincoln smiled, grateful. "Yes, Elizabeth. I know."

Elizabeth woke abruptly in the dark of night to an incessant pounding on her door. "Mrs. Keckley," someone called. "Mrs. Keckley, please get up!"

Disoriented, Elizabeth sat up, groped for her dressing gown, and pulled it on. The pounding and calling persisted as she climbed from bed and hastened to the door. "Miss Brown?" she said, confused, as she discovered her boardinghouse neighbor in the hall. "What's the matter? Is there a fire?"

"No, no, not a fire, but terrible news, terrible news!" Miss Brown wrung her hands, tears on her cheeks. "Mr. Lincoln has been shot, and the entire cabinet has been assassinated!"

Elizabeth's heart lurched. "Assassinated?" Images of the men she had seen through the years at the White House — smiling, scowling, whispering urgently in corners, striding intently about the president's business, laughing at his stories — flew through her mind. Her blood felt as if it had been frozen in her veins, and her lungs as if they would collapse for want of air. "Dear God, all of them dead? And Mr. Lincoln? Was he badly hurt?"

Miss Brown shook her head. "No, praise heaven. He was not mortally wounded."

"Oh, thank God. And Mrs. Lincoln?"

"Unharmed — at least, I have heard nothing about any injury done to her."

Heart pounding, Elizabeth thanked her neighbor and hurried back into her room to dress. It was after eleven o'clock, but sleep had fled, and she could not bear to sit patiently awaiting news when it felt as if the house could not contain her. She dashed outside, where the streets were full of wondering, fear-struck people. Rumors flew thick and fast, some confirming Miss Brown's account, others contradicting it, still more offering even wilder, more terrible reports. Elizabeth grew ever more frustrated and frightened until worry compelled her back indoors, where she woke Walker and Virginia and told them the president had been shot. "I must go to the

White House," she said, her voice breaking. "I cannot remain in this state of uncertainty."

"Elizabeth, dear," said Virginia, her face stricken beneath her muslin nightcap. "You must calm yourself. Mr. Lincoln must be recovering just fine, or the bells would be tolling all over the city."

"Virginia's right," said Walker, but he too looked apprehensive. "You've had a shock. Go back to sleep. You can call on Mrs. Lincoln first thing in the morning."

"No, no." Elizabeth shook her head, her heart jumping and fluttering like a trapped bird in her chest. "I must go to her now. Even if the president was only slightly injured, Mrs. Lincoln will be upset, and she will want me."

The Lewises exchanged a silent look, and then Walker agreed that Elizabeth should go, but she should not go alone. Elizabeth paced in the foyer while the couple dressed and told Jane to look after her younger sisters. It seemed an eternity until Virginia and Walker joined her and they headed out into the night. They made their way swiftly through the milling throng, scores of confused and alarmed people questioning one another and repeating rumors and sometimes breaking into loud, gasping sobs. On the way through Lafayette Square, they passed the residence of Secretary Seward and were shocked to find it surrounded by armed soldiers, bayonets drawn to keep back all intruders. Alarm quickening their pace, they hurried on until they reached the White House and found it too surrounded by soldiers. Every entrance was strongly guarded, and no one was permitted to pass.

Elizabeth drew herself up, summoned all her strength of will, and addressed a guard at the gate firmly. "I am Mrs. Elizabeth Keckley, the First Lady's personal modiste and friend. If she is in distress, she will want me."

The soldier ignored her, his gaze moving steadily over the crowd gathering in front of the White House, his grip tightening around his rifle. Elizabeth felt Virginia nudge her discreetly, and so she quickly took another breath and said, "Ask the doorman who I am. I am here at the White House several times a week. He will know me."

The soldier again ignored her, but another standing a few feet away took pity on her. "I'm sorry, ma'am, but no one is allowed to enter tonight."

Quickly, desperately, Elizabeth whirled upon him. "Would you please have the doorman send word to Mrs. Lincoln that I am here? I know she will tell you to let me in."

The guard, a red-haired, freckled lad little older than George would have been, shook his head. "She isn't here, and the president hasn't been brought home either."

The first guard sucked in his breath through his teeth and glared at the red-haired soldier, who promptly tore his gaze away from Elizabeth and snapped to attention. Neither of them would say anything more, so reluctantly, and with an increasing sense of sickening dread, Elizabeth, Virginia, and Walker left the White House. As they made their way through the milling throng toward home, Elizabeth felt weak from grief and anxiety. A few blocks along, she glimpsed a gray-haired elderly man passing, and something of the kindness and sorrow in his expression compelled her to reach out, touch his arm gently, and imploringly ask, "Will you please, sir, tell me whether Mr. Lincoln is dead?"

"Not dead," he said, "but dying. God help us!" With a heavy step he continued on his mournful way.

"Not dead but dying," said Virginia, her voice trembling. "Then indeed, God help us all!"

Eventually, in bits and fragments they collected on their way to Twelfth Street, they assembled the shocking story. The president lay mortally wounded, some said in a residence across the street from Ford's Theatre, but no one knew for certain. The popular actor John Wilkes Booth had stolen into the president's private box while he watched the performance with Mrs. Lincoln and their guests, and had shot him in the back of the head. Mr. Lincoln was not expected to live until morning.

Hearts crushed and broken, Elizabeth, Virginia, and Walker returned home.

Once there, Elizabeth could not sleep. She imagined Mrs. Lincoln wild with grief and wanted to go to her, but she did not know where she might be, and she had no choice but to wait until morning. Never had the nighttime hours dragged so slowly. Every minute seemed an eternity, and Elizabeth could do nothing but pace and wait and watch the eastern sky through her window for the coming of dawn, hugging her arms to her chest as if warding off a bitter wind.

Morning came at last, gray and somber. At half past seven, a distant church bell began to toll, and then another joined it, and another, until all the bells in Washington resounded with the terrible news. The president was dead, Elizabeth thought numbly, and then a sob escaped from her throat, and she flung herself onto her bed, anguished and weeping. She covered her ears with clenched fists, but nothing would block out the mournful sound.

She lay there still, exhausted and drained, at eleven o'clock, when a carriage drove up to the boardinghouse and a messenger rapped on her door. "I come from Mrs. Lincoln," he said. "If you are Mrs. Keckley, come with me immediately to the White House."

Elizabeth hastily threw on her shawl and bonnet, and within moments she was seated in the carriage and speeding toward the White House through a cold and dismal rain. The gas streetlamps were usually extinguished by that time of day, but that morning they had been left burning. The streets were unnaturally hushed for a late Saturday morning. Flags hung in cheerless folds at half-staff, and here and there, shops and houses were draped in black crepe. A lone sentry paced back and forth in front of a house, and in front of another farther along, and after a moment of bewilderment Elizabeth recognized the residences as those belonging to cabinet members. Miss Brown had been mistaken when she had told Elizabeth that they had all been assassinated, but at nearly the same time Mr. Lincoln was shot, Secretary Seward had been attacked in his own home, in bed where he lay recovering from a carriage accident. If not for the neck brace he wore due to his injuries, he likely would have been stabbed to death. As it was, he had been terribly wounded and might yet perish, and no one could say what plots against the other secretaries had been thwarted, had been abandoned, or had yet to be enacted.

Soon the carriage reached the White House, where Elizabeth saw hundreds of colored folks, mostly women and children, milling about on the lawn, weeping and lamenting their loss. Unlike the previous night, this time she easily passed through the gate and by the guards and up to the very front door, but once she crossed the threshold into the silent, somber house, she felt as if a heavy shroud of grief had been draped over her shoulders. Steeling herself, she removed her bonnet and hurried upstairs, but Mrs. Lincoln was not in her bedroom, nor in the family sitting room. Before long, a servant with red-rimmed eyes guided her to a small spare bedroom that had been made up for Mr. Lincoln to use during the summer, when the family resided mostly at the Soldiers' Home and Mr. Lincoln spent only occasional nights alone at the mansion. "The First Lady refused to be taken into any of the family bedrooms," the servant confided. Elizabeth thought of how Mrs. Lincoln still avoided the room where her son Willie had been laid out for his funeral, and she understood why Mrs. Lincoln could not have gone to the chambers she had shared with her husband.

Elizabeth hesitated with her hand on the door, taking deep breaths to push back the sorrow that threatened to rise up and choke her. When she had composed herself, she entered the room and plunged into darkness. Her eyes adjusted, and she made out the dim shapes of a woman tossing and turning restlessly upon the bed, and another sitting in a chair by the window, where the curtains had been drawn so barely a beam of pale sunshine leaked in. After a moment Elizabeth recognized Mrs. Mary Jane Welles, the wife of the secretary of the navy and one of her patrons. Nodding to her, Elizabeth hurried to Mrs. Lincoln's bedside and murmured her name.

"Elizabeth?" Mrs. Lincoln's voice was the barest of whispers. "You have come at last?"

Elizabeth took her hand. "Yes, Mrs. Lincoln. I'm here."

Mrs. Lincoln slowly rolled over and looked

up at her bleakly, her eyes red and swollen, her cheeks pale, her expression shocked and haggard. "Why did you not come to me last night, Elizabeth? I sent for you."

Elizabeth blinked back tears. "I did try to come to you, but —" She fought to keep her voice steady as she lay her palm upon Mrs. Lincoln's brow, which felt strangely feverish to the touch. "I could not find you."

"I sent three messengers."

"I'm sorry." Elizabeth sat down on the edge of the bed, clutching Mrs. Lincoln's hand in both of hers. "I did come. I did come, but you weren't here."

"They did not bring us here." Mrs. Lincoln's voice was distant, disbelieving. "They took my husband across the street from the theater to Mr. Peterson's boardinghouse. My husband was too tall for the bed. They had to lay him upon it diagonally." She choked on a sob and began to keen.

"Hush now," Elizabeth said, stroking her brow. "Hush."

While Elizabeth soothed her, Mrs. Welles, who did not look at all well and had left her own sickbed to answer Mrs. Lincoln's summons, quietly excused herself and departed for home, entrusting Mrs. Lincoln to Elizabeth. She was nearly exhausted from grief, but Elizabeth endeavored to calm her. After she had quieted, Elizabeth gently asked if she might go pay her respects. When Mrs. Lincoln nodded, Elizabeth slipped her hand free and quietly left the darkened chamber and went alone to the guest room, where the president lay in state. As she crossed the threshold, heart pounding and legs trembling, she suddenly recalled the sight of young Willie Lincoln lying in his coffin in the same place where his father's body now lay in repose. In her mind's eye she watched again as the president wept over the pale, beloved face of his boy, and she thought of how kindly Mr. Lincoln had spoken to her the last time she saw him alive, how generously and respectfully he had described the vanquished General Lee. The Moses of her people had fallen in the hour of his triumph. His tragic death was all the more heartbreaking because he had not lived to enjoy the peace he had toiled so long to achieve.

Several members of the president's cabinet, a few army officers, and other dignitaries were grouped around the body of their fallen chief, some weeping openly, but they made room for her as she approached. Reverently she lifted the white cloth from the pale face of the man that she had so greatly admired — not merely admired, but looked upon as someone as divine as he was human. Her pounding heart grew calm as she looked upon his face; notwithstanding the violence done to him, she discovered something beautiful as well as grandly solemn in his expression — the sweetness and gentleness of childhood, the stately grandeur of inspired intellect. She gazed long upon him, until she was obliged to turn away, her vision blurred by tears, her throat constricted in grief.

Fighting to regain her composure, she returned to Mrs. Lincoln's room to find her in a new paroxysm of grief — wailing, keening, convulsing terribly. Robert bent over her, murmuring, his expression pained and tender, while young Tad crouched at the foot of his mother's bed, his face a world of agony. Elizabeth quickly went to her and bathed her brow with cool water, struggling to soothe the violent tempest as best she could. Tad's grief was no less than his mother's, but her frightening outbursts had shocked him into silence. Suddenly he threw his arms around her. "Don't cry, Mama," he begged, his voice muffled as he pressed his face against her neck. "Don't cry, or you will make me cry too! You will break my heart."

Mrs. Lincoln could not bear to hear her youngest son cry, and with a great effort, she clasped him to her heart and struggled to calm herself, but she could not restrain her grief for long, and soon it burst forth again, alarming and heart wrenching to behold.

In the days following the assassination, every room in the White House was darkened, every voice low and subdued, every footstep heavy and muffled. Mrs. Lincoln sequestered herself in the small guest room with the curtains drawn, sometimes silent, sometimes weeping or shrieking. She could not bear to view her husband's body, but the construction of a tall platform in the East Room to display her husband's coffin intruded upon her seclusion. "When will they be finished?" she asked through clenched teeth, sitting up in bed, rocking back in forth in misery. "Every nail they drive is like a pistol shot."

On April 17, the president's casket was set upon the finished catafalque beneath a black canopy, mirrors and chandeliers draped with black crepe, seats on risers covered in black cloth erected for the mourners. The mood was hushed and somber as an honor guard of two generals and ten other officers kept watch day and night. Nearly twenty-five thousand people passed through the East Room to pay their respects the following day, and on April 19, invited guests returned for the funeral service. Mrs. Lincoln and Tad could not bear to attend, but Robert did, the sole representative of the family. Elizabeth wanted to see the president one last time before he was laid to rest, but Mrs. Lincoln needed her more, so she remained at her side.

After the service, a funeral procession carried the president's remains to the Capitol, where he lay in state in the rotunda so that thousands more could file past and pay their respects. On Friday, April 21, nearly a week after the president's death, a nine-car funeral train bedecked with bunting, crepe, and a portrait of Mr. Lincoln on the cowcatcher left Washington on a seventeen-hundred-mile journey westward to Springfield, carrying three hundred passengers and the remains of the president and his young son Willie. The Lincoln Special traveled at only five to twenty miles per hour out of respect for the thousands of mourners who had assembled along the rail lines, lighting the way with bonfires at night. The train made scheduled stops in twelve cities, where tens of thousands gathered to mourn and to bid farewell to their fallen leader.

For six weeks Elizabeth remained at the White House with the distraught widow, sleeping on a lounge in her chamber at night, comforting and soothing her as best she could throughout the long, sorrowful days, rarely leaving her side. Mrs. Lincoln's closest friends in Washington, Mrs. Mary Jane Welles and Mrs. Elizabeth Blair Lee, attended her sometimes too, but she denied admittance to nearly everyone else. The new president, Mr. Andrew Johnson, did not try to come to see her, nor did he send even so much as a brief note to express his sympathies. It was said that on that terrible night he had tried to enter the Peterson residence to see the president on his deathbed but had been turned away lest the sight of him upset the First Lady. However much that might have offended him, in Elizabeth's opinion, the only right, respectful, and dignified thing to do was to put aside his hurt feelings for the sake of the grieving widow. At first Elizabeth attributed his neglect to the demands of his sudden elevation to head of state, but as time went on and he still sent no condolences, she became appalled and indignant. She only hoped that Mrs. Lincoln in her sorrow would not take notice of his inexplicable affront.

Mrs. Lincoln did not often speak of Mr. Booth, her husband's murderer, but Elizabeth knew she brooded over who else might have been complicit in the assassination. A new messenger had accompanied the Lincolns to the theater that terrible night, and it had been his duty to stand at the closed door of the box throughout the performance, guarding the president and his party from intrusion. It soon came to light that this new messenger had become engrossed in the play, and had neglected his duty and gone off to watch it, allowing Mr. Booth easy admission to the box. Mrs. Lincoln had convinced herself that this man was implicated in the plot against her husband.

One evening, Elizabeth was lying on her lounge near Mrs. Lincoln's bed when a servant entered the room and Mrs. Lincoln asked her who was on watch that night.

"Mr. Parker, madam," she replied. "The new messenger."

"What?" Mrs. Lincoln exclaimed. "The man who attended us to the theater on the night my dear, good husband was murdered! He, I believe, is one of the murderers. Tell him to come in to me."

From Mr. Parker's wide-eyed and wary expression upon entering, Elizabeth knew he had overheard Mrs. Lincoln's words through the door, which had been left ajar.

"So you are on guard tonight," Mrs. Lincoln fiercely addressed him. "On guard in the White House after helping to murder my husband!"

"Pardon me, but I did not help to murder the president," Mr. Parker protested, trembling. "I could never stoop to murder — much less to the murder of so good and great a man as the president."

"But it appears that you *did* stoop to murder."

"No, no! Don't say that," he pleaded. "God knows that I am innocent."

"I don't believe you. Why were you not at the door to keep the assassin out when he rushed into the box?"

"I — I did wrong, I admit," he stammered, "and I have bitterly repented it, but I did not help to kill the president. I did not believe that anyone would try to kill so good a man in such a public place, and the belief made me careless. I was attracted by the play, and did not see the assassin enter the box."

"But you should have seen him," Mrs. Lincoln snapped. "You had no business to be careless. I shall always believe that you are guilty. Hush!" she exclaimed as he attempted to reply. "I shan't hear another word. Go now and keep your watch." She dismissed him with an imperious wave of her hand. White-faced and stiff, Mr. Parker

411

turned and left the room. As soon as the door closed behind him, Mrs. Lincoln fell back upon her pillow, covered her face with her hands, and burst into sobs.

Robert Lincoln was tender and solicitous of his mother in her grief, but his haggard looks revealed that he suffered greatly and shouldered his new responsibilities as head of the household heavily, though he never failed to put up a brave, strong front in his mother's presence. Robert endured his mother's fits of anguish better than his poor younger brother, who had lost one parent to death and feared losing another to grief. Often at night, when the bereft Tad was awakened by his mother's sobs, he would pad down the hall from his room to hers and climb into her bed. "Don't cry, Mama," he would say, hugging her tightly. "I cannot sleep if you cry! Papa was good, and he has gone to heaven. He is happy there. He is with God and brother Willie. Don't cry, Mama, or I will cry too." And Mrs. Lincoln would again endeavor to stop crying for his sake.

Elizabeth's heart went out to the boy. He and his father had adored each other, but as much as Mr. Lincoln had doted on him, especially after losing Willie, Tad had never grown spoiled. Despite his youth, he had seemed to understand that he was the son of a president, and that this had bestowed upon him both privileges and responsibilities. Early one morning, Elizabeth passed by his room when his nurse was dressing him. "Pa is dead," she heard him say to his nurse soberly. "I can hardly believe that I shall never see him again. I must learn to take care of myself now."

Her heart aching for him, Elizabeth drew closer to the door to listen.

"Yes, Pa is dead," he went on, mournful and matter-of-fact, "and I am only Tad Lincoln now, little Tad, like other little boys. I am not a president's son now. I won't have many presents anymore." He sighed, a soft and forlorn sound. "Well, I will try and be a good boy, and will hope to go someday to Pa and brother Willie, in heaven."

Elizabeth pressed her lips together and hurried on before she broke down. She had to be brave. Mr. Lincoln would have wanted her to be strong for his wife and family. It was the last service she could do for him, and she could not bear to fail.

Mr. Lincoln's sons understood the practical matter of their new circumstances sooner than their mother, whose grief had consumed her every thought, waking and sleeping, since her husband's death. President Johnson, in a singular act of generosity, had allowed the grieving family to remain in the White House while he lived under guard at a residence on Fifteenth and H streets and worked out of a small office in the Treasury Building. Eventually, however, Mrs. Lincoln realized that his patience would not last forever, and she had to prepare to leave.

"God, Elizabeth," she once exclaimed, after the bleak awareness dawned, "what a change! Did ever a woman have to suffer so much and experience so great a change? I had an ambition to be Mrs. President; that ambition has been gratified, and now I must step down from the pedestal. My poor husband! Had he never been president, he might be living today. Alas! All is over with me!"

Elizabeth tried to comfort her, but her words rang hollow, and she knew it.

Mrs. Lincoln folded her arms and rocked herself back and forth. "My God, Elizabeth, I can never go back to Springfield! No, never, until I go in my shroud to be laid by my dear husband's side, and may heaven speed that day! I should like to live for my sons, but life is so full of misery that I would rather die."

Keening, she pressed her fists against her

eyes and wept hysterically, and although Elizabeth desperately wished to give her solace, she knew nothing she could do would suffice, nothing she could say would bring her peace. Time would do what she could not, Elizabeth hoped grimly, as she watched and waited by Mrs. Lincoln's side.

CHAPTER THIRTEEN

May–June 1865

Mrs. Lincoln could not bear to go to Springfield, but she had to go somewhere.

Some of Mr. Lincoln's closest friends urged her to return to Springfield, to the home she still owned there, at least until her husband's estate was settled. He had died without a will, so although his property would eventually go to his wife and children, they would not receive their shares of his estate until the legal knots were untangled. Mrs. Lincoln adamantly rejected the idea of returning to Springfield. She had burned too many bridges in her former hometown and had become the subject of gossip. She was estranged, at least in part, from her sisters and half sisters, even Little Sister Emilie and the faithful Elizabeth Edwards. Most of all, as she confided to Elizabeth, she could not bear to set foot in her once-happy home on Eighth and Jackson, where she knew she would be tormented by memories of the early years of her marriage and the husband and children she had lost. But Elizabeth knew, as the well-meaning gentlemen did not, that Mrs. Lincoln also had to take care to find a residence she could afford, since her debts to her favorite stores had climbed to at least seventy thousand dollars. Elizabeth thought it a blessing that Mr. Lincoln had not learned of his wife's debts before he died, and had been spared that anger and embarrassment.

In the meantime, letters of condolence continued to arrive from all corners of the nation and from foreign heads of state. Mrs. Lincoln read them all, quoted aloud to Elizabeth from the most tender and sympathetic, and replied to as many as she could, tears streaming down her face as she wrote. One letter in particular she cherished above all the others.

Osborne, April 29, 1865

Dear Madam,
Though a stranger to you I cannot remain silent when so terrible a calamity has fallen upon you & your country, & must personally express my *deep & heartfelt* sympathy with you under the shock-

ing circumstances of your present dreadful misfortune.

No one can better appreciate than I can who am myself *utterly brokenhearted* by the loss of my own beloved husband, who was the *light* of my life — my stay — *my all* — what your sufferings must be; and I earnestly pray that you may be supported by Him to whom alone the sorely stricken can look for comfort in this hour of heavy affliction.

With the renewed expression of true sympathy, I remain, dear madam,

Your sincere friend, Victoria

"The queen indeed understands my suffering," Mrs. Lincoln said the first time she read the letter, and said again, with greater feeling, each time she reread it. Once, as she returned the letter to its envelope, she added that the queen was truly blessed in that no one had driven her from her home the moment she became a widow. "That, Elizabeth," she noted with a sad, tearful smile, "is the difference between being a widowed First Lady of America, and a widowed Queen of England."

Elizabeth was glad Mrs. Lincoln found comfort in Queen Victoria's words, and, wanting to be kind, she did not point out that no one had driven Mrs. Lincoln from her home the moment she had become a widow either. Elizabeth would allow that President Johnson had been more than patient, permitting her to stay on for weeks and weeks, forgoing the use of the White House residence, offices, and reception rooms that were rightfully his. But that scant, unspoken acknowledgment was all that Elizabeth would grant him. Mrs. Lincoln had become aware that Mr. Johnson had never sent any written condolences, nor had he called upon her to express his sympathies. Robert, who had taken responsibility for communicating with the new president's staff during the transition, complained indignantly about Mr. Johnson's neglect of proper form, but his mother was even more upset and angry. If the Queen of England could find time to write a thoughtful letter, surely a new president elevated by his predecessor's death could too. It was shameful, Mrs. Lincoln declared, absolutely shameful, that a letter could cross the Atlantic Ocean in less time than Mr. Johnson required to cross the street.

But the White House *was* his, after all, and though Mrs. Lincoln desperately clung to the tatters of her former life as long as she could, eventually, reluctantly, she decided to settle in Chicago. Mr. Lincoln had intended to retire there after his second term, she said, and it was a city that had always been good to him. It was in Chicago that he had received his first nomination as the Republican candidate for president, a place reminiscent of triumph, not despair. The city was also reasonably close to Mr. Lincoln's tomb in Springfield, where Mrs. Lincoln imagined she might seek solace in the years to come.

Almost as soon as the matter was settled, Mrs. Lincoln asked Elizabeth to come with her.

Startled, Elizabeth could not speak for a moment, so intensely did she not wish to go. "I cannot go west with you, Mrs. Lincoln."

"But you must go to Chicago with me, Elizabeth," Mrs. Lincoln implored. "I cannot do without you."

"You forget my business, Mrs. Lincoln." Though she knew Mrs. Lincoln's moods by that time, Elizabeth was still astonished that she would make such a request. "I cannot leave it. Just now I have the spring trousseau to make for Mrs. Douglas, and I have promised to have it done in less than a week."

Mrs. Lincoln dismissed her objections

with the wave of a hand. "Never mind that. Mrs. Douglas can get someone else to make her trousseau." Seeing that Elizabeth was unpersuaded, she tried a more practical line of argument. "You may find it to your interest to go. I am very poor now, but if Congress makes an appropriation for my benefit, you shall be well rewarded."

"It is not the reward, but —"

"Now don't say another word about it, if you do not wish to distress me." Already Mrs. Lincoln's mouth was tightening, her eyes becoming tearful and beseeching. "I have determined that you shall go to Chicago with me, and you must go."

Elizabeth had been with Mrs. Lincoln so long, and Mrs. Lincoln had become so dependent upon her, that she felt as if she could not refuse. She clung to one thread of hope: that Mrs. Douglas, the lovely young widow of the late senator Stephen A. Douglas from Illinois and one of Elizabeth's favorite patrons, would insist that she remain in Washington to complete her trousseau as agreed. But when the gracious Mrs. Douglas learned of Mrs. Lincoln's request, she told Elizabeth, "Never mind me. Do all you can for Mrs. Lincoln. My heart's sympathy is with her."

Never before had Elizabeth wished for a

patron to be unkind and selfish, just once.

Realizing that no excuse would suffice, Elizabeth prepared to go to Chicago with Mrs. Lincoln and her sons, packing a satchel, explaining her absence to Virginia and Walker and paying a few months' rent in advance, and distributing her sewing among her assistants.

Although Emma had admired Mr. Lincoln very much and thought his widow deserved the nation's sympathy and consideration, she thought Elizabeth was making a terrible mistake. "When will you return?"

"I don't know." Elizabeth looked around the workroom and let her gaze rest on the young women in her employ, her heart sinking with a distinct sensation of dread. She intended to leave her most important, difficult sewing in Emma's capable hands, but while her favorite assistant was honored and had assured Elizabeth she would satisfy their clients' every request, Elizabeth was nonetheless worried. In her absence, would her loyal patrons place their orders with Emma, trusting that her assistant could attend to the easier tasks until Elizabeth returned to finish the more difficult, or would they choose another dressmaker, one of her competitors? "I'll come back as soon as Mrs. Lincoln doesn't need me anymore."

A corner of Emma's mouth turned down in a wry grimace. "In other words, you're never coming back?"

"Now, Emma —"

"What shall I tell your patrons? Some of them insist that you sew every stitch yourself."

"Show them some of your handiwork. I'm certain you'll win their confidence."

"I must tell them something," Emma insisted. "Will you return in a week? A month? Two?"

"Tell my patrons —" Elizabeth hesitated. "Tell them I will return as soon as I am able."

Emma nodded, relenting, but Elizabeth knew she was not pleased — and that she was nearly as worried about the future of the business as Elizabeth herself.

Once Mrs. Lincoln resigned herself to leaving Washington, she threw herself into the tedious work of packing — but first she gave away nearly everything intimately connected with her late husband, just as she had done with Willie's belongings after his death. She could not bear to be reminded of the past, and so, with Elizabeth acting as her agent, she gave away articles to those whom she regarded as the warmest and most sincere of Mr. Lincoln's admirers. Mr.

Lincoln's faithful messenger, William Slade, received one of Mr. Lincoln's many canes and his heavy gray shawl, while his wife received the black-and-white striped silk dress Mrs. Lincoln had worn to the theater on the night of the assassination. Mrs. Lincoln sent other canes from his collection to colored abolitionists Frederick Douglass and the Reverend Henry Highland Garnet, the minister of the exclusive Fifteenth Street Presbyterian Church, where Virginia and Walker worshipped and Elizabeth hoped to someday, if her application and interview met with approval. Another cane went to Senator Sumner, with a note explaining that the gift of "this simple relic" paid tribute to his "unwavering kindness to my idolized Husband, and the great regard *he* entertained for you." She gave the suit Mr. Lincoln was wearing when he was shot to a favorite White House guard, and the last hat he wore to Reverend Dr. Gurley, who had officiated at both Mr. Lincoln's and Willie's funerals. The lively goats whose antics had given the president so much enjoyment went to Mrs. Elizabeth Blair Lee, one of the few friends who had looked after Mrs. Lincoln in the days of her most intense, anguished grieving. To Elizabeth Mrs. Lincoln presented the bonnet and cloak she had worn that terrible night, stained with the president's blood, as well as Mr. Lincoln's overshoes and the comb and brush that Elizabeth had often used to dress his hair. They were precious mementoes of the great man, and Elizabeth accepted them with deepest gratitude. Her vow to cherish them always brought a rare smile to Mrs. Lincoln's face.

What were not distributed as relics and mementoes were loosely packed into fifty or sixty boxes and a score of trunks. Privately Elizabeth believed that many of the things Mrs. Lincoln insisted upon taking with her were not worth carrying away, but she went along with it when she observed that the work of sorting and folding and packing occupied Mrs. Lincoln so completely that she had far less time for lamentation.

Into the boxes and trunks went all the bonnets Mrs. Lincoln had brought with her four years before from Springfield, along with every one she had purchased since coming to Washington. "I may find use for the material someday," she replied when Elizabeth carefully asked if she meant to take even those that were no longer in fashion and had not been worn in years. "It is prudent to look to the future."

Elizabeth, still unhappy with her reluctant

decision to accompany Mrs. Lincoln, pressed her lips together rather than declare that she wished Mrs. Lincoln's foresight with regard to the future had not been confined to the present moment, and to worn-out clothing. Patience, she counseled herself. She knew she was tired and disgruntled, and grieving too in her own way. Mrs. Lincoln needed her to be steadfast and sensible. First Ladies — and queens too, she supposed — could fall apart from grief, but women like Elizabeth could not.

During their time in the White House, Mrs. Lincoln and her children had received many gifts from admirers and dignitaries, and those too were packed up for Chicago. Mrs. Lincoln took no furniture with her save a dressing stand her husband had particularly liked and that the commissioner had given her permission to keep for Tad. Mrs. Lincoln replaced it with another, equally fine piece, but Elizabeth observed that other furnishings had disappeared from the executive mansion, carried off by servants and visitors after the steward was dismissed and no one was superintending affairs. Elizabeth was dismayed to see so much of Mrs. Lincoln's lovely and expensive refurbishment of the White House being stealthily undone, day by day, but Mrs. Lincoln seemed too distracted to notice.

Robert was often in the room where his mother and Elizabeth were packing boxes, and he argued in vain that she should set fire to her vast stores of old goods, or at the very least leave them behind. "What are you going to do with that old dress, Mother?" he asked, scowling and nudging a box with the toe of his boot as she folded yet another garment and tucked it away.

"Never mind, Robert," she replied. "I will find use for it. You do not understand this business."

"And what is more, I hope I never may understand it," retorted Robert, gesturing impatiently to the piles. "I wish to heaven the car in which you place these boxes for transportation to Chicago would take fire, and burn all of your old plunder up." He turned on his heel and strode from the room.

Elizabeth had watched his tirade from the corner of her eye, saying nothing. She agreed with him that Mrs. Lincoln would probably never put any of the old clothes to good use, but she disapproved utterly of his arrogant, disrespectful tone.

"Robert is so impetuous," Mrs. Lincoln said, making excuse for her son, as if she could read Elizabeth's thoughts. "He never

427

thinks of the future. Well, I hope that he will get over his boyish notions in time."

"I'm sure he would not speak to you this way if he were not grieving."

"He has spoken to me this way for years," Mrs. Lincoln reminded her, and then she sighed. "Elizabeth, I may see the day when I shall be obliged to sell a portion of my wardrobe."

"What do you mean?"

"If Congress does not do something for me, then my dresses someday may have to go to bring food into my mouth, and the mouths of my children."

"Surely it will never come to that," Elizabeth hastened to assure her. She did not like to imagine the dresses she had so painstakingly fashioned being haggled over like apples in a market, sold off for as much as they could fetch before they spoiled.

Later, upon reflection, Elizabeth realized that perhaps Robert thought quite a bit about the future. His had certainly undergone enormous change in the weeks since his father's murder. On April 14, he was a proud Union officer, courting the lovely young Miss Mary Harlan and intending to study the law. Now he was the head of a household, planning to leave Washington for Chicago — and like herself, he knew

428

not for how long. In the midst of his own grief, he surely also felt terribly disappointed for himself, responsible for his only surviving brother, and worried about his unstable mother. That did not excuse his impertinence, but it did make his behavior more understandable, and more forgivable.

At last everything, worthless and invaluable alike, was packed, and the day of their departure arrived. As she accompanied Mrs. Lincoln from the White House, Elizabeth was stunned almost breathless by the stark contrast with Mr. Lincoln's final leave-taking, when his casket was carried from the hall in a grand and solemn state. Thousands had gathered to bow their heads reverently as the plumed hearse bore him off to the Capitol rotunda surrounded by the mournful pomp of military display — battalions with reversed arms, the riderless horse with boots turned about in the stirrups, the flags at half-staff, the melancholy strains of funeral dirges. Mrs. Lincoln left to complete indifference, the only music the chirping of birds, with scarcely anyone to bid her farewell. The silence was almost painful.

On the threshold, Mrs. Lincoln paused for a moment, drew a deep, shaky breath, and took Tad's hand in hers. "Come along," she said, eyes fixed straight ahead. She left the White House without looking back, boarded her carriage, settled herself as the rest of her party climbed in after her, and said nothing more as they drove to the depot to board the private green railcar that had so often carried Mrs. Lincoln to and from the capital and New York City.

Before long the train puffed and chugged away from the station. Until they left the city limits, every exhalation of steam from the engine seemed to Elizabeth a great sigh of relief — Washington City, glad to see the last of Mrs. Lincoln, who had never been good enough for their great, martyred president and now could be forgotten.

They were a small party — Mrs. Lincoln, Robert, and Tad; Elizabeth; Dr. Anson Henry, a longtime friend of the family and Mr. Lincoln's former personal physician; and Thomas Cross and William Crook, two White House guards who had been assigned to escort the Lincoln family back to Illinois. Not long after the train headed westward, Mrs. Lincoln began to complain of one of her terrible, head-splitting migraines, so Dr. Henry dosed her with laudanum, and Elizabeth bathed her temples with cool water. "Lizzie, you are my best and kindest friend,"

430

Mrs. Lincoln told her drowsily, reclining with her eyes shut, her face pale. "I love you as my best friend. I wish it were in my power to make you comfortable for the balance of your days."

"That's very kind of you, Mrs. Lincoln," said Elizabeth, touched. "For now, let's think about how to make *you* comfortable."

Mrs. Lincoln grasped her arm. "If Congress provides for me, depend upon it, I will provide for you."

Gently Elizabeth patted her hand, thanked her, and urged her to rest quietly.

Mrs. Lincoln slept soundly that night, and the next morning she felt well enough to sit up and gaze out the window. For hours she seemed distracted, dazed, while Elizabeth sat sewing quietly nearby, keeping an eye on her.

"What's that you're making?" Mrs. Lincoln suddenly asked. "A quilt?"

"That's right." Elizabeth set her needle and fabric pieces on her lap and handed her one of the completed sections, seven small pieces joined together, a light center hexagon encircled by six dark. "I've just begun. You know I'm not accustomed to idleness, and dressmaking is too difficult to do well with the motion of the train."

"Such small pieces, and such fine

stitches." Mrs. Lincoln peered closer. "These fabrics look familiar."

"They're scraps left over from making your dresses," said Elizabeth. "I'm glad you recognize them. Each one seems to me like an old friend, and when my gaze falls upon one, I remember the gown cut from the same cloth, and the grand occasion for which it was made."

"What a lovely idea." Mrs. Lincoln returned the quilt pieces, and her gaze went back to the window. "A memory album made of fabric. It is just the thing."

She paused so long, Elizabeth thought she was finished, but then she added in a barely audible whisper, "Unless it is too painful to remember."

Fifty-four hours after they set out from Washington, their train arrived in Chicago. No one met them at the station; Elizabeth did not know who might have met them, if indeed anyone knew they were coming. Mrs. Lincoln had arranged for rooms at the Tremont House, a luxurious hotel on the southeast corner of Lake Street and Dearborn. "My husband began his Senate campaign from that balcony," Mrs. Lincoln said as they descended from the carriage, indicating the place above by lifting her chin.

"Back in 1860, it served as the headquarters for the Illinois Republican Party during the Republican National Convention. My, how they rallied around my husband here in those days!"

Robert glanced at the impressive edifice, tugging on his ear thoughtfully. "Isn't this also where Senator Douglas died?"

Mrs. Lincoln's lips thinned. "Yes," she said sourly. "It is that too." She swept inside, and without another word, they all trailed after her.

Elizabeth was astounded by her sumptuous room. Never had she stayed anyplace so fine, and her heart sank with dismay when she estimated the likely expenses. Mrs. Lincoln had become accustomed to the grandeur of the White House, and she apparently expected to keep herself in that style. Elizabeth realized that as her friend and companion, it fell to her to warn Mrs. Lincoln that she would soon bankrupt herself if she persisted in that way. Just as she gathered her courage, Mrs. Lincoln spared her the onerous duty by reaching the same conclusion herself. "Everything here is so very fine, and so very dear," she confessed to Elizabeth, sighing heavily. "We cannot stay. I cannot fall into further financial embarrassment."

She dispatched Robert to find them less expensive accommodations, and within a week Robert proposed they move to the Hyde Park Hotel, a quiet retreat seven miles from the city center on the shore of Lake Michigan at Fifty-third Street. The village of Hyde Park, population five hundred, was a cool, lovely spot that had become a popular summer escape for well-to-do Chicagoans. The hotel's owner, Mr. Paul Cornell, a Chicago lawyer and developer for whom Mr. Lincoln had once done some legal work, told Robert that he would consider it a great honor if Mrs. Lincoln decided to reside there.

And so she did.

They traveled by train, arriving in Hyde Park at about three o'clock on a Saturday afternoon. Elizabeth was struck by the newness of the hotel, which had opened only the previous summer and still smelled faintly of pine boards. The accommodations were markedly different from Tremont House, the rooms comfortable but small and plainly furnished. Most of Mrs. Lincoln's boxes and trunks had been stored in a warehouse upon their arrival, but what remained they unpacked. Elizabeth helped Mrs. Lincoln put away her clothes, and then she assisted Robert as he unpacked his books and arranged them on shelves in the corner of his room. They chatted pleasantly all the while, and when they were finished, Robert folded his arms, stood by the mantel, and gazed into space as if the weight of his change of fortune, the dramatic contrast between the past and the present, had just become real to him. "Well, Mrs. Keckley," he eventually said, "how do you like our new quarters?"

"This is a delightful place," said Elizabeth, "and I think you will pass your time pleasantly."

He studied her quizzically for a moment, as if he had expected a different answer. "You call it a delightful place. Well, perhaps it is." He looked around the small but neat room, and she realized then that he saw it quite differently than she — cramped and spartan. "Since you do not have to stay here, you can safely say as much about the charming situation as you please. I presume that I must put up with it, as my mother's pleasure must be consulted before my own. But candidly, I would almost as soon be dead as be compelled to remain three months in this dreary house."

If he had not said "almost," Elizabeth thought wryly, she might have accused him of exaggeration. She watched as he went to the window and gazed out upon the lovely scenery with a moody, querulous expression. Muffling a sigh, she excused herself, left him to his brood, and went to check on Mrs. Lincoln, who had retired to her room to rest before they sent down to the kitchen for their supper. Elizabeth had listened to Mrs. Lincoln's sobbing for eight weeks, so she was not surprised to find her lying on the bed, weeping as if her heart was broken. Elizabeth backed quietly into the hallway and slowly began to pull the door shut, but Mrs. Lincoln had heard her enter and rolled over to see who had disturbed her.

"What a dreary place, Elizabeth," she lamented, propping herself up on her elbow and wiping tears from the corner of her eyes with her other wrist. "And to think that I should be compelled to live here, because I have not the means to live elsewhere. Ah! What a sad change has come to us all."

"It is not so bad," Elizabeth said, seating herself in the spindle chair beside the bed. "The views are lovely, and the breeze from the lake is refreshing." She reached out her hand. "Come and see it with me."

Mrs. Lincoln shook her head and fell back against the pillow. "I couldn't bear it. How could I enjoy any small beauty when my husband lies in his grave and I know not what will become of me and my poor sons?"

Elizabeth sighed softly. "Very well. As you wish." She excused herself, found Tad playing alone in his room, and took him outside instead. He held her hand and chattered excitedly as they walked to the lakeshore, and once there he tore himself free and ran whooping and hollering down to the water. Together they walked along the beach, picking up smooth, round stones, stacking the prettiest and most interesting in a pile by the grass to take back to their rooms, flinging the rest into the lake one by one so they might enjoy the satisfying splashes.

Sunday dawned quiet and peaceful. From her window, Elizabeth looked out upon the beautiful lake, only one of many enchanting views from the hotel she had discovered. The wind rippled the broad, blue expanse of the water, and sunbeams made the waves sparkle like scattered jewels. Here and there a sailboat silently glided by or disappeared below the faint blue line of the horizon. Her thoughts turned toward the heavenly realm to which she aspired, the sunbeams on the water suggesting crowns studded with the jewels of eternal life. Elizabeth could not fathom how anyone could consider Hyde Park a dreary place, when it shone so brilliantly with light and life. She would be happy to rest there. She had seen so much trouble in her life, and she was weary, and knowing that she had to shepherd Mrs. Lincoln through her misery made her wearier still, and reluctant to leave her room and face the day. She would almost prefer to fold her arms and sink into an eternal slumber, so that the great longing of her soul for peaceful rest would at last be gratified.

Robert spent the day in his room with his books, while Elizabeth remained in Mrs. Lincoln's, describing the many charming features of their new accommodations Mrs. Lincoln had perhaps not noticed in her grief, speaking plainly but gently about how Mrs. Lincoln's present circumstances were different from what she had come to expect as her due and encouraging her to plan for the future. Mrs. Lincoln refused to think beyond the summer, insisting that she wanted to live in seclusion all that while. "Old faces will only bring back memories of scenes I wish to forget," she said, "and new faces could not possibly sympathize with my distress, or add to the comforts of my situation."

Elizabeth disagreed but could not persuade her otherwise. Overnight, however, Mrs. Lincoln evidently relented enough to allow herself to ponder Tad's future, for on Monday morning, after Robert went into Chicago on business, she told Tad that he was going to have a lesson every morning, beginning that very day.

Tad protested that he did not want a lesson, to which Mrs. Lincoln replied that in that case she supposed he wanted to grow up to be a great dunce. "You must do as Mother tells you, Tad," she said firmly. "You are getting to be a big boy now, and must start school next fall. You would not like to go to school without knowing how to read."

Tad considered her words, perhaps imagining his humiliation if he were the only boy in his class who could not read, and then bounded to his feet, declaring that he did want a lesson after all and that he must have his book and start right away. Elizabeth looked on, amused, as Mrs. Lincoln seated herself in the easy chair and Tad pulled his own smaller chair up alongside, his book on his lap. The scene would have pleased Mr. Lincoln very much, Elizabeth thought. Tad had been humored and pampered by his parents, especially by his father. Tad suffered from a lisp and had never been sent to school, and so he did not know his book at all well. Elizabeth had never understood how two parents who valued knowledge and learning as much as the Lincolns did could have neglected Tad's education, so she was pleased to see that Mrs. Lincoln meant to make up for lost time. It was not only for Tad's sake that Elizabeth approved of this new plan. As much as Tad needed to learn his letters, Mrs. Lincoln needed some worthy endeavor to occupy her time and thoughts.

Tad opened his book and slowly spelled the first word. "A, P, E."

"Well," his mother prompted, "what does A, P, E spell?"

Tad glanced at the small woodcut illustration above the word. "Monkey."

"Nonsense," Mrs. Lincoln exclaimed. "A, P, E does not spell monkey."

"Does too spell monkey!" Tad pointed triumphantly at the picture. "Isn't that a monkey?"

"No, it is not a monkey."

Tad's mouth fell open in disbelief. "Not a monkey! What is it, then?"

"An ape."

"An ape! That's not an ape. Don't I know a monkey when I see it?"

"Not if you claim that is a monkey."

"I do know a monkey," he insisted. "I've seen lots of them in the street with the organ grinders. I know a monkey better than you do, 'cause I always go out to see them when they come by and you don't."

"Tad, listen to me. A monkey is a species of ape. It looks much like a monkey, but it is not a monkey."

"It shouldn't *look* like a monkey then. Here, Yib —" This was the name he had adopted years before for Elizabeth, when his youth and speech impediment had conspired to render her name impossible to pronounce. "Isn't this a monkey, and don't A, P, E spell monkey? Ma don't know anything about it." And with that he thrust the book at Elizabeth, earnest and excited.

Elizabeth could not help it; she burst out laughing. Tad drew back, very much offended. "I beg your pardon, Master Tad," she gasped, fighting to chase away her mirth. "I hope that you will excuse my want of politeness."

He bowed his head, forgiving her as graciously as a little lord, but then he persisted, saying, "Isn't this a monkey? Don't A, P, E spell monkey?"

"No, Tad," she said kindly. "Your mother is right. A, P, E spells ape."

"You don't know any more than Ma." Indignant, Tad slammed the book shut. "Both of you don't know anything."

At that moment, Robert entered, home

from Chicago, and Tad immediately posed the question to him. It took some doing, but eventually Robert convinced his younger brother that Mrs. Lincoln and Elizabeth did indeed know what they were talking about, and that A, P, E did not and never would spell monkey. Once Tad accepted this irrefutable truth, the rest of the lesson proceeded with far less difficulty.

Elizabeth watched from the corner of her eye while she pieced her quilt, biting her lips together until the urge to laugh had passed. Then it occurred to her that if Tad had been a colored boy rather than the son of a president, and a teacher had found him so difficult to instruct, he would have been ridiculed as a dunce and held up as evidence of the inferiority of the entire race. Tad was bright; Elizabeth knew that well, and she was sure that with proper instruction and hard work, a glimmer of his father's genius would show in him too. But Elizabeth knew many black boys Tad's age who could read and write beautifully, and yet the myth of inferiority persisted. The unfairness of the assumptions stung. If a white child appeared dull, he and he alone was thought to suffer from a lack of intelligence or a deficient education, but if a colored boy appeared dull, the entire race was deemed unintelligent. It seemed to Elizabeth that if one race should not be judged by a single example, then neither should any other.

Thomas Cross and William Crook returned to Washington to resume their duties at the White House, taking with them the last vestiges of Mrs. Lincoln's former rank. As the days passed, having lost her husband and then her status, Mrs. Lincoln became consumed with fears of her incipient poverty. It had been demoralizing enough to leave the elegant Tremont House because she could not afford to live in such fine style, but to have fallen so far, so suddenly, felt like shameful exile. At first, acquaintances attempted to call on her at the Hyde Park Hotel, but Mrs. Lincoln could not bear for anyone to see her in such reduced circumstances, so she turned them all away. "I had hoped for a much different reception when I decided to move here," she confided to Elizabeth. She had expected the Chicago elite to embrace her upon her arrival in their city; she had anticipated an outpouring of sympathy for her as the widow of the slain president. Elizabeth suspected that she had also hoped that some wealthy Republican benefactor would settle her in a residence more befitting her status and insist upon

443

paying her expenses. But no guardian angel appeared, no offers were forthcoming. Time after time Mrs. Lincoln grasped thin straws of hope that one or another of her husband's wealthiest supporters or a friend who had acquired great wealth due to his patronage would come to her aid, and time and time again, her hopes were dashed to pieces.

Humiliated, Mrs. Lincoln withdrew further into her seclusion, seeing no one, expressing her grief and worry to confidantes in lengthy letters. The weight of her debts threatened to crush her, but she was determined to pay back every cent. She penned elaborate pleas for government compensation in recognition of her husband's sacrifice for the nation, asking for all of the salary he had expected to earn in his second term as president. When Congress did not promptly make a provision for her, she decided to write directly to some of the newly wealthy, influential men who had earned fortunes from the appointments Mr. Lincoln had granted them, hoping that by reminding them what they owed the man, they would be moved to help the widow. She might have succeeded had the press not reported that Mr. Lincoln had left behind an estate worth seventy-five thousand dollars. Of course, it was bound up in a snarl of legalities, and it would be split three ways between Mrs. Lincoln and her sons, and even when her inheritance did come to her, she would not be given the principal to live on, but only the annual interest. But since the newspapers neglected to mention those details, Mrs. Lincoln's claims of poverty rang hollow. No one, not even her husband's closest friends and greatest admirers, was inclined to offer her sympathy or charity when her plaintive appeals seemed to paint a false portrait of her circumstances.

Worsening matters were reports that when the Johnson family moved into the White House, they found the place ransacked, the public rooms nearly emptied of furniture. Although unscrupulous visitors and unfaithful servants had spirited away the goods, gossip lay the blame upon Mrs. Lincoln's shoulders — or rather, within the scores of boxes and trunks she was known to have taken with her to Chicago. Thus while Mrs. Lincoln passed her lonely days feeling neglected and impoverished in remote Hyde Park, the public was gleefully relishing the new campaign against her, devouring each new sordid tale, no matter how improbable it would seem to a less prejudiced reader.

The public's scornful perception of her drove Mrs. Lincoln deeper into self-pity and

445

despair. She rejected the ongoing, insistent assertions of her husband's executor — Justice David Davis, Mr. Lincoln's campaign manager in 1860 and his nominee to the Supreme Court in 1862 — that she could live comfortably on her existing income if only she would move back to her home in Springfield. She begged friends to write to congressmen on her behalf, to use their influence to secure her the government pension she urgently needed. As First Widow, she believed that her sacrifice should be acknowledged by the government as well as the public, and lifting her above indigence was the very least they should do. Her tireless, frenzied letter writing took on the air of a crusade — to redeem her reputation, to regain the status she had lost, to receive the honors she felt herself entitled to, and to preserve her husband's legacy. She pored over newspapers to stay informed about what was being said about Mr. Lincoln and by whom, and she filled her letters with astute observations about politics and current affairs. Any honors or provisions bestowed upon others greatly affronted her, for she believed they did not give enough credit to the slain president to whom they owed everything.

Memorializing President Abraham Lincoln became her great cause — in addition, of course, to raising Tad and seeing Robert independent, established, and content. She often confided to Elizabeth that if not for her sons, she would be quite relieved to take her own life.

While Mrs. Lincoln wrote letter after letter, Elizabeth too kept up her own correspondence, sending courteous letters to favorite patrons eager to know when she might return, and writing more intimate missives to Virginia and Emma, to whom she poured out her concerns about Mrs. Lincoln and her business. Virginia offered her sympathy and urged her to come home at the earliest possibility, while Emma told her, simply and frankly, that her business was faltering in her absence. Emma and her other assistants had completed the dresses Elizabeth had begun before her departure, but new orders had become few and far between once word spread that the renowned Madam Keckley would not wield the needle herself. Out of necessity, Emma had let go half of the assistants, for there simply was not enough work for them all. "All the ladies ask when you will return," Emma wrote. "If you come back soon I believe we can entice them back in time to sew dresses for the next social season etc., but I fear if you stay away too long they will find someone else to attend them. They will not look half as pretty but they must wear something I guess."

Elizabeth's worst fears seemed to be coming to pass. She had invested everything into her dressmaking business — her money, her time, her toil — and now she felt as if she were watching it crumble to pieces from across a great chasm. The Lincolns were settled in their new home, though less happily than Elizabeth wished, and she had begun to wonder how much longer Mrs. Lincoln would require her to stay. The government had given Mrs. Lincoln a small sum to hire Elizabeth as her paid companion — thirty-five dollars a week for her services, one hundred dollars for travel expenses and lodging, and fifty dollars for mourning attire — but the income she lost neglecting her business in Washington vastly exceeded what she earned in Chicago. Also, although she would never distress Mrs. Lincoln by inquiring about the fund, she was certain that it would be depleted soon.

Elizabeth kept up with the news too, though not as fervently as Mrs. Lincoln, who read several newspapers from New York, Washington, and Chicago each day, and Elizabeth's heart skipped a beat whenever her gaze fell upon a story about Mr. John Wilkes Booth and his conspirators. All along, Mrs. Lincoln had seemed strangely indifferent to news about the death of her husband's assassin, the rounding up of his conspirators, and their upcoming trial, but Elizabeth hung on every word. She also found herself searching the columns of print for any mention of Mr. and Mrs. Jefferson Davis, who had fled deep into the South until they and their small party were finally captured early one May morning near Irwinville, Georgia. Newspapers reported that when the fugitives heard Union soldiers approaching their camp, Mr. Davis threw on one of his wife's dresses in an attempt to disguise himself and began to walk off into the surrounding forest. But a sharp-eyed corporal noticed that the very tall woman was wearing a man's boots and ordered him to halt, while another soldier raised his rifle. Still in her nightclothes, Mrs. Davis ran to her husband and flung her arms around him, and the soldier, unwilling to shoot a woman in the back, lowered his weapon. Elizabeth knew that Varina Davis had probably saved her husband's life, since the officers had orders to take the Confederate president dead or alive.

Elizabeth wished she could send a kind

word to Mrs. Davis, whom she had always liked despite their disparate views on the very significant matters of slavery and secession, but she did not know where to send a letter. According to newspaper accounts, Mr. Davis was in prison at Fort Monroe, but Elizabeth did not know what had become of his wife and children.

In the last week of May, Elizabeth read that Chicago would soon host its second Great Northwestern Sanitary Fair. Throughout the war, the United States Sanitary Commission and its chapters throughout the North had raised essential funds in support of the war effort, its volunteers hosting countless fairs to earn money to purchase food, blankets, bandages, hospitals, uniforms, bedding, and nearly everything else the soldiers desperately needed. Even though President Johnson had declared the fighting officially over, the work of the Sanitary Commission went on, for the soldiers' needs, though different in nature, were as great as ever. Proceeds from the Chicago fair would benefit impoverished veterans, wounded soldiers who could not work, and the widows and orphans of soldiers killed in battle.

For the first Great Northwestern Sanitary Fair in the autumn of 1863, President Lincoln had donated the original draft of the Emancipation Proclamation, and it had sold for three thousand dollars. President Johnson or one of his advisers must have decided that a similar gesture was expected of him, for Elizabeth learned that the catafalque upon which President Lincoln's casket had rested had been sent from Washington for the event. It was hoped that ticket sales to view the exhibit, which would include other artifacts from the war, would raise an impressive sum for the worthy cause.

Intrigued, Elizabeth wanted very much to attend, but she could not persuade Mrs. Lincoln to accompany her. "An outing would do you good," Elizabeth told her, "and I know the cause of the Union soldiers is very dear to your heart."

Mrs. Lincoln shuddered. "The soldiers are indeed very dear to me, but not even for them do I wish to look upon something so intimately associated with my husband's death."

"The pavilion is so vast, that even if you do not go near it, you will still have many other things to see."

"And what would the people say if I refuse to go near my husband's catafalque?" Mrs. Lincoln countered. "They would say I do not show him proper respect. They would say I do not mourn him and that I am indifferent to his memory. Such lies would fill the papers tomorrow. No, Elizabeth, I do not wish to be seen there, and even if I wore a heavy veil, I would be known."

Elizabeth was disappointed, but she understood, and so she decided to go alone. She took the train north, and after a short ride into the heart of the city, she arrived at the station and walked the short distance to the fair's Trophy Hall on Michigan Avenue. She paid her admission fee and began touring the exhibits, reading the placards and studying the artifacts. She deliberately chose her route to save President Lincoln's display for the end, and her heart felt heavier with every step toward it.

The catafalque looked nearly as it had in the East Room, but strange and small and out of place in the unfamiliar, noisy, bustling setting of the pavilion. The simple bier was about seven feet long, two and a half feet wide, and perhaps two feet tall, draped in black silk trimmed in white, with heavy black tassels hanging at the four corners, deep swags of silk along the sides, and long fringe adorning the edges all around. A glass dome covered it, studded with stars, and at its base lay souvenirs of slavery taken from Southern plantations during the war — an enormous ball and chain, a pair of heavy shackles, an assortment of whips, and other items so bleakly, painfully reminiscent of her youth that Elizabeth had to turn away. She remembered how distraught Mrs. Lincoln had been when the catafalque was being constructed in the East Room, because every strike of a hammer against a nail sounded to her like a pistol shot. How thoughtless she had been to invite Mrs. Lincoln to attend the fair with her! Why on earth would any grieving widow subject herself to the sight of the bier upon which her husband's casket had rested?

Shaking her head and silently chiding herself, Elizabeth quickly walked away from the catafalque. She had seen nearly all she had wanted to see and was inclined to leave, but then her gaze fell upon a crowd gathered around another display on the opposite side of the hall. Curious, she drew nearer and spied an iron bell with a sign proclaiming that it had been taken from the Mississippi plantation of Jefferson Davis — but that object, though it drew many a curious eye, did not account for the crowd. The fairgoers were waiting in line to pay twenty-five cents to see a wax figure depicting Jefferson Davis at the moment of his capture in Georgia.

Elizabeth could not resist. She joined the queue, paid her fee, and when her turn came, stepped beyond the curtain with a handful of other spectators to view the display. A wax figure bearing a fairly good resemblance to Mr. Davis stood on a platform, clad in a man's suit with a woman's floral garment over it, a strangely familiar garment —

"Oh, my goodness," Elizabeth exclaimed. "It's Mrs. Davis's chintz wrapper!"

The other visitors in her group started at her outburst. "It's what now?" one gentleman queried as all eyes turned her way.

Her gaze fixed on the garment, Elizabeth gestured, utterly disbelieving. "It's — it's one of the two chintz wrappers I made for Mrs. Davis back in January of 1861, right before she and her husband left Washington." From the corner of her eye, she saw two ladies regarding her with astonishment as they whispered to each other. "I am a seamstress," she explained. "I'm visiting from Washington City, where I have a dressmaking business. Mrs. Davis was one of my customers, and Mrs. Lincoln was too, and still is."

She was not sure why she added the last, perhaps because the doubt in their eyes unsettled her. She became aware then of other fairgoers peering around the curtain, drawn by her exclamations or wanting to see what was holding up the line.

The first gentleman to speak to her told them, "This colored woman claims she made this wrapper for Mrs. Davis."

The people murmured excitedly, and some pushed their way to the front while still more peered around the curtain. Elizabeth instinctively took a step backward.

"Is that so?" a woman asked excitedly. "Can you prove it?"

Others joined in the call for her to prove her claims, and Elizabeth looked from one to another to the next in dismay, wishing she could flee. "How?" she managed to say. "How shall I prove it?"

"Tell us how you made it," an elderly woman prompted.

That Elizabeth could do well enough. Steeling herself with a deep breath, she stepped closer to the wax figure and told them how Mrs. Davis had purchased the fabric herself, how the specter of war had compelled her to economize, how she had needed Elizabeth to complete the garments quickly because she anticipated — correctly, as it turned out — that her husband would soon decide to leave Washington. These first details came out in a rush, but then Elizabeth began to talk about how she had made the garment, how a particular technique was a signature of her style, and that part came easily.

While she spoke, the curtain was shoved out of the way so a large crowd could gather around her. It grew by the minute as Elizabeth proved, as best she could, that she knew firsthand that the garment had belonged to Mrs. Davis because she was the seamstress who had made it. She knew that words were not proof — for all her listeners knew, she could be a very good actress or a particularly skilled liar — but her self-confident manner and knowledgeable descriptions of the wrapper's finer details seemed to convince them of her veracity.

"This colored woman says she made the dress old Jeff Davis wore when he was captured," a man shouted over his shoulder, beckoning others to gather around.

"I make no such claim," Elizabeth protested. "That is to say, I did indeed sew this garment for Mrs. Davis, but I have no idea whether Mr. Davis ever wore it as a disguise. I would think that he did not, that he could not have done, for his shoulders are far too broad and the bodice too narrow —"

They interrupted her explanation with jeers and protests that she must not defend him, so she quickly steered the subject back to the making of the wrapper. In the meantime, someone had run to fetch the chairwoman of the fair, who stood among the crowd, listening as eagerly as the others. The spectators had expected to enjoy amazing sights at the fair, but nothing quite like this, and they had not even had to pay the extra twenty-five cents for the privilege.

"Will you swear to all this?" someone called out when she finished. The crowd was pushing forward and she was becoming a little uneasy.

Elizabeth agreed, because she could not imagine what the mob's disappointment would compel them to do if she refused. The fair's chairwoman, Mrs. Bradwell, dashed off to find a notary public, and while Elizabeth waited, she answered questions and demurely avoided others about the Davis family and the Lincolns. At last Mrs. Bradwell returned with a short, dark-haired, portly gentleman who quickly produced paper, pen, and the seals of his office. He and Mrs. Bradwell advised her what to say, but she changed the wording slightly as she wrote her oath:

I hereby certify that I, Elizabeth Keckley, was originally the dressmaker for Mrs.

Jefferson Davis, that I have recently been dressmaker for Mrs. President Lincoln and have attended her from Washington to Chicago; that I have seen the figure of Jefferson Davis now on exhibition at Trophy Hall, and recognize the dress upon said figure as made by me for Mrs. Jefferson Davis, and worn by her.

Elizabeth Keckley
Chicago, June 6, 1865

Three witnesses, including Mrs. Bradwell, signed the document after she did, and the notary stamped and sealed it and held it up for all to see. They burst into cheers, and in the confusion Elizabeth managed to slip away, flustered and breathless, but not before she glimpsed Mrs. Bradwell affixing the signed and notarized document to the display.

The next day, Elizabeth was surprised and chagrined to read about her little adventure in the Chicago *Evening Journal.* Her oath had been printed in its entirety, and it was noted that after she had verified the authenticity of the wrapper, ten thousand fairgoers had spent a total of twenty-five hundred dollars on lottery tickets for a chance to win the garment.

"Twenty-five hundred dollars," Elizabeth

mused aloud, impressed. She decided that her small embarrassment had been well worth it, since it had helped to raise a substantial amount of money for a very worthy cause.

It was almost mid-June when the fund to pay for Elizabeth's services ran out and Mrs. Lincoln could no longer afford her room and board. Mrs. Lincoln begged her to remain a little while longer regardless, but Elizabeth, missing her own home and worried about her dressmaking business, was secretly not altogether disappointed that she could not.

By that time she had persuaded Mrs. Lincoln to leave her rooms occasionally and take the air, and as the day of Elizabeth's departure approached, they often strolled together in a nearby park that Mrs. Lincoln had become quite fond of, or along the lakeshore, where they enjoyed the refreshing breezes.

On their last day together, Mrs. Lincoln was melancholy and tearful, and since Elizabeth realized that nothing she could say would ease the pain of her departure, she spoke very little but instead listened attentively while Mrs. Lincoln lamented. "It almost appears to me that I am on the seashore," said Mrs. Lincoln sadly, gazing out at the lake. "How wide is it, do you suppose?"

"I believe it is some seventy-five miles in breadth."

"Well, then, it is little wonder I cannot discern the opposite shore." Mrs. Lincoln sighed heavily, dejected. "My friends thought it would be quieter here during the summer months than in the city, and they were right, but it will be far too quiet without you, Lizzie."

"If I could stay, I would." Elizabeth spoke truly. She needed not hurt Mrs. Lincoln's feelings by adding that she was relieved that she could not stay.

"Tell me, how can I live without my husband any longer?" Mrs. Lincoln suddenly cried. "This is my first awakening thought each morning, and as I watch the waves of the turbulent lake under our windows I sometimes feel I should like to go under them."

Elizabeth felt a chill every time Mrs. Lincoln spoke thus, but she said firmly, "You thought you couldn't live after Willie died, and yet you did. You have Tad and Robert to live for if you don't care about living for yourself. You must think of your sons, and rally."

Mrs. Lincoln inhaled deeply and shuddered. "You are the only person who talks to me this way. Tad becomes frightened when I sink into despair, and Robert becomes impatient. You are the only good, kind friend I have anymore, and I don't know how I shall get along without you."

"You would perhaps have more friends if you would allow them to see you instead of sending them all away."

Mrs. Lincoln was silent for a long moment. "I suppose there is something to what you say." She threw Elizabeth a beseeching look. "Promise me, that if Congress makes an appropriation for my benefit and I can bear your expenses, you will come with me to visit my husband's tomb on the first anniversary of his death."

"I have already promised you that," Elizabeth reminded her, smiling fondly, "but if it will comfort you to hear me say it again, then I promise, again, that I will."

"And promise me that you will write."

"I will, but —" Elizabeth hesitated. "I confess that I am not a good writer."

"You don't think you are, but you are," Mrs. Lincoln declared with a little of her old fire, "and I wouldn't care if you were not. Write to me as often as you can."

So Elizabeth promised that she would.

CHAPTER FOURTEEN

June 1865–September 1866

In the middle of June, Elizabeth returned to Washington with Mrs. Lincoln's best wishes for her continued success in business. She also assured Elizabeth that she still considered her to be her personal modiste, though hundreds of miles would soon separate them. "You know my form as well as I do myself," Mrs. Lincoln remarked. "I will still ask you to make new dresses for me, when I have the occasion and the means to have a new dress made. I must insist that you sew every stitch yourself, as you have always done; I am no longer First Lady, and I'm sure your assistants are quite good, but they cannot be your equal."

"I will always consider it a great privilege to sew your dresses with my own hands," Elizabeth assured her.

The train ride east was long and tiresome, but each mile brought her closer to home.

The front door of her boardinghouse on Twelfth Street was a welcome sight, and as she approached, Virginia and Walker hurried out to greet her, taking her satchel and embracing her and declaring how good it was to see her again. After she settled herself in her room, which Virginia had kindly aired and dusted in anticipation of her arrival, she accepted the couple's invitation to join the family for dinner.

After they finished eating and the children left the table, little Alberta in Jane's arms and Lucy trailing along behind, Virginia and Walker queried Elizabeth about her time in Chicago and what she planned to do next. "First I intend to salvage my dressmaking business," she said. "I have some duties to attend to at the White House on behalf of Mrs. Lincoln, and of course I want to resume my work with the Freedmen and Soldiers' Relief Association." The charitable organization that she had founded to assist the contraband seeking refuge in Washington City had changed its name in 1864 to reflect the changing times and emancipation.

"Have you sent business cards to President Johnson's family?" asked Walker. "Or maybe you plan to leave one at the White House when you take care of Mrs. Lincoln's business?"

"I don't intend to do so at all," Elizabeth said. "I have no desire to work for the new president's family."

"Why not?" asked Virginia. "Mrs. Lincoln was your best customer. Why wouldn't you want to sew for the new First Lady?"

"Or in this case, all three of them," said Walker. "Mrs. Johnson is said to be so often indisposed that her daughters have taken responsibility for most of the duties of White House hostess."

"Is that the problem?" said Virginia, smiling as if she couldn't believe it. "Too many First Ladies to please and too much work?"

"That's not it at all." How lovely it was to be among her friends again, enjoying their teasing. "Mr. Johnson was never a friend to Mr. Lincoln, and he failed to treat Mrs. Lincoln with common courtesy in the hour of her greatest sorrow."

"You don't have to sew for him," Walker observed. "His wife and daughters surely did nothing wrong."

Elizabeth hesitated. He made a fair point, and yet she could not overcome her reluctance. She would feel disloyal to Mrs. Lincoln if she sewed for her successor. Also, if she sewed at the White House again, she was likely to encounter Mr. Johnson as frequently as she had seen Mr. Lincoln, and she had no desire to spend any time in his company.

She took a day to rest and recover from her journey, and then she called at the White House to transact Mrs. Lincoln's business. Her heart filled with dread as she passed through the front doors, for every familiar sight and sound and smell bitterly reminded her of the past. Inside, she discovered that its new occupants had already altered the mansion significantly, and more refurbishments were in progress. The walls had been painted here and new wallpaper hung there. Stained and damaged upholstery had been concealed within linen slipcovers. The wood floors, doors, and trim had been refinished and repainted to a glossy sheen. Taking in the scene, Elizabeth was reminded painfully of Mrs. Lincoln's extensive beautification efforts, and how all her hard work had been undone by unscrupulous staff and greedy treasure seekers.

When Elizabeth completed her errand and departed, which she did as quickly as she could, she fervently hoped that she had crossed the threshold for the last time.

Elizabeth had promised Mrs. Douglas that

she would create her long-overdue spring trousseau as soon as she returned from Chicago, so after setting Emma to the task of delivering notes to her favorite patrons to inform them she was back in business, she called on Mrs. Douglas to meet their engagement. Mrs. Douglas looked very pleased to see her, but also quite surprised. "Why, Mrs. Keckley," she exclaimed, "can it really be you? I did not know you were coming back so soon. It was reported that you would remain with Mrs. Lincoln all summer."

Elizabeth acknowledged that she had expected to stay longer too. "Mrs. Lincoln would have been glad to have kept me with her had she been able."

"Able?" Mrs. Douglas echoed. "What do you mean by that?"

"Only that she is already laboring under pecuniary embarrassment, and was only able to pay my expenses, and allow nothing for my time."

"You surprise me. I thought she was left in good circumstances."

"So many think, it appears," said Elizabeth ruefully. "I assure you, Mrs. Lincoln is now practicing the closest economy." She went on to tell her of Mrs. Lincoln's fruitless efforts to obtain a widow's pension from the government and the withholding of her inheritance due to the delays sorting out her husband's estate.

In the days and weeks to come, Elizabeth would share the tale of Mrs. Lincoln's woes to mutual acquaintances and sympathetic patrons — Mrs. Lee, Mrs. Welles, anyone kind enough to listen and perhaps to advocate her cause to their influential husbands and friends. If the truth about Mrs. Lincoln's circumstances came to light, perhaps Congress would be compelled to make a provision for her.

With Mrs. Douglas's spring trousseau at last under way, Elizabeth gathered her assistants, polished her sign, and, to her great relief, soon had her business going along at a steady pace. As word of her return to Washington spread, orders soon began to come in faster than Elizabeth could fill them. One day in late June, the girl attending the door found Elizabeth in the cutting room, where she was hard at work on a lovely rose silk gown. "Mrs. Keckley," the youngest of her assistants said, "there is a lady below who wants to see you."

Caught in the middle of a difficult section, Elizabeth finished cutting before she answered. "Who is she?"

"I don't know. I didn't learn her name."

Elizabeth did not want to interrupt her work at that moment, but she also didn't wish to offend an important patron. "Is her face familiar? Does she look like a regular customer?"

The girl shook her head. "No, she is a stranger. I don't think she was ever here before. She came in an open carriage, with a colored woman for an attendant."

"It might be the wife of one of Johnson's new secretaries," Emma mused.

"Do go down, Mrs. Keckley," urged another assistant.

Their curiosity had fanned the flames of her own, so she set down the shears, brushed loose threads from her skirt, and went below. When she entered the parlor, a tall, brown-haired, plainly dressed woman rose and asked, "Is this the dressmaker, Mrs. Keckley?"

"Yes," Elizabeth replied. "I am she."

"Mrs. Lincoln's former dressmaker, were you not?"

"Yes, I worked for Mrs. Lincoln."

The woman smiled. "And are you very busy now?"

Elizabeth spread her hands and laughed, indicating the workroom just beyond, where the sounds of her industrious assistants hard at work could not be mistaken. "Very, indeed."

"Can you do anything for me?"

"That depends what is to be done, and when it is to be done."

The woman tapped her chin with her forefinger, thinking. "Well, say one dress now, and several others a few weeks later."

Elizabeth quickly ran through her mental list of work she had already accepted. "I can make one dress for you now, but no more," she said with a hint of polite regret. "I cannot finish the one for you in less than three weeks."

"That will answer," the woman said, her manner cheerfully decisive. "I am Mrs. Patterson, the daughter of President Johnson. I expect my sister, Mrs. Stover, here in three weeks, and the dress is for her. We are both the same size, and you can fit the dress to me."

For a brief, disquieting moment, Elizabeth wished she had asked the woman for her name before agreeing to sew for her, but they soon arranged satisfactory terms. After Elizabeth measured Mrs. Patterson, she bade her good morning, entered her carriage, and drove away.

When Elizabeth returned to the workroom, her assistants were naturally eager to learn who her visitor had been. "It was Mrs. Patterson," she replied. "The daughter of President Johnson."

"What?" exclaimed one of the girls. "The daughter of our good Moses. Are you going to work for her?"

When Elizabeth spoke, it felt like an admission of guilt. "I have taken her order."

"I fear that Johnson will prove a poor Moses," said Emma, frowning, "and I would not work for any of the family."

Several of the young women murmured agreement. It was not until that moment that Elizabeth realized how little they liked Mr. Lincoln's successor. That Mrs. Lincoln disliked him, Elizabeth knew, and that he had made a bad impression when he had arrived drunk for his own inauguration, all of Washington was well aware. But since Mr. Johnson had taken office, Elizabeth had been either sequestered with the grieving First Widow in her White House chambers or hundreds of miles away in Hyde Park. She knew very little about any policies he might have enacted or speeches he had made in the past few weeks, but clearly, he had not won over the women in that room.

Elizabeth wondered if Mr. Johnson would turn out to be as poor a leader as Emma predicted, or if her assistants were merely biased against him because he was not Mr. Lincoln, the Great Emancipator they had all admired and respected. That, Elizabeth thought, with the first pang of empathy she had felt for him, was not his fault, and he should not be condemned for it.

Before long she finished the first dress for Mrs. Patterson — or rather, her sister — and was pleased when it was received with great satisfaction. She agreed to make additional dresses for the sisters, and as the summer passed, she discovered that both Mrs. Patterson and Mrs. Stover were kind, plain, unassuming women, making no pretensions to elegance. One day when she called at the White House, she found Mrs. Patterson busily at work with a sewing machine. The novelty of the sight struck her, because although Mrs. Lincoln knew how to sew and had owned a lovely sewing machine in a solid redwood full case, silver plated and adorned with inlaid pearl and enamel, Elizabeth had never seen her use it, nor could she recall having ever seen Mrs. Lincoln with a needle in her hand.

But as pleasant as the sisters were, and as kindly as they treated her, Elizabeth was never entirely happy in their employ. She rarely glimpsed Mr. Johnson, so he was not the problem, although she could not forget how he had slighted Mrs. Lincoln by neglecting to offer his condolences after Mr. Lincoln's death. She could not cross the threshold of the White House without remembering the pleasant hours she had once spent there or the kind familiarity Mr. Lincoln had always shown her. She missed collaborating with Mrs. Lincoln on a stunning new gown, as the sisters took little interest in fashion and preferred simple, long-sleeved garments with high necklines and collars and scant ornamentation. She missed hearing Mr. Lincoln address her as "Madam Elizabeth" and "combing down his bristles" before he escorted his wife to a levee. She even missed his silly, rambunctious goats. The White House held so many vivid associations for her that every step she took, every direction she turned, evoked a memory from a past more satisfying than the present. It pained her to be in the White House when Mr. and Mrs. Lincoln no longer could be.

In August, Elizabeth had recently finished two light summer linen dresses, one for each sister, when Mrs. Patterson sent her a note requesting her to come to the White House to cut and fit another, warmer dress for her in anticipation of autumn. Some strange mood possessed Elizabeth in that moment, and she curtly wrote back that she never cut and fitted work outside of her workrooms. This brought her business relations with the president's daughters to an abrupt end.

Emma regarded Elizabeth curiously when she explained why they would not be sewing anything else for the White House hostesses. "You told them you never cut and fitted dresses except within your workrooms, but you used to do so for Mrs. Lincoln."

"Yes, on occasion, but Mrs. Lincoln never objected to coming here. In fact, I think she enjoyed it — perhaps even preferred it."

"I remember." Emma regarded her from beneath raised brows. "I also recall that you used to say that you never approved of ladies attached to the presidential household coming to your rooms. You said it was more consistent with their dignity to send for you, and have you go to them."

"Well —" Elizabeth paused, thinking, but it was no use. "You're quite right. I have said that, and I did feel that way. I *do* feel that way. I cannot explain why I responded to Mrs. Patterson as I did."

"*I* can explain," said Emma, as if it were obvious. "You don't want to work for them, but you don't know how to refuse them."

"I must be mad to do so," said Elizabeth,

pressing a hand to her forehead. "They've been perfectly agreeable patrons, and who turns down work from the president's daughters?"

"The most popular modiste in Washington City, that's who." Emma swept her arm toward the busy workroom, where all of her assistants were industriously sewing, sitting up straight as she had taught them to avoid backaches and neck strain. "You're not mad at all, nor were you impertinent. You didn't refuse to work for Mrs. Patterson; you agreed to work for her, so long as the cutting and fitting took place here, and she declined."

Elizabeth sighed. "I suppose that is one way of looking at it."

"It's the only way to look at it." Emma smiled fondly and shook her head. "You can choose your customers, Elizabeth, and you can afford to be particular."

Looking around the workroom, Elizabeth realized that indeed, perhaps she could.

By the end of summer, Elizabeth's business had prospered so much that she opened a second shop in the market, but Mrs. Lincoln's prolific correspondence revealed that she was faring far less well. She said virtually nothing about the June trial and July execution of the four conspirators condemned to die on the gallows for their part in her husband's assassination, but she poured out her sorrow when she informed Elizabeth of the death of Dr. Anson Henry, one of the few friends from her Springfield days who had not abandoned her. "I will never forget how tenderly and solicitously he cared for me in the weeks after my beloved husband's death," she lamented. "To think of him lost at sea is almost more than I can bear."

Mrs. Lincoln also felt control of her husband's legacy slipping from her grasp. She had won an important early skirmish when she overruled the Illinois dignitaries in choosing the location of her husband's memorial and tomb, but another battle was brewing against an opponent she had not seen coming. Her husband's former Springfield law partner, William H. Herndon, hoped to write a revelatory book about the president's "inner life" and had taken to poking about asking Mr. Lincoln's friends and acquaintances to confide their memories to him. Mrs. Lincoln was troubled by Mr. Herndon's actions, but Robert was incensed. It was one matter to study a politician, he declared, because having his private life exposed to the public was part of the price he paid for his office. It was another thing altogether to subject his wife and children to such uninvited scrutiny, to compel them to live inside a "glass house."

All the while, the beauties of Hyde Park continued to elude her. "I am miserable," Mrs. Lincoln wrote later in July. "I remain sequestered in my rooms except to take an occasional walk in the park, and of course I see no one, becalmed as I am on the *far off* shores of Lake Michigan." In August, she quit the Hyde Park Hotel and moved herself and her sons to the Clifton House, a respected residential hotel at Wabash Avenue and Monroe Street in central Chicago. Tad enrolled in a local school and was determined to catch up to his peers, and Robert apprenticed at Scammon, McCagg & Fuller, a prominent Chicago law firm. But any satisfaction she might have found in her new residence and her sons' accomplishments was dimmed by her ongoing torment. Grief stricken and feeling abandoned, Mrs. Lincoln remained terrified of poverty and debt, and it seemed she could think of little else. Her creditors had hesitated to pester her about her overdue bills when she was First Lady, but recently they had begun threatening to sue her and to publish lists of her debts in the papers. She wrote to friends, former White House staff, and members of the House of Representatives pleading her case and asking them to use their influence to assist her, and Elizabeth could well imagine the alternately desperate, hectoring, flattering, and relentless tone of her letters. Although her husband's frequent critic Horace Greeley, editor of the *New York Tribune,* astonished Mrs. Lincoln by taking up a subscription to raise money for "the late president's grieving widow and her fatherless sons," her own efforts seemed all in vain.

Elizabeth offered Mrs. Lincoln what encouragement and comfort she could through the mail, but it was never enough. It was a national shame, Elizabeth thought indignantly, that President Lincoln's widow could not be better provided for. He had given his life for his country the same as any soldier, the same as her own dear George, and the least the government could do was to care for his widow and his children, the same as any soldier's.

In autumn, a woman — a stranger, Elizabeth believed — called on her at her boardinghouse. "You are surprised to see me, I know," the woman greeted her happily. She was not a customer, nor anyone Elizabeth recognized from Washington, and yet her face was familiar. "I have just come from Lynchburg, and when I left cousin Anne, I promised to call on you if I came to Washington." The woman beamed, spreading her hands. "I am here, you see, according to promise."

"Cousin Anne?" said Elizabeth, bewildered. "Pardon me, but —"

"Oh, I see you do not recognize me," the woman exclaimed. "I am Mrs. General Longstreet, but when I was a girl, you knew me as Bettie Garland."

"Bettie Garland," Elizabeth gasped. Bettie Garland was the cousin of her former master, Hugh Garland, and had often visited the family at their former residence near Dinwiddie Court House in Virginia. "Is this indeed you?"

The woman nodded, beaming, and they clasped hands, exclaiming with the delight that only an unexpected reunion could bring.

"I am so glad to see you," said Elizabeth, offering her guest a chair and seating herself. After buying her freedom, she had kept in touch with her former mistress and her children — especially the daughters whom she had raised and loved — but their ties had been severed by the outbreak of war.

Elizabeth had often wondered what had become of them, although whenever she mentioned their names and expressed concern for their welfare, her Northern friends would roll their eyes and ask how she could possibly spare a kind thought for those who had kept her in bondage. Try though she might, Elizabeth could not make them understand that despite the grave injustice done to her, and without condoning any part of it, she still felt a deep and abiding affection for a few particular members of the families that had owned her — though certainly not all of them. "Where does Miss Anne live now?"

"Ah! I thought you could not forget old friends," said Mrs. Longstreet. "Cousin Anne is living in Lynchburg. All the family are in Virginia. They moved there during the war." Then her jubilance dimmed. "Fannie is dead. Nannie has grown into a woman and is married to General Meem. Hugh Junior was killed in the war, and now only Spotswood, Maggie, and Nannie are left."

"Fannie, dead!" Fannie was the Garlands' third-eldest daughter and had been especially fond of Elizabeth's mother, who had served as her nurse. "And poor Hugh! You bring sad news as well as pleasant." Her thoughts flew to Nannie, who had been her special charge. She had shared Elizabeth's bed, and Elizabeth had watched over her as if she had been her own child. Indeed, Elizabeth could not have loved her more if she had been. "I can hardly believe it. She was only a child when I saw her last."

"Yes, Nannie is married to a noble man. General Meem belongs to one of the best families in Virginia. They are now living at Rude's Hill, up beyond Winchester, in the Shenandoah Valley. All of them want to see you very badly."

"I should be delighted to go to them," Elizabeth declared. "Miss Bettie, I can hardly realize that you are the wife of General Longstreet, and just think, you are now sitting in the very chair in the very room where Mrs. Lincoln has often sat!"

"The change is a great one, Lizzie," she said, laughing ruefully. "We little dream today what tomorrow will bring forth. After fighting so long against the Yankees, my husband is now in Washington, suing for pardon, and we propose to live in peace with the United States."

Elizabeth was very pleased to hear it.

She had many questions about old friends, and the time passed swiftly in conversation, but all too soon Mrs. Longstreet's visit ended. Before she left, she gave Elizabeth the Garlands' address, and the next day Elizabeth wrote to them, telling them of her life in Washington and expressing hope that she would be able to see them before long.

When she told Virginia and Emma about Mrs. Longstreet's visit and the letters she had sent to Miss Anne and her daughters, Emma shook her head in wonder, frowning. "I don't know why you miss them so. I never, never wish to see any of my masters or mistresses again."

"I don't wish to see *all* of my old masters," Elizabeth pointed out. "There are some I can never forgive. But I understand why you feel the way you do, Emma. Your break with your last master and mistress was particularly unpleasant. They should never have refused to abide by your mistress's will, so they have only themselves to blame for the lawsuit. I bought my freedom. Perhaps that makes the difference."

"I hope you won't be disappointed, Elizabeth," said Virginia, her brow furrowing with concern. "I suspect your old mistress and her daughters have forgotten you. Surely they're like all of their kind, too selfish to give a single thought to you now that you're no longer their slave."

"Perhaps so," said Elizabeth, "but I cannot believe it. Did they not ask Miss Bettie to call on me? You don't know the Southern people as I do. Though master and slave, we had a warm attachment."

Virginia and Emma exchanged a dubious look, and Elizabeth suspected that they could debate the matter forever and her friends still would not understand her point of view. "You have some strange notions, Elizabeth," Emma remarked, shaking her head.

Of all her acquaintances, only Mrs. Lincoln seemed to understand her enduring affection. "Certainly the Garlands will not have forgotten you," she responded after Elizabeth wrote to her about Mrs. Longstreet's visit. "I have never forgotten my beloved Sally, and how tenderly she cared for me throughout my early years. I do not mean to speak ill of my dear mother when I say that Sally raised me. After my mother died, I do not know what I should have done without Sally, as my father's new wife considered all of us stepchildren a burden, and was much preoccupied with her own children. No, Elizabeth, they cannot have forgotten you."

Heartened, Elizabeth waited anxiously for a reply to her letters, and she did not have long to wait. Her heart soared when the first of many long missives came from various members of the family, warm affection filling every line. For months they exchanged letters, and in the winter, Miss Nannie — now Mrs. General Meem — wrote that she and her husband would be very glad to have Elizabeth visit them in the summer. "You must come to me, dear Elizabeth," Miss Nannie entreated. "I am dying to see you. We are now living at Rude's Hill. Ma, Maggie, Spot, and Minnie, sister Mary's child, are with me, and only you are needed to make the circle complete. Come — I will not take no for an answer."

Elizabeth was delighted to accept, and after consulting with Emma and considering the likely state of dressmaking orders at one time and another, she wrote back telling Miss Nannie to expect her in August.

Mrs. Lincoln was delighted for her but sorry for herself, that someone else would have the pleasure of Elizabeth's company when she could not. Throughout the autumn, she had tried to sell some of her jewels and other luxury items, and had tried to return others to the stores where she had purchased them, but the effort proved futile. Shortly before Christmas, Congress informed her that they would not give her Mr. Lincoln's salary for his entire second term, as she had asked, but would only part with one year's pay, which after deductions amounted to little more than twenty-two thousand dollars, equal to only a small fraction of her debts. Later that winter, Congress granted President Johnson seventy-five thousand dollars to refurbish the White House, and humiliating criticism appeared in the New York *World* and other papers saying that Mrs. Lincoln had left behind a ransacked mansion and mountains of overdue bills that continued to plague merchants throughout the city. The persistent Mr. Herndon had succeeded in collecting letters, interviews, and statements from people who had known Mr. Lincoln — some quite well, some barely at all — and was delivering lectures drawn from the material, which he hoped to publish as a book. Still eager to interview Mrs. Lincoln, he had sent his request to Robert, but both he and his mother were unsettled by his phrasing: "I wish to do her justice fully — so that the world will understand things better. You understand me." Mrs. Lincoln did not clearly understand him at all, she fretted to Elizabeth. "What precisely does he mean by *do me justice fully*?" she had written to Elizabeth. "He puts on a foreboding tone that I do not like. And yet I feel it may be necessary to speak with him. If I do not give him *my truth,* he may invent his own."

Worse yet had been the anniversaries of days that had brought Mrs. Lincoln anguishing memories of loss — November 4, her first wedding anniversary without her husband; December 13, her forty-seventh birthday; December 21, Willie's birthday; New Year's Day, marking the start of another year without the loved ones she mourned; February 1, the date of her son Eddie's death; and February 12, Mr. Lincoln's birthday. All of these melancholy dates built up to the worst, most unbearable anniversary, April 15, the date of her husband's assassination. She suffered too on March 30, Good Friday, for it was on the night of Good Friday that he had been shot. "I am desperately unhappy and do not think I will be able to get through the day without you by my side," she wrote to Elizabeth as the end of March loomed nearer. She reminded Elizabeth of the promise she had made upon her departure from Chicago, that if Congress had granted her a widow's pension, Elizabeth would return and accompany her to Springfield to visit her husband's tomb on the anniversary of his death. The appropriation was not made, and so Elizabeth could not go. Mrs. Lincoln traveled with Tad instead, arranging her travel plans at odd times and along circuitous routes to avoid encountering any old friends.

Elizabeth could not go to Illinois that spring, but she did go to Virginia in summer. On August 10, the fourth anniversary of her son George's death, Elizabeth boarded the train for Harpers Ferry, eagerly anticipating her reunion with the Garlands. The journey was not without mishaps. The train arrived at Harpers Ferry at night, but Elizabeth slept through the stop and was carried to the next station, where she was obliged to wait for another train to take her back. Once there, she intended to change cars for Winchester, but she had missed the train and was detained another day. Arriving at last in Winchester, she learned that the only way to reach Rude's Hill was by a series of stagecoaches. The drive commenced in the evening and would last through the night, but Elizabeth was so exhausted she could scarcely keep her eyes open. A young gentleman riding in the stage told Elizabeth that he knew General Meem well and that he would tell her when they had reached the proper place for her to disembark. Thus reassured, Elizabeth drifted off to sleep.

"Aunty." Someone was shaking her. "Aunty, didn't you want to get out at Rude's Hill?"

"Yes, I did." Elizabeth straightened in her seat, rubbing her eyes. "Are we there?"

As she spoke, her gaze fell upon the young man who had promised to wake her, and she discovered him softly snoring.

"More than there," the man who had woken her said. "We have passed it."

"Passed it?"

"Yes. It is six miles back. You should not sleep so soundly, Aunty."

"Why did you not tell me sooner?" Elizabeth cried. "I am so anxious to be there."

"Fact is, I forgot it," he said with a shrug. "Never mind. Get out at this village, and you can find conveyance back."

Elizabeth had little choice but to do exactly that. The town, New Market, was in a sad, dilapidated condition that spoke plainly of the heartless destruction of war. Climbing down from the stage and collecting her satchel, she found her way into a hotel, really little more than a house, where she was able to buy a cup of coffee and gather her wits. When she inquired about a ride back to Rude's Hill, the landlord told her that the stage would return that evening.

"This evening?" Elizabeth's spirits plummeted. It was only just dawn. "I want to go as soon as possible. I should die if I had to stay all day in this lonely place."

She didn't mean to insult the residents of the tiny hamlet, but fortunately few of them were present to hear. The landlord shrugged and said there was nothing he could do, so she settled down for a long wait, utterly dejected.

She had not sat there long, sipping her cooling coffee, when the colored man behind the bar came over to her table. "I'm sorry for your troubles, ma'am."

She managed a tremulous smile. "That is very kind of you."

"I know Gen'ral Meem's place. I can drive you over in 'bout an hour."

Elizabeth seized her chance. "Oh, could you? That would be the most joyful news I've heard in days."

He assured her it would be his pleasure, and in turn she thanked him and urged him to set out as soon as possible.

She finished her coffee and waited outside the door of the hotel for her courteous driver to bring his wagon around. While she stood there, fighting to conceal her impatience, a fat old lady spied her from across the street and waddled over to greet her. "Ain't you Elizabeth?"

"Yes, I am," she replied, startled that the stranger should know her name.

"I thought so." The woman smiled, revealing several missing teeth. "They been expecting you at Rude's Hill every day for two weeks, and they do little but talk about you. Mrs. Meem was in town yesterday, and she said that she expected you this week certain. They will be mighty glad to see you."

At this news, Elizabeth's spirits rose slightly. "I will be even gladder to see them."

"Well, as to that I couldn't say," the woman said, chuckling hoarsely. "They've kept a light burning in the front window every night for ten nights, in order that you might not go by the place should you arrive in the night."

"Thank you," Elizabeth said fervently, feeling much restored. "It's pleasant to know that I'm expected. I fell asleep in the stage, and failed to see the light, so here I am instead of at Rude's Hill, where I meant to be."

As the woman clucked sympathetically, the man from the hotel pulled up in his wagon. Elizabeth climbed aboard, and soon they were on the road to General Meem's country seat. "That's Rude's Hill," her driver remarked, nodding to a picturesque green rise encircled with tall trees as they approached. Elizabeth shaded her eyes with her hands as they climbed the hill, eager for her first glimpse of her old acquaintances. She spied a young man standing in the front yard, quickly tallied the years and subtracted from his apparent age, and deduced that he must be Spotswood — or Spot, as everyone called him, shortening the old family name. She had not seen him in eight years, but when she beckoned to him, he cried out with joy and came running. His happy shout drew the attention of the rest of the family, who had been waiting by the windows or on the veranda but now came hurrying to the wagon. "It is Elizabeth! It is Elizabeth," she heard them cry happily, and eager to be among them, she stepped from the wagon to the top of the stile — but when she attempted to leap down, her hoopskirt caught on one of the posts, and she fell sprawling to the ground.

"Elizabeth," someone exclaimed. Her palms stung and her right knee throbbed from the impact, and she lay there, dazed, the smell of fresh Virginia soil with a pungent undercurrent of manure filling her senses.

Spot reached her first and hauled her to her feet, and a moment later she was in the arms of Miss Nannie, Miss Maggie, and

Mrs. Garland. She scarcely had time to properly thank her kind driver before they whisked her into the house, tended to her soiled hands and skirts, and settled her into an easy chair by the hearth. All the while, the servants looked on in amazement.

Beaming with joy, Miss Nannie clung to her hand as if she would never let go. "Elizabeth, you are not changed a bit," she declared, kissing Elizabeth again on the cheek, her eyes filling with happy tears. "You look as young as when you left us in St. Louis, years ago."

"I cannot say the same," Elizabeth replied, laughing. "You have quite grown up!"

Miss Nannie smiled proudly and beckoned to a tall, graceful young woman. "Here, Elizabeth, this is Minnie, Minnie Pappan, sister Mary's child. Hasn't she grown?"

"Minnie," Elizabeth exclaimed, extending her hand to the young woman, who smiled, took it, and sat down on the footstool. "I can hardly believe it. You were only a baby when I saw you last. It makes me feel quite old to see how tall you have grown. Miss Minnie, you are bigger than your mother was — your dear mother whom I held in my arms when she died." Elizabeth had to pause to compose herself, wiping a tear from each eye.

"Have you had your breakfast, Elizabeth?" asked Mrs. Garland.

When Elizabeth shook her head, the children let out a chorus of vows that they would take care of that right away. "It is not necessary that all should go," Mrs. Garland said, laughing, as Nannie, Maggie, and Minnie headed for the kitchen. "The cook is there. She will get breakfast ready."

But the three young ladies did not heed her. They rushed to the kitchen, and soon they brought Elizabeth a delicious hot breakfast on a tray. While Elizabeth ate, the cook observed the commotion from the doorway, astonished. "I declare, I never did see people carry on so," she said, shaking her head. "Wonder if I should go off and stay two or three years, if all of you would hug and kiss me so when I come back?" The Garlands laughed and teased her, saying that they could not spare her so she must not test the theory.

Soon after Elizabeth finished her breakfast, Miss Nannie's husband arrived. "Elizabeth, I am very glad to see you," he greeted her. "I feel that you are an old acquaintance, I have heard so much of you through my wife."

"And me," Miss Maggie interjected.

General Meem smiled. "Yes, and you, and your mother. Welcome to Rude's Hill, Elizabeth."

In the days that followed, Elizabeth learned that during the war, General Stonewall Jackson had used Rude's Hill as his headquarters, and he had slept in the very room Elizabeth was given as a sitting room. General Jackson was the Southern ideal of a soldier, and admirers from far and near still came to Rude's Hill to pay tribute to their fallen hero, to walk in his footsteps. Elizabeth observed that nearly every visitor would tear a splinter from the walls or windows of her sitting room, which they would carry away and treasure as a priceless relic. The Garlands' plantation was beautiful, but the scars of war were visible everywhere upon the house and the landscape. General Meem had taken up planting, and he employed many laborers to tend the fields and servants to care for the home.

Elizabeth soon discovered that she evoked great curiosity in the neighborhood. Her association with Mr. Lincoln, and her attachment to the Garlands, her former owners, had garbed her in the disguise of a tragic heroine from a sentimental romance. Elizabeth thought it was nonsense, but she did not complain. She was comfortably quartered at Rude's Hill, and the Garlands showed her every attention. They passed the days sewing together or talking of old times, and every day they either drove about the countryside or rode on horseback.

Elizabeth and Mrs. Garland — Miss Anne, as Elizabeth would always think of her — had many long talks alone. For the first time Elizabeth searched her former mistress's face and discovered features that resembled her own. She wondered if the long, quiet looks Miss Anne often gave her meant she was doing the same. Miss Anne was only eight years older than she, they were children of the same father, and yet their lives could not have been more different.

Once, while they were out walking through the new flower garden Miss Anne had only recently begun to cultivate, Elizabeth asked her what had become of her aunt Charlotte, her mother's only sister. She had been maid to the elder Mrs. Burwell, Miss Anne's mother.

"She is dead, Lizzie," Miss Anne said gently. "She has been dead for some years." She sighed, and her eyes seemed to gaze back through the years. "A maid in the old time meant something different from what we understand by a maid at the present time. Your aunt used to scrub the floor and milk a cow now and then, as well as attend to the orders of my mother."

"I remember," said Elizabeth, clasping her hands behind her back as they walked. She supposed she probably knew better than her former mistress what her aunt's chores had included.

"My mother was severe with her slaves in some respects, but then her heart would be full of kindness."

Elizabeth mulled that over. "I suppose that's fair to say."

"She had your aunt punished one day —"

"For what offense?"

"I don't recall what she did, or didn't do," Miss Anne admitted, "but my mother punished her. Not liking her sorrowful looks, my mother made your aunt two extravagant promises on the condition that she would look cheerful, and be good and friendly with her again."

Silently, Elizabeth cheered for her stubborn aunt. "What did she promise?"

"First, that Charlotte might go to church the following Sunday, and second, that my mother would give her a silk dress to wear on the occasion."

"Extravagant indeed," remarked Elizabeth. "I assume that my aunt accepted?"

495

"Oh, certainly. Now, my mother had but one silk dress in the world, silk being not so plentiful in those days as it is now, and yet she gave this dress to her maid so they would be friends again." Miss Anne laughed merrily.

"Did your mother's plan work?" Elizabeth asked. "Were they friendly again?"

"Oh, her plan worked all right, and it was fortunate for Mother that it did. Two weeks afterward, she was invited to spend the day at a neighbor's house, but when she inspected her wardrobe, she discovered that she had nothing fit to wear in company."

Elizabeth felt a slow smile grow on her lips. "Is that so?"

Miss Anne nodded, amused. "She had but one alternative, and that was to appeal to the generosity of your aunt Charlotte. So, she was summoned, and the problem was explained to her, and the maid offered to loan her silk dress to the mistress for the occasion, and the mistress was only too glad to accept. She made her appearance arrayed in the silk that her maid had worn to church on the preceding Sunday."

They laughed together over the incident, although perhaps not for the same reasons.

"Elizabeth —" Miss Anne broke off, and they walked in silence for a long moment before she spoke again. "During the entire war I used to think of you every day, and have longed to see you so much. When we heard you were with Mrs. Lincoln, the people used to tell me that I was foolish to think of ever seeing you again — that your head must be completely turned."

"And of course you believed their wise counsel," said Elizabeth lightly, "because people who have never met me are always the best judge of my character."

"Of course not," Miss Anne protested. "I knew your heart, and I could not believe that you would forget us. I always insisted that you would come to see us someday."

"How could I forget the people I grew up with from the time I was a baby?" asked Elizabeth. "My Northern friends used to tell me that you would forget me, but I told them I knew better, and I didn't lose hope."

"Love is too strong to be blown away like gossamer threads," Miss Anne said. "The chain is strong enough to bind life even to the world beyond the grave." Abruptly she halted and placed a hand on Elizabeth's forearm to bring her to a stop too. "Elizabeth," she said, suddenly anxious. "Do you always feel kindly toward me?"

Elizabeth chose her words carefully. "To tell you candidly, Miss Anne, I have but one unkind thought, and that is that you didn't give me the advantages of a good education, which was my heart's desire. All I have learned has been the study of later years."

Miss Anne pressed her lips together and nodded. "You're right," she said unhappily. "I didn't look on things then as I do now. I've always regretted that you weren't educated when you were a girl." She paused and managed a wan smile. "But you haven't suffered much on this score, since you get along in the world better than we who enjoyed every educational advantage."

Elizabeth did not contradict her. Miss Anne was a widow dependent upon the generosity of her brother-in-law, whereas while Elizabeth was also a widow, she was independent and self-sufficient, a prosperous businesswoman. She had been an intimate of the Lincoln White House, and except for the death of her son, she had not suffered from the war as the Garlands, Meems, and Pappans had.

She would not trade places with her former mistress, Elizabeth realized, despite Miss Anne's privileges and advantages. She was proud of all she had done for herself without them, and she was proud of the woman she had become.

Elizabeth remained at Rude's Hill for five

weeks, and parted from Miss Anne and her children with heartfelt wishes on all sides that they would meet again someday.

CHAPTER FIFTEEN

October 1866–February 1868

When Elizabeth returned to Washington, she had much business to attend to and mail to sort. Most of the letters were from Mrs. Lincoln, who struggled on as lonely and miserable as ever. In the summer she had become so weary of boarding that she spent nearly all of her husband's remaining 1865 salary granted to her by Congress on a fine stone home on West Washington Street in Chicago. She and Tad had settled there, in a popular neighborhood near Union Park, while Robert had moved into a bachelor apartment, where he was no doubt much happier.

After much consideration, Mrs. Lincoln had also warily consented to speak with Mr. Herndon, but when they met in Springfield in September, Mrs. Lincoln had tried to flatter and charm her husband's would-be biographer into leaving her out of his book

500

altogether. "I told him that it was not unusual to mention the existence of the wife, in the biography of her husband, with nothing more than to note that the two were married on this particular date in such and such a place," she wrote to Elizabeth. "I *wish* he would say nothing at all of me, but I *hope* he will say no more of me than that. I do not know if my pleas will convince him. He has disliked me since we met at a dance at the home of Colonel Robert Allen, shortly after I first came to Springfield. Mr. Herndon engaged me for a waltz, and afterward, he told me that I had glided through the dance with the grace of a serpent. A serpent, Elizabeth! Hotly I replied, 'Mr. Herndon, comparison to a serpent is rather severe irony, especially to a newcomer,' and I promptly left him. I believe he has harbored a grudge against me ever since, but as he was my husband's law partner, we were often thrown together, and our relations were civil, if not friendly. I can only trust that his fond memory of my husband will prevent him from taking out any lingering resentment upon me. I do believe he means to exalt my husband in his book, in which case it is my duty as his widow to share my memories of him, which are more intimate than anyone else's."

Elizabeth received Mrs. Lincoln's letter too late to write back and advise her against the interview, but she consoled herself with the realization that it might not have mattered in any case. Mrs. Lincoln could have disregarded Elizabeth's misgivings, or Mr. Herndon might have written whatever he pleased even without speaking with Mrs. Lincoln. Elizabeth hoped that whatever Mr. Herndon chose to do, it would be of so little consequence that no one would ever hear of it, but in this matter she was disappointed. In November, Mr. Herndon delivered another lecture, which he arranged to distribute widely on broadsides in advance and which was reprinted in newspapers throughout the nation. In his lecture, the perfidious Mr. Herndon claimed that Mr. Lincoln had never loved his wife, but instead pined for Miss Ann Rutledge, to whom he had been engaged until her untimely death in 1835. After that, he had never addressed another woman with love and affection. He had even signed his letters to Miss Mary Todd "Your Friend Abraham Lincoln" rather than "Yours affectionately," and he had eventually married her only out of obligation to honor. Thus Mary Lincoln was not to blame for the well-known difficulties in the marriage, because Mr. Lincoln had never loved her.

When Elizabeth read the shocking assertions, her heart went out to Mrs. Lincoln. If Mr. Herndon's intention had been to wound the grieving widow, he could not have chosen a more devastating tactic. On the first anniversary of her husband's death, Mrs. Lincoln had written to Elizabeth, "It was always music in my ears, both before and after our marriage, when my husband told me that I was the only one he had ever thought of, or cared for. That will solace me to my grave." Now Mr. Herndon had stolen that comfort from her. And on what shaky grounds? Was Mr. Herndon constantly at Mr. Lincoln's side, day and night, year after year, so that he could with all certainty confirm that Mr. Lincoln had never addressed any other woman but Miss Ann Rutledge with love and affection? Had he read every letter Mr. Lincoln had written to his wife, heard every word uttered? Elizabeth could not count how many kind, affectionate phrases she had heard Mr. Lincoln speak to his wife through the years. Admittedly, they had quarreled from time to time, but so did every husband and wife of Elizabeth's acquaintance, and however hotly their tempers flared, Mr. and Mrs. Lincoln had always been anxious to make up soon afterward.

It comforted Elizabeth very little — and as she would learn in letters yet to come, Mrs. Lincoln not at all — that Mr. Herndon was roundly disparaged for his lectures. The people were shocked and appalled that he would violate all standards of decorum by addressing such intimate details of the martyred president's life, and many were sure that Miss Rutledge was a figment of his imagination. A furious Robert Lincoln took measures to discredit and silence the aspiring biographer, warning that the subject of the Lincoln family was strictly off-limits for his manuscript in progress. The Lincolns' pastor from their Springfield days, Dr. James Smith, wrote a scathing rebuke, addressed to Mr. Herndon but widely published in the newspapers, including the *Chicago Tribune,* which was where Mrs. Lincoln discovered it. The pastor had read Mr. Herndon's lecture "with feelings of mingled indignation and Sorrow, because coming as it did from his intimate friend and law partner, it was calculated to do the character of that great and good man an incalculable injury, deeply to wound the feelings of his heart broken widow and her orphan boys, and to place that whole family both the dead and living, in their family relations, in a most unenviable light before the public." He emphatically asserted that no man was better placed to know Mr. Lincoln's heart than his pastor, esteemed and respected by the family, entrusted with their spiritual care, intimate with all the joys and sorrows of their lives, relied upon for his advice and counsel. "During the seven years when he and myself were at home," he wrote, "scarcely two weeks ever passed during which I did not spend a pleasant evening in the midst of that family Circle." Dr. Smith's intimacy with the Lincoln family had convinced him that Mr. Lincoln was "utterly incapable of withholding from the Bride he led to the Altar that which was her due, by giving her a heart dead and buried in the grave of Another; but that in the deep and honest sincerity of his Soul, he gave her a heart overflowing with love and affection." He was certain that Mr. Lincoln "was to the Wife of his bosom a most faithful, loving and Affectionate husband."

Mrs. Lincoln must have felt a certain sense of vindication to have her husband's own pastor publicly confirm that Mr. Lincoln had loved her most tenderly, but even so, Mr. Herndon's claims had dealt her a terrible blow. "There are hours of each day, that I cannot bring myself to believe, that it has not *all* been some hideous dream," she lamented to Elizabeth. "In my bewildered state, I sometimes feel that my darling husband, *must and will* return to his sorrowing loved ones. This I know shall never be, in this World, and if not for Tad I would all too willingly join him in the Next."

In the first few weeks of 1867, Mrs. Lincoln's letters often alluded to her sinking fear that she would not be able to afford her home on West Washington Street much longer, and that she would be obliged to take cheap rooms for herself and Tad elsewhere, rent out the house, and live off the income. In March she wrote again to confess that her fear had become a certainty. She had struggled long enough to keep up appearances, but that mask at last had to be thrown aside, for she simply could not live on her meager allowance. "As I have many costly things which I shall never wear," she wrote, "I might as well turn them into money, and thus add to my income, and make my circumstances easier. It is humiliating to be placed in such a position, but, as I am in the position, I must extricate myself as best I can. Now, Elizabeth," she continued, "I want to ask a favor of you. It is imperative that I should do something for my relief, and I want you to meet me in New York, between the 30th of August and the 5th of September next, to assist me in disposing of a portion of my wardrobe."

Elizabeth knew that Mrs. Lincoln's income was modest, only seventeen hundred dollars a year, and that her collection of elegant gowns, packed away in boxes of trunks since her move from Washington, was of no tangible value to her any longer, since she would almost certainly never wear the dresses again. Elizabeth decided that since Mrs. Lincoln's need was urgent, it would be prudent to dispose of the gowns quietly, and that New York would be the best place to transact such delicate business.

"Why do you take this on?" Emma asked when Elizabeth explained why she might have to leave the dressmaking business in her care or shut it down altogether while she traveled on behalf of Mrs. Lincoln. "You have already done so much for her, and she is never any better for it."

"I think she is better for knowing she can rely on me," Elizabeth countered. "Everyone else has betrayed or abandoned her, except her sons. The question should not be why I help her so much but why other people help her so little." Mrs. Lincoln was the wife of the Great Emancipator, the martyred president who had done so much good for their race. How could Elizabeth refuse to do anything that would be to her benefit?

On September 15 Elizabeth received a letter from Mrs. Lincoln announcing that she would arrive in New York City on the night of the seventeenth. She instructed Elizabeth to come beforehand and secure rooms for them at the St. Denis Hotel under the name Mrs. Clarke, an alias she had sometimes employed while traveling as First Lady.

Startled, Elizabeth read the letter again to be sure she had not misunderstood it. She had never heard of the St. Denis Hotel, which suggested that it was not a first-class establishment and was unlikely to be up to Mrs. Lincoln's standards. She also was perplexed by Mrs. Lincoln's decision to travel without protection under an assumed name, and forgo the trust and deference due to her as the First Widow. Most dismaying of all, she knew it would be difficult if not impossible for her as a colored woman to engage rooms at a strange hotel for a person about whom the proprietors knew nothing.

"What is she thinking?" Elizabeth murmured, shaking her head as she scanned the letter. If only she could ask! Mrs. Lincoln would already be en route to Washington before a letter could reach her in Chicago, and a telegram was out of the question, because Elizabeth could not expose the delicate business to every curious operator along the line. Caught in an impossible predicament, Elizabeth's only hope was that at the last moment, Mrs. Lincoln would send word that she had changed her mind. So Elizabeth remained in Washington, waiting for a letter or a telegram, her anxiety increasing each day. When Mrs. Lincoln sent no word by September 18, the morning after she had said she would arrive in New York, Elizabeth immediately telegraphed "Mrs. Clarke" at the St. Denis Hotel and told her she would join her there soon.

She took the next train to New York, and after an anxious ride by rail and then by stage, she arrived at the hotel, a six-story building at Broadway and East Eleventh Street. Pulling the bell at the ladies' entrance, she inquired with the boy who answered whether a Mrs. Clarke was staying there. He did not know, but went off to check with the manager, and soon returned to reply that Mrs. Clarke was indeed their guest. "Do you want to see her?" he asked.

"Yes."

"Well, just walk right there." He gestured in an indefinite direction. "She's down here now."

Hesitating, thinking that perhaps Mrs. Lincoln was in the parlor with company, Elizabeth gave him one of her business cards. "Take this to her, if you please," she said, but at that moment, Mrs. Lincoln came into the hall, drawn by the sound of her familiar voice.

"My dear Elizabeth, I am so glad to see you," she exclaimed, crossing the room and giving Elizabeth her hand. "When I arrived last night and you were not here, I was simply frantic."

Elizabeth had not seen Mrs. Lincoln in more than two years, and her pale, haggard appearance momentarily rendered her speechless. "I sent a telegram," she managed to say.

"Yes, but I have only just received it. It has been sitting here all day but it was never delivered until this evening. Come, and let us find out about your room."

She led Elizabeth into the office, where the clerk, like all modern hotel clerks, was exquisitely arrayed, highly perfumed, and too self-important to be courteous. He eyed Elizabeth with disdain as Mrs. Lincoln approached. "This is the woman I told you about," she said. "I want a good room for her."

The clerk's eyebrows rose. "We have no room for her, madam."

"But she must have a room. She is a friend of mine, and I want a room for her adjoining mine."

"We have no room for her on your floor" was his pointed reply.

Elizabeth understood his meaning perfectly, and she regarded him with steady, dignified silence. She would like nothing more than to quit his establishment and find a room for herself at a hotel run by a courteous colored proprietor, but night had fallen and she dared not venture out again, nor could she leave Mrs. Lincoln alone.

Mrs. Lincoln drew herself up, frowning. "That is strange, sir. I tell you that she is a friend of mine, and I am sure you could not give a room to a more worthy person."

"Friend of yours or not, I tell you we have no room for her on your floor." He paused and reluctantly added, "I can find a place for her on the fifth floor."

"That, sir, I presume, will be a vast improvement on my room," declared Mrs. Lincoln imperiously. "Well, if she goes to the fifth floor, I shall go too. What is good enough for her is good enough for me."

"Very well, madam." The clerk heaved a sigh and checked his register and room keys. "Shall I give you adjoining rooms, and send your baggage up?"

"Yes, and have it done in a hurry. Let the boy show us up. Come, Elizabeth." Mrs. Lincoln turned away from the clerk with a haughty parting look. The boy who had met Elizabeth at the door led them to the stairs, which they climbed and climbed until Elizabeth began to suspect that they would never reach the top. When they did, and the boy opened the doors to their rooms, Elizabeth could not have said which of them was more appalled. They had been given a pair of cramped, dingy, scantily furnished, three-cornered rooms in the servants' garret that smelled of dust and damp and sweat. Never in her life would Elizabeth have imagined a president's widow in such humble accommodations.

"How provoking," Mrs. Lincoln exclaimed, sinking heavily into a chair, panting from the effort of scaling the tower of stairs. "I declare, I never saw such unaccommodating people. Just to think of them sticking us away up here in the attic. I will give them a regular going over in the morning."

"You forget they do not know you," Elizabeth reminded her. "Mrs. Lincoln would be treated differently from Mrs. Clarke."

"True, I do forget. Well, I suppose I shall have to put up with the annoyances." Mrs. Lincoln's expression turned woebegone. "Why did you not come to me yesterday, Elizabeth? I was almost crazy when I reached here last night, and found you had not arrived. I sat down and wrote you a note — I felt so badly — imploring you to come to me immediately."

"I thought perhaps you would change your mind," Elizabeth admitted. "I also knew I would have great difficulty securing rooms for 'Mrs. Clarke.' "

"Well, based upon what we have seen so far I cannot fault you for suspecting as much." Then she gave a little start. "You have not had your dinner, Elizabeth, and you must be hungry. I nearly forgot about it in the joy of seeing you. You must go down to the table right away."

Elizabeth was famished, but the thought of a good meal partly revived her. Mrs. Lincoln pulled the bell rope, and when a servant appeared, she ordered him to give Elizabeth her dinner. Elizabeth followed him downstairs, where he led her into the dining room and seated her at a corner table. She was giving him her order when the steward approached. "You are in the wrong room," he said gruffly.

Elizabeth regarded him mildly. "I was brought here by the waiter."

"It makes no difference. I will find you another place where you can eat your dinner."

Elizabeth's stomach rumbled as she got up from the table and followed him from the dining room. "It is very strange," Elizabeth said tightly when they reached the hall, "that you should permit me to be seated at the table in the dining room only for the sake of ordering me to leave it the next moment."

The steward halted and regarded her over his shoulder. "Are you not Mrs. Clarke's servant?"

"I am with Mrs. Clarke," Elizabeth replied, emphasizing the distinction.

"It is all the same." He turned back around and continued down the hall. "Servants are not allowed to eat in the large dining room. Here, this way. You must take your dinner in the servants' hall."

Humiliated and hungry, Elizabeth followed the steward through the rear corridors of the hotel, knowing that it was the only way she was likely to get a bite to eat. On reaching the servants' hall, the steward tugged on the knob only to find the door locked. He left Elizabeth standing in the passage while he went to inform the clerk. A few minutes later, the obsequious clerk came blustering down the hall, the scent of his perfume preceding him. "Did you come out of the street, or from Mrs. Clarke's room?"

"From Mrs. Clarke's room," she replied politely, refusing to mirror his ill temper.

"It is after the regular hour for dinner. The room is locked up, and Annie has gone out with the key."

For a moment Elizabeth hoped that he might allow her to return to the dining room, but when he said nothing more, her pride would not allow her to stand waiting in the hall any longer. "Very well," she said, turning toward the staircase. "I will tell Mrs. Clarke that I cannot get any dinner."

He scowled as she began to climb the stairs. "You need not put on airs," he called after her. "I understand the whole thing."

"I don't think you do," Elizabeth muttered under her breath as she reached the first of far too many landings. "If you understood the whole thing," she huffed as she climbed, "it is strange that you should put the widow of President Abraham Lincoln in a three-cornered room in the attic of this miserable hotel."

Murmuring to herself what she could not say to his face only made her feel worse. When she finally reached Mrs. Lincoln's room, tears of humiliation and frustration blurred her vision.

At the sight of her downcast expression, Mrs. Lincoln's brow furrowed in concern. "What is the matter, Elizabeth?"

"I cannot get any dinner."

"Cannot get any dinner? What do you mean?"

Elizabeth sank into a chair and told her all that had happened since the servant had led her downstairs. "Those insolent, overbearing people," Mrs. Lincoln exclaimed, furious. She seized the armrests of her easy chair and pulled herself fiercely to her feet. "Never mind, Elizabeth. You shall have your dinner. Put on your bonnet and shawl."

"What for?"

"What for?" Mrs. Lincoln put on her bonnet and stood at the mirror, tying the strings. "Why, we will go out of the hotel, and get you something to eat where they know how to behave decently."

Warily, Elizabeth said, "Surely, Mrs. Lincoln, you do not intend to go out on the street tonight?"

"Yes I do. Do you suppose I am going to have you starve, when we can find something to eat on every corner?"

"But you forget. You are here as Mrs. Clarke and not as Mrs. Lincoln. You arrived alone, and the people here already suspect that everything is not quite as you say. If you go outside the hotel at night, they will accept that as evidence against you."

"Nonsense. What do you suppose I care for what these low-bred people think? Put on your things."

"No, Mrs. Lincoln," Elizabeth said firmly, though her stomach rumbled a protest. "I shall not go outside of the hotel tonight, for I understand your situation, even if you do not. Mrs. Lincoln has no reason to care what these people may say about her, but Mrs. Clarke wishes to remain incognito, so she must be more prudent."

With some difficulty, Elizabeth finally persuaded Mrs. Lincoln to act with caution. She was so frank and impulsive that she never gave enough thought to how her words and deeds could be misconstrued. Elizabeth bade her good night and went off to her own room, but not until she was settled in bed and had turned down the lamp did it occur to her that Mrs. Lincoln could have ordered dinner to be served to

Elizabeth in her room, so that she would not have had to retire hungry.

The next morning, Mrs. Lincoln knocked on Elizabeth's door before six o'clock. "Come, Elizabeth, get up," she called. "I know you must be hungry. Dress yourself quickly and we will go out and get some breakfast. I was unable to sleep last night for thinking of you being forced to go to bed without anything to eat."

Elizabeth too had slept poorly in her uncomfortable, lumpy bed, kept from restful slumber by her growling stomach. Swiftly she dressed, and before long she and Mrs. Lincoln were taking their breakfast at a restaurant on Broadway about a block away from the St. Denis Hotel. Afterward, they strolled up Broadway and entered Union Square Park, where they seated themselves on a bench beneath a canopy of trees bright with autumn colors, watched the children at play, and discussed Mrs. Lincoln's plan to sell her wardrobe. Mrs. Lincoln soon revealed that the previous day, while Elizabeth was en route from Washington, she had called on a diamond broker after seeing an ad in the *Herald* at the breakfast table. "I tried to sell them a lot of jewelry," Mrs. Lincoln said. "I gave my name as Mrs. Clarke. The first gentleman I spoke with was pleasant, but we were unable to agree on a price. He stepped back into the office to confer with another gentleman, and just as I concluded they were plotting to hurry me out the door, a third gentleman entered the store. He looked over my jewelry — he was, as I later learned, Mr. Keyes, a silent partner in the firm — and discovered my name engraved inside of one of my rings."

"Oh, dear," said Elizabeth.

"I had forgotten about the engraving," Mrs. Lincoln confessed. "When I saw him looking at the ring so earnestly, I snatched it from him and put it in my pocket."

Elizabeth smothered a laugh. "I'm sure that didn't provoke his curiosity at all."

"I did not want to wait around to find out. I hastily gathered up my jewelry and started to leave, but they had become much more interested in my wares, as you can imagine. I left my card, Mrs. Clarke at the St. Denis Hotel. They are to call to see me this forenoon, when I shall enter into negotiations with them."

"Is that wise?" Elizabeth asked carefully. "Surely they've figured out that you are Mrs. President Lincoln."

"Or that I am her thieving maid."

"Not likely, I think." Earnestly, Elizabeth said, "With such delicate business, should you trust a firm that you have never heard of before, one that you chose only because you spied their ad in the paper? Wouldn't it be more prudent to seek a recommendation from an acquaintance, or work through a jeweler you've done business with before?"

"More prudent but impossible," Mrs. Lincoln replied. "I could not ask friends for introductions or go to my favorite jewelers without exposing myself. Even if Mr. Keyes knows who I am, the rest of the city must not suspect. I could not bear the humiliation."

Elizabeth understood, and after enjoying the sunshine and cool breezes a little while longer, they returned to the hotel. Shortly after their arrival, Mr. Keyes called, and after they withdrew to a parlor to chat, Mrs. Lincoln confirmed her true identity. He was, as Elizabeth suspected he would be, elated, and he willingly admired the shawls, dresses, and fine laces Mrs. Lincoln displayed for him. When Mrs. Lincoln explained why she was compelled to sell her wardrobe, Mr. Keyes was much affected by her story and severely denounced the government for its ingratitude. He was disgusted by the tale of their ill treatment at the St. Denis too, and he urged Mrs. Lincoln to move to another hotel without delay.

Mrs. Lincoln agreed, and as they rode to the Union Place Hotel, Elizabeth said, "Perhaps when we arrive, you can confide in the proprietor, and give him your true name without registering, to ensure the proper respect." Hesitantly, Mrs. Lincoln agreed, but by the time they reached the hotel, she had changed her mind again, and registered as Mrs. Clarke. Even so, they were treated with far more courtesy — perhaps because Mrs. Lincoln's real name was discernible on some of her trunks, if one looked carefully, and the staff knew who she was but pretended otherwise.

After they had settled into their new accommodations, Mr. Keyes and Mr. Brady called on Mrs. Lincoln often over the next few days, for they had much to discuss. Mrs. Lincoln was anxious to dispose of her garments and return to Chicago as quickly and discreetly as possible, but to Elizabeth's consternation, the gentlemen would hear nothing of this. "Put your affairs in our hands," Mr. Brady declared, "and we will raise you at least one hundred thousand dollars in a few weeks. The people will not permit the widow of Abraham Lincoln to suffer. They will come to her rescue when they know she is in want."

This was precisely what Mrs. Lincoln wanted to hear, in both financial and emotional terms, and so she agreed to work with W. H. Brady & Co. They advanced her six hundred dollars for her expenses while she remained in New York, and they assured her that their plan, once they devised it, would succeed.

The Union Place Hotel was comfortable, and the brokers' confidence was heartening, but even so, Mrs. Lincoln and Elizabeth remained wary of discovery. On Sunday they took a carriage ride through Central Park, but they took no pleasure in it, because despite the heavy veil Mrs. Lincoln wore to conceal her identity, they could not throw open the window for fear of being recognized. They also narrowly escaped being run into by another carriage, and they were terribly alarmed not 'only for the harm that might have come to them, but because an accident would have drawn attention and their masquerade would have been exposed.

Elizabeth disliked the subterfuge more every day, but when Mr. Brady and Mr. Keyes came to Mrs. Lincoln with their plan for disposing of her goods, she began to dread that the scheme was a disaster in the making. Mr. Brady believed that the prominent Republican men who owed their fortunes to Mr. Lincoln would be willing to advance her money rather than let it be made known that his widow was so impoverished that she was compelled to sell her wardrobe. To that end, he urged Mrs. Lincoln to write letters describing her unhappy circumstances, addressed to him but dated as if she had written them weeks earlier while still in Chicago. The brokers wanted her to imply that she had saved letters compromising various politicians and businessmen who had profited from wartime contracts. Mr. Brady and Mr. Keyes would show the letters to the gentlemen in question in hopes of embarrassing them into providing for her. If that failed — if her plight, their loyalty to the Republican Party, and their own sense of self-preservation did not move them — Mr. Brady would threaten to publish the letters.

To Elizabeth the plan smacked of blackmail, and the moment Mr. Brady and Mr. Keyes left, she urged Mrs. Lincoln not to go along with it. "I fail to see how any good could come of dishonesty and threats," she said. "You said you wanted to dispose of your wardrobe quickly and quietly. I fear these letters will only draw the matter out and bring you unwanted attention."

"I have been ignored long enough." Mrs. Lincoln sat down at her table and took out pen, ink, and paper. "Mr. Brady and Mr. Keyes believe that I must do something to gain the attention of the gentlemen best placed to assist me."

"You will gain their attention, certainly, and also the attention of the wider world." Elizabeth despaired of convincing her, and yet she could not be silent. "The worst of what the papers have written about you in the past will be nothing compared to the disparagement and scorn they will heap upon you over this."

" 'Dear Sir,' " Mrs. Lincoln said aloud as she began her first letter, making a show of ignoring her that Elizabeth thought unkind. " 'A notice that you sold articles of value on commission, prompts me to write to you.' See, Elizabeth, there is an honest beginning. You cannot fault me for following Mr. Brady's advice if I say nothing that is not true."

"The date, as well as your location." Elizabeth gestured to the page, barely keeping her frustration in check. "Chicago, September 1867. That is already untrue."

"Those are small details, and of no consequence."

Elizabeth muffled a sigh and resisted the

524

urge to fling her hands in the air in exasperation. She peered over Mrs. Lincoln's shoulder as she wrote, ostensibly to Mr. Brady, of how urgent necessity compelled her to part with valuable gifts from dear friends. Mrs. Lincoln finished that letter and began another, dated Chicago, September 14. "My dear sir," she addressed Mr. Brady. "Please call and see Hon. Abram Wakeman. He was largely indebted to me for obtaining the lucrative office which he has held for several years, and from which he has amassed a very large fortune. He will assist me in my painful and humiliating situation, scarcely removed from want. He would not hesitate to return, in a small manner, the many favors my husband and myself always showered upon him. Mr. Wakeman many times excited my sympathies in his urgent appeals for office, as well for himself as others. Therefore he will be only too happy to relieve me by purchasing one or more of the articles you will please place before him."

Elizabeth's dismay deepened with every dip of Mrs. Lincoln's pen into the inkwell. Mr. Wakeman was a former New York congressman and postmaster of New York City, whom President Lincoln had appointed surveyor of the Port of New York, second only to the Custom House as the most coveted patronage post the administration could bestow. He was also a sharp, shrewd politician, and Elizabeth could not imagine his fearing embarrassment so much that he would allow himself to be bullied by a diamond broker with questionable ethics.

"Please, Mrs. Lincoln, take care," Elizabeth urged her. "If you insist upon writing these letters, at least use the mildest language possible."

"Never mind, Elizabeth," said Mrs. Lincoln briskly, signing her name. "Anything to raise the wind. One might as well be killed for a sheep as a lamb."

So Elizabeth sighed and said no more, not even when Mrs. Lincoln began a new letter with "You write me that reporters are after you concerning my goods deposited with you . . . and also that there is a fear that these newsmen will seize upon the painful circumstances of your having these articles placed in your hands to injure the Republican Party politically." Not for the world would Mrs. Lincoln do anything to injure their cause, she wrote, "notwithstanding the very men for whom my noble husband did so much unhesitatingly, deprived me of all means of support and left me in a pitiless condition." The phrases were designed to put the fear of exposure in the press into the gentlemen's hearts, and considerable guilt regarding Mrs. Lincoln's circumstances besides, but Elizabeth could not imagine powerful men meekly throwing money Mrs. Lincoln's way to make the potential scandal disappear. They were far more likely to throw Mr. Brady from their offices in utter contempt.

But Mrs. Lincoln would not hear her.

The letters were written and delivered to Mr. Brady and Mr. Keyes, who immediately commenced showing them to the gentlemen Mrs. Lincoln had named. Soon thereafter, it occurred to her that the brokers' scheme was designed to bring her income without parting with any of her clothes, so she decided to dispose of her wardrobe another way. She instructed Elizabeth to make appointments for several dealers in secondhand clothing to call on "Mrs. Clarke" at the Union Place Hotel, but although they duly came, and seemed interested in her goods, they could not agree on a price. Thwarted, but not daunted, a few days later Mrs. Lincoln and Elizabeth packed a bundle of dresses and shawls into a carriage and drove along Seventh Avenue, stopping at first one store and then another, seeking buyers. They soon discovered that the dealers wanted the goods for little or nothing, and although Mrs. Lincoln met them squarely, her tact and shrewdness accomplished nothing. Discouraged, they returned to the hotel disgusted with the whole affair, but they could not abandon it.

In the meantime, their strange behavior had drawn the attention of the hotel staff and other guests, who cast curious, suspicious looks upon them wherever they went. The large trunks in which Mrs. Lincoln's wardrobe was stored had been kept in the main hall rather than carried upstairs, and they had become the objects of scrutiny and speculation. First one reporter, then another, noticed that the faint outlines of Mrs. Lincoln's name appeared on the lid of one trunk, even though the letters had been rubbed out. Mrs. Lincoln and Elizabeth became ever more wary and uncomfortable with the speculative glances and whispers, until Mrs. Lincoln finally decided that they must escape. They packed their smaller trunks, had the larger ones delivered to the offices of W. H. Brady & Co. at 609 Broadway, paid their hotel bills, and quickly departed for the country, where they remained for three days to throw the reporters off the scent. When they returned to the city, Elizabeth suggested that Mrs. Lincoln go to the Metropolitan Hotel, where she had stayed on previous occasions, and confide in the proprietor, who had always been courteous and respectful to her. Mrs. Lincoln refused. Instead they took rooms at the Brandreth House, where Mrs. Lincoln registered as "Mrs. Morris."

Elizabeth had grown weary of the aliases and the clandestine skulking, but she endured it, wanting to believe that eventually it would benefit Mrs. Lincoln. As the weeks passed, she lost hope that any good would come of their efforts, but she felt no vindication when Mr. Keyes and Mr. Brady were finally forced to admit that their scheme had failed. They had shown the letters to numerous prominent Republicans, but not one had responded favorably. With the exception of a few dresses sold at low prices to secondhand dealers, Mrs. Lincoln's wardrobe was still packed away in her trunks. The six hundred dollars the brokers had advanced was nearly spent, and Mrs. Lincoln had nothing to show for her time in New York — in fact, with gossip circulating about the mysterious, heavily veiled widow peddling her wardrobe, it would be fair to say she was worse off than when she had left Chicago.

In the first week of October, her funds and

patience spent, Mrs. Lincoln reluctantly agreed to allow Mr. Brady to exhibit her wardrobe in their showrooms for sale, and to widely publicize that it was hers. "People who were not interested in Mrs. Clarke's clothing will be very eager to acquire Mrs. Lincoln's," Mr. Brady declared, but Elizabeth was not reassured. Mrs. Lincoln also agreed to allow the brokers to publish her letters in the New York *World,* a Democratic newspaper more than willing to expose Republicans to ridicule. After resigning herself to the new plan, discouraged, anxious, and missing young Tad dreadfully, Mrs. Lincoln left New York the same morning the letters appeared in the paper, leaving Elizabeth behind in charge of her affairs.

Elizabeth wanted very badly to return home too, and to reopen her business. Mrs. Lincoln had promised to pay her a commission from the sale of her wardrobe, but no sales meant no pay. She could not afford a hotel, so she found lodgings in a private home, economized, and hoped that putting Mrs. Lincoln's wardrobe on display would stir up interest that would lead to profitable sales.

In the end, she received only part of what she hoped for.

The first sign of impending disaster came not from 609 Broadway or the press, but from a letter Mrs. Lincoln sent to Elizabeth within hours of returning to Chicago. On the train west, she found herself in the peculiar situation of sitting behind two gentlemen who had just read her letters in the *World* and were discussing her pecuniary embarrassment. Later, she went to the dining room and was shown to a table where sat none other than her friend from Washington Senator Charles Sumner, who recognized her immediately despite the black veil doubled over her face. His pity was so tangible that she knew he too was thinking of the letters and the public display of her wardrobe, and she was so discomfited that she invented an ill friend who needed her and fled from the table. She was embarrassed to tears, later, when the compassionate senator brought a cup of tea to her car. In a second letter, written only hours after the first, Mrs. Lincoln lamented, "I am writing this morning with a broken heart after a sleepless night of great mental suffering. R came up last night like a maniac, and almost threatening his life, and looking like death because the letters of the *World* were published in yesterday's paper. I could not refrain from weeping when I saw him so miserable."

Elizabeth needed a moment to parse out her meaning, and when she deduced that Mrs. Lincoln meant the falsified letters had been printed in the Chicago papers, her heart plummeted so quickly it left her light-headed. She should have expected the scandal to be too big and too interesting to remain confined to New York.

"I weep whilst I am writing," Mrs. Lincoln wrote on. "I pray for death this morning. Only darling Taddie prevents my taking my life." She was nearly losing her reason, she concluded, and she instructed Elizabeth to tell Mr. Brady and Mr. Keyes not to put a single line more of hers into print.

In the weeks that followed, more and more letters came from Chicago, and although Mrs. Lincoln begged Elizabeth to write to her every day, it was all she could do to take care of the business already entrusted to her. The curious and the contemptuous visited the offices of W. H. Brady & Co. to examine dresses piled up on a long table, shawls hanging over the backs of chairs, furs and laces and jewels in a glass case. The publication of the letters had indeed stirred up interest, but while many people browsed, no one bought. As one reporter sniggered in the *Evening Express*, some of the dresses "if not worn long, have been worn much; they are jagged under the arms and at the bottom of the skirt, stains are on the lining, and other objections present themselves." The extravagantly high prices on the labels dangling from the articles, the reporter said, had no doubt been conceived by the dressmakers, overproud of their labors. "The peculiarity of the dresses," he added, "is that the most of them are cut low-necked — a taste which some ladies attribute to Mrs. Lincoln's appreciation of her own bust."

That report, and other similar pieces that followed in other papers, only worsened from there. Reporters and gossips alike began referring to the situation as "Mrs. Lincoln's Old Clothes Scandal." Democrats sensed an opportunity to injure their opponents by pouncing upon the *World* letters as evidence that Republicans had bought favors from Mr. Lincoln's White House. In response, Republican newspapers denounced Mrs. Lincoln's rash, improper, and unwomanly actions and fell over one another in their haste to repudiate her. "It appears as if the fiends have let loose, for the Republican papers are tearing me to pieces in this border ruffian West," Mrs. Lincoln wrote Elizabeth on October 9. "If I had committed murder in every city in this *blessed Union,* I could not be more traduced. And you know how innocent I have been of the intention of doing wrong."

But Elizabeth could not consider her entirely innocent, for she had, after all, agreed to compose the false letters. Always Elizabeth wanted to believe that Mrs. Lincoln's intentions were good, but she could not quite convince herself this time.

While Mrs. Lincoln pored worriedly over the papers and tried to make amends to Robert and groused about her maltreatment in letters to Elizabeth and other sympathetic friends, Elizabeth remained in New York, assisting the brokers as she could, trying to prevent the damage to Mrs. Lincoln's reputation from worsening. Eventually, as the scandal dragged on, so many false reports were circulated that Elizabeth, at a suggestion from Mrs. Lincoln, granted interviews to the sympathetic *Herald* and the *Evening News* to set the record straight. None of it seemed to make any difference. The vitriol increased, the wardrobe sat pawed over and collecting dust at 609 Broadway, and Elizabeth worked herself close to exhaustion. She began to take in sewing to make ends meet, but such intermittent piecework brought in a meager living compared to what she had earned running her own dressmaking business. She moved to a boardinghouse on Broome Street, whose proprietress, Mrs. Bell, was a cousin of William Slade, Mr. Lincoln's former messenger. But those measures were not enough.

Elizabeth remained in New York throughout the fall and winter, struggling to serve her former patron's best interests while neglecting her own. At her lowest moments, she wondered why she persisted when she had lost almost all hope of success. By November she was wretchedly low-spirited and wanted desperately to return to Washington, but Mrs. Lincoln urged her to remain in New York a little while longer. Perhaps later, she suggested, after the whole sorry business was resolved, Elizabeth could join Mrs. Lincoln in Chicago. "Had you not better go with me and share my fortunes, for a year or more?" she implored, apparently oblivious to the pleasant, productive, satisfying life Elizabeth had left behind in the capital, and how she longed to return to it.

Nevertheless, duty compelled her to persist in the cause of Mrs. Lincoln's relief. Drawing upon the connections she had made on behalf of the Contraband Relief Association, Elizabeth wrote to leaders of the colored community proposing that collections for Mrs. Lincoln should be taken up in colored churches. The idea met with strong approval, because freeborn and freed slave alike recognized Abraham Lincoln as their great friend, and they were anxious to show their kind interest in the welfare of his family in some way more earnest and substantial than simple words. "You judge me rightly," Mr. Frederick Douglass wrote in his reply. "I am willing to do what I can to place the widow of our martyr President in the affluent position which her relation to that good man and to the country entitles her to." To that end, he proposed arranging a series of lectures by the best speakers in the country — and he himself would be honored to participate. The fees this venture would raise, combined with the generous donations from the colored community, would at last relieve Mrs. Lincoln's financial distress and allow her a great measure of comfort.

Gratified, Elizabeth wrote to Mrs. Lincoln about the plan, elated to have good news to share at last. But to her consternation, Mrs. Lincoln resisted. As desperate as she was for relief, she did not want to accept help from Negroes. "I want neither Mr. Douglass nor Garnet to lecture on my behalf," she decreed abruptly on the second day of November. Bewildered, and not a little disappointed, Elizabeth had no choice but to inform Mr. Douglass of Mrs. Lincoln's wishes, and the project was immediately abandoned. Less than two weeks later, Mrs. Lincoln changed her mind, but her initial rebuff had surprised and disappointed colored leaders, and their enthusiasm for helping her had cooled.

"Write to me, dear friend, your candid opinion about everything," Mrs. Lincoln begged as the scandal swirled about her. "I pray God there will be some success," she wrote on another occasion, "although, dear Elizabeth, entirely between ourselves, I fear I am in villainous hands." "Alas! Alas!" she lamented the very next day. "What a mistake it has all been!" Mrs. Lincoln asked Mr. Brady and Mr. Keyes to return her wardrobe, and ordered Elizabeth to collect it, only to have the brokers defer her requests again and again. With Mrs. Lincoln losing heart, Elizabeth found it next to impossible to keep her own spirits aloft.

In early January, in one last, desperate attempt to raise money from the "Old Clothes," Mr. Brady and Mr. Keyes took a portion of the wardrobe to Providence, intending to launch a traveling expedition at Remington's Hall, charging the "moderate consideration" of twenty-five cents each for admission. "The exhibition will bring in money," Mr. Keyes told Elizabeth, "and as money must be raised, this is the last resort." He assumed Mrs. Lincoln would approve, and Elizabeth assumed that he had consulted her beforehand, but both were mistaken. "Why did *you* not urge them *not* to take my goods to Providence?" Mrs. Lincoln demanded by return mail when informed of the plan, already under way. "For heaven's sake see K & B when you receive this, and have my wardrobe immediately returned to me, *with their bill.*" Although advertisements ran in *The Providence Journal* announcing the exhibit, it never opened, for the Providence board of aldermen refused to grant the brokers a license. Nevertheless, Mrs. Lincoln was not mollified.

Elizabeth soon inadvertently upset Mrs. Lincoln again. The needs of her own race, especially their education, were always in her thoughts, and it pained her that Wilberforce University, the school her son had attended, had burned to the ground on the day of President Lincoln's assassination. Although she was preoccupied with discharging Mrs. Lincoln's business, Elizabeth had agreed to lead a fund-raising drive to rebuild the college. She arranged with Reverend Daniel Payne, one of the college's founders and a witness to her pension statement, to loan some of her Lincoln relics — Mr. Lincoln's hat, cloak, gloves, comb, and brush, as well as Mrs. Lincoln's bonnet and blood-spattered cloak — for an exhibition that would tour Europe. At the news of yet another exhibit linked to her name, Mrs. Lincoln became frantic. "Your letter announcing that my clothes were to be paraded in Europe — those I gave you — has almost turned me wild," she immediately responded. "Robert would go *raving distracted* if such a thing was done. If you have the *least regard* for *our reason,* pray write to the bishop that it *must* not be done. How little did I suppose you would do *such a thing;* you cannot imagine how much my overwhelming sorrows would be increased. May kind heaven turn your heart . . . For the sake of *humanity,* if not *me* and my children, *do not* have those black clothes displayed in Europe. The thought has almost whitened every hair of my head."

The withering rebuke was almost more than Elizabeth could bear, and she immediately did as Mrs. Lincoln demanded.

With dwindling hopes of ever receiving a

commission from the sale of Mrs. Lincoln's wardrobe, and with increasing worries about the damage to her reputation for her very visible role in the "Old Clothes Scandal," Elizabeth realized that she must do something for herself, and rely no longer upon ephemeral expectations.

She had accumulated several memory sketches since the summer day she had learned that the woman she had escorted around Washington City's contraband camps was Miss Harriet Jacobs, the runaway slave from North Carolina who had bravely published her autobiography in 1861, using a pseudonym to protect herself from recapture and return to her horrifically abusive owner. Many other former slaves had also written their own life stories, including Mr. Frederick Douglass, whom she greatly admired. Though illiterate, Sojourner Truth had dictated her memoirs to a friend, and they had been published to great interest and acclaim. Why could Elizabeth not do the same? Mrs. Lincoln and Mr. Douglass, as well as the Garlands, had complimented her writing. Why should she not tell her own story?

And so she took her memory sketches and began to fashion them into a memoir. She envisioned her book as tracing her life from her birth into slavery, through the sorrowful years of her youth, and on to her triumphant emergence into freedom. She would describe her years as Mrs. Lincoln's personal modiste and White House intimate, and share her observations of the great, martyred president. She hoped to place Mrs. Lincoln in a better light before the world by revealing the innocent motives that had spurred her often misunderstood actions. Lastly, she would offer a detailed account of the so-called "Old Clothes Scandal," to redeem her own good name as well as Mrs. Lincoln's.

"Do all you can, dear Mrs. Keckley," Mr. Douglass had exhorted her as they planned the thwarted lecture series for Mrs. Lincoln's benefit. "Nobody can do more than you in removing the mountains of prejudice toward that good lady."

Elizabeth believed he was right. No one knew Mrs. Lincoln the way she did, and no one could explain and justify her actions better than she, a friend and confidante who understood her good intentions.

Elizabeth could do this much for Mrs. Lincoln, and since no one else would, she had to. She owed that much to the grieving widow — and even more so, to the memory of the noble, martyred president who had done so much for her race. For both of them, she resolved to try.

CHAPTER SIXTEEN

March–June 1868

At first, Elizabeth was too embarrassed to confide in any of her New York acquaintances that she was writing her memoirs, even though many friends and patrons throughout the years had told her she ought to, since she had lived such an extraordinary life. But as the pages accumulated, she mentioned her manuscript to one friend, and then another, and eventually the tale found its way to Mr. James Redpath, a friend of Mr. Frederick Douglass and an editor with the publishing house G. W. Carleton & Company. Elizabeth had already met Mr. Redpath, but only in passing, and it was not quite accurate to say they knew each other. When she was living in St. Louis, some of her friends had spoken with the staunchly abolitionist Mr. Redpath when he came to the city to interview slaves for a book he was writing. He had also visited the White House often to advise President Lincoln on matters concerning Haiti, but although she had seen him there, they had never spoken. Having heard of her fledgling memoir, however, he was eager to make her acquaintance, and mutual friends introduced them.

The red-haired, fiery Scotsman called on her at her Broome Street boardinghouse, where she sat anxiously in the chair opposite his while he read the opening chapter of her memoir, the story of her birth and early childhood. She held her breath, waiting for his verdict, perching on the edge of her seat until he set her handwritten pages on his lap and said, "This is a promising start."

She exhaled deeply. "Thank you, sir."

"The story of Little Joe sold off by the pound and his poor mother running after the wagon as it sped away from the plantation . . ." Mr. Redpath shook his head, grim. "Tragic. Absolutely heartbreaking. I don't suppose you know if they ever reunited?"

"I wish I knew," said Elizabeth. "Perhaps, after the war, they were able to find each other, but Little Joe was no more than four years old when he was sold to the Petersburg slaver. I imagine it would have been very difficult for him to retrace the path of dim childhood memories."

Mr. Redpath grunted and nodded. "Tragic indeed." He held up the pages of her manuscript. "Where have you taken the story after this, and where do you intend to go?"

She explained her plan for the book, and his eyes lit up with eagerness when she mentioned that she hoped to devote a significant portion to her White House years and "Mrs. Lincoln's Old Clothes Scandal." She intended to share the profits of her book with Mrs. Lincoln, and to reveal the truth, the good and the bad, so that the world would better understand the former First Lady, who had been so unfairly maligned.

"I admire your loyalty," Mr. Redpath remarked. "Rest assured, Carleton and Company wants the truth presented to the world as much as you do — the good and the bad."

Within days Mr. Redpath brokered an agreement between Elizabeth and his publisher, and told her that they would like to publish her memoir as soon as possible, by spring at the latest. "But I have only just finished writing about how I purchased my freedom," Elizabeth replied, her joy and alarm creating a dizzying muddle of her thoughts.

He assured her that he would help, and so

they agreed to meet several times a week to collaborate on the rest of the manuscript — daily, if necessary, as the deadline approached.

From then on, by day Elizabeth attended to Mrs. Lincoln's business and took in sewing to earn her keep, and by night she wrote in the quiet seclusion of her garret room. In the evenings, Mr. Redpath would call on her at her boardinghouse, and they would meet in the public parlor to review her previous night's work. Sometimes, necessity and haste required her to merely jot down her recollections rather than writing lengthy paragraphs of elegant prose. On such occasions she would read aloud from her notes to Mr. Redpath, elaborating where needed, while her editor took notes of his own, which he took back to his office, combined with hers, and revised.

Elizabeth passed her fiftieth birthday working with Mr. Redpath on the twelfth chapter of her memoir, an account of Mrs. Lincoln's departure from the White House after her husband's assassination. The next day, she received a letter from Mrs. Lincoln, who was despondent because she had forgotten her pocketbook, which held her entire allowance for the month, on the streetcar. "The loss I deserve for being so careless," she lamented, "but it comes very hard on poor me. Troubles and misfortunes are fast overwhelming me; may *the end* soon come."

Mrs. Lincoln had so often said that only Tad kept her from taking her own life that Elizabeth did not know whether by "the end" she meant the end of her troubles or the end of everything. After so much repetition, laments of that sort should no longer have bothered Elizabeth, but they unsettled her anew every time.

Every other scheme having failed, Mr. Brady and Mr. Keyes decided to put what remained of Mrs. Lincoln's wardrobe — which was nearly all of it — up for public auction. Unwilling to dispose of her goods in such a manner, Mrs. Lincoln adamantly insisted that the brokers return everything to Elizabeth and settle her account. They took their time about it, but eventually they allowed Elizabeth to collect the unsold goods — at which time they presented her with a bill for $820, the charge for their services. They also kept several hundred dollars more that they had received for selling Mrs. Lincoln's diamond ring and a few other items — for their expenses, they explained. Elizabeth promptly packed up Mrs. Lincoln's wardrobe and shipped it back to her in Chicago, and when Mrs. Lincoln sent her a check for the bill, Elizabeth delivered it to Mr. Keyes personally. When she left his office on March 4, receipt in hand, she felt a wave of relief, resignation, and disgust wash over her. The whole ugly, ill-conceived business was over at last. Not only had it failed to raise any money for Mrs. Lincoln's support, it had also cost her hundreds of dollars in brokers' fees and incalculable damage to her reputation. But finally it was done.

Although Elizabeth missed her home and friends in Washington City and urgently needed to reopen her dressmaking business, she decided to remain in New York until her manuscript could be completed. Since she no longer needed to reside within a convenient distance of W. H. Brady & Co., she moved to a less costly, fourth-floor garret room at No. 14 Carroll Place, the home of Mrs. Amelia Lancaster, a successful hairdresser to New York City's elite.

As she drew closer to the final chapters of her book, a certain sense of unease compelled Elizabeth to write to Mrs. Lincoln and tell her about it. After Mr. Herndon's shocking lectures, Elizabeth expected Mrs. Lincoln to have misgivings, so she emphasized in the warmest terms that everything she wrote was designed to place Mrs. Lincoln before the world in the best possible light. Mrs. Lincoln acknowledged Elizabeth's confession with a single line in her next letter: "It would appear that every former inmate of my beloved husband's White House *must* inflict a memoir upon the public — I can only trust that my *dearest friend* would not write anything *unkind,* or betray any confidences." Elizabeth had hoped for her to more explicitly bestow her blessing upon the project, but she accepted Mrs. Lincoln's remarks as tacit permission to proceed. She could not have abandoned the book then in any case; she had invested too much of her time and industry, as well as Mr. Redpath's.

A few days later, Elizabeth finished writing her account of the disastrous attempt to sell Mrs. Lincoln's wardrobe, the final chapter of her book. After Mr. Redpath read it, he praised her for her unflinching frankness and honesty in describing what surely must have been as embarrassing an episode for herself as it was for Mrs. Lincoln.

"Unflinching?" echoed Elizabeth. "On the contrary, I did flinch, quite often, as I wrote it. I confess I'm very concerned about divulging Mrs. Lincoln's private conversations and personal thoughts to the world."

Mr. Redpath's brow furrowed in sympathy. "I understand completely. I promise you, nothing published in the book will hurt Mrs. Lincoln."

Elizabeth was relieved to hear it. "That pleases me very much."

"You're nearly finished," Mr. Redpath remarked, gathering the day's pages into a neat stack. "You must be looking forward to completing the manuscript and returning to Washington."

"I am," said Elizabeth tentatively. She had thought the manuscript *was* finished. "What else would you like me to add?"

"Well, there's the preface, which should describe your purpose and qualifications for writing a book of this nature."

"Oh, of course. I'll begin it right away."

"I had another thought as well. The letters you've included from Mr. Douglass and the Garland ladies are most illuminating. Do you have any letters from Mrs. Lincoln? I'm sure your readers would find them fascinating."

Elizabeth felt a thrill of excitement and fear when he spoke of her readers, as if they already existed in eager multitudes. "I have many, but I simply could not include them in the book, fascinating or not. Mrs. Lincoln would not approve."

Mr. Redpath shrugged, thoughtful. "She allowed several letters to be printed in the *World*."

"Yes, and she deeply regretted it afterward."

"Ah." Mr. Redpath nodded, thinking, and then ventured, "I don't suppose you would let me read them?"

"Are you merely curious?"

"I am *very* curious, but not *merely* curious. Reading Mrs. Lincoln's letters would give me a sense of her manner and intonation, which will be of great help to me as I edit your manuscript. The facts her letters include, too, will help me verify dates and details you have provided. And there is the matter of your credibility. Some foolish people will argue that a former slave never could have written such a fine book, nor gained admission to the most intimate circles of the White House in the first place. I cannot emphasize enough the importance of personal correspondence in establishing the authenticity of a biography."

"I understand," said Elizabeth. She had heard of other former slaves' memoirs that had been unfairly dismissed as works of fiction, and she knew many people who, after knowing her but a little while, insisted that she was far too dignified and talented to have ever been a slave. She could not bear to have anyone question her integrity, but such accusations were probably inevitable. If she could forestall them or at least limit their number by sharing Mrs. Lincoln's letters with her editor, she would be wise to do so.

She went to her garret room and returned with a bundle of Mrs. Lincoln's letters, neatly bound with a black ribbon left over from trimming one of her many bonnets. She gave them to Mr. Redpath with the understanding that they were precious mementoes and must be returned to her undamaged as soon as he was finished with them, and that they were only meant to assist him in editing her manuscript, not to become a part of it.

Mr. Redpath assured her that he would publish nothing from Mrs. Lincoln's letters that would embarrass her, and with that, he left Elizabeth to write her preface.

Alone in her room, she held her pen hovering above the page, unable to begin. A twinge of doubt struck — who was she, to think she could write a book? Immediately she chased the thought away, impatient with her timidity. Who was she, indeed. She *had* written a book, so the question of whether she *could* had already been answered. Now all that remained was to explain why she had, and to what purpose.

"I have often been asked to write my life, as those who know me know that it has been an eventful one," Elizabeth wrote. "At last I have acceded to the importunities of my friends, and have hastily sketched some of the striking incidents that go to make up my history. My life, so full of romance, may sound like a dream to the matter-of-fact reader, nevertheless everything I have written is strictly true; much has been omitted, but nothing has been exaggerated."

Elizabeth paused. A sudden vision filled her mind's eye — Mrs. Lincoln picking up her book, examining the cover, and turning the pages, her frown deepening with every paragraph. Elizabeth drew in a deep breath, exhaled slowly, and refreshed her pen in the ink. "In writing as I have done, I am well aware that I have invited criticism." Elizabeth figured she could probably compose an accurate list of those who would be first and loudest to complain. "But before the critic judges harshly, let my explanation be carefully read and weighed."

The critic might refuse, but it wouldn't hurt to ask.

Elizabeth next ruminated briefly on slavery, a topic she would return to in a more personal, revelatory way early in her memoir. Then her thoughts again turned to Mrs. Lincoln. "It may be charged that I have written too freely on some questions, especially in regard to Mrs. Lincoln," she acknowledged. "I do not think so; at least, I have been prompted by the purest motive. Mrs. Lincoln, by her own acts, forced herself into notoriety. She stepped beyond the formal lines which hedge about a private life, and invited public criticism."

But was that fair? The nagging question brought Elizabeth's pen to a halt. Mrs. Lincoln had not run for office and had not been elected First Lady; the role had been bestowed upon her by virtue of her husband's choices and actions. It was, admittedly, a role she had relished, a title she had desired since childhood. She had reveled in the attention, so long as it was favorable, and she had certainly enjoyed the benefits and privileges of being, as she had sometimes called herself, Mrs. President. So yes, Elizabeth decided, it was fair to say that Mrs. Lincoln had chosen a public life.

Even so, the people had judged her too harshly. "The people knew nothing of the secret history of her transactions, therefore they judged her by what was thrown to the surface." Indignantly, Elizabeth rebuked a few prominent personages who had been especially unkind and certain newspapers who had taken excessive glee in exposing Mrs. Lincoln's faults, but then she thought better of it and scratched out the lines. "Mrs. Lincoln may have been imprudent, but since her intentions were good, she should be judged more kindly than she has been."

If she could persuade her hypothetical readers of nothing else, Elizabeth hoped she would convince them of this. Suddenly she wondered if Mr. Herndon had entertained similar thoughts as he composed his lectures.

Her spirits dipped, but she firmly reminded herself her book and Mr. Herndon's scribblings had nothing in common except for purporting to be about Mr. and Mrs. Lincoln. Their motives — and their degree of truthfulness — could not be more dissimilar.

And yet worry nagged at her. Would Mrs. Lincoln agree?

"If I have betrayed confidence in anything I have published, it has been to place Mrs. Lincoln in a better light before the world," Elizabeth wrote, her hand firm and steady around the pen. "A breach of trust — if breach it can be called — of this kind is always excusable." She took a deep breath and steeled herself; the next admission would not be easy. "My own character, as well as the character of Mrs. Lincoln, is at stake, since I have been intimately associated with that lady in the most eventful periods of her life. I have been her confidante, and if evil charges are laid at her door, they also must be laid at mine, since I have been a party to all her movements."

To defend herself, she had to defend the lady she served, and as Elizabeth wrote the words, she realized this truth had compelled her throughout the entire writing of her memoir. She had long been admired for her integrity and dignity, but the unfortunate business at 609 Broadway had tainted her sterling reputation with scandal. She had to redeem herself, and she could not do that without redeeming Mrs. Lincoln.

Elizabeth finished the preface, hoping she had written everything Mr. Redpath wanted her to write, that she had said everything she needed to say. Readers might disregard her lengthy explanation and decide for themselves that her motives were not pure, but she knew the truth. She also knew that nothing within the pages of her book could cause Mrs. Lincoln to be regarded in a worse light than that in which she presently stood, so the secrets Elizabeth revealed could do Mrs. Lincoln no harm.

"I am not the special champion of the widow of our lamented President," Elizabeth emphasized. Mistrustful readers would say that she could not be honest about the former First Lady's faults, since they were friends. She must make them believe otherwise. "I wish the world to judge her as she is, free from the exaggerations of praise or scandal. The reader of the pages which follow will discover that I have written with the utmost frankness in regard to her — have exposed her faults as well as given her credit for honest motives."

Had she inadvertently weighted the scales too much in one direction or the other? The question had plagued her with every word she had written. She had tried her best to be fair, and Mr. Redpath assured her she had been. She hoped the world would agree.

She especially hoped Mrs. Lincoln would agree.

On April 1, Mr. Redpath brought her a copy of the *American Literary Gazette and Publishers' Circular,* opened it to a page he had marked, and twice tapped an advertisement at the top of the left column. "Mr. Carleton and I and everyone at our publishing house are tremendously proud to have

557

you as one of our authors," he said. "We have great expectations for the success of your book."

Elizabeth glanced away from the page to thank him, but she immediately turned back to it and began to read:

G. W. Carleton & Co.

Will publish early in April

A REMARKABLE BOOK ENTITLED

BEHIND THE SCENES

By Mrs. Elizabeth Keckley, for thirty years a household slave in the best Southern families, and since she purchased her freedom, and during the plotting of the rebellion, a confidential servant of Mrs. Jefferson Davis, where, "Behind the Scenes," she heard the first breathing of that monster, SECESSION. Since the commencement of the rebellion, and up to date, she has been Mrs. Abraham Lincoln's modiste (dressmaker), confidante, and business woman generally: a great portion of her time having been spent in the White House in the president's own family. Being thus intimate with Mrs. Lincoln and her whole family, as well as with many of the distinguished members of Washington society, she has much to say of an interesting nature in regard to men and things in the White House, Congress, Washington, and New York. She discloses the whole history of Mrs. Lincoln's unfortunate attempt to dispose of her wardrobe, etc., which when read will remove many erroneous impressions in the public mind, and place Mrs. L. in a more favorable light.

The book is crowded with incidents of a most romantic as well as tragic interest, covering a period of forty years. It is powerfully and truthfully written, and cannot fail to create a wide-world interest, not alone in the book, but in its gifted and conscientious author. It is perfectly authentic. One vol. 12 mo. 400 pp. Cloth. Illustrated with portrait of the author. Price $2.

"What do you say to that?" said Mr. Redpath, smiling.

"I say it is quite wonderful," said Elizabeth, with a warm but tremulous laugh. Although she had been working on her memoir for months, somehow the advertisement made it seem real, immediate, tangible. Hesitantly, she asked, "It says that I was thirty years a slave, but I was actually a slave for thirty-seven years, almost thirty-eight."

"An insignificant difference," Mr. Redpath assured her. "Thirty is a nice round number. Although you are right to say that it is not entirely accurate, it sounds better in the advertisement."

"Of course," Elizabeth said, regretting her criticism. "Thank you for your kind words about me and my book. You make it sound so intriguing that if I had not written it, I would be first in line to buy it."

Mr. Redpath smiled. "You deserve abundant praise. The book is remarkable, and its author even more so." To Elizabeth's surprise, he took her hand and raised it to his lips. "It has been an honor working with you, Mrs. Keckley. The privilege would not have been greater if I had worked with the First Lady herself."

"Don't ever tell her that," Elizabeth quickly warned him, without thinking. Laughing, Mr. Redpath assured her he would not.

A few days later, Mr. Redpath called on her again and placed her finished book in her hands. For a long moment she held it, unmoving, disbelieving. "Learn your book," her father had urged her in his letters. How proud he would be to know that she had become an author.

Elizabeth's hands trembled, and as Mr. Redpath looked on smiling, she opened the red clothbound cover and turned the first few blank pages. She paused at the engraved portrait of the author — she didn't think it was a very flattering likeness, but never mind. Next she came to the title page:

BEHIND THE SCENES.
by
Elizabeth Keckley,
FORMERLY A SLAVE, BUT MORE RECENTLY
MODISTE, AND FRIEND TO MRS. ABRAHAM
LINCOLN.
OR,
THIRTY YEARS A SLAVE, AND FOUR YEARS IN
THE WHITE HOUSE.

So Carleton & Company had not corrected the number of years she had been a slave. Well, she supposed, what harm would it do to have people think she was a few years younger?

"How does it feel to see your words in print for the first time?" asked Mr. Redpath.

"It feels wonderful," Elizabeth said. Her heart was pounding so quickly that she had to take a deep breath to quiet it. She turned to her preface and read again the familiar words that until then she had seen only in her own imperfect handwriting. Then an unfamiliar turn of phrase caught her eye, and another. Her brief musings on slavery had been embellished greatly. The sense of her original words was still evident, but it had been cloaked in more ornate prose than she liked. Feeling Mr. Redpath's eyes upon her, she was careful not to allow her expression to betray her surprise and disappointment. Everyone knew that editors changed an author's words, she chided herself. An author of a first book should expect even more assistance, especially from such an experienced editor.

She paged through the book carefully, her joy soon returning when she discovered that the rest of the memoir had not been altered as drastically. Then she reached the end of her tale, and discovered an unexpected appendix.

Joy turned to shock when she discovered the letters from Mrs. Lincoln she had lent to Mr. Redpath to assist him in editing her manuscript. They had been reproduced almost exactly as Elizabeth remembered, with only a few inconsequential phrases omitted. Ironically, Mrs. Lincoln's warning that her confidences were meant to be "BETWEEN OURSELVES" had been preserved, including the emphatic capitalization.

She felt as if all the air had been squeezed from her lungs. "Mr. Redpath," she managed to say in a strangled voice. "Mrs. Lincoln's private letters —"

"Yes. We thought they contributed to the authenticity of your work."

"But I let you borrow them only to assist you in your editing," protested Elizabeth, distressed. "You agreed not to publish them."

Mr. Redpath's brow furrowed. "No, Mrs. Keckley, no," he said, shaking his head. "We agreed that I would not publish anything from the letters that would embarrass Mrs. Lincoln."

She held out the book to him and quickly paged through the appendix. "I assure you, this will embarrass her!"

"I disagree," he replied. "The letters reveal her thinking, the motives behind her actions. You always said that if people understood her good intentions, they would be more forgiving of her . . . outbursts and mishaps, as it were. I fail to see how that should embarrass her."

He failed to see because he did not want

563

to see. Sick at heart, Elizabeth sank into a chair, the book on her lap. Mrs. Lincoln would view the publication of her private correspondence as the worst sort of betrayal. She would never forgive her.

"Mrs. Keckley, please do not distress yourself." Mr. Redpath either truly was utterly bewildered by her reaction or he was a shrewd actor. "These letters — in fact, your entire memoir — will serve their purpose. They will inspire Mrs. Lincoln's critics to abandon their misconceptions and rally to her side. Mark my words."

She pressed her lips together and nodded, hoping he was right. There was no point in arguing with him. What was done was done. She could not go from bookstore to newsstand tearing the appendix from every copy of *Behind the Scenes*.

And, as it happened, Mr. Redpath's prediction proved true to some extent, but not as he had expected.

On April 12, a woman for whom she did some sewing, a native of Boston, greeted her with the cryptic remark "I'm glad to see you doing so well. You should not give a care for what they say in Springfield."

Elizabeth's heart thudded, and her thoughts flew to Mrs. Lincoln. "What do they say in Springfield?"

Her patron's quick, guarded expression revealed that she assumed Elizabeth already knew. She didn't want to explain, but after some coaxing, she reluctantly told Elizabeth that a brief item about her forthcoming book had appeared in the *Springfield Daily Republican.* Although Elizabeth was relieved to learn that her patron referred to Springfield, Massachusetts, rather than the former hometown of the Lincoln family, she still needed to steel herself before asking her patron to bring her the clipping.

The headline read "Kitchen and Bed-Chamber Literature," and the review — if it was right to call it a review, before the book was published — was worse than Elizabeth could have imagined.

A disreputable New York publishing house announced a book to be entitled *Behind the Scenes,* by Mrs. Elizabeth Keckley, who professes to have been Mrs. Jeff Davis's confidential servant while the rebellion was being cooked, and Mrs. Abraham Lincoln's dressmaker while the rebellion was going on. Such a book may be written in good taste, be interesting, be instructive, be decorous; but the chances are as the Bank of England to a filbert, that it is a sensational enterprise of the worst sort, after the order of Gen. Baker's "Secret Service," unprincipled, false, scandalous, indecent. The very idea of domestic servants being persuaded to write books about the secrets of their employers, being crammed by literary adventurers with what they ought to say, and their lumbering and halting narration being helped at every stage by perhaps the very class of men who edit the flash papers of our cities, must be repulsive to every person of an ordinary degree of refinement. We hope it will prove to be a good book. We greatly fear it will be an exceedingly bad one.

At first Elizabeth was too flabbergasted to speak. "Should they not first *read* my book before they condemn it?" she eventually managed to say. "Indecent? My memoir? I was told what to write by 'literary adventurers'? How could they possibly believe such terrible things?"

"I'm so very sorry," her patron said, thoroughly miserable. "I wish I had never mentioned it."

"You're not to blame." Elizabeth blinked back angry tears and fought to maintain her composure. "You are only the bearer of bad news. You didn't write these cruel things."

"Those newspapermen will eat their words after they read your book," her patron said comfortingly. "I for one am no less interested in reading your memoir now than I was before they attempted to discourage me."

Elizabeth managed a wry smile. "Perhaps, but you know me."

"Think of it, though," her patron mused. "The *Republican* might have done you a favor."

"In what way? I don't see how."

"They have made the people curious about your story. Everyone will want to buy your book now. They will read it and make up their own minds. You shall see."

Elizabeth hoped she was right, but an ominous cloud seemed to blot out the sun, casting shadows upon what she had expected to be a bright and happy day.

Undeterred by the newspaper's grim predictions, her New York friends were immensely proud of her and excited about her book, and her landlady threw a party for her on the first day of its release. Emma, the Lewises, and other friends sent congratulatory telegrams from Washington City. Their enthusiasm lifted Elizabeth's spirits somewhat, but Mrs. Lincoln had not responded to her letter confessing the matter of their private correspondence made public, and silence from such a prolific letter writer made Elizabeth uneasy.

On April 15, a new advertisement appeared in the *American Literary Gazette and Publishers' Circular,* but with a dramatic new headline that described her memoir as "A Literary Thunderbolt." Most of the book description remained the same, although what Elizabeth had to say "in regard to men and things in the White House" was no longer described as merely "interesting," but now also "startling."

"Oh, no, no, no," Elizabeth murmured, setting the paper aside. Her insightful, poignant memoir had been transformed into a spectacle.

Behind the Scenes outraged the press, who were swift, scathing, and merciless in their response.

The New York *Citizen:* "Has the American public no word of protest against the assumption that its literary taste is of so low grade as to tolerate the back-stairs gossip of Negro servant girls?"

The Washington *National Intelligencer:* "Where will it end? What family that has a servant may not, in fact, have its peace and happiness destroyed by such treacherous creatures as the Keckley woman?"

The New York Times, after offering three columns of excerpts and noting that Mrs. Lincoln was in financial distress: "Mrs. Keckley, we also learn, is likewise in trouble. Mrs. Lincoln is unable to pay her, and she supports herself by taking in sewing — and by writing a book. She would much better have stuck to her needle. We cannot but look upon many of the disclosures made in this volume as gross violations of confidence. Mrs. Lincoln evidently reposed implicit trust in her, and this trust, under unwise advice no doubt, she has betrayed. But only in a restricted sense can the book be called her own. It is easy to trace, all through its pages, the hand of a practiced writer — of one who has prejudices to gratify and grudges to repay. As mere gossip, the book is mainly a failure. Mrs. Keckley really knew very little about life in the White House, and she ekes out her scant stock of story and anecdote with extracts from newspapers, moral reflections and other expedients of like character. The public will be disappointed when they come to read her book. They will find it less piquant, less scandalous, than was expected, considering its source, while as a literary work it can lay claim to very little merit indeed."

And the *Springfield Daily Republican,*

which seemed all too delighted to discover that its dire predictions about the quality of her book had been fulfilled: "One would suppose the public had been treated to Mrs. Lincoln and her affairs *ad nauseam,*" the reporter sneered, "but scandal is always a marketable commodity, and this book contains plenty of it."

The theories about the diffusion of knowledge and the education of the masses, are all very fine, and within certain limits work very well. It is not pleasant, to be sure, to have a cook so literarily inclined as to be continually removing all your pet books from the library to the kitchen, and who insists on the first reading of the morning paper while she is getting breakfast; or a housemaid who prefers reading your letters to attending to her own proper duties. But all these can be patiently endured in consideration of the many benefits that are supposed to accrue to Bridget and Dinah on account of a smattering of knowledge. But when Bridget or Dinah takes to writing books instead of reading them, and selects for themes the conversations and events that occur in the privacy of the family circle, we respectfully submit that it is carrying the thing a little too far. The line must be drawn somewhere, and we protest that it had better be traced before all the servant girls are educated up to the point of writing up the private history of the families in which they may be engaged.

The vitriol stunned and sickened Elizabeth, and yet she was compelled to read on, nor could she ignore the other withering criticisms and condemnations that threatened to bury her in an avalanche of newsprint and ink. The reviews were overripe with ridicule and condemnation, and often contradictory. *Behind the Scenes* was both badly written, and written so well that it could not have come from the pen of a "treacherous Negro servant." Her memoir was worthless trash, and yet deserving of multiple newspaper columns for excerpts. Except for the *Chicago Tribune,* which emphasized the presence of notable Illinoisans in her memoir, praised certain sections as "interesting" and "affecting," and concluded that she was a woman "of more than ordinary intelligence," the reviews were unanimous in their disgust and outrage, and they seemed less concerned with commenting on her book than with denouncing Elizabeth for writing at all. To her astonishment, the same papers that had spent the past eight years gleefully pillorying Mrs. Lincoln now became her staunch defenders against the villainous "White House Eavesdropper" she had unwisely trusted.

In that sense, Mr. Redpath's prediction that *Behind the Scenes* would compel the public to rally around Mrs. Lincoln came true.

Mr. Redpath no longer called on her at No. 14 Carroll Place, most likely because they had parted on uncomfortable terms over the printing of Mrs. Lincoln's letters, but when the attacks upon her and her book became unbearable, Elizabeth visited him at his office and asked him what she should do about the terrible, unfair reviews. "Ignore them," he advised her simply.

"I cannot," Elizabeth insisted. "Nor should I. They are in the wrong. These reporters cannot offer any specific examples of poor writing in my book. They can only claim that it is worthless in a general sense while they impugn my character. And all the while they insist upon referring to me as Mrs. Lincoln's Negro servant as if I were a — a housemaid or a kitchen girl rather than an accomplished seamstress. They say I desecrated the memory of President Lincoln, a man I admired and respected with all my heart. I cannot let those accusations stand unchallenged."

Seeing that she was resolved, Mr. Redpath reluctantly suggested that she write a rebuttal, which he would forward to the editor of the New York *Citizen,* a gentleman who happened to be one of Carleton & Co.'s best-selling authors. Immediately Elizabeth took up her pen in her own defense, challenging her critics to read her book alongside the pages and pages that respected newspapers from across the nation had committed to the "bitter crusade" against Mrs. Lincoln. Which of them, she asked, had truly betrayed and scandalized the former First Lady? "Is it because my skin is dark and that I was once a slave that I am being denounced?" Elizabeth demanded. "As I was born to servitude, it was not fault of mine that I was a slave; and, as I honestly purchased my freedom, may I not be permitted to express, now and then, an opinion becoming a free woman?"

The resoundingly unanimous response of the public was that she could not.

Not long after her refutation appeared in the *Citizen,* someone left a small, flat package for her on the doorstep of her boardinghouse, wrapped in brown paper with "Mrs. Kickley" printed in block letters upon it.

Curious, Elizabeth unwrapped it — and suddenly discovered that the misspelling of her name had been no accident. The gift of her anonymous enemy was a booklet entitled *Behind the Seams; by a Nigger Woman who took work in from Mrs. Lincoln and Mrs. Davis.* The ostensible author, "Betsey Kickley (nigger)," had signed the book with an X, indicating that she was illiterate.

Her heart thudded as she opened the booklet and allowed her gaze to skim over the lines of text, enough to determine that it was a cruel, vicious parody of her memoir. Sickened, she threw it away, but she could not erase the taunting image from her thoughts — stacks and stacks of the booklet flying off newsstands and bookstore shelves, people throughout the country savoring its ugliness with malicious glee.

Her own book, she soon discovered, had become much harder to find. The controversy and the accusation that it was an "indecent" book had discouraged many booksellers from stocking it, and as time passed, Elizabeth heard convincing rumors that a furious Robert Lincoln had ordered her publisher to recall the book, and when that failed, he and his friends bought up all the copies they could, and had them burned.

Elizabeth felt as if she had plunged into a

nightmare. She wrote impassioned, apologetic letters to Mrs. Lincoln but never received so much as a single word in reply. When she discovered that Robert Lincoln was visiting the city, she sent him a note imploring him to let her call on him so she could apologize in person, but he flatly refused to see her. White people closed ranks against her, the colored woman who had dared scrutinize someone so high above her station, and even those who disliked Mrs. Lincoln denounced Elizabeth for betraying her and for dishonoring Mr. Lincoln's memory by revealing intimate scenes from his family life. Her own people were upset with her because they worried that white employers would be reluctant to hire colored servants, for fear that their own secrets would be written up in scandalous books. Despondent, smoldering with indignation and disappointment and embarrassment, Elizabeth nonetheless held her head high, even when several of the seamstresses for whom she had sewed suddenly discovered that they no longer had any piecework to assign her.

With her income sharply diminished, sales of her book became more important than ever. When she called on Mr. Redpath to inquire about receipts, he said that the book

575

had not yet sold enough to pay for the costs of printing and distribution. To help increase sales, he proposed arranging public lectures, one in New York and one in Boston, and if those went well, they would consider expanding the series to other cities. "Chicago, perhaps?" prompted Elizabeth, eager for an opportunity to call on Mrs. Lincoln and offer her in person the apologies and explanations she deserved.

"We'll see," said Mr. Redpath affably.

In the third week of June, Elizabeth read aloud from her book to an audience of no more than three dozen ladies and gentlemen at a Manhattan bookstore, a third of them her own good friends who had come to show their support. As for the rest, Elizabeth soon realized from their queries and comments that they could be divided into three groups: the curious, drawn by the press's claims of indecency and scandal and hoping to witness some of each; people who despised Mrs. Lincoln and were glad to see her brought low; and unrepentant secessionists and other political enemies seeking evidence to confirm their suspicions of treachery, indecency, and corruption in the Lincoln administration. At the end of the evening, only Elizabeth's friends went home satisfied.

"Mrs. Elisabeth Keckley, the eavesdropper of the White House, seeks to increase the sale of her dirty book by reading selections from it," the *Springfield Daily Republican* sneered two days later. "She attempted at New York, Tuesday evening, but failed utterly and deservedly, and to-night will make an effort at Boston. She reads more poorly than she writes, and that is as bad as can be."

Notwithstanding the power of the newspaper's warning to beckon curiosity seekers, the turnout at the Boston event at Lee & Shepard was slighter than that of her first reading but composed of much of the same sort of people. Thus Elizabeth was relieved rather than disappointed when Mr. Redpath informed her that Carleton & Co. did not intend to arrange any more lectures for her, although they certainly encouraged her to do so on her own, if she wished.

Elizabeth emphatically did not.

She had too much dignity to rail against the unfairness and injustice of her circumstances. She understood that she was mired in scandal and that every movement she made to climb out of it only dragged her in deeper.

She could not count how many times through the years had she observed Mrs.

Lincoln similarly entangled. Mrs. Lincoln's instinct had been to fight ferociously to salvage her reputation, sending scores of letters to garner support, evoking the power of her husband's high office to demand the deference due to her as his wife, using patronage to forge alliances and appease enemies, and, when all else failed, fleeing the scene and leaving faithful friends to clean up the mess she left behind.

Mrs. Lincoln's tactics had never succeeded, not that Elizabeth could remember.

If Mrs. Lincoln's example had taught her nothing else, it had shown her that the only way to redeem oneself from scandal was to live an exemplary life every day thereafter.

And that was precisely what Elizabeth intended to do.

CHAPTER SEVENTEEN

1868–1893
When the furor subsided, Elizabeth quietly
moved back to Washington, where Virginia,
Walker, and Emma welcomed her warmly
— and kindly said nothing of her book or
the scandal. She reopened her dressmaking
business, summoned her former assistants,
and sent out letters to her patrons announcing her return, but during her long absence,
many of her assistants had found other
employment or had gone into business for
themselves. Some of her favorite patrons
soon placed orders with her for garments
for the winter social season, but many more
demurred. Although they never said so, Elizabeth was certain they stayed away because
of her book.

She wrote again to Mrs. Lincoln seeking
forgiveness, to let her know she had returned to Washington if Mrs. Lincoln
wanted to reply. The next time Mrs. Lin-

coln visited Washington, Elizabeth vowed, she would apologize sincerely and profusely in person. And Elizabeth would present to her a gift of her heart and hands three years in the making, and as yet unfinished — the quilt she had begun on the train to Chicago, when she had accompanied the grieving widow on her departure from the White House.

Pieced of silks left over from Mrs. Lincoln's gowns, the quilt struck the eye as predominantly red, blue, gold, and white, although other colors appeared too, tans and lavenders and ashes of rose. In the center Elizabeth had appliquéd and padded a bold eagle clasping a flag in his talons, wings outspread, the word "Liberty" embroidered beneath him in gold. Around the central emblem she had added three concentric borders, the first of gold silk embroidered with flowers along the sides and black silk cornerstones. The second was simpler, tan pieces along the top and bottom and a black-and-white stripe along the sides. Next she had attached borders of dark blue and blue-gray, and cornerstones of light tan, intricately embroidered with flowers, sprigs, and other ornaments. She planned to frame the central medallion with borders of Grandmother's Flower Garden hexagons joined in clusters of seven and separated by contrasting rhombuses, giving the traditional design the effect of a radiating star, but those segments were still in progress. After that, she did not think the quilt would be quite finished; it would need another concentric border or two, and perhaps another embellishment, such as a scalloped edge or fringe, something she could not yet envision. For a while she worked swiftly — fewer patrons meant fewer dresses, which meant more idle hours to fill — hoping to complete the quilt in time to present it to Mrs. Lincoln when she next returned to Washington.

But although Mrs. Lincoln returned to the capital in September for her son Robert's marriage to Miss Mary Harlan, she seemed to abhor the city, for to the best of Elizabeth's knowledge, she made no other visits. Elizabeth was sure she would have heard if she had, for the newspapers continued to follow her comings and goings, her struggles with her finances, and her attempts to persuade the government to raise her pension.

It was from the newspapers that Elizabeth learned Mrs. Lincoln and her son Tad had left for Europe, where they were expected to embark upon a lengthy tour. Mrs. Lincoln reportedly hoped to recover her health, which had worsened of late, and to seek respite from the disappointments and humiliations at home. Some wags, recalling the notorious memoir of Mrs. Lincoln's dressmaker, noted that she had once declared that she would prefer to leave the country and remain absent throughout his term of office should General Grant be elected president of the United States. Perhaps, they impertinently suggested, that was why she planned to stay abroad so long. Elizabeth did not believe for a moment that Mrs. Lincoln had taken Tad abroad to avoid the Grant administration. Surely Mrs. Lincoln was fleeing grief and unhappy memories — one of which, Elizabeth could only assume, was the ruin of their friendship.

With a pang of regret and sorrow, Elizabeth carefully packed the unfinished quilt in the trunk where she kept the leftover fabric from Mrs. Lincoln's gowns. She hadn't the heart to work on it anymore, not knowing when, or if, she would ever see her estranged friend again.

Even practicing the closest economy, Elizabeth found it difficult to make ends meet. The book that had cost her so much had paid her nothing, so quietly she sued Carleton & Company for half of the profits from her memoir. She did not prevail in court, and therefore she did not receive a single cent, nor were Mrs. Lincoln's letters ever returned to her.

From time to time, Elizabeth would spot Mrs. Lincoln's name in the newspaper and read about her travels in Germany, Scotland, England, France, and Italy. In 1870, while Elizabeth was struggling to rebuild her dressmaking business, she learned that Senator Charles Sumner had pushed through Congress a bill granting Mrs. Lincoln an annual pension of three thousand dollars, which President Ulysses S. Grant promptly signed. Delighted, Elizabeth immediately wrote Mrs. Lincoln a congratulatory letter, expressing her heartfelt joy at the well-deserved benefit and long-overdue justice. She said nothing of their estrangement, hoping that perhaps Mrs. Lincoln's long months away had given her time to reflect on the great many occasions Elizabeth had demonstrated her loyalty and friendship, and that perhaps she might extend a hand in forgiveness. Elizabeth sent her letter to the residence in Frankfurt am Main last reported in the papers, but no reply came. Not long thereafter, in May 1871, she read that Mrs. Lincoln and Tad had left Germany for England a few months after Elizabeth had written to her and from there had returned to Chicago. Wistfully, she wondered if her letter had arrived too late, and if even at that moment it sat unopened on a table in Mrs. Lincoln's unoccupied rented rooms in Germany. How tragic it would be, she thought, if that letter would have provoked the tender, forgiving reply she had longed for, but the opportunity for reconciliation had been lost, all for the mischance of one letter gone astray.

Yet knowing that Mrs. Lincoln had returned to the United States rekindled Elizabeth's hopes, spurring her to unearth the abandoned quilt and resume working on it in earnest. Though Mrs. Lincoln was hundreds of miles away, she had not been so close in years, and if she returned to the capital — and was it not likely that eventually some official business would summon her there? — Elizabeth wanted the quilt to be ready.

But to her shock, the next news Elizabeth read of Mrs. Lincoln was not of an impending visit to Washington, but of the death of her son Tad.

Tears ran down Elizabeth's face as she read the grim report. As mother and son had sailed to America from England, where eighteen-year-old Tad had been enrolled in boarding school, the young man's weak lungs had suffered in the storms and damp. Upon his arrival in Manhattan, he was diagnosed with a serious chest ailment and put on bed rest at a hotel until he regained enough strength to continue on to Chicago by train. Eventually Tad's doctors pronounced him fit enough to travel, and after a long train ride that Elizabeth could well imagine from her own experience of it, they reached Chicago and settled into Robert Lincoln's new home, which he shared with his wife and daughter. Mrs. Lincoln and Tad soon moved into Clifton House, where Mrs. Lincoln could better nurse him, but her tender efforts were all in vain. On July 15, Tad Lincoln died from a dropsy of the chest.

Elizabeth sent condolences but neither expected nor received a reply. Elizabeth prayed for Mrs. Lincoln and for Robert, and worried about them both, but especially Mrs. Lincoln. She could not count how many times in the years since President Lincoln's assassination the despondent widow had declared that if not for Tad, she would gladly join her husband in the grave. By her own admission, only Tad and her responsibility for him had kept her from taking her own life.

What would Mrs. Lincoln live for now?

Elizabeth kept her beloved, familiar rooms in the Walker Lewis boardinghouse for a while longer, but eventually her financial troubles obliged her to move elsewhere. For the next few years she boarded with one family and then another, always within the capital. Later, after her dear friend Virginia passed on, she moved back into the Lewis boardinghouse to help Walker care for their youngest daughters, still at home — pretty Alberta, her goddaughter, and sweet Elizabeth, born after the war. Sewing work still came in sporadically, but fashions had changed with the times, and other dressmakers, including Emma, now married with a son and daughter, were more eagerly sought after by the Washington elite. In her success Emma had never forgotten who had trained her and launched her career, and she frequently sent work Elizabeth's way. Elizabeth was grateful for the assistance and very proud of her most accomplished apprentice.

From the little she gleaned from the press, her own troubles were nothing compared to Mrs. Lincoln's, whose erratic behavior had only worsened in the wake of Tad's death.

In May 1875, after a shocking trial, every sordid detail of which was breathlessly recounted in the papers, Robert Lincoln had his mother declared insane and committed to an asylum in Batavia, Illinois, about forty miles west of Chicago. Powerless to help or to comfort her former friend, Elizabeth followed the heartbreaking story in the newspapers, stunned by reports that Mrs. Lincoln had tried to commit suicide by taking an overdose of laudanum the day before the verdict was delivered. The attempt had been thwarted by a wary druggist, who had recognized her and had substituted a solution of burnt sugar and water for the medicine she demanded.

For weeks afterward, Elizabeth was haunted by visions of Mrs. Lincoln languishing in a cold, ominous institution, devoid of all warmth and comfort. She imagined her keening endlessly as she had when Willie died, weeping and shrieking as she had after Mr. Lincoln had been killed. Elizabeth had been her most faithful companion in those dark days, but she had been unable to offer Mrs. Lincoln any solace when Tad passed away, nor could she do anything for her now.

Then she remembered the quilt, and she worked upon it feverishly. She finished the

Grandmother's Flower Garden borders, and then added one final border, ivory silk with four more proud eagles, one on each side echoing the dark eagle bearing a flag in the center, but made of gold silk, stuffed and embroidered, with more intricate floral embroidering all along the sides. As it neared completion, she wrote to Dr. Richard J. Patterson at Bellevue Place and asked if she might be permitted to visit Mrs. Lincoln. "I have made her a precious gift, which I hope she will accept as a token of my enduring sympathy and friendship," she wrote. "It is my great hope that this quilt, with its pieces reminiscent of happier days of years gone by, will offer her diversion, comfort, beauty, and solace in her confinement."

She had grown so accustomed to sending letters to Illinois only to receive no reply that she was almost startled when Dr. Patterson responded within a fortnight. He offered her his compliments and said that he was "most gratified to know that Mrs. Abraham Lincoln was not forgotten by her Washington friends," but that he must discourage Elizabeth from attempting to call on Mrs. Lincoln, especially since she would be obliged to travel hundreds of miles to do so. Often Mrs. Lincoln was unfit to receive callers, he explained, and when she was, she almost always refused to see anyone.

Remembering how Mrs. Lincoln had turned away many kind-hearted visitors during the early days of her widowhood in Hyde Park, Elizabeth was disappointed but not surprised.

As for her gift, Dr. Patterson wrote, "It is with great admiration for your generosity that I must respectfully urge you not to send this quilt — which sounds truly extraordinary, a masterpiece of the form — until Mrs. Lincoln is better able to appreciate it. At this time she abhors all tokens of the past. Objects, places, and anniversaries that evoke memories a sane person would find pleasantly diverting, are an anathema to her. I regret that as finely made as your quilt surely is, Mrs. Lincoln would find no comfort in it. I encourage you to keep the quilt safe, and to deliver it to her after she has been restored to reason, at which time I am sure she will thank you for it."

She wouldn't, Elizabeth realized. She never would. It was not a symptom of Mrs. Lincoln's insanity that she could not bear souvenirs of the past. She had always shunned them. She had quickly, almost frantically, given away Willie's toys and books after his death. She had readily parted with Mr. Lincoln's relics in the weeks following his assassination, not only to express gratitude and respect for his dearest friends, but also to get them away from her, far away, where she would never have to look upon them again.

Blinking back tears, Elizabeth packed up the quilt, certain that this time would be the last. What a fool she had been to think Mrs. Lincoln would ever want to look upon scraps of the dresses she had worn at the height of her power as First Lady, dresses she had tried to part with in what turned out to be the most humiliating scandal in a life that had known too many.

What a fool Elizabeth had been to assume that Mrs. Lincoln would want anything from her.

From time to time, brief news reports would address Mrs. Lincoln's incarceration. One journalist from the *Chicago Post and Mail* who had come to view the sanatorium's grounds was inexplicably granted an interview with the ailing widow, and when Elizabeth read that he found her clad in a shabby dress with her hair gone completely white, her heart sank. When the reporter noted that she rambled in conversation, and that if left alone in her room she spoke to imaginary companions, Elizabeth felt so heartsick for her that she could not finish reading the article. Expecting Mrs. Lincoln's decline to continue inexorably, Elizabeth was delighted to read little more than a month later that she had been pronounced well enough to leave the asylum and visit her sister, Mrs. Elizabeth Edwards, in Springfield. "It is not likely that she will return to Bellevue Asylum," the paper's Chicago correspondent reported. "She is decidedly better, sleeps and eats well, and shows no tendency to any mania; but whether the cure is permanent or not the test of active life and time will prove."

Elizabeth rejoiced at this good news, and again when, in June 1876, headlines declared that Mrs. Lincoln had officially been declared restored to reason. She resided with her sister Elizabeth in Springfield, their old estrangement apparently forgotten. Elizabeth's faint hope that Mrs. Lincoln might find it within her heart to forgive her too diminished yet again when she learned that Mrs. Lincoln had sailed for France on October 1 and would likely spend many years abroad.

Mrs. Lincoln did not return to the United States until the autumn of 1880, and only then because, at sixty-two years of age, she was too ill to live alone. She returned to her sister Elizabeth's home and care, and Elizabeth knew then that Mrs. Lincoln would never again visit Washington.

On July 2, 1881, Robert Lincoln was walking with the newly elected president James Garfield through a Washington railway station when a disgruntled office seeker shot the president twice in the chest. Mr. Garfield survived the attack, but as the summer waned, infection set in and he declined, suffering eighty days until death finally claimed him on September 19. As shocked and horrified as the rest of the nation, Elizabeth found herself unable to sleep, worrying about Mrs. Lincoln, who was surely in anguish as the new tragedy forced her to relive her own husband's assassination.

Elizabeth was tempted to write to her again — to offer sympathies, to assure Mrs. Lincoln she had at least one friend thinking about her in those troubled times — but she sat at her desk staring off into the distance, waiting for words that would not come. Eventually she abandoned the letter as a futile effort, having never once touched pen to paper.

Elizabeth read about Mrs. Lincoln twice more in the national papers. The first occasion came in November of that year, shortly after Congress granted the newly widowed Mrs. Garfield an annual pension of five thousand dollars, two thousand dollars greater than Mrs. Lincoln's. Her campaign to get Congress to increase her own pension to match put Mrs. Lincoln in the headlines once again. In January of 1882, Congress agreed, and with unexpected generosity also voted to grant her back pay as well as a fifteen-thousand-dollar bonus. Elizabeth privately cheered the decision, glad to know that Mrs. Lincoln would surely at last be released from the financial worries that had plagued her for years.

But Mrs. Lincoln did not have long to enjoy her triumph.

The next time Elizabeth discovered her name in the Washington papers was the day after she died in Springfield on July 16, 1882.

With all hopes of reconciliation forever lost, Elizabeth no longer had any reason to finish the medallion quilt, but while the nation mourned and remembered and eulogized the former First Lady, she found herself compelled to take the unfinished top from the trunk. At first she considered adding a wide band of black silk all around the outer edges to signify mourning, but just as she was about to put shears to fabric, she decided against it. Mrs. Lincoln had spent nearly two decades in mourning, and although Elizabeth knew it was a strange notion, she could not bear to consign the quilt to the same unhappy end. Instead she trimmed the quilt in long red fringe, which reminded her of the glamour and patriotism of Mrs. Lincoln's best days in the White House. Then, in recognition of Mrs. Lincoln's passing, Elizabeth added four red tassels, one in each corner, because they reminded her of the tassels that had hung from the black silk drape on Mr. Lincoln's catafalque. That was the single note of mourning Elizabeth allowed in the quilt, although she knew it was unlikely anyone else gazing upon the quilt would recognize it for what it was.

It's over, Elizabeth thought when the quilt was finished.

She had been working doggedly until then, keeping herself so busy that she had no time for contemplation, but the realization that it was truly over cracked the façade of her serene resignation, and all the grief pushed out through the fissures, and she wept.

In 1890, eight years after Mrs. Lincoln was beyond caring what Elizabeth did with the precious relics entrusted to her, Elizabeth found herself in such difficult financial circumstances that she was obliged to sell her mementoes of Mr. Lincoln, which she had cherished and protected for thirty-five years. Overcoming her wariness of brokers, she enlisted the services of W. H. Lowdermilk & Co. and sold her treasures to Mr. Charles F. Gunther of Chicago, a candy manufacturer and collector of curiosities. To Mr. Gunther went the bloodstained cloak Mrs. Lincoln had worn to the theater on the night of her husband's assassination, the right-hand glove Mr. Lincoln had worn at the first public reception after his second inauguration, and everything else. The only mementoes Elizabeth kept for herself were a pair of Mrs. Lincoln's earrings, the pieces of fabric left over from sewing Mrs. Lincoln's dresses, and the medallion quilt, which to Elizabeth seemed a relic of that time, although she had finished it later.

Word of the sale found its way to Wilberforce University near Xenia, Ohio, where the news must have evoked Bishop Daniel Payne's curiosity and concern. He had never forgotten how Elizabeth had once offered to donate her Lincoln relics to the university, so they might be exhibited in Europe to raise money to rebuild the school's main building, which had burned down on the day President Lincoln was assassinated. Mrs. Lincoln had objected so vehemently that Elizabeth had apologetically withdrawn her offer, but Bishop Payne had understood her dilemma and had respected her decision. Mrs. Keckley must have fallen upon hard times indeed to sell her cherished mementoes now.

Elizabeth was pleasantly surprised to receive Bishop Payne's letter inquiring about her health, and she enjoyed his pleasant reminiscences and his description of how the university had grown and prospered since the days her son, George, had studied there. Then he proposed a change to the faculty that astonished her so much she had to ease herself into a chair: He offered her a position as head of Wilberforce University's Department of Sewing and Domestic Science.

She immediately wrote back to thank him profusely, but to decline. She was no professor, she reminded him. It was true that she had learned her letters in childhood, even though it had been illegal for her to read and write, and she had endeavored all her life thereafter to obey her father's wish that she "learn her book." She had always loved to read, especially the Bible, but she had enjoyed nothing in the way of a formal education. Would not university students expect a more learned instructor?

Not at all, Bishop Payne promptly responded. Students in the Department of Sewing and Domestic Science expected instructors who knew their craft inside and out and could skillfully pass on their knowledge to others. Elizabeth fit that description perfectly, and her experience as a mantua maker in the highest of Washington's social circles would be invaluable. That she had accomplished so much without the benefit of formal schooling attested to her strength of character — her determination, perseverance, and love of learning, values she could impart to her students.

Although Elizabeth had taught sewing to freedwomen in contraband camps and ambitious young ladies in her workrooms, she had never taught in a classroom. How very different it would be, she reflected, imagining herself standing before a class of eager pupils, patiently demonstrating how to make flawless darts and lecturing them on the benefits of proper posture in avoiding neck and back strain.

She agreed to visit the campus, to meet the faculty and students and to learn more about the position. She traveled by train and was entertained so graciously by everyone she met there that after two days at Wilberforce University, she gladly accepted Bishop Payne's generous offer. And so it was that after thirty years in Washington, at the age of seventy-four, she packed up her few belongings, bade farewell to Walker Lewis and his daughters and Emma and her many friends from the Fifteenth Street Presbyterian Church, and moved out west to Ohio.

Never once in her blessedly peaceful and rewarding years there did she regret her decision.

Elizabeth thrived in the classroom and on peaceful strolls around the campus chatting with her cheerful, inexhaustibly curious, impossibly young students, all of them born after the war, never having known a single day when slavery was the law of the land. Dressmaking had changed since she had honed her skills in the art, but she adapted, and she soon discovered that experience trumped even the most newfangled tricks and contraptions. Among themselves, her students whispered stories about her and would come to her later, wide-eyed and awestruck, to ask what President Lincoln had really been like and whether it was true that his wife had been insane. Elizabeth would never fail to respond with serene praise for president and First Lady alike, and she would never allow anyone to disparage Mrs. Lincoln in her presence.

Sometimes Elizabeth would invite a group of favorite, promising students to her home and show them the silks and satins and other fine fabrics she had saved from making Mrs. Lincoln's garments. On occasion, she would reward an accomplishment with a gift of a small scrap of the precious fabric, which the lucky student could make into a pin-cushion, a small, useful White House treasure of her own. Her students and a few faculty members alike marveled at her quilt, and they sympathized when she expressed her regret that she had been unable to give it to Mrs. Lincoln as she had intended.

Elizabeth found it strange that not one of her students seemed aware of the scandal that had led to her estrangement from Mrs. Lincoln. Some of them had heard that she had written a memoir, although none of them had ever read it, which surprised Elizabeth not at all since Robert Lincoln had done his utmost to reduce the inventory.

Eventually it dawned on her that perhaps she had triumphed over the scandal after all.

In 1893, Wilberforce University participated in the World's Columbian Exposition in Chicago, a grand and glorious event in commemoration of the four hundredth anniversary of Columbus's discovery of the New World. When the event was in the planning stages, exhibit proposals from colored Americans were summarily rejected, but after strong protests from the black community led by Frederick Douglass and Ida B. Wells, the exposition organizers relented and allowed very limited participation, including displays of needlework and drawings in the Women's Building. Knowing that many skilled artisans and scientists of her race had been unfairly excluded diminished Elizabeth's pleasure in the honor bestowed upon Wilberforce University, and if it had been up to her, she would have withdrawn from the exhibition in solidarity. But it was not her decision, and, as she told herself, her hardworking students deserved to have their excellent work displayed and their achievements noted. Only by taking their rightful place among whites and presenting their handiwork before the eyes of a skeptical public could they hope to influence prejudiced minds.

Elizabeth felt herself drawn along by the strong pull of memory as she and several of her students traveled by train to Chicago.

When she closed her eyes, she could see her former patron and lost friend as she had been in those grief-stricken weeks in Hyde Park, lamenting alone in her darkened room, staring unhappily across the vast dark blue of Lake Michigan. She had never ceased mourning, Elizabeth knew. She had never gathered up the shards of her broken life and reassembled them into something new, something endurable, if not happy. Even though Mrs. Lincoln had passed beyond all human suffering, and had been reunited at long last with her youngest sons and her beloved husband, Elizabeth was moved to pity for her anew.

The exposition was a wonder to behold. Elizabeth had assumed that it would be much like the Great Northwestern Sanitary Fair she had attended in the city in June of 1865, but the World's Columbian Exposition far surpassed it. Fifty nations participated, and when she wasn't tending her department's exhibit, Elizabeth and her students toured the various buildings and pavilions, marveling at clever new inventions, tasting strange and often delicious foods, and listening to music from different countries far across the sea. A wistful ache filled Elizabeth as she waited safely on solid ground while her bold, young students

braved a ride on a dangerous-looking con-
traption called a Ferris wheel. The exposition's vast grounds were so close to Mrs.
Lincoln's former Hyde Park residence that
Elizabeth could have walked there, if she
wished — but she knew she would find no
comfort or satisfaction in revisiting that
unhappy chapter of her past.

She would rather continue to explore the
exposition, which seemed to represent the
future with all its newness and wonder and
innovation, and to pass pleasant hours at
the Wilberforce University exhibit, which
was firmly rooted in the present. Their
exhibit resided within the Manufacturers
and Liberal Arts Building, and in their modest portion of the vast space, wooden figures
clad in garments designed and made by
Elizabeth and her students showed off the
department's skill and artistry, and a revolving showcase displayed photographs and
biographies of their graduates.

Observing passersby as they admired the
garments, and watching her students as they
answered questions with grace, intelligence,
and poise, Elizabeth felt her wistfulness
recede as the warm glow of joy and pride
filled her heart almost to bursting. This was
her legacy, she realized, not the beautiful
wardrobe she had sewn for Mrs. Lincoln or

even the book she had written with such good intentions. These young women, and the apprentices she had instructed and advised back in Washington, and the runaways and freedwomen she had provided with the fundamental skills to care for themselves and their families — they were her legacy. Their success and independence and confidence were her true gifts to the world.

Her greatest legacy could not be measured in garments or in words, but in the wisdom she had imparted, in the lives made better because she had touched them.

CHAPTER EIGHTEEN

1901

Elizabeth gazed out upon the streets of Washington through the carriage window, thinking of how much the capital had changed since she had first settled there as a younger, more ambitious woman in 1860. In her mind's eye she could still envision it as it had been then — the unfinished Capitol dome, the muddy streets, the slaves in chains being led from harbor to holding pen.

How the world had changed since then. How she herself had changed.

Her weekly carriage rides were prescribed by her doctor, who insisted that she get out and about to increase the vigor of her constitution. Ever since she had moved back to Washington after a mild stroke had obliged her to resign from Wilberforce University, she had resided in a basement room at the Home for Destitute Colored Women and Children on Fifteenth Street.

It amused her to refer to it as *her* home, not only because she lived there, but because it had been endowed in part by donations from the Contraband Relief Association she had founded so long ago. She liked her solitary room, small and neat, the little table with a pitcher and bowl in one corner, a straight chair in the other, a rocking chair near the bed, and the old trunk containing her clothes and what remained of her cherished mementoes. Over the dresser hung a picture of Mrs. Lincoln, and through the window Elizabeth could watch young colored men and women on their way to and from classes at Howard University. No one but her pastor and a few friends knew that she resided there, who she was and who she had been. And that was the way she liked it.

When the carriage pulled to a stop in front of the home, Elizabeth slowly and gingerly stepped down, accepting the driver's assistance with thanks. Straight and tall, unbowed by age or infirmity, she crossed the threshold, exchanging polite greetings with the residents and staff she passed. "You have a visitor in the parlor," one woman told her, and so Elizabeth headed down the hall, curious, because she was not expecting anyone, or she would have gone driving earlier.

In the parlor she discovered a most welcome guest, her goddaughter Alberta, or Mrs. Alberta Elizabeth Lewis-Savoy as she was now called, whom she had known since the moment of her birth. "My dear girl," Elizabeth greeted her happily, embracing her and kissing her cheek. Alberta would always be a girl in Elizabeth's eyes, though she was thirty-seven with children of her own. "To what do I owe this unexpected pleasure? I didn't expect to see you until Sunday."

Alberta smiled warmly, but her manner was somehow hesitant, a guarded look in her eye. "I stumbled upon an interesting article in the newspaper this morning, and I thought you might want to see it."

She took a clipping from her handbag and gave it to Elizabeth, who held the page without unfolding it. "It was so fascinating you could not wait a few days?"

Alberta looked as if she might speak, but then she shook her head, smiled weakly, almost apologetically, and guided Elizabeth to a chair. Elizabeth muffled a sigh as she seated herself, wondering what on earth it could be this time. Peering closely at the paper, she read the headline aloud: " 'Negro

Authors.' Hmm." Suddenly wary, she glanced up at Alberta, who gestured for her to read on.

NEGRO AUTHORS.

THREE HUNDRED BOOKS BY THEM ON EXHIBITION IN BUFFALO

BUFFALO, NY — Some three hundred books written by American Negroes form a part of the Negro exhibit at the Pan-American Exposition. The collection contains the best work of the race in the field of authorship, and is unique. Examination of these books furnishes new data by which to rate the civilization of the Negro.

At this, Elizabeth sighed and shook her head.

We may as well be entirely frank in the appraisal. Much of it is rubbish. None of it is very great.

This judgment evoked an ironic laugh. "Keep reading," Alberta urged her, and Elizabeth reluctantly complied.

There has been no Negro Homer, Shakespeare, or Dumas — no American counterpart of the great French mulatto. But a great deal of this work has better qualities than the world has reason to expect, when it remembers the condition of its origin. Its chief value, the one thing that makes it worthy of attention, has no concern with the graces of literary form, but lies in the fact that here is the world's best record of the evolution of the Negro recorded by the Negro himself.

"Do you suppose," Elizabeth mused aloud, "that when our white friends write and speak in this manner, they have any idea how insulting they are?"

"I believe most of them don't," Alberta replied. "And of those that do, many wouldn't care."

Elizabeth sighed and read on, through admiring reviews of the poems and letters of Phillis Wheatley, a pamphlet by Reverend Daniel Crocker, and several scholarly works. Praise for the exceptional works of Mr. Frederick Douglass and Wilberforce University professor W. E. B. Du Bois followed, and then Elizabeth held her breath as she glimpsed her own name one paragraph below.

As may be supposed the collection is rich in what may be called literary curios. One of them, *Behind the Scenes,* by Elizabeth Keckley, "formerly a slave, but more recently modiste and friend to Mrs. Abraham Lincoln," had considerable vogue in its day (1868) because of its singular revelations.

" 'Considerable vogue'?" Elizabeth echoed, unsure whether she should be amused or alarmed. The reporter apparently had not done his research, or he would have chosen a much different descriptor.

"I thought you should be aware that your book is on display, and apparently attracting notice," said Alberta, looking profoundly sorry. She knew well the story of how Elizabeth's slim red volume of remembrances had been received upon its publication. Considerable vogue, indeed.

"Thank you, my dear," Elizabeth said, reaching for her hand and smiling fondly. "I am safely forewarned. Let us hope nothing else comes of this. It is nice, I suppose, to have been included in the exposition, but the world has moved on, and I suspect my 'literary curio' will soon be forgotten again."

She hoped so, but she was much mistaken.

Less than a week later, she received a letter from a journalist, Mr. Smith D. Fry. He had read about the Negro exhibit, and, intrigued by the brief description of *Behind the Scenes,* he wished to interview the authoress. "I was only a lad when your memoir was published," he recalled, "but my mother owned a first edition. It had a red cover, I recall, and I remember her saying that it was so vividly written that she felt as if she had been in the room with you and Mrs. Lincoln during some of the most significant events of the Civil War years, some moments triumphant and others tragic."

Elizabeth realized then that she was apparently as susceptible to flattery as the next woman, because although she had been quite determined to decline his request, that paragraph changed her mind. The detail about the red cover convinced her that he described a true memory and not a fiction meant to win her over. The newspaper had not mentioned the color of her book's cover, nor was it likely that Mr. Fry had glimpsed a copy more recently. She was also both charmed and amused by his proud boast that his mother had owned a first edition, as if there had been a second.

Still, she gave herself a day to reflect before replying that she would grant his request.

On the morning of the appointed day, she dressed herself with her usual care in a black silk dress with a white fichu tied about her shoulders. Mr. Fry was waiting for her in the parlor when she came down, and as they exchanged greetings she silently gave him credit for punctuality. He looked to be about fifty years old, stout and a bit jowly, and mostly bald, but he was courteous and pleasant, and in his eye she detected keen intelligence and a strong desire to learn all he could about his subject — dissecting her, if necessary. She would have to be on her guard.

She settled herself into a high-backed, upholstered chair, fixed a demure expression in place, and awaited his first question.

"Mrs. Keckley," he began, pencil and paper at the ready, "I regret that I must begin with a delicate question."

She prepared herself for the worst. "Very well."

"My readers will want to know, but I dread asking." He hesitated. "May I say that you are eighty years of age?"

"You may," said Elizabeth, though she was eighty-three.

He nodded and scribbled something on his pad. "It is said that you were Mrs. Lincoln's dressmaker, but you were really much more than that, weren't you?"

"I was her modiste," Elizabeth replied, as

if the title were explanation enough.

"And that means you sewed for her, and dressed her for important occasions, is that not so?"

It was so much more. "I dressed Mrs. Lincoln for every levee," she said. "I made every stitch of clothing that she wore. I dressed her hair. I put on her skirts and dresses. I fixed her bouquets, saw that her gloves were all right, and remained with her each evening until Mr. Lincoln came for her. My hands were the last to touch her before she took the arm of Mr. Lincoln and went forth to meet the ladies and gentlemen on those great occasions."

"I imagine you must have seen the president quite often then."

"Yes."

"They considered you part of the family?"

Elizabeth reflected briefly upon how Mrs. Lincoln had behaved toward the women of her family. "I would not make such a claim. I would say that I was a dear and trusted friend."

"To Mrs. Lincoln?"

"To them both, although I was certainly much closer to Mrs. Lincoln." For a moment she was lost in thought, but then she fixed her gaze upon Mr. Fry and said, "Mr. Lincoln was a good friend of mine, but he never knew what a good friend of his I was, and have ever been." When Mr. Fry watched her expectantly, waiting, she added, "I was Mr. Lincoln's friend, am his friend now, and will always protect his memory by keeping my mouth closed concerning the many things which he unhappily suspected or imagined were going on around him officially and unofficially."

"I assume you feel very loyal to him," Mr. Fry remarked. "So many Negroes do, or so I am told, because he was the Great Emancipator."

Elizabeth wondered at his line of questioning. She thought he had come there to discuss her book, but he seemed to be more interested in learning about Mr. Lincoln. That suited her fine. She would much prefer to talk about the great president, but if Mr. Fry entertained any hopes that she would giddily rattle on with malicious gossip, he would be sorely disappointed. "I was born a slave, but bought my freedom, and so was under no obligations to Mr. Lincoln for emancipation," she said. "But I loved him for his kind manner toward me and for his great act of giving freedom to my race. I know what liberty is, because I remember what slavery was." She smiled, and for a moment she almost felt sorry for the reporter, who was likely a father and perhaps a grandfather but to her seemed very young. "You who have never suffered cannot understand the full meaning of liberty."

Mr. Fry had been writing swiftly the entire time she spoke, but at that, he paused. "No," he said thoughtfully. "I don't suppose we do. I don't suppose we can."

Suddenly she warmed to him, although she could not bring herself to trust any journalist completely. "I have almost worshipped Abraham Lincoln," she admitted. "He was as kind and considerate in his treatment of me as he was of any of the white people about the White House. In that he manifested the consistency of his belief that all human beings are created equal in the sight of God."

Unlike his successor, Elizabeth thought, but prudently did not say aloud. Mrs. Lincoln had judged Mr. Johnson's character rightly from the moment he stumbled drunkenly onto the national stage. He had undone many of the reforms Mr. Lincoln had put into place, and his policies had flung obstacles into the path of people of color as they marched toward equality. Many of the gains they had made during the war had been thwarted under President Johnson, but progress moved ever forward, and Elizabeth had not lost her hope for a better future for her race.

"And did you feel the same about Mrs. Lincoln?"

Elizabeth considered his question. "She was a very different person than her husband. He was a remarkable man, the greatest man I have ever known. If I were to use him as a measuring stick for Mrs. Lincoln or anyone else, including myself, we should all fail to measure up."

"We should indeed." Mr. Fry's gaze was on his pad as his pencil rapidly scratched upon the page. "Do you ever feel that you failed to measure up to the trust the Lincolns placed in you?"

"I never betrayed a secret in the days when secrets were worth gold, and gold was scarce," Elizabeth said, a trifle sharply.

"And yet, there is the matter of your book."

So he *was* aware of the controversy. "Yes," she said evenly. "I wrote a book about my life, which included my years in the White House. I did it with the best of intentions, but as you are no doubt already aware, it did not turn out at all as I had expected."

He studied her for a moment, brow furrowing, and then he asked, "Were you troubled at all, afterward, to know that you profited from exposing Mrs. Lincoln's foibles to the world?"

"Sadly, her foibles were well-known before I ever wrote a word about them." Suddenly Elizabeth felt very tired. "As for profit, I never received a dollar from the publication of that book. They kept it all. However, I need not regret that, because they printed many things which ought not to have been printed, many things which caused heartaches, because they were untrue." She sighed and glanced away, feeling tears threatening. "The book was printed, and my name was on the title page as the author of everything contained between its lids."

"And you were not?" Mr. Fry asked, prompting her, when she had been silent for a while.

"No, indeed." She could tell from his expression that he wanted an example. Oh, how the press rejoiced when you gave them enough rope for them to hang you by! But perhaps she was being unfair. This man had never written an unkind word about her. It was unfair to hold him accountable for the actions of others of his profession. "They told the story of how Mrs. Lincoln tried vainly to sell her expensive and costly wardrobe in New York, but they did not tell it right. I was with Mrs. Lincoln at that time and did my best to help her dispose of her valuable things —" Suddenly, prudence prevailed and she thought better of telling him how Mr. Redpath had strayed from her version of events. "But it would do no good now to say anything about the details of that venture. I merely mention it because they made it a part of the book which made money for them, but the publication of which brought me no money, while it made some enemies for me who should have always been my friends."

She felt herself sinking into a mournful reverie, but after a time, Mr. Fry quietly asked, "You made dresses for other well-known ladies too, didn't you?"

Elizabeth nodded. "I made dresses for Mrs. Lincoln, the ladies of President Andrew Johnson's family, and also for the ladies of the Grant administration. And Mrs. Jefferson Davis too, before secession." She recalled that Mrs. Grant and Mrs. Davis had become quite good friends after the war. At the time she had thought that if the wives of Union General Grant and Confederate President Davis could become friends, then surely she and Mrs. Lincoln could reconcile. But it was not to be.

"You must have been quite famous in those days."

Elizabeth regarded him skeptically. "I was acquainted with famous people. That does not mean that I garnered any fame for myself."

"Mrs. Keckley, I believe you're being too modest," he protested, smiling. "You should be proud of your fame."

He *was* young, not to understand how foolhardy it was to take pride in something so fickle, so fleeting, as fame. "I was famous, in my line, for many years," she acknowledged. "I was proud; yes, very proud. But fame and pride do not last, as I have found to my sorrow. They don't bring food to an old woman when she is forgotten or when her friends have passed away —"

Abruptly she fell silent. She had not meant to broach that unhappy subject, nor would she care to return to it, no matter how long Mr. Fry sat there regarding her with plaintive, hopeful, puppy-dog eyes beneath a furrowed brow. "I understand you have fallen upon hard times," he eventually said, all frank sympathy.

Slowly drawing in a deep breath, Elizabeth nodded. She did not want his pity. "When I am in most distress," she said with an effort, keeping her voice calm and even, "I think of what I often heard Mr. Lincoln say to his wife: 'Don't worry, Mother, because all things will come out right. God rules our destinies.' "

Mr. Fry's pencil hovered above the paper. "He truly said so? He believed that?"

Elizabeth nodded. "Many and many a time have I heard him say those words, when disasters surrounded the Union armies, and also when domestic troubles came." His words had comforted Mrs. Lincoln, and Elizabeth too, though he had not intended them for her. "Yes, that good man's memory helps me, for I recollect very many of his sayings, showing faith in God and His goodness."

"It is good to find comfort in memories," Mr. Fry said gently.

"Yes." Elizabeth smiled wistfully, her gaze faraway. "I have always thought so."

They chatted awhile longer, and Elizabeth tried not to lament too much about her poverty, or her loneliness, as she had outlived so many of her friends. When she grew tired, Mr. Fry noticed and promptly stood, shook her hand, thanked her profusely, and showed himself out.

She wondered, as she watched him leave, what he had seen that she had not intended to reveal to him. She wondered if he would invent dialogue and sighs and long, sad looks to fill in the gaps in the story he had surely already composed in his head before she had spoken a word, gaps she had neglected to fill because she did not have the pieces his story required. Why should one write the story to fit the facts, she thought wryly, when nothing could be easier than to invent one's own facts to suit a more provocative story?

She sighed, pulled herself slowly to her feet, and made her way alone to her solitary room. She would learn soon enough what Mr. Fry thought of her, and after his story ran in the papers, a brief flash of notoriety might again illuminate her quiet life before it faded into embers. And when it was gone, it would be gone. Such was the nature of fame. Soon she would be forgotten again, except for the few dear friends yet living who mattered to her most.

Her life was smaller than it had been at the height of her success and fame as Mrs. Lincoln's dressmaker, but she was older now, and wiser, and did not require so much as she once had.

She was a free woman in a nation united and at peace. She had lived a full and fascinating life. She had known the most remarkable people of the age, and she had never refused to help the humble and downtrodden. Despite its disappointments and losses and heartbreaks, she would not have wished her life a single day shorter — nor, when the time came for her to join the many friends and loved ones who had gone on before her, would she demand an hour more.

She was ready to lay down her burdens and rest, and perhaps to find in heaven the reunion and reconciliation that had eluded her on earth.

AUTHOR'S NOTE

Elizabeth Hobbs Keckley lived out her remaining years in Washington, DC, at the Home for Destitute Colored Women and Children. There, after a brief illness, she died in her sleep of a paralytic stroke on May 26, 1907, at the age of eighty-nine. According to John E. Washington, author of *They Knew Lincoln* (Dutton, 1942), she was laid to rest in the Columbian Harmony Cemetery "on a beautiful knoll, facing the east beneath a spreading elm tree" among "most of the illustrious colored people who loved and served Lincoln while he was in Washington."

The controversy surrounding Elizabeth Keckley's memoir lingered on after her death. In 1935, a Civil War historian, journalist, and self-proclaimed "unreconstructed Southerner" named David Rankin Barbee contended that not only had Elizabeth Keckley not written *Behind the Scenes,* but no such woman had ever existed. The memoir was a fraud, he insisted, a fiction created by the outspoken "abolitionist sob sister" and Washington correspondent Jane Swisshelm. Barbee apparently had not considered how many friends and acquaintances of Elizabeth Keckley were yet living, and one can well imagine his feelings when they promptly came forward to refute his claims and to testify that Elizabeth Keckley had indeed existed. In the face of such adamant opposition, Barbee partially retracted his statements, explaining that what he had meant to say was that "no such person as Elizabeth Keckley" could have written *Behind the Scenes.* "Scholars, with whom I cannot class myself, have long been bothered over the authorship of this book," he stated in Washington's *Evening Star* on November 26, 1935. But despite the attempts of Barbee and others to deny Elizabeth Keckley's authorship and to erase her from memory, her memoir, so denounced in its day, is now widely regarded as a significant historical artifact offering invaluable insight into the Lincoln White House and the private lives of Abraham and Mary Lincoln.

The provenance of the exceptional quilt attributed to Elizabeth Keckley is even less certain than that of her memoir. At the time of this writing, the earliest documented appearance of the Mary Todd Lincoln quilt was in 1954, when its owner, the quilter and author Ruth Ebright Finley, mentioned it in a lecture. Finley reportedly claimed that Elizabeth Keckley pieced the quilt from scraps of fabric left over from sewing Mary Lincoln's dresses, and that she had presented the quilt as a personal gift to the First Lady, who used it as a counterpane on her bed in the White House and took it with her when she departed after President Lincoln's assassination. When Finley died in 1955, her quilt collection passed to her nephew, Bill Dague, who kept the quilt until 1967, when he and his wife sold it at a yard sale at their family farm in Sharon, Ohio. The quilt was purchased by Ross Trump, an antiques collector and dealer and family friend of the Finleys and Dagues. In 1994, Trump donated the quilt to the Kent State University Museum, where it remains to this day. However, other accounts question whether Elizabeth Keckley ever gave the quilt to Mary Lincoln, or indeed whether she was the quiltmaker who made it. I was unable to establish the quilt's provenance before Ruth Ebright Finley's ownership, and so, in the absence of historical evidence,

I created a history for the quilt that best suited my story.

In the 1950s, after years of neglect, the Columbian Harmony Cemetery was sold to a land developer, and the remains of approximately thirty-seven thousand people — including Elizabeth Keckley — were moved to the new National Harmony Memorial Park Cemetery in Landover, Maryland. Whether due to neglect or mischance, the headstones were not relocated, and thus Elizabeth Keckley's remains were reinterred in an unmarked grave. For decades, historians believed that her gravesite would remain forever unknown, but in 2009, a self-described amateur historian named Richard Smyth was researching historical graves within the cemetery's ledgers and records when he discovered the plot and section where Elizabeth Keckley had been buried. For two years, Smyth worked with National Harmony Memorial Park and several other organizations, including the Surratt Society, Black Women United for Action, the Lincoln Forum, and the Ford's Theatre Society, to raise funds to purchase a memorial honoring Elizabeth Keckley's role in presidential history. On May 26, 2010, the 103rd anniversary of her death, the new bronze and granite grave marker was erected. The inscription reads:

ELIZABETH KECKLEY
1818–1907
ENSLAVED MODISTE CONFIDANTE
BORN INTO SLAVERY, ELIZABETH KECKLEY
PURCHASED HER FREEDOM USING HER
EXCEPTIONAL SKILLS AS A SEAMSTRESS.
AFTER ESTABLISHING HER OWN BUSINESS,
SHE WAS EMPLOYED AS A MODISTE
(DRESSMAKER) BY MARY LINCOLN,
BECOMING HER TRUSTED FRIEND AND
CONFIDANTE. MRS. KECKLEY'S
AUTOBIOGRAPHY "BEHIND THE SCENES"
PROVIDES INTIMATE DETAILS ABOUT LIFE
INSIDE THE LINCOLN WHITE HOUSE.

ACKNOWLEDGMENTS

I offer my heartfelt thanks to Denise Roy, Maria Massie, Liza Cassity, Christine Ball, Brian Tart, Kate Napolitano, and the outstanding sales teams at Dutton and Plume for their support of my work and their contributions to *Mrs. Lincoln's Dressmaker.*

I owe a debt of gratitude to the people who graciously assisted me during the research and writing of this novel. Geraldine Neidenbach, Heather Neidenbach, Marty Chiaverini, and Brian Grover were my first readers, and their comments and questions proved invaluable throughout the writing of this book. Nic Neidenbach willingly responded to my frantic questions when technology failed me, proving once again how wonderful it is to have a computer guru in the family. I always appreciate the support and encouragement of Marlene and Len Chiaverini, and Marlene's enthusiasm for this story in particular was especially heartening. Karen Roy and Alyssa Samways went on library research expeditions and sent me copies of crucial historical documents that I could not have obtained on my own; and Sara Hume of the Kent State University Museum not only provided me with a personal tour and viewing of the Mary Todd Lincoln quilt but also offered intriguing and informative replies to the many questions that occurred to me after my visit. Many thanks to you all.

I am fortunate indeed to live so close to the Wisconsin Historical Society, whose librarians, staff, and excellent archives I have come to rely upon in my work. Of the many resources I consulted, the following proved especially valuable and instructive: Jean H. Baker, *Mary Todd Lincoln: A Biography* (New York: Norton, 1987); Joan E. Cashin, *First Lady of the Confederacy: Varina Davis's Civil War* (Cambridge, MA: Belknap Press of Harvard University Press, 2006); Catherine Clinton, *Mrs. Lincoln: A Life* (New York: HarperCollins, 2009); Daniel Mark Epstein, *The Lincolns: Portrait of a Marriage* (New York: Ballantine Books, 2008); Jennifer Fleischner, *Mrs. Lincoln and Mrs. Keckly: The Remarkable Story of the Friendship Between a First Lady and a Former Slave* (New York: Broadway Books, 2003); Ernest B. Furgurson, *Freedom Rising: Washington in the Civil War* (New York: Knopf, 2004); Becky Rutberg, *Mary Lincoln's Dressmaker: Elizabeth Keckley's Remarkable Rise from Slave to White House Confidante* (New York: Walker and Company, 1995); Justin G. Turner and Linda Levitt Turner, *Mary Todd Lincoln: Her Life and Letters* (New York: Knopf, 1972); and John E. Washington, *They Knew Lincoln* (New York: Dutton, 1942).

Of course, no work was more important than Elizabeth Keckley's own memoir, *Behind the Scenes* (New York, G. W. Carleton & Company, 1868). Though I regret the unhappiness its publication brought her, I am deeply grateful that Elizabeth Keckley left behind such a rich and evocative account of her life.

As always and most of all, I thank my husband, Marty, and my sons, Nicholas and Michael, for their continuous love, support, and encouragement. I tell you every day how much I love you, but there are times when words cannot suffice, and this is one of them.

ABOUT THE AUTHOR

Jennifer Chiaverini is the author of the *New York Times* bestselling Elm Creek Quilts series, as well as five collections of quilt projects inspired by the novels. *Mrs. Lincoln's Dressmaker* is her twenty-first novel and first stand-alone work of historical fiction. A graduate of the University of Notre Dame and the University of Chicago, she lives with her husband and sons in Madison, Wisconsin.

The employees of Thorndike Press hope you have enjoyed this Large Print book. All our Thorndike, Wheeler, and Kennebec Large Print titles are designed for easy reading, and all our books are made to last. Other Thorndike Press Large Print books are available at your library, through selected bookstores, or directly from us.

For information about titles, please call:
(800) 223-1244

or visit our Web site at:
http://gale.cengage.com/thorndike

To share your comments, please write:
Publisher
Thorndike Press
10 Water St., Suite 310
Waterville, ME 04901